ONE—RIO DE JANEIRO

Pinnned to the canvas deck chair by a merciless sun, Julia Elliott stared through a rippling heat-haze at the blue-green water, mesmerized by tiny, white crested waves lazily slapping the sand. Her eyelids were heavy and, with the sun burning through her hair, she could almost relax and imagine that she was back in Venice Beach with her daughters. Almost, but not quite. The knot of anxiety that had recently lodged in the pit of her stomach now denied her any degree of calm and peace.

Cocooned by cliffs hugging the cove on both sides, one of sheer rock stretching upward toward the cloudless sky and the other covered with dense forest, she watched sailboats and ships of all kinds and sizes appear and disappear on a bay dotted with islands jutting from the water like gigantic boulders. Overhead, cable cars dangled and swayed in the sultry breeze as they ascended to the famous Rio de Janeiro landmark, Sugar Loaf, or Pão de Açucar, as it was known in Brazil. A gentle gust of air lifted strands of her short, taffy-colored hair and cooled the perspiration soaking her light cotton blouse. She floated, out of body, out of mind, anxious and tense.

Suddenly, Mary Beth's voice shattered the oddly soothing hum of a helicopter, distant traffic and the slap of nearby water.

"I'm totally cooked. Want to take a walk?" She waved vaguely in the direction of the rocky precipice on the left where a broad, paved path, shaded by the overhanging cliff, had been cut into the stone. Gradually, it rose from the beach to curve out of sight high above the bay.

With an effort, Julia sat up, tipped the last of her *caipirinha* into her mouth and crunched the slivered ice to bits. Carefully placing her glass on top of the table, she turned her head toward Mary Beth and, with a grimace and slightly lifted eyebrows, nodded toward her husband Jack, and then toward Mary Beth's spouse. The latter was deeply engrossed in texting while Jack frowned at a laptop balanced on the table and mumbled into his cell phone. Mary Beth's forehead dropped to the table and, when she straightened a moment later, she was silently laughing, her shoulders shaking.

Both women stood and Julia turned to her husband. "Want to come?" She knew the answer and unconsciously braced herself against the sting of rejection.

Without pausing in his phone conversation, Jack shook his head, waggled one finger and scribbled something in a small notebook.

Of course not, she thought, looking at Mary Beth's husband. "How about you, Jim?"

He grinned, lifted his *caipiriniha* and shook the tumbler. "I'll keep Jack company." Almost immediately, he returned to his cell phone.

"Okay, we'll be back."

As they left the restaurant veranda, Julia tried, and failed, to recapture the excitement she had felt on arrival in Rio yesterday.

"Aren't they a barrel of laughs? You can't take them anywhere," commented Mary Beth.

"I did warn you about Jack's new devotion to work," Julia said. "It goes way beyond responsibility."

Best friends since their years as college roommates, the two women began the gradual ascent and again Julia was mesmerized by the view. The higher they climbed, the more islands appeared in the bay, while the early afternoon sun was reflected in dazzling flashes on the dancing, green water. Suddenly, Mary Beth stopped and gestured toward two fishermen far below. Perched precariously on a craggy boulder surrounded by turbulent surf, the pair chatted and baited their hooks while ignoring the churning water at their feet and the occasionally drenching spray that shot overhead.

"Look at that."

"How did they get down there?" Julia asked, her stomach oddly queasy as she peered down at the men.

"I haven't the faintest idea. What I'd like to know is how do they keep from falling in?"

Tearing her attention away from the fishermen, Julia waved one arm to encompass the sparkling bay and islands beyond. "You know, before we came to Brazil, this is what I imagined it would be like. A dream, not a nightmare."

Mary Beth stepped back and leaned against the cliff, her arms folded as she shrewdly studied her friend. Small, with olive skin, brown eyes and mahogany hair, Mary Beth was often mistaken for a Brazilian. She had a natural talent for languages, greatly enhanced in this case by a junior year spent in Belo Horizonte, and now, after only ten days in Brazil, spoke Portuguese fairly well. Julia, still struggling to master the basics of the language after one year, tried hard to overcome her envy.

"Rio isn't São Paulo, Julia. You live in the business and banking capitol of South America that's also the third largest city in the world. Rio has six million people and São Paulo has something like twenty-two. It makes a difference. A big one"

Mary Beth pushed away from the cliff, dusted off the back of her shorts and the women slowly continued along the trail.

"I know all that but..." Julia paused to pluck a leaf from a cliffside shrub and absently tore it to shreds as the vague perception that something was not quite right once again caught the breath in her throat. "It's a hard place to live," she explained uncertainly, gazing steadily at her friend. "I don't seem to fit in." Firmly, she pressed her lips together, realizing too late that she sounded like one of whiney wives she detested.

Mary Beth glanced at her friend. "Fit in with whom? What's the actual problem?" she asked sharply.

That's a good question, isn't it? Julia thought. They were higher now, with trees as well as shrubs growing along the edge of the path, the foaming water far below. For a moment they both looked back at the cove, the line of restaurants fronting a small, clean beach dotted with tiny figures and a spreading oasis of dark green just beyond.

Julia frowned, wondering about the true answer to her friend's question. "I really don't know. I had a successful career and terrific friends and gave them up. Remember, this was supposed to be a fantastic opportunity to live in an exotic country, but I feel completely off-balance." She paused, suddenly infused with exasperation. "And Jack is certainly different. Look at him back there, making business calls on Sunday when we're on a four-day vacation."

"Ah-ha", Mary Beth exclaimed, running one palm idly over the sheer rock on their left, "now we're getting to it. Everybody told you that ex-pat men down here, especially in São Paulo, turn into workaholics."

"Jack wasn't like this at home," Julia said defensively.

"Julia, come *on*. Think. One of the first things you found out was that Brazil is often a dead end for executives, not the stepladder to a posting in London or Paris or a promotion to the head of the company that they all hope it will be. You told me that yourself. Remember your stories about the two top execs who went back to flunky jobs in the States, and another one found no job at all when he got there. So of *course* Jack's working his butt off...he's scared silly."

The pair stared at one another.

"So stop obsessing about it and get a life."

Compressing her lips, Julia bit back a curt retort. Mary Beth had always cut right to the heart of any situation and could usually see a number of solutions. In this case, though, Julia herself couldn't grasp the real problem, the source of her apprehension, and certainly couldn't verbalize it, not even to Mary Beth, nor even to herself. What she did know was that it involved more than Jack's work habits.

Shrugging, she moved forward. "You're right, I suppose."

Even though shaded by the heavy tangle of vines and trees, Julia found the heat oppressive. Sweat stinging her eyes and breathing heavily, the two women struggled along the path that now angled sharply upward. Suddenly, the women rounded a curve and found the path blocked by a large, permanent sign prohibiting any further travel without an official guide. To the left of the notice was a tiny, steep trail, muddy and overgrown, that disappeared into thick shrubbery.

"Wow," commented Julia. "I wouldn't try that one *with* a guide."

Edging into a small clearing on their right, they had an unimpeded view of the bay and islands beyond. Julia pointed to a large, vermilion freighter moving slowly out to sea.

"Look at that bright red ship."

"I wonder who thought up the paint job."

"Don't know, but I like it."

Silently they watched the ship as it disappeared behind an island.

Two husky young men in tee shirts and Bermuda shorts thundered up the path, squeezed past the sign and plunged ahead, using hanging roots and branches to pull themselves up the trail. One man vanished from sight but the other slipped backward in the mud, paused to reposition his feet and then hesitantly followed his companion.

Mary Beth raised her eyebrows and looked steadily at Julia.

"See? There are nut cases in Rio even though it's a beautiful and clean city."

"Maybe one of them was a guide."

They both laughed.

"Let's go find our husbands and have another caipirinha. Since our vacation's only two weeks long, I have to make the most of it." She grinned and moved downhill.

Julia fanned herself with cupped hands and turned for one last look at the bay, now a deep emerald shot with turquoise and sprinkled with whitecaps. Heat pressed the color from a milky blue sky and caused the thick vegetation on the distant islands and cove opposite to waver slightly as though moved by a breeze. Julia had forgotten how calming she had always found the sea, how a walk on Venice beach, her bare toes digging into the wet sand and spray from the breakers enveloping her in a fine mist, had smoothed her mind even in a storm. At night the surf's heavy rhythm had ushered in an unbroken sleep and, until moving to Brazil, she had always wondered if she could live away from the water. Well, she thought, turning to follow Mary Beth back down the path, São Paulo was inland and she had better get used to it—along with everything else that went with her new home.

Out of the corner of her eye she saw a burst of crimson and stopped abruptly. Leaning forward, her blue eyes sparkling with silent laughter, Julia watched as the scarlet freighter flashed into view and then vanished again behind another island. Either the ship was a total misfit in the world of transportation or the belle of the ocean. Either way, it was amusing and also impossible to overlook in the world of deep greens, grays and blues through which it moved. As she turned to slip and slide downhill, Julia felt an odd sense of affinity with the strange little boat ploughing its way through the sea. Abruptly, the familiar clench of apprehension and anxiety slid over her like a shroud; the sailing vessel was forgotten as she puzzled over the true answer to Mary Beth's question.

TWO—VENICE BEACH, CALIFORNIA

Unaware that her orderly life was about to disintegrate, Julia pulled clippers from her gardening belt, turned to the rose bushes and frowned thoughtfully. Sterling Silver, one of her favorites, looked a little sick. Maybe she'd pruned it too severely, or perhaps it needed bone meal.

Later, Julia remembered this moment as the calm before the storm, even though actual downpours in Venice Beach were heralded, not by serenity, but by gusting winds, snapped and broken palm fronds that skittered over the pavement and a sinister, gunmetal-gray, out-of-control ocean. At that moment, however, nothing marred the near perfection of the day, and Julia's contentment was enhanced by the soothing scent of blooms from nearby mature plants as she lowered four new bare root roses into a bucket of water. Straightening, her eyes rested on the stained glass windows in the front of the house. Although the four panes were obscure and dark in the sunlight, she could nevertheless see the black outlines of three geese soaring over a field of long-leaved grasses into a brilliant sunset. To her, the birds symbolized freedom and a will to keep going even though the day was nearly over, and they never failed to lift her spirits.

Absently, she stripped off her worn gardening gloves and turned to watch her youngest daughter Sydney slice through the water in the lap pool. Contentedly, Julia reflected on her good luck She was the only person in her circle of friends that didn't have some kind of major health, financial or marriage problem; no wonder the others told her, with more than just a hint of envy, that she was moving smoothly through a charmed life.

The French doors from the master bedroom at the far end of the house opened and Jack Elliott emerged, briefcase in hand, tie still neatly knotted. Surprised, Julia stared, all thoughts of roses and geese instantly evaporating. Jack wouldn't dream of hanging out in the garden wearing his suit and tie: the first thing he did after work was change into a swimsuit and jump into the pool or jog to the beach for a plunge into the surf. Hastily, Julia replaced the clippers in her belt and moved forward, stumbling over Angelique, a fluffy male cat, who was batting furiously at their leaping miniature poodle.

"Leave him alone, Oso," she automatically ordered the dog, with no results at all. Eyes on her husband, she stepped over the tussling animals.

"Hi," she called, eyeing his suit. "I like your new swimwear."

"Very witty. I've got something important to tell you."

His voice carried an odd note of subdued tension. With the sun low over the palm trees and directly behind Jack, Julia couldn't see his face but she experienced a moment of panic. He couldn't have lost his job, that wonderful Financial Director position that paid for their elegant lifestyle and the girls' very expensive private education. Well, why not? All around them executives were being felled like wheat in a Kansas harvest. Chop, chop, down you go, and Jack was forty-seven, which seemed to be over the hill in most companies. Could she support the family with her job at the T.V. station? Certainly not in this style. Squeezing her hands together, she moved toward her husband, keenly aware of Sydney rhythmically gliding from one end of the pool to the other, not realizing that, in the next few minutes, a kaleidoscope might seem stable compared with her life.

"What is it?" She stepped to one side, forcing her husband to turn so that he was bathed in the sun's soft, flattering light. Anxiously, she scanned the tanned face framed by iron gray hair for signs of defeat or dismay. Instead, the startlingly blue eyes sparked with happiness.

"I've been offered a fabulous job. It's a huge step up."

Relieved, her muscles relaxed and her fists unclenched. "Oh, that's great. Is it another company?" Jack had been headhunted in the past but had never found the jobs sufficiently tempting. Or maybe he wasn't up to the risk of the unknown.

"Still Claymore Cable..." He smiled, erasing the slight furrows between his dark eyebrows and deepening the lines around his cheeks, and Julia wondered fleetingly why wrinkles on a man were so much more attractive than on a woman. His even teeth flashed, the white enamel intensified by his dark beard and mustache, and Julia realized with a start that Jack was more handsome and much more sensual than he'd been when they'd married.

"Well, are you going to tell me?" she asked impatiently.

"It's as president," he began. Julia gasped, her eyes wide. Behind her, Sydney continued to slip through the pool, the water only slightly disturbed by her dipping arms and fluttering legs. "President of Claymore Brazil. There are some irregularities in the company books and I'm being sent to the rescue."

Confused, Julia simply stared. It had never occurred to her that Jack would consider work that involved leaving their Venice Beach home in California.

"Well?" he prompted, still smiling.

"Brazil?" There was a Brazil in Indiana not too far from Terre Haute, and she thought there was one in Tennessee, but neither sounded very tempting. Her eyes flicked over the large, two-story house that they had built, the peach, fig and apricot trees they had planted and her beloved rose garden, now numbering forty-eight carefully tended plants. Julia's brief spurt of enthusiasm was replaced by a feeling of loss.

"Brazil the country, of course. We'll be living in São Paulo, the third biggest city in the world."

That was an enticement? Stunned, she continued to stare at her husband.

"Have you accepted the job?"

"Of course!" His smile was a bit less brilliant. "This is a fantastic opportunity for all of us. A new country—an exotic one with new friends and places to visit. More money and...what's the matter?"

His smile was gone and so was hers.

"You're supposed to talk it over with me *before* accepting the job. And they should send us to see the city and the office and then decide."

"They offered to do that but there was no point since I really have no choice. If I turn it down, I'll never be offered another promotion, and you know it."

She did know it but now she was confused and annoyed. "No choice? What about my job, which pays very well."

"For a woman..." It was a calm, factual statement that only served to fan the flames of anger.

"Yes, what a pity I can't grow a penis." She'd worked hard for years to become the first woman Public Relations Director at the Business Channel; she was proud of herself, her achievement and the independence and status it gave her. She was now forty-four and, once she relinquished this job, she'd never get it back in age-conscious Los Angeles. Quite clearly Jack didn't give a damn about anything but himself. She was glad he was going bald on the top of his head.

"Sarcasm kills, Julia."

"And what about *Angel and Friends*? They depend on me." Every Saturday, Julia, joined occasionally by Sydney, packaged and dispensed food staples to undocumented Hispanics at the local Center. It was work she loved.

"There are plenty of other volunteers."

"Oh, yes, let's flush everything away—my job, volunteer work and this house. You aren't thinking of me at all."

His face grew pink and his soft voice had lost its confident tone. "You're wrong. I'm thinking of this whole family, Julia. While we're there I'll make double my current salary and the company's going to pay for everything— rent, condo fees, taxes, electricity, and car. It's the chance of a lifetime. And," he added hopefully, "you can have a vacation from work and your charity activities." He ran his hands affectionately up and down her arms. "You're going to love it there."

Jack was her best friend, the husband she had adored above all else for years and now he looked and sounded so miserable and beaten that Julia felt heartsick. Briefly, she stroked his cheek, her eyes softening.

"I probably will," she conceded. "At least I speak Spanish *almost* fluently."

He lifted his shoulders apologetically. "It's Portuguese in Brazil."

"Portuguese," she repeated tonelessly.

Unnoticed by either of them, Sydney had finished her daily aquatic workout and now stood nearby, drying her tanned, slender body with a towel that matched her blue tank suit. Angelique sped along the ground closely pursued by Oso and then lifted in a graceful, furry leap to the veranda railing where, hissing occasionally under the soaring geese, he peered regally down at the dog.

"What were you two arguing about?"

"We're discussing, not arguing."

"Sure you are." In an earlier era, Sydney's perfectly oval face with just the hint of a cleft chin would have been described as elfin; now it was referred to as delicate. Brushing her extremely short cap of straight brown hair forward with the fingers of one hand, she slung the towel over her shoulder and looked from one parent to the other. "So what's this discussion about?"

"Your father has accepted a job in Brazil."

"*What?*"

"It's a wonderful chance for all of us," Jack said defensively. "It's only for two years, which isn't a lifetime. *And* they pay for everything, including your school fees."

"They'll pay for Marlborough?"

"Well, not really. You'll have to come down with us and enroll in the American School."

Gray fur flattened by the wind, Angelique arced overhead, claws extended and, as soon as his paws touched earth, chased after a speedily retreating Oso. Both disappeared around a corner of the house.

"Dad, it's my senior year," she wailed. "What about my friends? And the Swim Team schedule, and performances of The Runner Stumbles? In case you've forgotten, I'm first understudy for Sister Rita, the female lead."

"They probably put on high school plays in São Paulo."

"I'm absolutely not changing schools, especially to one in a foreign country where they speak a language nobody else understands and I have no friends. I'll fail and have to work at Target or McDonalds instead of going to college."

"Don't be absurd." Usually, Jack was lenient, even permissive, with both the girls but now his voice was cold and harsh.

"I'll kill myself." Sydney began to cry. "I'm staying here with Angelique and Oso. And Auntie Gail."

Julia took a deep breath. Grasping both her husband and daughter by their forearms, she turned them toward the house.

"This is way out of hand," she said, her anger receding

in the face of Sydney's obvious fear and near-hysteria. And her daughter did have a point. Changing schools in one's senior year was always problematic, but moving to another country where the language, culture, customs and food were unfamiliar was a recipe for disaster. "Jack, why don't you go for a swim and Sydney can shower and change and I'll have a big glass of hemlock on the rocks while I get dinner. Let's all calm down and talk about it later."

Clearly, Jack was going to Brazil, and if she wanted to stay married to him she would have to go too, whether she liked it or not. Two years was a long time and there were always women that were happy to accompany a handsome, abandoned company president. Goodbye job where she was well paid (considering that she was a woman), and goodbye *Angel and Friends* where there were so many other volunteers that she wasn't really needed. Her stomach clenched with resentment. Get over it, she told herself sternly, and start thinking about what Sydney should do.

THREE—VENICE BEACH, CALIFORNIA

Gail Sanders knocked twice on Julia's front door and then flung it open, stepping inside as Oso and Angelique rushed out. Although it was Saturday, Gail was wearing a chic double-breasted, double-belted, moss green Bermuda shorts suit and carried a huge leather handbag, indicating to anyone who knew her that she was either on her way to or from a business appointment.

"Yoo-hoo, it's your baby sister bearing gifts," she called, glancing into the empty living room and moving quickly toward the kitchen. "Where is everybody?" She stopped and closed her eyes, lifting her face dramatically toward the ceiling. "And what is that heavenly chocolate smell?"

"Hi, Gail," Julia answered from the door of the library. "I just made an apple fudge pie, and if you're very nice we can have two tiny pieces. With whipped cream..." Julia turned and flapped one hand into the library. "I'm thinking of putting a pothos plant in here, but I don't know if there's enough sunlight."

Gail frowned at her sister as the pair moved into the library. "Why are you worrying about that now? You're going to be gone in a month." Rummaging in her handbag, she extracted a book. "Here's your present. This is supposed to be the best English language guide to Brazil. I kind of glanced at a few pages and it's got tons of different stuff. There's information about parrots that live to be eighty years old and addresses of some incredible stores and restaurants, and even pictures of skimpy bikinis. Nothing about Buenos Aires, though."

"Buenos Aires is in Argentina, not Brazil," Julia corrected automatically, looking alternately at her sister and the book. Accepting the gift, she collapsed onto an overstuffed chair. She really didn't want to discuss this with Gail, not after all the arguments she'd had with Jack and then the rows with Sydney. Thank God Stephanie was at college and didn't really care where her parents lived.

"Thanks for the book, but I don't know if I'm going to Brazil."

Dramatically, Gail dropped her handbag on the floor. For a moment the two women stared at one another and then Gail leaned forward, her body rigid, her tone sharp.

"What are you talking about? Are you crazy? You've got this fabulous opportunity that most people would kill for and you're going to stay here?"

Exasperated, Julia snapped back, "That's easy for you to say. You have your own business, no children, no pets and no husband, so you could just pick up and go." She lifted a hand, fingers spread, and began ticking off items with her other hand. "I have this house that I don't want to rent and can't leave empty, a dog and a cat that obviously can't go with us and a daughter that refuses to leave. My job will not be waiting when I get back and I'm very attached to the people at *Angel and Friends*."

"Who certainly *will* be waiting when you get back..."

It was an old argument. Legally, *Angel and Friends*

should turn their clients over to Immigration rather than feed them and try to help with jobs and legal assistance but, as far as Julia was concerned, that would also be calloused and immoral.

"Oh please," she said. "You know as well as I do that California restaurant and farm and factory owners are only too happy to hire people with no papers and pay them half minimum wage. And no benefits either." As always, she felt exasperation begin to rise at her sister's stubborn stance.

In a gesture of helplessness, Gail flung her arms wide. "Do stop, I'm not up to a sermon. So staying here is all your idea, not Jack's?"

"Yes, it's mine."

"You are a ninny. I need a restorative drink." Gail strode to the built-in bar and mixed two gin and tonics, her face set. After handing one to her sister, Gail perched on a chaise-longue and said, "I read in that book that they have a fabulous drink in Brazil called a caipirinha." Looking directly at her sister, she asked, "Where is everybody?"

"Sydney's with her friends, Jack's playing tennis."

"So we can speak freely?"

"We always do."

Gail flipped an errant blond curl off her forehead, sipped at her gin, and then raised her eyebrows, indicating disapproval. Julia watched her warily, both envying and resenting Gail's ability to bounce through life seemingly unaffected by problems and disasters. She was always on top of every situation while Julia seemed to struggle with even the simplest decision.

"So, let's talk about this. What does Jack say about you staying here?"

"He's not very happy."

"Ha! I'll bet. And Mary Beth?"

Mary Beth Paulson and Julia, closest friends and confidants, spoke on the phone almost every day. "She can't believe it."

"I think you're a fool."

Julia sat rigidly in the chair, suffused with growing anger. "Thanks."

"Well, you are! Before you married Jack you said a hundred times that you hoped he wasn't a letch like Dad. Now you're going to turn your husband loose for two years in a country that's known to have some of the most beautiful women in the world while you stay here and trudge off to the TV studio each day. Explain that logic to me."

"We've been married twenty years, and I have no reason to believe that Jack is an incorrigible womanizer. Or would he turn into one..."

Gail crossed one leg over the other and pointed an index finger at her sister.

"Trust me, under the right circumstances, any man will wander. Not like our esteemed father, of course, but they'll all chase a few skirts given the opportunity. You're paving the way for Jack to become a walking phallus."

Swallowing an angry, defensive retort, Julia stood and stepped to the bar where she rummaged about on a crowded shelf and finally selected an open jar of macadamia nuts. Although her sister was sensitive to the subject of extracurricular women since one of her husbands had been caught with a prostitute on Hollywood Boulevard, thus explosively ending that marriage, Gail was echoing Julia's own doubts. She fished out two nuts and handed the jar to Gail.

"Okay, assuming you're right and I'm pushing Jack into irresistible temptation, how do you see me just taking off for two years?"

Gail looked at her Patek Philippe watch and hastily swallowed a few macadamias. Instead of answering the question, she said, "I have to go pretty soon. I have an appointment with that bizarre Marcia Markel, which will ruin my day."

Puzzled, Julia sat down, took a sip of gin and tonic and

asked, "Who?"

"Oh, I told you about her. This is the third wedding I've planned for her wimpy daughter, but Mama never likes the prospective grooms and always manages to break it off. I suppose that's what's happening this time too." She sighed. "The joys of being a wedding consultant." She paused thoughtfully. "Although, with all my husbands I admit I am an expert." She gazed inquisitively at Julia. "So, let's go through the problems."

"Sydney, for one. She won't come with us and I'm not leaving her with her friend Gretchen Bauer for the next year, even though the Bauers would be happy to have her. That family seems to have no rules at all."

Gail glanced briefly at the ceiling, or perhaps it was a wordless plea for heavenly intervention. "When we were growing up we didn't either."

"Don't start that again." As a child and teenager, Gail had relished the nearly total freedom they enjoyed, but now, in her adult years, she viewed this lack of parental attention as serious neglect, while Julia looked upon the benign indifference bestowed upon them by their socially oriented mother and libertine father as a blessing.

"Well," Gail broke into her thoughts, "you can always leave Sydney with me for her senior year."

Speechless, Julia stared at her sister and then said, "But you've never had any children."

"My dear Julia, Sydney is not a child. She is seventeen and I certainly know how to deal with adolescents. Most of my clients are teenagers, mentally and emotionally if not in actual fact."

Julia slowly thought this through. It was an incredible offer that might be the best of very limited options.

"Are you serious?"

"Oh, for God's sake, of course I am. Besides, it would give us an excuse to come visit you in exotic and tropical Brazil."

Julia began to smile. "I have to talk to Jack, of course,

but it sounds fantastic to me. Thanks, baby sister. We need to leave you money for Sydney's expenses and—"

Gail waved her into silence. "What other major problem?"

"The house and pets."

"I was thinking about that," Gail said slowly. She drained her glass and placed it carefully on the coffee table. Leaning forward, both elbows on her knees, fists supporting her chin, she looked at her sister. "As I recall, Jack has a nephew going to Loyola Marymount who lives in a dump of an apartment out by the airport."

"Yes, Carl. God, that apartment is gross. And planes fly about ten feet overhead every half second."

"Exactly! So wouldn't he and his roommates love to live in a beautiful house with a pool in Venice Beach for a year or two? Their fee for this would be the care and feeding of the very loveable resident dog and cat."

Part of Julia jumped eagerly at the suggestion, but then she visualized the boys' current habitat with its encrusted dirt in the kitchen, molding remnants of food throughout the apartment along with unwashed crockery, heaps of clothes, both dirty and clean mixed together, sagging filthy sofa, grimy floors and windows. She looked around her library. Floor to ceiling mahogany bookcases lined with neat rows of books, built-in bar set into one corner of the silk-papered walls, rattan chairs and sofa upholstered in a bright bird-of-paradise print and glass doors onto the small verandah framed by draperies that matched the walls. She could just envision what four sloppy boys would do to her carefully designed and meticulously maintained house. Mouth drawn in a tight, disapproving curve, she shook her head.

"I know what you're thinking," said Gail. "That they'll turn the house into a pig pen in two minutes. Don't forget that place they're in now was just plain vile when they rented it. They've simply retained its natural charm and beauty."

They both smiled, remembering their shared shock when, on Carl's moving day, they had stopped by with his mother to see how he was progressing. "I don't understand why the university doesn't build more dorms and get rid of the lottery system for on-campus housing," commented Gail.

"No more land, I suppose, and they probably want to use any spare space for more educational buildings." Julia shrugged, her mind now elsewhere. Would it work to have four unsupervised twenty-year-old men here, or would she return to find the property destroyed? "Agnes Murphy down the street rented out a house they own in Bellflower, and when they checked up on it they found the tenants had built a bonfire in the middle of the living room floor. Stan had to take two weeks off and hire a crew of workmen to put it all back together."

Gail looked at her in disbelief, glanced at her watch and stood up.

"First off, this is not Bellflower, and I can just imagine the tenants she had in that part of L.A. No one I know would even drive through the area, and they certainly wouldn't *live* in Bellflower." She stooped and hoisted her handbag. "As far as I'm concerned, the boys could manage here quite well. They're all from decent families, have good manners, are juniors in college and probably do like to party and screw around but not demolish homes. Think about it. Right now I've got to deal with surly Marcia and her insipid daughter. Thanks for the drink. It'll help see me through the ordeal. I'll be back later for some fudge pie. And not a tiny piece, either."

Long after her sister had dashed through the living room and out the front door, Julia sat and unseeingly studied the palm and banana trees that screened the neighboring property. She felt suddenly weightless with relief. Thanks to her sister, whom she had always thought of as an air-head, she might be able to go with Jack after all. For the first time since her husband's Brazilian bombshell had dropped on the household, a small thrill of excitement built in the pit of her stomach and spread throughout her body.

Silently, Jack and Julia watched the visa official at the Brazilian Consulate shuffle through the papers they had presented. Only open from ten till noon, three days a week, the office was normally jammed with prospective immigrants and was sadly understaffed with workers that seemed to advertise the languid pace of their home country. The couple had arrived promptly at ten and found six or eight others already in line.

"Next time we'll get here at seven", Jack murmured. It was nearly eleven forty-five.

"Next time?" Julia whispered incredulously. It was their third trip to the consulate; although they had received an official list of documents and papers that were required for Julia's visa, every time they arrived, they were advised to bring additional items.

"*Senhor*," the middle age woman said, looking at Jack and ignoring Julia, "I told you we must have the original birth certificate and also the original marriage certificate. This," she held up a certified copy of their marriage certificate, "is not original."

Julia felt her face flame with anger and gripped the edge of the counter. "I'm sorry," she interjected, "we were married here in Los Angeles, and in California you get only one original certificate. If you want more, you must have a court order." The woman lived and worked in California, so she must have heard this a thousand times, Julia thought in exasperation.

"Our rules say the original."

"Well, you can't have it. This is a certified, notarized copy, and it will have to do."

"After we issue the visa we'll return the original to you."

"No."

Julia felt Jack's arm snake around her waist and give her a warning pinch while the two women stared hostilely at one another. Without another word, the woman picked up the certificate, wheeled around, and with more energy than had been previously displayed in the visa section, marched across the room and vanished into another room.

"For God's sake, Julia, they're going to deny your visa altogether if you keep this up," Jack whispered crossly.

Her eyes flashed. "I haven't decided I'm going yet."

"Well, please make up your mind. I'm only going through this to help you. Claymore would have gotten both our visas if you hadn't spent nearly a month refusing to even think of Brazil."

They lapsed into chilly silence, broken by the return of the clerk some fifteen minutes later.

"The Consul says he will accept this," she said grudgingly as she ruffled the papers again. "But we need your furniture declaration."

"How soon?"

"At once! It has to be sent to Brasilia and returned. And you have only a limited period of time to ship your belongings."

"And we come back here with the list?"

"Of course."

The front door opened and Jack, carrying a clipboard, emerged from the house followed by Julia bearing a shrimp paté surrounded by crackers. Both paused on the deck and looked across the front lawn where, next to the swimming pool, a green and white striped beach umbrella shaded a round, white metal table. Sydney and three of her friends, all of whom looked remarkably alike in shorts, scoop-neck tee shirts, hoop earrings and oversized sunglasses, were sprawled on deck chairs around the table, chatting and giggling with Carl. Julia waved and called, "I thought you girls were going to the beach."

In unison, necks swiveled, and then the women rose,

wobbling slightly on their roller blades as they tottered across the grass toward the gate. It's amazing, Julia thought, they're all imitating each other. She and Jack exchanged easy smiles as they descended the stairs and watched the girls approach. Behind them, Carl stood beside the table, cracking his knuckles.

"We lost track of time," Sydney said, eyeing the paté.

"You don't have to leave," Jack said. "We have some things to explain to Carl but we can do that inside."

"That's okay, we're going to skate down to Redondo on the bike path, so we have to get going." Sydney scooped some paté with a cracker, popped it into her mouth and indicated her friends should do the same. "Yum!"

"That's pretty far to skate."

"She means we're going *toward* Redondo," amended a girl with long black hair tied into a ponytail. They all snickered, said goodbye to Jack and Julia and filed out the gate. Julia's smile faded as she watched them with a sudden pang of regret, aware that she was giving up a life she adored to step into the unknown. When she and Jack returned from Brazil, Sydney would be an adult, and nothing would be the same.

"See ya, Carl," one of the girls called.

"Maybe at the party tonight?" he asked. They giggled again and left.

"They think they're so adult," Jack muttered with a twisted smile as the couple again moved across the lawn.

"And they know absolutely everything," added Julia. "It's scary how far behind we are."

Jack chuckled and waved Carl in the general direction of a chair. "Have a seat," he said as he and Julia sat down. Julia slid the paté across the table. "Help yourself, Carl."

As he leaned forward, Jack spoke again.

"I've had a contract drawn up here. Because you're my nephew, I'm explaining it to you first, and then you can talk it over with the others."

"Okay."

"I hope so. If you all agree with it, I want you four here next Saturday to sign it."

"We'll agree," he said eagerly.

Carl eyed the remains of the paté, and then grinned at his aunt. "Thanks for the terrific nosh, Aunt Julia. You should open a restaurant."

For the first time Julia really felt she was cutting her ties. Mixed with excitement and anticipation, there was still a tiny thread of doubt about her decision.

FOUR—SÃO PAULO, BRAZIL

"I hope Sydney's all right." Firmly grasping the handrail, Julia followed her husband onto the escalator. They had just exited the plane and were on their way to Immigration in Sao Paulo's Guarulhos Airport. Jack gave a snort, and then broke into a series of chuckles, each one spawning the next. Julia shot him a quizzical glance. "What's so funny about hoping our daughter's doing well?"

"It's not that." His laughter died, and then erupted again. "Sydney will be fine, but a resident teenager may cramp your flaky sister's style—especially since she's never had children."

"Gail is not all that flaky or *A Ring and Roses* would have failed a long time ago."

"Oh, she's a good businesswoman, I'll grant her that, especially since her field is weddings and her hobby's getting married."

Julia had heard this before: "Jack, what a nasty thing to say." Her attention was instantly diverted by the milling crowd of passengers that had just come into sight on the

26

ground floor. "Look at that. It's unbelievable."

"Four international flights landed at almost the same time and the passengers must all go through immigration here," a heavily accented voice just in front of Jack informed them. Briefly Julia closed her eyes, listening as the voice brought more unwelcome news. "If you're Brazilian, you go quickly through that inspection on the left, but everyone else must queue here."

They stepped off the escalator and immediately melted into a mob that was guided into a line snaking back and forth between a parallel ropes across the enormous room. The flight, direct from Los Angeles to São Paulo, had been long and exhausting, somewhat dampening the enthusiasm Julia had managed to generate once she realized that this radical move was actually going to happen. Amazingly, everyone was happy. Stephanie and Gail were thrilled by the prospect of future exotic vacations. And, after Sydney was assured she could move in with Gail and finish high school with her class, she became such a big promoter of the move that Julia suspected her youngest daughter joyously anticipated a lifestyle of total freedom with no rules in her idiosyncratic and quirky aunt's house.

Caught up in all this eagerness, a constant round of goodbye parties, envious friends, packing, and dealing with the bureaucratic whims of the Brazilian consulate, Julia's attitude had altered. It *was*, she decided, a rare and exciting chance to know another country in depth without cutting all ties and torching every bridge. And lately she had been feeling overworked and underpaid—burned out-at the TV station. Why not be a lady of leisure for two years and let Jack support her? After Brazil, Jack might possibly be sent on another foreign assignment like Bob Jenkins, the vice-president for sales, who had recently spent almost three years in London.

Inching forward, Julia felt a surge of excitement at the sudden realization that they were actually in Brazil. Her eyes snapped with joy; she'd never thought of herself as an adventurous person but this was quite bold. Intertwining her fingers with Jack's, she resolved to make this the best period of her life.

Much, much later they passed through immigration, collected their luggage and were waved through customs inspection. As they approached the double frosted glass doors that separated them from the outside world, Julia and Jack smiled at one another, sharing a wordless moment of intimacy before passing a uniformed guard and watching the automatic doors swing open.

They stepped into another world, trading frosty air-conditioning for damp heat that pressed heavily against the skin, the piquant odor of fresh coffee in the air. Involuntarily, they stopped. The waiting area of the airport was a press of people of all ages and colors; a substantial number waving Brazilian flags and banners, and all shouting and cheering each time the double doors opened. Held back by a metal railing separating the forbidden halls of the customs area from ordinary folk, those in front were holding a long banner that read, *PARABÉNS CORINTHIANS* that they waved back and forth in time to percussion loudly played by out-of-sight drummers.

The doors opened again and a raucous cheer erupted, instantly drowned out by frenetic drumming. A tiny, white-uniformed porter materialized.

"Taxi?" he asked

Jack nodded.

"I thought the company was sending a driver," Julia shouted over the din.

"I told them not to bother. Planes are late more often than not, and then there's customs and immigration. The guy might stand here for hours."

Quickly, as though afraid his clients might change their minds, the porter took charge of their luggage cart, easing around the fringes of the crowd and into an empty area of the waiting room. Julia and Jack slowly followed.

"What is this?" Julia gestured toward the mob.

"Corinthians is a Brazilian soccer team," Jack said with an authority born of very recent research, "and I guess they must have gone somewhere and won a game. Or a tournament."

"Their fans don't dress very formally."

Jack laughed. Most of the women wore skin-tight tank tops or halters with mini-skirts, shorts or trousers, the latter also seemingly several sizes too small. Footwear appeared to be exclusively flip-flops.

"How do you think they get into those clothes?" Julia mused in amazement.

Several other instruments joined the percussionists and they swung into an obviously popular melody; the crowd immediately stopped cheering and began to sing. Julia and Jack stopped.

"Noisy bunch, aren't they?" he said. Dancing was a hobby they shared, and they both stared in fascination at the crowd. In addition to singing, Brazilian bodies now were moving in time to the tune; arms, legs and hips moved rapidly, gracefully and sensuously.

"We could tango," Jack suggested.

"Julia shook her head. "It doesn't work with this music."

"I forgot; it's the samba here."

"Which we never learned..."

A woman detached herself from the crowd and danced toward them, her feet moving with small, quick steps, her arms and shoulders twisting rapidly from side to side. A few feet from the couple, she turned her back toward them. Julia gasped. "How does she do that?" The woman's bottom bounced quickly from side to side while the rest of her body was almost motionless.

"Her feet are moving."

"But just in place."

The woman turned to face them and, for a fraction of a second, her clear, gray-green eyes caught Jack's. A tiny, seductive smile curved her lips before she swung around and danced back into the crowd.

"Wow", commented Julia, lit by an unexpected flash of jealousy and taken aback by the unexpected tableau from which she had been pointedly excluded.

"This is Brazil." Jack gently kissed her, then took her hand and changed the subject. "Where's our luggage? Everybody said you have to watch it all the time."

"It's right here," she said. Three feet away, their porter rested against the cart, his friendly smile displaying a scarcity of teeth in his brown, wrinkled face.

Later, in the taxi, Jack squeezed her kneecap, and then massaged her thigh. "This is a whole new life," he announced happily.

I will be cool, not anxious, Julia told herself resolutely as the taxi whipped down the highway, alternately tailgating cars and trucks while darting in and out of narrow openings in traffic. Staring out the side window, she was startled to see the green of the countryside suddenly replaced by a jumble of hovels made from broken bricks, cardboard and scrap metal. The dwellings seemed to be heaped together, with open holes for windows and doors, with makeshift ladders allowing access to the higher levels. As traffic thickened and their driver was forced to slow, she could see laundry draped from windows and ladders and hung upon wires that looked suspiciously like electrical lines suspended over narrow dirt pathways. Neatly dressed men and women emerged from the hidden interior, joining children who played ball and flew kites alongside the highway and older people who sat on rickety benches watching the traffic. The taxi passed a shack crowded with men drinking from bottles on the counter and she glimpsed a thin horse shackled to an empty wooden cart. Nearby, a woman bent intently over her toddler's mop of curls from which she diligently picked nits.

Julia was stunned. "I can't believe people actually live here," she whispered.

"I think this is what's called a *favela*."

"My God," she breathed. Jack nodded briefly.

They drove into a haze of pollution, a forest of high rise buildings appeared on the horizon, the traffic slowed to a crawl and then stopped, while drivers flung obscene gestures at one another. Just like L.A., Julia thought. And then she remembered the tumbled hovels, children at play a scant foot from the highway, the woman searching for lice in her child's hair. "Or maybe not," she amended.

FIVE—SÃO PAULO, BRAZIL

*W*ith Jack beside her, Julia perched rigidly on a linen-upholstered sofa in the service flat that was their temporary home. Papers were stacked in an orderly fashion on the small oblong table that separated the couple from Flavia Cavalcante, the bilingual employee of an agency that settled foreign corporate families into the community. Flavia peered intently at Julia and Jack.

"You're very lucky we could find this apartment for you." Julia winced; the thunder of jackhammers on the opposite corner of the street where an enormous luxury hotel was being built made it difficult to hear even though the door onto the tiny balcony and all the windows had been tightly closed. "It's right in the heart of the Jardims district where the best restaurants and nightclubs are located," Flavia shouted. Julia nodded mutely. "And the shopping," Flavia intoned, clutching her breast with one hand and resting the fingers of the other lightly on her forehead. "International designer shops, antiques, chocolates, *everything* is all right here." She leaned forward, her very dark hair sweeping both shoulders, and smiled. "Better than Rodeo Drive." Automatically, Julia returned the smile. Flavia's dark eyes bored insistently into Julia's. "You *are* happy?"

Julia looked around the small room that held the sofa and one chair, a corner bar/kitchen with two stools and, behind the bar, four burners and a tiny refrigerator. Her main hobby, her great passion, was cooking, and there was no chance of creating a gourmet meal here, or cooking much more than a boiled egg or two. A folding door concealed a double bed that took up all but a few inches of the bedroom, a minute closet and a door to the tiny bathroom.

"Of course, for the moment, but when can we move into the house?"

In spite of warnings that apartments were much more secure and safe, Julia wanted a house with a large garden in which she could grow some of the marvelous tropical plants and shrubs that were considered exotic rarities in California, and also an adequate kitchen. For nearly four weeks, Flavia had escorted them through dozens of houses that ranged in size from large to enormous, but nothing seemed quite right. Especially difficult were the kitchens which, in Brazil, were normally used only by the maids, and were therefore tiny and primitive. With every residence, Jack grew more cranky and irritable until finally, tired of the search, the couple had selected a rental, about to be vacated, in Chacara Flora, a walled area that was considered the safest in the city.

"When your shipment arrives," announced Flavia, crossing legs that were encased in very tight, brown leather pants.

"And when will that be?" The shipment, for which all ex-pats waited anxiously and nervously, contained furniture, kitchen utensils, cooking equipment, bed, bath and table linens, crystal, and most of their clothes—everything sent from home that was needed to set up housekeeping.

Flavia shrugged, lifting her shoulders inside a clinging, crème-colored, sweater. "Maybe three months..."

Julia gasped. "We've been here one month already."

"What?" The jackhammers had been joined by the groaning and grinding of other heavy machinery. Clouds of dust and dirt mushroomed past their twelfth floor windows.

"This is a perfect flat," Flavia shouted. "It has a chair on the veranda so you can watch the sunset."

"There's only *room* for one chair and you can't see the sunset for all the cranes and machinery and dust." Julia's throat felt dry. "Why is the shipment taking so long?" Jack snuck another quick look at his watch.

"Because this is Brazil, and once it arrives, which it hasn't, you must give a little gift to the customs people."

"A bribe," Jack stated flatly.

"Of course, but maybe not just one. Your shipping agent has to decide how much and to whom the gratuities will go. It's very complicated."

"I can see that."

"And the dock workers may be on strike. They often are."

"How long do the strikes last?"

Again an expressive shrug. "Who knows? Right now, today, we must discuss the question of servants. It's very important, because I think I've found the perfect couple."

"A couple?" Julia felt that something had spun out of control. She had grown up in a California household where she, her mother and sister did the cooking, washing and cleaning, just like their friends and neighbors. Not a servant in sight. "I told you that I didn't really want anyone, but I would have a maid since I obviously can't take care of that huge house myself."

"No, you can't, and in Brazil no one does. You either are a maid, or you have one, but in that house you will also need a gardener, a pool man and a handyman for house repairs; and if you get a couple, the man can do all of that plus heavy housework. He's called a *caseiro,* and he often puts on a little white jacket and helps serve at the dinner parties that the cook prepares."

Jack, the corners of his lips twitching, lifted one eyebrow and looked at Julia who gazed back in a combination of resignation and amusement. They were both thinking that she had been the cook and gardener, and Jack the pool man and butler, in Venice Beach...without uniforms, and happy with their jobs.

"I'll do the cooking," Julia announced flatly. "And I only need help in the garden with the heavy work, like pruning."

Flavia stared at her as though she had just announced that she was a Bird Flue carrier.

"Who pays for this caseiro and his bride?" Jack enquired.

"Normally, you do."

"I don't think so..."

"Alright, I can probably do a deal so that Claymore pays. And I've found a really exceptional couple that will be snapped up in a minute if you don't want them. Good references, experience, honest, trustworthy—what else do you want?"

Again, Jack and Julia looked at one another. Julia nodded almost imperceptibly in surrender. Might as well, as long as she could cook and poke around the garden and didn't have to pay for help she didn't want anyway.

"We'll give it a try," Jack agreed reluctantly.

"Wonderful! Now, if you'll just sign these papers that you approve of Djalma and Vera, I can officially negotiate with Claymore to hire them. They could move in now and take care of the garden and pool and do some house repairs."

Jack frowned. "House repairs already?"

Flavia flapped one hand dismissively. "Just tiny little jobs—nothing major."

Jack bent over the table, scribbling his signature on marked lines. The women stood up and moved to the balcony door where they stared down into a vast, deep hole nearly a block square. The air was thick and muddy-yellow.

"When are they supposed to finish that?" Julia asked.

"Oh, not for a long time. Three or four years, I think. It's going to be a fabulous hotel, but the contractor's already cheated on the building materials so they had to tear it down and start again."

"At least the government made them start over."

"No, the government wasn't involved. Part of the supporting columns collapsed before they got much of anything else in place so there was no choice."

Jack stood and Flavia turned, a swirl of brown leather, with matching hair, eyes and skin.

"Thank you." She looked at Julia as they moved toward the door. "Tomorrow I'll pick you up at about 10:00 o'clock and we'll go to the supermarket so you can practice writing checks, and then we'll eat at Emilio's. It's my favorite restaurant, and you can put it on your Claymore expenses. Then we'll interview more Portuguese teachers. *Tchau.*"

As the door closed, Jack and Julia swiveled toward one another before collapsing onto the sofa, both shaking with laughter. When Julia's merriment began to subside, Jack's gasps of hilarity caused a fresh eruption of mirth. Rolling to one side, Julia sat up, her eyes watering as she struggled for breath.

"Oh, my stomach hurts. Next thing you know, we'll have a butler."

"We already have one, as long as the gardener brings his little white jacket and remembers to wash his hands."

Julia rolled over on the sofa as both again convulsed with laughter. "Who would have thought it? My very own staff of servants," Julia chortled. "I wish my mother were alive to see this. She'd be so impressed that her daughter unwillingly has what she herself always wanted."

Across the street, a chorus of jackhammers boomed an excited refrain.

Energized by Flavia's visit, Julia strode confidently into the mom-and-pop that substituted for a supermarket in the crowded city center and made her way to the wine and beer section. Because the apartment offered almost no cooking facilities, she ate sandwiches for lunch and, after a Scotch and soda or two, she and Jack dined out. A beer might be nice just for a change, she thought, puzzling over the glass six-packs, all of which looked identical. Hesitantly, she chose one and joined the queue to pay.

Nudging the beer toward the cashier, Julia presented a heap of coins on one outstretched palm. Brazilian money was still a mystery, more so because the inflation rate meant that prices changed every day, sometimes every hour, and she was forced to rely on the honesty of strangers to select the right amount.

The cashier shook her head and said something that Julia failed to understand. Quickly, she took a paper bill and added it to the change, thinking she might not have enough. Again the clerk spoke, this time plucking an empty glass beer bottle from the shelf behind her and waving it dramatically between them. Her face hot and crimson with humiliation, Julia was aware of grumbling and shuffling in the growing number of customers waiting to pay.

"I'm sorry, I don't understand."

The scene was repeated and the whispers and coughs behind her increased. Biting her lower lip, Julia clenched her fist around the money and, leaving the beer on the counter, turned away, struggling to contain tears of embarrassment.

"Excuse me." The English was heavily accented and spoken by an old woman with a brown, lined face and dark sparkling eyes. "The cashier is telling you that you must bring empty bottles before you can buy beer."

Julia frowned, wondering if she had misunderstood. "You mean, I can't buy beer?"

"Not without empty bottles."

"I can pay for the empties. Buy them from the clerk."

"You can't. It's not allowed."

Frustration replaced mortification. "But I don't have empties."

"There are places that sell them."

This was bizarre. Could the woman be pulling her leg? Hearing the clink of glass, she half turned and watched a young woman count out numerous empty beer bottles for the cashier. Julia asked, "Where are these places? What are they called?"

"They don't have actual names. You must ask around."

Abruptly the old woman turned and walked toward the exit. Julia felt that she had wandered into another time zone. The purchase of beer had segued into a very difficult task, one that she would relegate to Jack and his bilingual secretary next time.

Still dazed, she walked to the post office two blocks away, retrieved a stack of postcards from her handbag, and approached a postal clerk.

"*Fala ingles*?" she asked.

"*Não.*" The negative reply was accompanied by a broad, friendly smile.

Of course not, Julia thought; Flavia must be the only English speaker amongst the twenty-one million people living in São Paulo.

She took a deep breath. "*Eu quero comprar doce seios, por favor.*"

Julia had been trying to study Portuguese on her own and hoped she'd nailed this sentence correctly. The clerk's smile broadened and Julia could see that she was stifling a small chuckle. Two more postal workers popped out of an inner door, giggling and staring at Julia while customers around her craned their necks and either chuckled or guffawed.

"*Perdão, que quer?*" asked the clerk.

Knowing that something was very, very wrong, Julia nevertheless persisted, pointed to the postcards and said, "*Doze seios.*"

Now it was outright laughter around the room and, for the second time in less than an hour, Julia's face was hot and her body perspired heavily. A soft, female voice at her elbow whispered, "The word is *selos, Senhora. Seios* is the word for stamps in Spanish, not Portuguese. You have just asked for a dozen breasts."

Spreading her coins on the counter, Julia stared straight ahead as the grinning clerk separated the payment and pushed the remainder back to her. Her face still flushed, Julia moved through the chuckling crowd, aware that she was the focus of attention. Would she ever get it right in this country?

"I guess we should start back to town pretty soon."

Jack grunted, signifying both agreement and disagreement, then slipped an arm around Julia's waist and pulled her close. "We should make a habit of this. Get out of the pollution and the stress of São Paulo," he commented.

Julia kissed him lightly on one ear lobe and nodded enthusiastically. "Absolutely! We could pick a different place every month or so, although we might not be as lucky as we were here. This is so quiet and peaceful."

"Really a beautiful place..."

"And you were right," she added. "I do love Brazil."

For a few moments the couple stood at the edge of the *pousada* property, gazing at the magnificent crags and densely green valleys of Itatiaía National Park where they had spent the last two days. Only a three-hour drive from São Paulo, it was known for its hiking trails that varied in difficulty from moderate to extremely difficult and dangerous, as well as its numerous waterfalls and abundance of animal and plant life. It had been Jack's spur-of-the-moment idea on Friday morning to take the guidebook, get in the car and go. They were thrilled with both the park and the pousada and had spent the weekend hiking the easy trails, swimming lazily in the pool, and making love. São Paulo seemed light years away.

A faint breeze rustled the leaves of the thickly interlinked trees and shrubbery while the clipped calls of birds hidden in the forest emphasized the calm tranquility of the wilderness. Taking Jack's hand, Julia reluctantly turned and began to walk toward the pousada.

"The one bright spot is that we aren't going back to the residence hotel."

Draping one arm over Julia's shoulders, Jack steered her along a path toward the parking area. Just three weeks ago, Julia had stared out at the jackhammers, cranes and bulldozers on the opposite corner, then picked up the phone and called Flavia, demanding entry into their rented home. The agent was appalled, insisting that highly-placed American executives couldn't live like squatters but in the end gracelessly acquiesced, promising to rent furniture until the arrival of "the shipment" at some still-unknown date. Two days later, a bed, breakfast table, and two chairs had been delivered along with assorted pots, pans and dishes which Julia suspected might have come from a garage sale. As a way of life it could easily be identified as monastic but was still a vast improvement over the cramped and noisy service flat. And at last Julia could cook, and work in the garden.

In silence they drove down the mountain, the winding road shaded by overhanging trees and high, thick shrubs on both sides. Sunlight filtered through the branches, flashing on a fast-running stream that appeared briefly on the right before vanishing into the trees. From time to time, small signs appeared designating the way to hotels, and very occasionally one passed a building that was nearly concealed by the forest. At the edge of the park the road flattened abruptly and not far ahead they could see a truck piled high with pineapples stationed on the shoulder.

"Look, Jack, let's buy a pineapple and take it home. It'll be much fresher and cheaper than those from the street market."

Jack slowed the car, and then stopped just beside the truck. One of two young men lounging under a tree stood up and strode toward Jack's side of the car.

"They don't have a price posted."

"We'll ask."

"We don't speak Portuguese."

"Not very well, but I've certainly learned how to say `how much'?"

Jack rolled down his window and the man squatted beside the car.

"*Pois não?*" he asked.

"*Quanto é?*" asked Jack.

He was greeted by a torrent of Portuguese, ending with an inquisitive smile. Julia and Jack exchanged baffled looks.

"Did you get that?"

"Of course not; my vocabulary is limited to twenty words and no conjugations."

Jack turned to the man and said, "*Repete, por favor.*"

Again there was a flood of totally incomprehensible Portuguese, this time accompanied by dramatic gestures in the direction of the truck. Still talking, the man rose, stepped to his vehicle and selected a pineapple, returning to smell it, bounce it from hand to hand and then offer it to Jack.

"This was such a bad idea," said Julia. "Shall we just buy one and go?"

"Sure." He looked at the Brazilian. "*Bem. Bom. Tudo bem.*"

He held out a twenty-*reais* bill, which the man pocketed before handing Jack the change and motioning to his companion. The latter jumped up and began unloading pineapples from the truck while the first man opened the back door of Jack's car. Very quickly, the pair pulled pineapples and more pineapples from the truck and deposited the fruit on the back seat and floor. Alarmed, Julia twisted to count the number just as the door slammed and the pair backed away.

"*Tchau e obrigado,*" they called.

Dazed, Jack started the engine and guided the car back onto the road. Julia slumped back into the passenger seat.

"What have we done?" asked Jack.

"Somehow, we've bought about a dozen very ripe pineapples."

For a few moments neither of them spoke. Julia began to laugh. "This is a minor disaster."

Jack nodded. "Yup," he agreed. "We don't have any friends to give them to, and we don't know the neighbors, and I don't want to go on the Brazilian pineapple diet."

Julia brightened. "You know what? We could give them to a church."

"You mean just trundle them in and leave them on the pews?"

"I guess maybe that's not such a brilliant idea. Let's think."

As Jack drove back to São Paulo they thought and then thought some more and failed to come up with a solution. When they reached the outskirts of the city, Julia suddenly cried, "Look, there's a *favela*"

"And..."

"Stop the car. We're going to give the pineapples to those people in the *favela.*" Every time Julia passed one of the city slums, she felt guilty over the disparity between her life of real luxury and the misery that must exist in these unspeakable hovels. She wanted to help alleviate the wretchedness but didn't know how; now there was something she could actually do.

Jack swerved and screeched to a stop. "Are you sure this is safe? We're also in front of a prison."

But Julia had jumped from the car, opened the back

door and begun handing pineapples to several women nearby. As though summoned by magic radar, residents emerged from the tumbled structures and crowded around the car as Julia continued distributing the fruit. Within seconds, she shut the back door and jumped into the passenger seat with a wide grin. "See? We got rid of them and made a dozen people happy."

"All of them? Didn't you save one for us?"

Julia grimaced, sighed and slowly shook her head. "Sorry about that.

"It was a fabulous weekend," Jack said as they turned into Chacara Flora and waving to the guards at the gate, "in spite of the Pineapple episode."

"Absolutely wonderful," Julia agreed. "One we'll remember." She had no idea how prescient her words were. Suddenly, she sat forward and pointed to a man walking along the side of the road. "Isn't that Djalma?"

"Wearing a suit?"

As Jack drove slowly down the cobblestone road, both of them peered intently through the film-darkened windows. As they passed the pedestrian, their expressions reflected disbelief.

"It is indeed our gardener," confirmed Jack, "and he's wearing my Armani suit."

"Are you sure? About the suit, I mean."

"Do you think our handyman has Armani suits of his own? Especially one a couple of sizes too big?" Jack frowned ferociously, rolled down the window and yelled, "Djalma! Get into the car."

The gardener smiled pleasantly and continued walking.

"And my best Hermes tie," Jack seethed. Twisting around, he opened the back door and gestured for Djalma to get in. The gardener/pool-man ambled across the road, slid into the back seat and shut the door.

"Call Flavia and tell her we have a problem," Jack growled as he threw the car in gear and raced over the cobblestones toward home.

Flavia's numbers—all of them—had been programmed into the cell phone and, unexpectedly, she answered on the first ring at her office. Not enough to do, Julia thought, or maybe she's bored.

"I need to have you listen to Djalma tell me why he's wearing my husband's suit."

She passed the phone to the gardener and heard a lengthy explanation in Portuguese before he handed the instrument back. With a deepening frown, she listened to the translation.

"Police? He says he wanted to look nice for the police but they wouldn't see him and Jack has to go himself. What's this about?"

Jack wheeled into the driveway and shot up the hill. Tersely, Julia spoke into the phone. "There was an attempted robbery yesterday? In our dressing room? That room's empty." Again she listened to the voice on the other end of the line, her forehead deeply creased.

Jack braked sharply in the garage and the couple sprang out of the car and sprinted toward the dressing room, the phone still pressed to Julia's ear. Turning into the hallway, they could see scattered papers; Julia felt a knot of dread in her stomach. With slowed steps, she moved closer and then inched around the dressing room door to stand beside Jack.

Unable to move or speak, they stared at the chaos. Someone had cut the safe out of the wall into which it had been cemented and then blown it open. The contents, comprised only of documents and papers, had been flung about the room, torn and trampled. Julia felt her muscles begin to tremble, as though the temperature had dropped to sub-zero. Finally, she found her voice and spoke briefly into the phone before pressing the disconnect button.

"I don't get it." Jack's voice was barely audible. "Why didn't our faithful and highly-paid butler and cook hear anything?"

"Flavia said they were in their quarters watching TV, but she also said she suspects that Djalma then went out on a date, not to the police station."

"A *date?*" He pursed his lips and shook his head skeptically. "Wearing my suit?" Baffled, he turned to his wife. "But why would anyone invade a practically empty house? And how did they get in?"

"Obviously through that broken window..." Julia waved toward scattered broken glass. Flavia says the house isn't secure enough and we need to get a guard. She also said that the previous tenants were very rich and that the thieves apparently knew they were moving out but thought they might have left jewelry or money in the safe. Now they know the rich folks are gone and have been replaced by paupers who don't even have furniture, so they probably won't be back." Too late, Julia understood why Flavia had stressed the safety of an apartment and regretted her own insistence on renting a house. She felt the shadows of the intruders as a physical presence along with the ruined vulnerability of an invaded house and wondered if she would ever feel safe in the house again.

Placing both hands on her shoulders, Jack turned her to face him. "Paupers? She said that?" They stared at one another for a moment or two and then Jack began to laugh. "Paupers. That should be good for a raise."

There was the sudden sound of crockery being smashed at the other end of the house and their servants' voices were raised in angry shouts. More china hit the wall and Julia's eyes narrowed.

"Maybe he actually had been out on a date."

SIX—SÃO PAULO, BRAZIL

*J*ulia stepped into the living room and sank onto the crewel-work sofa, the one that had finally arrived in their shipment from Venice Beach, and stared contentedly at the garden. Wide, floor to ceiling glass doors separating the living room from the patio had been pushed back into the wall, giving the impression that there was no barrier between the man-made dwelling and the sloping garden. The view was spectacular; surrounding an expanse of emerald green grass, palm trees and a towering Yellow Cassia almost completely covered with fragrant, yellow blooms shaded a jumble of smaller Ipê, Frangipani, Mimosa and other shrubs and trees that Julia had yet to identify. During the time they had lived monastically in the almost-empty house, she had spent many days weeding the flower beds, identifying the medley of flora and designing a vegetable garden. And, while working in the back yard, her eyes frequently strayed to the empty *orquidario* built well behind the swimming pool. Roses didn't do that well in São Paulo, but orchids were everywhere; she resolved that these delicate flowers would fill her back garden just as soon as she learned something about their cultivation.

Now that the furniture and paintings had arrived, Julia thought the house was quite beautiful. It was the kind of large but comfortable home in luxuriant surroundings that her friends in California would envy if they ever came to visit, which wasn't likely since most Americans, including many of her friends whom she considered intelligent, had the erroneous impression that São Paulo was a suburb of Buenos Aires. Following that idea would take them to the wrong country where they could all happily tango till they dropped.

A slight frown creased her forehead. In spite of promises to themselves, they still hadn't taken a course in samba dancing, and if Jack continued to work long hours, they never would take one. Since their arrival, they hadn't danced at all. A pair of black and yellow bem-ti-vis caught her eye and thoughts of dancing vanished as she watched them approach.

Before skimming above the swimming pool and disappearing over the treetops, the two birds pecked briefly but furiously at the half papaya and sunflower seeds that Julia deposited daily in a bamboo bird feeder. A flock of noisily conversing green parrots circled above and then settled into the leafy branches of a large mango tree. Although the pale blue sky was cloudless, an early morning storm had polished the foliage and grass that now flashed and glittered in the sun. Julia closed her eyes, hearing the birds, the whisper of breezes in the coconut palm and the faint barking of a dog and thought that a hammock on the verandah would make life just perfect.

Her sense of peace was short lived. Muted but angry voices were heard around the corner, indicating another quarrel between the caseiro and his wife, followed by a series of resounding bangs as a metal spike was driven into a cement wall by a hammer. Apparently, Djalma's lunch hour was over.

"Senhora?" Moments later, Vera appeared in the doorway and rattled off a short announcement in Portuguese followed by a question, none of which Julia understood. It had been years since she'd felt so incompetent and useless. Somehow, when envisioning this adventure, both she and Jack failed to factor in the culture change and the difficult language, both important oversights.

"The company's going to pay for Portuguese lessons when we get there, and with your Spanish you'll have no trouble at all," Jack had assured her. He'd been so wrong. Possibly if Spanish had been her mother tongue it would have been helpful, or maybe she just didn't have any flair for languages, but the more she studied Portuguese— without successful results—the more the Spanish slipped away.

Jack, of course, couldn't understand her frustration since his entire office staff spoke English. His secretary, Eliana Gazzinelli, whom Julia had never met, had replaced Flavia as her bosom telephone buddy, translating when necessary, which seemed to be most of the time. Vera repeated the announcement and, with a sigh, Julia reached for the telephone. Time to call on Eliana for enlightenment.

"Hello there". A female voice with a faint southern accent floated into the living room, and a moment later a woman with short blond hair and an enviable tan appeared behind Vera. "May I come in?" she asked.

Dropping the phone, Julia jumped to her feet and moved across the room to greet her guest.

"I'm so sorry," Julia said, reaching the entrance hall. "I guess Vera was trying to tell me you were here, but I just didn't understand. Please come in."

"None of us understands anything for a while," the visitor said, stepping into the living room. "Wow, this is really a great place, with a real fireplace and bookcases. And the colors!" Julia glanced at the walls that she had painted to match the greenery outside, the large Persian carpets, the books, sculptures, and framed photographs, and she had to agree with her visitor that the room looked pretty good. "But the windows and doors are totally open into the garden. How's that for security?" the woman continued.

She wasn't at all pretty, Julia observed, but she had a fascinating, mobile face, unimproved by make-up and lit by hazel eyes and a smile that dug a dimple into one cheek and revealed a set of white, almost perfect teeth. Nearly six feet tall, her posture was very straight and her figure on the thin side; she wore twill pants, a cotton sweater and leather sandals.

"The doors can be pushed back into the walls so they more or less disappear, like now, but everything's closed and double locked at night and when we're away," Julia explained. "We had a robbery before our shipment arrived, and it taught us a lesson, even though there was nothing to steal."

"Welcome to São Paulo. But this really is the nicest house I've seen yet, and we've lived down the road in the Chacara for three years, so I've seen most of them. I'm Laura Patterson, and my husband Alan is with Gessy Lever, which means we may be here awhile longer."

"I'm Julia Elliott. Please sit down and I'll go pantomime for the maid to bring us some coffee."

"No, not for me. I have two cafe com leite in the morning and that's usually it for the day." She turned to face her hostess and flashed that brilliant smile. "I'm on the board of Newcomers Club and your husband's company informed us that you're new to Brazil, so I thought I'd come over and welcome you." Stretching out her right hand, she leaned forward. "Welcome. Now you must learn to greet everyone the way they do here; usually a kiss on both cheeks."

"Everyone?" Julia's lips brushed her guest's cheeks.

"Not the workmen or maids, but basically everyone

else." Digging into her large handbag, Laura extracted a transparent sack with four round, yellow spheres the size of baseballs which she offered to Julia. "Here is your housewarming gift."

Puzzled, Julia accepted the bag and poked curiously at one of the hard balls. "Thank you, but what are they?"

Laura smiled. "Maracujá, an indigenous fruit. In the States they're called Passion Fruit." She held up a warning hand. "And before you ask, they're nature's tranquilizer, not an aphrodisiac. They have beautiful flowers that the missionaries in Brazil thought represented Christ on the cross, so they're named after the Passion of Christ."

Julia nodded, carefully placing the bag on an end table. "Thank you again for my first present in Brazil, and for the explanation." She gestured to the bamboo sofa and chairs upholstered in white linen with tan and green bamboo print on the patio. "Let's go outside."

As though on signal, furious hammering began again in the back garden.

Laura's face reflected amused surprise. "What on earth is going on?"

"Unfortunately, we've had workmen here since we moved in. The place looked great but there were all these little problems, like the electricity. When we turned on the bathroom light, the lights in the library also went on, but to turn both of them off you had to first switch on one of the small lamps in the bedroom. Fortunately, we have this fabulous caseiro who's a good supervisor and a wonderful handyman himself."

Laura grinned as they stepped onto the patio. "If that's all that's wrong, you lucked out. I've seen some high priced rentals that were absolutely unlivable because Brazilian landlords rarely take care of their property. They expect the tenants to be responsible for all the repairs, major and minor, as well as pay the property taxes, condo fees and just about everything else."

Julia sat down on a chair and waved her guest toward

the sofa.

"I'm finding that out. And we didn't luck out. After we moved in, we discovered door handles that fell off, the hot water faucet in our bathroom didn't work, the toilet seat in the maid's bathroom had disappeared and most of the light fixtures were taken out of the ceiling. We had to replace some of the pipes, which meant that workmen spent every day for an eternity chipping out the cement from around the pipes. Then they replaced the pipes, and can you believe it? They packed cement around them again." Julia had begun calmly but in her relief at unloading all these problems to someone other than her husband at the end of his long, workaholic day, her words had begun to tumble out and her voice to rise.

Laura chuckled and swatted at a mosquito.

"As I said, welcome to Brazil. But you either get used to it, or turn around and go home."

Julia was startled. Retreat had never been in the picture. "Just leave?"

"Oh, sure... Some women can't, or won't, adjust, and they make life so miserable for their husbands that the men refuse to stay. It's the end of their careers, of course. You have to remember that the men here generally work long, hard hours, and we're basically left on our own."

Julia smiled crookedly at her guest, hoping that Jack's work wouldn't be that demanding. Laura suddenly stood and moved into the living room where she picked up a photograph in a stained glass frame. Returning to her seat on the sofa, she held the picture toward Julia: "Your daughters?"

"That's right. They don't look much like me, do they?"

"Well, not a lot." She pointed to Stephanie. "This one could actually be Brazilian." Laughing, shaking her head, Julia leaned forward and looked at the picture of a beautiful girl with a straight nose, straight teeth, tanned skin and brown eyes flecked with yellow, all framed by masses of curly, very dark brown hair.

"Yes, well all those wild curls are thanks to a perm and a bottle of dye. She's at university and I never know what to expect when she comes home. Unlike my younger daughter Sydney, who is very predictable, conservative and clings to her home and friends."

"Sydney looks fragile."

"Probably because of that waif haircut and the faux Diane Keaton outfits."

Laura tilted her head to one side and gave her hostess a quizzical look.

"She's seventeen," Julia continued. "A few months ago she saw *Annie Hall* on Movie Classics and decided that those clothes were `just too cool'."

After replacing the photograph on an end table in the living room, Laura slid back onto the sofa. "Did you bring your furniture with you, or get it here?"

"We brought most of it. The bamboo stuff we bought here." She smiled. "We're lucky. Jack has a nephew in college who was living in a really dumpy apartment out by the airport with three other students, and they jumped at the chance to stay for free in Venice Beach, especially in an empty house. They brought their own Goodwill treasures, and Jack's brother checks up on them periodically, so everybody's happy."

The hammering began again with renewed vigor, and Laura squinted as though in pain. "What *are* they doing?"

"You won't believe it."

In unison, the women stood up and stepped from the patio onto soft, well-mown grass, then moved along the side of the house. Turning the corner, Laura stopped and gazed at the garden and pool. A deep verandah with another set of bamboo furniture, hanging ferns and potted shrubs ran the length of the house. At the foot of several tiled steps, a marble pool with a tower of large, angular rocks at one end shone in the sunlight, the intense blue serving to emphasize the deep green of the surrounding trees and plants. The soothing whisper of water trickling over the rocks and into the pool was lost in the ear-splitting racket that had intensified since they rounded the corner.

"Except for that noise, it's perfect," commented Laura.

"I've always loved gardening. And cooking..."

"You take care of this yourself?"

Julia nodded. "Most of it... Not the transplanting or pruning, of course, or the spraying, but everything else."

"I am filled with admiration," said Laura. "You even have an *orquidario*."

"Empty, at the moment."

Laura leaned forward as she focused on two men at the side of the house, a pile of ceramic roof tiles at their feet. Djalma was crouched at the top of a small, brick column, shouting to an unseen comrade inside the roofless structure while another workman chipped away at the exterior. "What's going on?" Laura asked.

"Well, you know the electricity shortage and the mandate we have to cut our usage?"

"Of course..." The two women retreated slowly across the grass.

"Our bill was just too high and Jack decided to check the water heater, but we couldn't find it. No one seemed to know where it was until we tracked down the gardener who used to work here. He said the owner decided to put it in a concealed place and built that tower, which I do not consider a thing of beauty. To get to the heater, we had to take off the roof tiles and then we found that some of the wall has to be taken down in order to attach a timer, which is what we want to do."

"And it all has to go back up when you're finished, right?" Laura asked with wicked delight.

"Absolutely!"

"Well, as I said, Brazil is different, and eventually it kind of gets under your skin. Hopefully..." She smiled and looked at her watch. "I've got to pick up my children. Tell you what: I'll take you to a Newcomers meeting day after tomorrow and you must come to Bridge Club next week. Do you play?"

"No."

"Want to learn?"

For a moment, Julia felt deeply discontented. Bridge, clubs, cooking and gardening: all of them ways to fill the days and stave off boredom. But they also accomplished nothing, contributed nothing and emphasized the current pointlessness of her life in São Paulo. "Thanks, but I don't think so."

After a thoughtful pause Laura said, "That's okay. We always have lunch and you can meet other women. A few are great and a few are not, just like everywhere I guess, but you can't simply garden and watch the workmen. One of our members has an even more bizarre story about electricity."

Julia raised her eyebrows enquiringly.

"Her night guard tried to tap into her electricity for his TV and accidentally did something to the meter so it's running backward. She's now way into the negative usage for electricity, even though she has a house and pool about this size. And the electric company keeps sending her letters of congratulation."

Julia burst out laughing. "You're kidding."

"I am serious. We're lucky to live in the Chacara where we don't have to hire a guard."

The smile vanished and Julia's forehead creased in anxiety. "After our robbery the agency said we should have a guard, although we haven't done anything about it. You don't have one?"

"No. Statistically, private security itself is involved in a huge percentage of São Paulo robberies and kidnappings." Slowly, they retraced their steps into the living room. "Actually, you have to be careful everywhere. Keep the doors locked, don't leave windows open at night, and don't let deliverymen into the house, that kind of thing. Thieves are almost never caught."

Julia shook her head. "That's so encouraging. I went to an American Society talk on security and it scared me half to death. Lock the car and don't drive with the windows down, don't stand chatting at the front gate of your house, look around before you get into the car, and if you see anyone suspicious go into the nearest shop. They just went on and on."

"Don't let it put you off. I've never had anything happen in the three years I've been here, and your robbery was probably a fluke." She looked at her watch again and shook her head. "The offspring will be wild."

"I'll walk you to the front gate, but we mustn't stand there and talk."

Laura hooted with laughter, a joyous sound that dispelled Julia's lingering fears. "This is the Chacara, for God's sake. You can be nearly normal in here."

The two women smiled companionably at one another. "I hope so," Julia said. "And I look forward to Newcomers and Bridge Club."

Waving goodbye to her visitor, Julia could scarcely wait to phone Mary Beth and share the latest mixed news about São Paulo.

When the front door closed that evening, announcing Jack's arrival, Julia turned off the fire under Chinese Chicken, stripped off her apron and jogged into the living room. "Guess what? I met a potential friend today." She stopped, arrested by her husband's scowl and his slightly untidy appearance. "What is it? What's the matter?" Her imagination veered from robbery to a vicious quarrel with his CEO.

"This country is never going to make it," he said wearily, sinking onto the sofa. Julia sat down beside him, sliding one arm across his shoulders and kissing him on the cheek. At least it didn't sound like he'd lost his job.

"I'm more or less used to the fact that contractors for roads charge a million for the work, pocket half of that and do a shitty, cheap job so that it has to be redone in a year, and that builders do the same with apartments and offices and get away with it because they bribe the inspectors, but you won't believe what happened to me today in my office."

"What?"

"Fernando Lins is a guy on my Board, and I never thought much about him one way or the other until he called this morning and said that he wanted a free airline ticket to Brasilia, and could I please think up a reason to call a meeting there this week so that his company would pay for it."

Julia's first impulse was to laugh at the blatant attempt at fraud, but one look at Jack's thunderous face squelched every trace of humor. "Just like that?" she asked. "What did you tell him?"

"I told him no, of course. But these guys are so damned dishonest I just wonder what they'll come up with next."

"He could be the one bad apple."

"Don't bet on it. I'm down here because Head Office told me there are irregularities down here in Claymore's books, and I can only imagine what *other* kind of convoluted shit I'm going to find."

Julia stood up. "Why don't you go for a swim while I get us a couple of drinks," she suggested. "I made roast pepper spread and found some pita toasts, so that should make us a little happier."

Moving across the room toward the bar, she felt the world slide out of focus. They had relinquished a stable, settled, happy life in Venice and traded it for...what?

SEVEN—SÃO PAULO, BRAZIL

*"T*his is just lovely," Julia exclaimed. Following behind Pearl DeMott, her hostess, she crossed the walled entry patio, moving between a tiled fountain and a bank of Crepe Myrtle that varied in color from white to various shades of pink to magenta. Passing under a brick archway, they stepped into a garden shaded by a number of tall trees with spreading, leafy branches. Julia stopped. "Is this an orchid?" she asked, awed.

Turning, Pearl glanced briefly at her guest and then at the plant in question. "Everyone notices that one."

"But it's unbelievable. Does it get some kind of special attention?" Unlike its more common relatives, this particular orchid was at least five feet high and three feet in diameter, more like a large shrub than a plant, and was covered with dozens, perhaps hundreds, of showy white blooms.

Pearl shrugged. "I have no idea. I leave the care and feeding of all the orchids to my orchid man."

"I'd like to talk to your gardener someday. Find out

exactly what he does for this plant."

For a moment Pearl stared sternly at her guest and the latter experienced a sharp spasm of uncertainty. Julia guessed her hostess's age at forty and, despite the lack of a single wrinkle in her stretched facial skin, and not the slightest hint of gray in her ebony hair, Pearl's expression was one of deep, permanent dissatisfaction. "My *gardener* has nothing to do with the orchids. They're looked after by a specialist."

How arrogant, Julia thought forcing a smile to her lips as she said, "He certainly does a wonderful job."

"That's what he's paid to do," Pearl responded with thinly veiled hostility, turning and leading the way through the trees.

Mild aversion to her hostess hardened into active dislike as Julie followed Pearl's slightly pudgy back as it wobbled around another lush, green corner of the garden. Mary Beth, Mary Beth, she called mentally, come down here so we can see the humor in this. Almost against her will, Julia was struck by the simple beauty and practicality of the property which was perfect for parties, including bridge. Flanked by an ivy-covered guest house and rimmed on one side by a wing of the main building, the pool was apparently untouched by any of the tanned, bikini-clad women that were currently draped on recliners and chaise lounges around its edges. A young male servant in a spotless white jacket carried a tray with drinks and bottles of wine, which he offered to each guest.

"Here we are," Pearl announced, waving at a large, covered patio. "Make yourself at home." And she vanished into the house, abandoning her guest who, baffled and uncertain, took in her surroundings. Bridge, Julia thought? I don't see anything that looks like bridge. White iron chairs, arranged around oval, marble-topped tables on the flagstone patio, were occupied by women of all ages, most of whom were drinking wine or what appeared to be caipirinhas, Bloody Marys or gin and tonics. At one table, several guests were eating pistachio nuts and then flicking the shells at each other. A trio of women conferred earnestly at a long table against the wall of the house, their heads bent toward one another. Hesitating at the edge of the patio, Julia just wanted to go home. From time to time, a new arrival drifted past with a covered dish. Maybe I should have brought something, Julia thought, like a cold roulade or ratatouille. Ignored and self-conscious, she decided to leave.

"Julia," a voice called. "Julia, over here!" Laura, one of the three women next to the wall, stood up, waved both arms and edged past some of the tables and chairs on the patio. With an enormous feeling of relief, Julia moved forward to plant a grateful kiss on both of Laura's cheeks.

"I don't know a sole except you," she said as they began to wend their way back toward Laura's companions.

"Of course not; that's why you're here, to meet people."

"The hostess didn't seem aware of that."

"Pearl only pays attention to her own navel. Ignore her."

I can do that, Julia thought. "So where's the bridge set-up?"

"Over in the guest house, but that's for later. First we gossip and then have lunch and then sometimes swim."

A shower of pistachio shells pelted the shoulders and backs of the two women as they approached Laura's table.

"Julia, this is Marilyn, a psychotherapist who's forever analyzing our behavior."

"Welcome."

She could be Brazilian, with long dark brown, very curly hair and bronze skin but Marilyn's accent was strictly American. Wearing a brief halter top and what appeared to be tight lace hipster trousers, her mischievous grin transformed an unremarkable, too-narrow face into a beguiling promise of fun.

"Thank you."

"Marilyn's husband is Dr. Mauricio Coelho, the plastic surgeon who has semi-secretly operated on half the women in this club," Laura informed her. "Look behind their ears and you'll know which ones."

"He's also lifted their knees, stomachs, elbows, breasts, given some of them bum-bums, changed their noses, saved burn victims," Marilyn interposed.

"He's very dapper and chic," commented the third woman widening her aquamarine eyes rimmed with thick, long lashes in a dramatization of awe. "Those white shirts and dark suits and bright ties are just stunning with his gray pony tail and monocle."

"But does he wear that eyepiece during operations?" asked Laura. "It's a riveting thought."

"Good question," responded Marilyn with another enormous smile.

"I hear he dropped it on the floor while he was lifting and tucking Dominica's body and the whole team had to stop and scrabble around on the floor for it."

"Could be," Marilyn said thoughtfully. "But I don't believe it was Dominica."

Intrigued, Julia glanced at the other guests, wondering which ones had gone under dapper Dr. Mauricio's knife, and if the results were worth it. A very beautiful, very young maid in a black uniform with a white, frilly apron and cap appeared and offered a huge tray of hour d'houvres. She was followed immediately by the white-jacketed young man who held out a tray bearing clean glasses and two bottles of wine.

"*Tinto ou branco, Senhora?*"

"You can have a Bloody Mary or Caipirinha or Gin and Tonic, or just about anything alcoholic, if you prefer," said Marilyn.

"Red will be fine, but isn't it kind of early for serious drinking?" asked Julia.

Her remark produced an explosion of laughter from the other three.

"Not in this group, as you'll soon find out," said the third woman. Slight, with short auburn hair and freckles, those intense blue eyes were by far her most arresting feature. "By the way, I'm Kathleen Lamb".

"I'm sorry," Laura apologized. "I need to go back to Good Manners School".

"Nice to meet you," said Julia accepting a glass of wine as another uniformed maid appeared with more aperitifs. "Pearl seems to have a lot of servants," she remarked.

"Cooks, maids, gardeners, guards and God-knows-who-else, and they're all family members of her husband Clyde's assembly line workers." Julia knew that Clyde was a director of one of the car companies. "They're paid only minimum wage, get no raises or bonuses, and they can't complain or the real bread-winners, the company employees, will lose their jobs."

Julia swallowed her tiny smoked salmon sandwich with difficulty as she grappled with this news. She knew such things went on in the world but it never occurred to her that it might be an open practice carried out by someone she knew—someone who was, in fact, her hostess. "I think that's truly sick."

"Not as sick as the fact that any attractive female is at risk from Clyde and Denver, including the employees."

"Especially the employees!" emphasized Marilyn.

"Who's Denver?" Julia asked.

"Clyde and Pearl's fifteen-year-old son."

Involuntarily, Julia's eyes flashed toward Pearl, now languidly sipping a Caipirinha and reclining on a nautically striped chaise lounge. One hand soaked in a large, porcelain bowl and one foot rested in the lap of a very fat, very black woman dressed entirely in white who was bent attentively over Pearl's toes. Julia wasn't sure what she'd expected of this excursion but it certainly hadn't included the discovery that her hostess's husband sexually harassed the servants rather than pay them.

"Does Pearl know this?"

"Everyone knows it."

"But how can anyone accept her hospitality?" What am I doing here, she wondered uneasily? This is just not me.

Julia's discomfort was transmitted very clearly to her companions who exchanged brief, meaningful glances. Marilyn waved to a nearby chair.

"Let's sit down and relax, and I'll explain a couple of things that you, as a recent arrival, probably haven't yet discovered." Aware that she had somehow blundered and yet was irritated with the situation in which she found herself, Julia sank onto one of the heavy, white iron chairs with thick canvas upholstery. "Although São Paulo is huge—around twenty-three million people—the English speaking ex-pat community is quite small. Everyone knows everyone else, and that includes children and husbands. The men are virtually all highly placed executives, and sooner or later do business with one another or extend favors like making introductions or arranging lunch meetings that will be helpful to others in the community. No one can afford to deliberately offend or snub anyone else. That's why we come to Pearl's house, and why she comes to ours, although we wouldn't even know her back home."

Julia started to speak but was stopped by Marilyn's upraised palm.

"It's mandatory to try, at least superficially, to get on with everyone. On the plus side, because it's so small, the community acts like an extended family, helping out when it's necessary, supporting one another."

Subdued by the mild rebuke, Julia nodded, feeling acutely isolated, a stranger in a culture she didn't understand. None of her female friends in Venice spent their days throwing nuts at one another or drinking excessively, nor did they have fleets of uniformed servants that they felt obliged to cheat. They worked, raised families and volunteered to help others less fortunate, while here everyone seemed to be preoccupied with simply filling in the time. As if on cue, two women strolled past, one complaining bitterly about a dish recently broken by her careless maid.

Julia nodded slowly. "Got it," she said, cutting short more unwelcome revelations about the ex-pat community. Involuntarily, she glanced toward her hostess, who was still supine in the chaise lounge with the white garbed woman bent intently over one foot. Following her gaze, Marilyn added, "Pearl thought having Hícia do manicures and pedicures for anyone who wanted them was a touch of class, so she's here for every Bridge Club. She's dressed in white because Pearl imagines that it looks medical." Kathleen waved toward a table just inside the house which seemed to be covered with jewelry of all kinds and surrounded by women picking over the goods. "She also invited Pedro, who is hidden by that mob at his table, to come and sell his wares."

"The quality of his stuff is terrible," added Laura, "but it's cheap and he's a good salesperson who's targeted the American ex-pat community as his market."

"But doesn't anybody have a job?" Julia asked.

"I do," said Marilyn, "but I'm married to a Brazilian and have a permanent visa, and I also speak pretty good Portuguese after all these years. The majority of Americans have temporary visas."

"Like me," interjected Julia.

"Like you, and that means you're forbidden to work. Some women teach English and are paid under the table, but that's risky. There are plenty of volunteer opportunities working with *favela* children or teaching literacy to adults, but you need to be fluent in Portuguese. So this is how a lot of women cope with loneliness and boredom."

At the mention of a *favela*, Julia again pictured the squalid slum beside the highway leading to the airport, and then looked at her luxurious surroundings. "Who lives in the *favelas*?" she asked. "What kind of people?"

At the unexpected question, all three stared at her for a

moment before Marilyn answered. "Maids, taxi drivers, policemen, most of the help that doesn't live-in. Most of the working class..."

"You forgot the drug lords and dealers," prompted Kathleen.

"Them, too. *Favelas* are big communities.

Laura rose, followed by Kathleen and Julia. "Let's go check on lunch."

"How do I get a permanent visa?" Julia asked.

"Through Jack, who has probably already applied for one. Bureaucracy is slow, though, so don't expect anything for a while, if ever. And remember, for almost any job, paid or not, you have to know the language."

"You should have taken Julia to a Newcomers meeting first," said Kathleen.

"I did. It was all very sedate."

"Have you warned her that the Brazilian women will all be after her husband?" Kathleen continued as they pushed past the crowd at Pedro's table.

Glasses raised, faces flushed, three women raced through the living room and out to the pool where one pushed another into the water. Shrieking, glasses flying, a few more followed suit; within minutes, the pool was filled with elegantly dressed, shouting women. Julia once again remembered the shacks by the airport.

Bending closer to Julia, Laura ignored the swimming pool and murmured, "Kathleen thinks that her husband Randolph is having an affair just because he works all the time and pays more weekend attention to his horse than he does to her. Now she's met a man on the Internet and wants to go to the US to meet him, but Randolph won't give permission for Heather to go. Heather is their ten-year-old daughter, and Randolph's devoted to her."

Stunned and suffering from information overload, Julia's voice was, nevertheless, calm. "Jack's a workaholic, but fortunately I don't have to worry about him and other women."

They entered the deserted dining room. With deep red walls and dark furniture, the room was blinding in its display of silver. A large tea set flanked by two enormous candelabras on one sideboard, an antique Samovar with an array of candlesticks on another, and a collection of candy dishes and another candelabra on a tea cart all reflected the light of a crystal chandelier. In the center of the room, a beautiful Ñanduti lace tablecloth had been spread over a large oval table on which silver bowls of salad and silver platters of cold meat, chicken and fish had been arranged. Tableware and pristine white folded napkins were at one end of the table, large silver baskets of rolls at the other.

Kathleen covered her eyes with one hand. "Oh, my God, I forgot my dark glasses."

After a glance at the food, Julia knew she could have produced better, and certainly wouldn't have displayed it so flamboyantly.

Laura, still considering her friend's remark about Jack, looked speculatively at Julia. "You know, though, it doesn't hurt to keep a sharp eye on your man. Brazilian women are more crafty and aggressive than Americans. And they certainly dress more provocatively."

Involuntarily, Julia looked at two women seated in the living room. Engrossed in a lively conversation in Portuguese, they were clearly Brazilian and obviously sensuous in an unmistakably non-American way that extended beyond their tight, very expensive clothing, perfectly manicured nails and carefully tousled hair. Her mind flashed back to that first day in Brazil and the *sambista* who had exchanged a slightly too-long, intimate look with Jack; for just a minute her faith in her husband's fidelity wavered.

Splashes and shouts could be heard from the pool, pulling Julia into the present.

"Bridge doesn't seem to be the main activity," she commented.

"It used to be," responded Laura. "When we started the

Bridge Club it was really nice, with just eight women who had a pot luck lunch and bridge every Tuesday. Then it expanded and expanded and got out of hand. We three no longer play, but those that do participate phone their maids to get the kids and feed them while they get totally blotto and finally leave here at nine." Laura helped herself to salmon and salad.

"You'll find that most of the ex-pat ladies here have never thought they'd be living in huge houses with maids, drivers and cooks, all paid for by somebody else, and a lot just don't know how to handle it," Kathleen added.

"I love to cook," said Julia, "and I'm actually pretty good at it."

Kathleen offered Julia a plate. "Come on, let's eat, and then you can have a bridge lesson."

Julia couldn't imagine anything worse. "Thanks so much, but I've never been very keen on playing games of any kind. I think I'll just eat and run. Maybe we can all have lunch next week," she suggested hopefully, looking at each of the women in turn. "You can come over and sample my cooking."

"Good idea," said Marilyn, wincing as she looked toward the pool. "Since these Tuesdays are so unpredictable, we almost never come, but Kathleen and I wanted to meet you and introduce you to some others, see if you were a bridge person."

"Thanks, but it's not for me."

Silently, seriously, the trio bent over the buffet table while Julia glanced covertly at the two Brazilian women and once again thought about Jack and the samba dancer.

EIGHT—SÃO PAULO, BRAZIL

Slowly, Julia disentangled her legs from Jack's and, with a heavy sigh, he rolled onto his back. She slipped her arm over his chest and idly brushed his skin with her fingertips, her mind a contented, post-coital blank. Hot and slick with sweat, her hair plastered to her neck, she listened as Jack's breathing was gradually transformed into a series of shallow wheezes, indicating that he had dropped into a deep sleep. Smiling, she moved her hand across his torso and caressed his forearm, basking in the peace and serenity of the moment, thankful that it was Saturday and her husband wouldn't be leaping from the bed to race to the office. Nothing to do but lie here and make love, then go to the Museum and perhaps out to lunch—all of which, she realized, they seemed to do with less and less frequency.

Julia frowned as this unwelcome thought pushed its way into her mind, chasing away her previous sense of calm relaxation. Jack had no time to dawdle in a museum or drive to the beach for lunch, and certainly could not spend a lazy weekend at Itatiaía as they had done just after their arrival. Nor was there a way that dancing could fit into their lives at the moment. And, as he had told her more than once, stress and late nights at the office, as well as early hours and weekend work, simply didn't combine well with any kind of sexual activity. "I can't just run home and fuck on demand, for God's sake," he had told her more than once.

The hand that had been stroking Jack's arm stilled as Julia remembered the sharpness of his tone, the cruelty of his words and the dismissive way he had stormed from the room. However, as had happened this morning, he did occasionally play the mating game, and in these instances was not only enthusiastically lascivious but seemed more sexually inventive than in the past. It was all mildly puzzling.

A crash was heard from the far end of the house and then muted voices. Julia groaned, rubbing both hands over her face and struggling, unsuccessfully, to recapture the blissful mood of early morning. A muffled thud was followed by the voices of Djalma and Vera shouting at one another, the words indistinct but the tone of both venomous. With a resigned sigh, Julia sat up, listening as the quarrel became louder and closer. Beside her, Jack, now restlessly sleeping, was having a conversation with an invisible friend; his lips moved in a whisper, while his muscles twitched spasmodically. A door slammed and then banged shut again. Jack's eyes flew open and he stared, disoriented, at the ceiling.

"Shit," Julia mumbled, climbing out of bed and pulling a silk dressing gown over her nude body.

"What the Hell is going on?" asked Jack. His face twisted into a grimace as he pushed himself up and out of bed.

"Our workforce is having another row," Julia explained, sliding into her slippers.

"God Almighty", murmured Jack, digging a polo shirt

and pair of Bermuda shorts from the laundry basket. "What about this time?"

"I have no idea, but we'd better find out before they destroy the house."

With short, angry movements, Jack dressed and followed his wife to the door and down the hall. Crossing into the living room, they saw Djalma and Vera playing tug-of-war with a battered suitcase while simultaneously screaming at one another. Pushing past Julia, Jack strode into the living room and roared, "*O que está acontecendo?*" "What's happening?"

Instantly silenced, the abashed couple, each one still gripping the suitcase, turned to their employers. A quick, horrified glance around the room informed Julia that one of the dining chairs had been tipped over and an end table shoved against the wall. Books and magazines were scattered on the floor and an amethyst geode lay on its side. Furious, she stepped toward the pair just as Jack shouted, "Get out, both of you, right now."

Now Julia was both angry and alarmed.

"Wait! You can't do that, Jack. Laura says if we fire them without cause in Brazil, then we have to pay a huge penalty in addition to their holiday wages and God knows what else or they'll sue and the labor court will find in their favor."

"This is cause," he snapped, one arm making a sweeping gesture around the room. "Look what they've done to our living room. And my weekend is completely shot, not that they give a damn."

Suddenly, Vera yanked the suitcase from her husband's hand and strode across the room. At the front door, she pivoted and announced in Portuguese, "I've had enough. I'm going back to my mother in Bahia."

"What?" asked Julia, understanding only a few words.

"Ask Djalma about his women," Vera continued shrilly. "All those nights he was supposed to be out with his macho friends. Then he comes home in the morning smelling of women and tells me lies that he thinks I'm stupid enough to believe. Well," she straightened up angrily and tilted her head, "I may not be able to read or write, but my nose is educated and it tells me that he stinks of other women."

Whipping around, she opened the door and flounced outside. Jack stared at Djalma while Julia leaned toward her husband.

"I didn't catch that last part," she whispered. Julia was baffled by Jack's increasing fluency in Portuguese and she was more than a little envious. While she used the language only when speaking with her teacher, conversing with the help and when shopping, Jack's staff all spoke English so he and she should be equal. Only they weren't.

"She said he's a womanizer and whores around, so she's leaving him."

"Ah," Julia breathed, comprehending the tension and quarrels between the two. "Now I get it." She stared coldly at Djalma who gazed at the floor, his shoulders rounded in humility. "Djalma wants to be a letch but he also wants his job."

"Well, he can't have his job without the other half of the couple."

"We could hire a daily maid," she responded hopefully. "Laura's maid has a sister that's looking for a job. That would work." Julia felt her stomach muscles tighten at the idea of a new search for domestic help.

"Think about it. Djalma's wife has just walked out on him because he's chasing tail, so imagine fresh, new blood right here in the house. Nope, Djalma's got to go."

The gardener stepped outside, grasped a broom and began vigorously sweeping the patio.

"Do you think he's learned some English?" asked Julia, wondering if Djalma had somehow understood their conversation.

"English? Don't make me laugh. He's learned *nothing*," snapped Jack, glaring at the hapless caretaker.

"Don't you think we should at least make sure that Vera isn't coming back?" Julia suggested desperately.

"No, I don't, because she is, fortunately, gone. May I remind you of all the quarrels, the banged pots and pans, the screams and shouts. Let's just take advantage of this lucky opportunity and send our busy friend on his way." Jack's tone did not invite discussion, especially when he raised his voice and, in Portuguese, yelled, "Djalma, come here!"

Carefully replacing the broom against the outside wall, Djalma slowly entered the living room.

"You realize, of course, that we hired you and Vera as a couple, and now half of that couple is missing." Jack's voice was controlled and firm, his Portuguese stilted and heavily accented but understandable.

"I can find a maid," he suggested, "someone that cleans better than Vera and loves to wash and iron. My cousin, maybe?"

"I don't think you understand. We hired two specific people and now there is only one, so both must go."

Julia realized her husband definitely wasn't going to give him a second chance and her throat constricted. So it was back to the agency and months spent training a couple that might turn out to be even worse than Djalma and Vera. The caretaker's face twisted in sudden comprehension. He was being given the boot.

"Get your things together right now and meet me in the study," Jack ordered. "I'll sign your *carteira* and give you a month's extra wages. And then, out you go."

Hesitantly, Djalma balanced on one foot and then the other, finally convinced that he had lost his job.

"Senhor Jack?" he asked.

"What is it?"

"I know a couple that are looking for work." Scowling, Jack waited for him to continue. "They're very reliable, good workers and I've known them for years."

Jack turned to Julia and said in English, "He knows a

couple looking for work, but being friends with this guy is not such a hot recommendation." He looked at Djalma again. After a moment's silence, he spoke in Portuguese. "If they're so wonderful, why are they looking for work?"

"Because their Austrian employer left."

Julia understood this without a translation and felt herself relax.

"They might be worth a try," she said to Jack, her voice earnest with hope. Anything but a return to the agency and an endless parade of mostly unsuitable candidates while her house grew dustier and her clothes more wrinkled. How had she managed in Venice without any help at all? Her lips curved in a wry smile as she came up with the answer. Sydney and Stephanie might not have been paid for it but they had always helped around the house, which was much smaller, and Jack used to tend to the pool and garden on Saturdays. Sometimes even after work. Times had changed.

"Do these people have references? Written ones and also phone numbers?" Jack asked.

"I think so."

"And do they have names?"

"Zé and Alda."

"All right, tell them to give me a call. And I'll see you in the study in fifteen minutes."

Djalma shuffled from the room.

Shrugging, Jack shook his head slowly. "Djalma's buddies may be okay, but I think we'd better see the agency anyway."

Dejection settled over her shoulders like a blanket. This was very easy for him to say but she was the one that had to deal with the help on a daily basis. "Okay, but I don't think they're open today."

"Certainly not, but you can go on Monday." Forestalling any protest, he added, "Since it's my money, I want to be sure we're hiring the right couple."

Of course, she thought, that was the final word. Gone

were the days when she could put her own earnings on the table and call a few shots. Jack looked at his watch.

"I'm going to the office as soon as I deal with Djalma."

"Perfect," she exclaimed angrily. "I thought we were going to the Museum and then out to lunch. That's what we had agreed, if you remember."

"No, actually I didn't remember." At least, she thought, he has the grace to look embarrassed. "And I can't cancel now because I asked Eliana to meet me there so we can work on the de Silva contract."

Eliana, Eliana, Julia mused darkly. My darling spouse sees much, much more of her than he sees of me. Hurt, feeling wretched and discarded, she adjusted her dressing gown, trying to exhibit a nonchalance she certainly did not feel.

"I wish you'd write these things down, Jack. You *do* remember we're giving a dinner party next Saturday, don't you?"

He nodded, his mind already elsewhere. "I'm sure Eliana put it in my agenda. First, I've got to change clothes and run. I'm late already."

He kissed her lightly, impersonally on the cheek and strode from the room. Staring out at the garden, she pulled her dressing gown even more tightly around her body, wondering how she could salvage the day. Saturdays weren't easy. Although the vast majority of upper-level Brazilians employed *babás*, or nannies, to care for their children, the English-speaking community tended to raise their own offspring, just as she had done in Venice. This meant that those with school-age children usually devoted weekends to family activities, as she herself had done when Stephanie and Sydney were younger. Which left out Laura, Marilyn and Kathleen as playmates for today, and those were the only women she knew very well.

Damn Jack anyway, she thought. It wasn't the first time this had happened but, as Laura and Marilyn had warned her, she was strictly on her own here.

At any rate, she wasn't going to sit at home and sulk. Pivoting slowly, Julia looked forward, without enthusiasm, to visiting the Pinocateca Museum and eating a solitary lunch in the museum restaurant afterward. The happiness and contentment she had felt earlier now seemed to be a vague dream she had experienced a long time ago.

NINE—SÃO PAULO, BRAZIL

"I wish you didn't have to work so much. We came to Brazil because it was different and beautiful, but so far we haven't seen much of it outside of São Paulo." Julia felt irritable and out of sorts even though this evening they were on their way to a São Paulo Independence Day Fling given by one of Jack's business associates, a party that promised to be amusing and fun. No one seemed to find it odd that this particular Independence Day celebrated the failure of São Paulo to win its freedom from Brazil. Anything for a holiday.

"For God's sake, not this again. We came to this country because of a job offer I couldn't afford to refuse. You have a life here that our friends in the States wouldn't believe. Alda does the housework and at least *tries* to help with the cooking, and Zé takes care of the rest, yet all I hear from you are complaints. If you want real problems you should step into my shoes for a minute." Jack gripped the steering wheel with both hands and stared straight ahead at the tangle of cars that had completely paralyzed traffic on the Morumbi Bridge.

Julia clamped her lips together, sealing a retort. What did *he* know about her life? On the other hand, he worked late six days a week and left home early every morning which, she had to admit, left little time for trips or concerts or even normal conversation about the lives either of them were leading. With a pang of wistfulness, she thought of the old days in Venice Beach when they had spent long hours sharing problems, helping one another find solutions, encouraging far-fetched dreams and laughing over daily events. And dancing...

"Wanderley, that shit, is constantly pressuring me to use companies that he owns, and to contract services from firms that are crappy but give him big kick-backs," Jack continued tersely. "And since he's CEO, he doesn't have to hear about quality if he doesn't want to."

And that, thought Julia, seems to be pretty typically Brazilian. The roads and buildings were nearly always in some state of disrepair because the contractor used sub-standard materials but charged the full price, and of course the sub-contractor did the same and then it all passed because the inspectors, if there happened to be any, were bribed. And if, by some miracle or accident, they were caught, nothing ever happened. She thought of Palacio II in Rio, a luxury high-rise apartment building. A few years ago, it collapsed into a heap, killing eight residents all because the owner/builder cheated on the content of the cement. It had been a scandal but the owner was still free and hadn't paid any fines nor indemnified the survivors, most of who were now living in hotels.

Punching the air conditioner closed, Julia turned her head to look at the Pinheiros River, source of the fetid smell of garbage and dead animals that permeated the air. After a wind or rain the odor was very faint but tonight it was an overwhelming reminder that São Paulo needed a number of major public improvements. Lights on the far side of the river twinkled in a postcard display of nocturnal beauty; one would never guess that much of the illumination came from favelas, those tumbled heaps of brick, cardboard and corrugated shacks, where the electricity had been bootlegged from the surrounding forest of expensive high rise apartment buildings.

Everyone knew that there was plenty of money to fund every public service in Brazil, but the cash kept finding its way into private pockets. She smiled faintly. Or into underpants, as in the case of the politician who was caught with thousands of illicit reais stuffed into his drawers.

"Of course, one of the many things they didn't tell me back home is that this arm of Claymore is owned 50% by Claymore US and 50% by a Brazilian consortium, which makes it impossible to find a solution for any problem." He pounded the steering when in frustration. "And you know what the guys in home office do when I tell them?"

Yes, she thought, I know.

"They blow it off. I was sent down here to straighten out some irregularities. Outright corruption is a better description, and I'm expected to go along with it because I'm making a lot of money. They picked the wrong guy for that."

"I know." Jack's ethics, honesty and fairness were three of the qualities that had attracted Julia so many years ago along, of course, with his rugged good looks. She flashed him a quick, appraising glance; he still resembled a pirate in a business suit and tie. Moving her hand to his thigh, she stroked his leg sympathetically.

"And nothing's going to change," he said, "no matter what I do."

Julia stared at the river's rippling surface as traffic finally began to flow over the bridge. Dark and dappled with reflected moonbeams, headlights and apartment illumination, nothing moved on the water. Forty years ago—maybe less—there had been swimming, boating and fishing on the Pinheiros. Now, such things were unthinkable. Recently, police had trapped an escaping thief on the riverbank. Rather than surrender, the criminal had jumped into the water and swum to the other side where he was met by the police who marched him to a nearby favela for a hosing down and change of clothes. Only then, sanitized, was he allowed to get into the police car.

"The problem isn't just Wanderley," he said. They left the bridge and continued on Morumbi Avenue. "It's Home Office. When Gary McGrath and Tim Hawkins come down here to see how we're doing, Wanderley takes them to fabulous restaurants, shows, the beach, you name it. Last time the three of them spent the weekend at Casa Grande in Guarujá, on company money, of course. And I strongly suspect Wanderley gets girls for them."

"Prostitutes?" That *was* a surprise.

"High caliber ones. Maybe low-lifes too—I know they've been to the 'My Love' more than once."

Torn between amusement and disbelief, Julia swiveled to face him. "That strip club downtown?"

Jack grimaced. "That's the one."

Julia shook her head. "How do you know?"

"Wanderley *told* me. The last time Gary and Tim came down they brought their wives, and the women wanted to see some of the city's seedy life after dinner. When they got to the club the doorman greeted the guys by name."

Julia laughed. "How stupid can those men be?" Almost immediately, she sobered, wondering about the women. "I guess I'm just old fashioned or something, but I can't imagine going to a strange city with you and asking to visit a strip club."

"No, I can't picture that either."

His tone was cool; stung, for a second she remembered Jack's late nights and working weekends. He swung the car into a wide, gently curving and severely pot-holed street lined with enormous houses almost entirely hidden behind very high walls. Empty and dark, the avenue was lit only by moonlight filtering through tall trees that arched overhead; Jack checked to make sure the car doors were locked.

"I think this is the right street," he said. "According to the map it is, but this looks pretty deserted."

Almost immediately parked cars appeared on both sides and, not far ahead, they saw uniformed *manobristas*, men who worked for valet parking services.

"Wow, that must be the place."

"It's huge". And ugly, she added mentally, gazing at the building that loomed over the street, its façade broken by narrow windows that reminded her of the slots in forts through which soldiers mowed down their attackers. It rose from the sidewalk to a height of three or four stories and stretched down the block to vanish into the darkness. An iron door stood open, flanked by two hefty men wearing black suits, black shirts, red ties and dark glasses even though it was ten o'clock at night.

"Why do guards always have to look like thugs?" Julia asked.

"Because they probably *are* thugs," her husband replied. "Plus the intimidation factor."

A manobrista held the car door open and Julia stepped out, transfixed by the view of the entry hall which was brilliantly lit by countless candles. They flickered in wall sconces, in tall bamboo candlesticks lining the walls, on the ground in square and round translucent containers and on an array of small pedestals.

"That's fantastic," she breathed as they moved toward the doorway. "Whose house is this? I know you told me, but I've forgotten." She gave an apologetic shrug.

"Moacyr Alonso. He's the president of Banco Manaus do Sul, one of the companies in the Brazilian consortium that owns fifty percent of Claymore International."

"Now I remember."

Jack gave his name to one of the guards who found it on a list, checked it off and allowed them to enter.

Jack lowered his voice to a whisper. "Moacyr's slimy, unethical jerk, a real pain in the ass who tries to out-fox me on a daily basis. He cheats at everything—business, his marriage, you name it. A few years ago a prostitute was found murdered in the garage here and he blamed one of the guards who, of course, then ran away and was conveniently never found."

Wordlessly, Julia scanned her husband's handsome face. When, she wondered, would she become immune to these horror stories, casually told by and about people they knew? She was beginning to understand why Brazil was said to be forever the country of the future.

They moved through the blaze of light to a circular, white Carrara marble staircase. Directly opposite the stairway was a dimly lit room with a closed, iron and glass door through which they saw the outline of floor to ceiling rows of bottles. Normally, Julia would have gawked at the sight of a huge, private wine cellar but she was still focused on Jack's analysis of their host. He sounds just charming, she thought, a possible soul-mate of the lawyer who was recently hospitalized after his involvement in a traffic accident. The intended victim of a car robbery, the lawyer had accelerated, run into another vehicle and as he was carted off on a stretcher, ten thousand reais was found in the trunk of his car along with a list of police to be paid off.

"But this really isn't the time for a character assassination of my colleague," cautioned Jack, smoothing his beard as they ascended the stairs.

In the months that they had been in São Paulo, Julia had been invited to numerous large residences that resembled baronial castles, most of them with non-descript décor and occupied by ex-pats from relatively modest backgrounds. This establishment, however, was entirely different. Despite its forbidding external appearance, the interior was elegant with white marble walls and floors, arched doors and a soaring, domed ceiling sliced with stained glass skylights. The far wall was made entirely of glass and looked onto an indoor pool banked by potted shrubs, flowers and trees and illuminated by fiber optic lighting. Almost concealed by the plethora of shrubbery, Julia could see an annex which she took to be a guest house or the servant's quarters or maybe even an exercise room.

"This is really beautiful." She forgot her husband's scandalous description of their host as she looked at the groupings of elegant sofas, chairs and lamps, the oriental rugs and the Brazilian paintings that graced the walls.

"Hello, and welcome," said a voice behind her. "I'm Diva Alonso."

Smiling, Julia turned. "Julia Elliott." They kissed on both cheeks.

"You're very brave to have this crowd in your house," Jack said to Diva with a smile.

"Not at all," she replied, exuding cheer and beaming back at him. "I enjoy it."

As her husband continued to chit-chat with the hostess, Julia searched the crowd for a familiar face. Her eye was caught by a very modern rope chair which she recognized from a photograph in the newspaper. Created by two brothers, famous Brazilian designers, it fit perfectly into the room and she marveled at the successful mixture of furniture and decorating styles.

"I hope you'll excuse me for a minute?" Jack enquired. "I've just seen one of my colleagues." He moved into the crowd and disappeared.

Although the two had never formally met, Julia had a nodding acquaintance with their hostess through various charity events where Diva was endlessly energetic, always visible and usually ran the show. She was Venezuelan, fine-boned with ivory skin and ebony hair swept into a chignon; Julia thought her the epitome of Latin elegance and breeding. What, she wondered, was such a sophisticated and chic woman doing with a man who sounded like the perfect slime-ball. Briefly, she lifted her eyes to the crystal chandeliers and reflected on the fact that money was a powerful motivator.

"I saw your name on the list of Newcomers Club members and I've been meaning to phone you and ask you to join the volunteers at Lar Christina Angelica," Diva said, linking her arm with Julia's and drawing her toward a marble pedestal on which rested a spot-lit bronze image of a waif peering through a window. Her slightly accented voice had the persuasive articulation and intonation of a natural salesperson. "It's a youth center for children in the nearby favela. Before and after school activities, games, classes with lunch and snack."

In that instant, Julia realized how much she had missed her volunteer work at *Angel and Friends,* where her care, attention and skills had a direct effect on those in need. Joyful at the prospect of once again making a difference, she quickly deflated and slowly shook her head. "I'd love to but my Portuguese is just too terrible."

"That doesn't matter. You can teach English. Do you know anything about crafts or sewing?" Julia again shook her head, feeling quite useless. She could see that a background in television and distribution of food to illegal immigrants wasn't going to count for much in São Paulo. "Well, Laura tells me you're interested in gardening." Diva persisted. A smile lit Julia's face.

"I love gardening. Along with cooking, it's my favorite hobby."

"There you go. Cooking's out because we don't have the facilities for such a class, and anyway the children are only interested in familiar foods which are mainly rice and beans. However, the older children need someone to help plant and grow vegetables." Diva's brown eyes grew thoughtful. "To be perfectly honest, it's a fairly long way to drive, and it *is* on the edge of a favela, which is why I have trouble recruiting volunteers."

"I could probably manage if I had written directions. Or I could go with someone else."

Diva smiled. "That's a possibility. Let's talk next week.

And you really should join the Garden Club." One arm swept upward toward the bronze. "Isn't this sculpture amazing? The artist's a professional and she still finds time to be on the Boards of American Society and Newcomers and to help out at Vivenda, Casa da Paz and Cheshire Homes."

Julia nodded, fatigued by the thought of this artist's boundless energy and speculating, not for the first time, about the number of Newcomers members who were long term residents of the city rather than just recent arrivals. Pearl drifted past, waving at Diva and ignoring Julia. A hand lifted in greeting from the thickening crowd; it was Laura, thank God. Her dark eyes flashing attentively around the room, Diva spotted a bewildered pair hesitating at the top of the staircase

"Ah, Casey and Clair have arrived. If you'll allow me, I must welcome them." Diva stepped close and lowered her voice. "Three armed men held them up outside their house last week when they came back from the Alfa Theater. They were lucky they just lost their car and some cash." She leaned fractionally closer and lowered her voice to a whisper. "And I did want to say that I'm terribly sorry about the trouble your husband is having at the office."

Her skin feeling suddenly cold in the tropical night, Julia stared at her hostess. "What trouble?" she asked softly.

Lifting her hands expressively, Diva smoothly buried her blunder. "It's nothing, I'm sure. Moacyr brings home the most tangled stories, most of which are completely wrong. Please excuse me."

As Diva hurried to greet the new arrivals, Laura, tall and elegant in a long, powder-blue crepe dress and short, satin jacket in the same hue took her place beside the sculpture. "What's up?"

Rubbing one bare forearm, Julia shook her head. "Diva just told me that Jack's in some kind of trouble, but when she realized she'd put both feet in her mouth, she clammed up. Do you know anything about it?"

Laura flipped impatient fingers through her hair and grimaced at Julia. "This community lives on gossip of one kind or another, you know that. You also are aware that São Paulo businesses run on crises. I'm sure that you'd be the first to know—from *Jack*—if there was something radically wrong at work."

Remembering the conversation with her husband in the car, Julia's anxiety dissolved. "I'm sure you're right."

"So how's the new couple working out, speaking of crises and gossip."

"You mean Alda and Zé?"

Laura nodded, lifting a glass of champagne from a passing waiter. Before answering, Julia raised both eyebrows and turned her lips down. "Ouch," commented Laura with a grin. "That bad, are they?"

"Better than anything the agency could come up with, even though they *are* Djalma's friends. Zé's excellent, but Alda is worse than useless. She doesn't clean well...in fact, Zé had to show her how to sweep under the furniture, and besides, she's sick all the time. First she had a skin disease, and then we found she has high blood pressure as well as hearing problems, and bad eyesight too!"

Laura began to laugh. "Is that all?"

"It's not funny. She's not smart either, which means she can't *learn*. One day she scorched a pair of Jack's pants and I got really pissed and yelled at her. It was in English, but she was bright enough to get my general drift and ran to tell Zé who complained to Jack that I had insulted his wife and if I did it again they'd have to leave."

Laughing, Laura deposited her empty champagne glass on the pedestal and covered her face with both hands. A smile curved Julia's lips as she watched her friend's shoulders shake with hilarity.

"Okay, chuckle away. I supposed it does sound comical to others. What I can't figure out is why Djalma recommended them."

Sobering, Laura peeked through her fingers at Julia and then reached out and took her friend's hands in her own. "I'm sorry, but you have had the worst luck. Did you check their references?"

"Yes and no. Since the last bosses they had are somewhere in Austria we couldn't talk to them, but the written recommendations seemed fine. They're probably fake," she added glumly.

"Get another couple."

Julia widened her eyes in horror. "To tell you the truth, I'm not sure there *are* better couples, although other people seem to have them." Hearing her name, Julia turned to see Marilyn edging around a group of animated guests, all of whom seemed to be speaking at once.

"You look fabulous," Julia exclaimed, feeling a rush of combined admiration and envy at the sight of the long, olive-green satin gown with a matching sequined-lace over-dress. It was a color she couldn't wear but was perfect with Marilyn's darker skin and hair. Marilyn shrugged.

"Thanks. I got sick of wearing black to everything like a professional mourner, so I had my dressmaker run this up." Julia and Laura looked at Julia's black dress; Julia sucked in her cheeks dolefully and Laura pressed one hand to her lips and rolled her eyes comically.

"By the way, have you seen Kathleen around?" Marilyn asked.

"No."

"She's rushing around telling everyone that she's going to Seattle to meet the mystery man tomorrow night. Apparently, Heather stays here with Randolf since he won't let her leave. Personally, I don't understand why she wanted to take a ten-year-old on an assignation."

"I guess Randolf didn't either since he wouldn't sign the document," commented Laura.

"What document?" Julia asked in confusion.

"Under Brazilian law, both parents must give notarized, written permission before a minor can leave the country, which Randolf refused to do," Laura explained.

"Kathleen's just acting out an ex-pat syndrome," Marilyn continued. "In your home territory you have jobs, friends, family, you know the language and the culture and the area and then you come here and have none of that. Women react in different ways; in Kathleen's case it's with an extremely peculiar affair."

It was an assessment that Julia would remember many months later.

"She needs therapy, not a plane ticket," declared Laura flatly. She looked around. "Where are the waiters with the drinks?

As though summoned by a genie, a white-jacketed servant appeared with a tray holding three clean glasses, a tumbler filled with ice cubes, a bottle of whiskey, one of soda and several caipirinhas.

Both Laura and Julia selected caipirinhas while Marilyn ordered a whiskey and ice. Grasping her drink, Julia sipped, looking at the crowd over the rim of the glass, wondering where Jack had gone.

"Besides trying to freak you out about Jack, what else did Diva have to say?" Laura asked. "I'll bet she tried to bring you into her volunteer fold."

"Yes, and she succeeded."

"You're going to do what?"

"Work in the garden with some kids. At someplace called Lar Christina Angelica."

Laura laughed, tossing her hair. "Perfect! I just started teaching embroidery there so we can go together."

Julia grinned. "Thanks. I'd probably never find it on my own." Still surreptitiously looking for her husband, she felt a small knot of resentment beginning to gnaw at her stomach. Slipping off to see his buddies was okay, but he should come back to her occasionally.

"Diva also mentioned the Garden Club," Julia said.

"Great idea! I don't know why I didn't think of that myself." Laura shook her head. "So tell me, what's up with your daughter?"

Julia widened her eyes dramatically, temporarily forgetting about Jack. "I suppose you mean Sydney. It just gets worse and worse. She used to be a model student and daughter and my sister tells me that, in the eleven months we've been gone, she's taken up smoking, refuses to acknowledge Gail's curfew and is dating a divorced or divorcing sculptor with three pre-teenage daughters."

"Late bid for independence, perhaps?" Marilyn suggested. "She may be furious because her parents left."

"I have no idea, but I've strongly suggested that both girls and Gail come down for a couple of weeks of family bonding. I hope they take me up on it."

"Or you could take a run up there to see what's happening," Laura suggested.

Again Julia briefly scanned the room for any trace of Jack, her sense of unease growing. For a moment, Marilyn studied her friend with shrewd eyes and then spoke.

"You know, maybe it's not a great idea, especially if Jack's having problems at work," she said.

A shrill voice at her elbow spared Julia the necessity of a reply.

"Having problems at work is he?" The three women exchanged despairing glances before turning to face Celeste Monroe. "I thank God every day, and all the angels and saints, that I'm single and childless."

Alarmingly overweight, Celeste was nevertheless stylish in a long black skirt and black and white print silk blazer. Probably forty, an art historian and a confirmed spinster, she was on a year-long sabbatical to study Brazilian naïf painting and had decided the ideal location for her project was São Paulo.

"Hello, Celeste," the trio chorused unenthusiastically.

"What kind of problems?" she persisted, moving very close without lowering her voice. Nearby, heads turned quizzically.

"We were speaking hypothetically," Julia answered.

"How is your work going?"

Dramatically, Celeste pressed both hands to her ample bosom, briefly closed her eyes as if in prayer and slowly shook her head, her blunt-cut, hennaed hair swinging from side to side. "Not well, not well at all." Opening her eyes, she announced, "All I ever wanted was to be rich and famous, and it's just not going to happen."

"Art history professors generally are neither rich nor famous," Julia commented dryly.

Ignoring the comment, Celeste declared, "If I can't have some kind of recognition, I'm going to become a nun and help the poor."

Julia's breath caught on a suppressed chuckle. "But you aren't Catholic."

"That can be changed," Celeste announced confidently. "I've already contacted several orders and they are *amazed* at my knowledge of this country. And impressed by the fact that I'm still in mourning", she waved one hand at her black skirt and print blazer, "for Princess Di six years after her death. I would love to stay in Brazil, but the Religious tend to work in the Amazon or the outback, and I had Rio or São Paulo in mind. It's a problem."

"I should point out that nuns aren't rich or famous either."

Tilting her head, Celeste's scarlet lips curved in a sly smile. "Not true," she crowed, shaking an admonishing index finger. "Think of Mother Teresa, for one. And Sister Dorothy right here in Brazil in our own day and age."

"They were never rich, and Dorothy was only famous after she was murdered. How about going to find some food?" Marilyn invited.

"No, thank you," answered Celeste. "I've cruised the buffet table and it has shrimps and patés and cheese...all the things I don't eat."

"See you later then," Julia responded. As they moved slowly through the throng, she murmured, "That is a sad case."

"Very," agreed Marilyn. "Her family history, which she'll tell you at the first opportunity if she hasn't already, is not a happy one. Against that background, Celeste herself is a success story."

Julia shook her head sympathetically, then lightly grasped Laura's forearm and smiled. "There's Jack. See? Over there talking to Maricarmen and someone else."

"That's Maricarmen's husband."

"And who's the other woman?" Julia's smile had faded.

Everyone in the ex-pat community knew Maricarmen who, although she was Brazilian, was on the Boards of both Newcomers Club and Canadian International Women's Society and was one of the orchid judges in the São Paulo Garden Club. Carefully coiffed and made-up, she nevertheless managed to look matronly in a long navy-blue skirt and matching lace top. Not so the second woman, whose tanned back, bared by a long, diagonally striped gown cut dangerously low on the buttocks, was turned to Julia. Jack was conversing with the group but it was the softening of his facial expression when his eyes came to rest on the second woman that caused Julia to catch her breath. She knew that look very well; she'd bathed in it when he proposed, when they were married and when the girls were born, but that had been a long time ago. Her muscles were paralyzed and her skin icy as she watched her husband.

"I'll see you later," Marilyn said, turning to greet an acquaintance.With reluctant steps, Julia followed Laura and was introduced to Maricarmen's husband Valdir. Half turning in Jack's direction, she stared at her husband's female companion. With perfectly straight, white teeth, a generous mouth, dimples, dark, winged eyebrows over mahogany eyes and a casual tousle of coffee-brown hair, she was quite beautiful. Her dress, as Julia had noticed from the back, was a second skin, the scarlet and white stripes emphasizing her tanned, perfect body. Silver or white gold earrings dangled from her ears and a matching necklace drew attention to her long, smooth neck. Julia's mouth was dry and she felt the blood flood her face as the woman graced her with a brilliant smile.

"You must be Dona Julia. I'm Eliana Gazzinelli, Mr. Elliott's secretary. It's a great pleasure to meet you, especially after all our phone conversations."

This was Jack's Eliana whom Julia had imagined as a middle aged, dowdy spinster bending over her computer, a telephone pressed to one ear? As Eliana leaned forward to kiss her cheeks, Julia was overwhelmed by the cloying scent of *Arpege* and her own rank odor of jealousy.

TEN—SÃO PAULO, BRAZIL

*I*t was Tuesday, one of Julia's mornings to teach the boys gardening at Lar Christina Angelica. Although this was only her fourth month as a volunteer, she loved the work, satisfied that finally she was doing something worthwhile with her time.

"Look," she said, squatting in the dirt beside a tomato plant around which several young boys hovered. "First we must tie this up. And then we have to water it regularly." She picked her Portuguese words carefully and spoke slowly while demonstrating the way to stake the plant. She pointed to the row of tomatoes and smiled at the group. "Let's see if you can do it." Quizzical faces stared at her.

Embarrassed, Julia stood up and called to Laura. "Could you please help me out?"

After a quick glance, Laura whispered to the girls seated around the table, put down her embroidery and stood up. Concerned, she strode to the vegetable patch. "What's up?"

"I thought I told them that we need to tie up the plants.

Those expressions tell me that I did not exactly hit the mark."

Turning to the boys, Laura spoke. To Julia it sounded exactly like the words she had just used, but the result was entirely different. Immediately, the group moved along the row of tomatoes, carefully securing them to the stakes just as Julia had demonstrated.

"I feel really stupid," Julia said glumly. "I study this stuff, I've had two lessons a week forever, and it's just useless."

"Don't be silly. Children want perfection," Laura replied cheerfully. "At least they didn't laugh at you, which used to happen to me."

Pulling her lips downward, Julia ran one hand through her tawny, shoulder-length hair and shrugged. "This language is impossible."

"You usually do okay."

I usually do okay because I've learned to fake it, Julia mused, thinking of the innumerable times she'd mentally rehearsed a sentence or two before verbalizing it. And then she had to wade through a morass of rapid Portuguese, trying to unravel the response. She'd learned to catch a key word and then try to guess the rest, along with developing a response. "Ta" was a gem she used often and could signify almost anything. Of course, her Portuguese teacher was full of praise, probably because the woman's fees were outrageous and she wanted to make sure Julia didn't become discouraged and quit. Laura's voice cut into her thoughts.

"You're just nervous because your girls and Gail arrive next week."

"Thank you, Doctor Freud, but that has nothing to do with it," Julia responded, knowing Laura had hit on at least a partial truth. It would be the first time her family had visited Brazil and she wanted everything to be perfect so that they would have a wonderful two-week holiday.

"Anyway, these kids adore you and they work hard, as

we can see from all the leafy green things growing around here, so don't worry about your Portuguese."

Julia didn't feel reassured. Spanish had been no problem, so why was she such a dunce in Portuguese? This whole adventure was a lot different than anything she'd envisioned back in Venice Beach when Jack had assured her that she would love Brazil. Laura tucked an arm through Julia's and glanced at her watch. "If we're going to see that movie, we'd better be on our way."

In Los Angeles, Julia would never have found time for a movie in the afternoon, which she still found somewhat decadent. Wise enough not to voice this opinion to Laura, she said goodbye to the children.

Before entering the car, Julia stood for a moment and surveyed the grounds of Lar Christina Angelica. Built in the gritty Embu-Guaçu municipality, it was an oasis of peace where impoverished children could play on the new asphalt basketball court, practice musical instruments inside the immaculate, three-room clubhouse and, after or before school, participate in classes such as gardening, embroidery, sewing and dance. Lunch, cooked by two female caretakers in a tiny kitchen on an old, two-burner gas ring, was provided at long tables on the veranda, along with badly needed instruction in table manners and hygiene. The region was hilly, the surrounding neighborhood had no vegetation, and ramshackle concrete block buildings interspersed with cardboard and plywood shacks rose from plots of bare earth. Inside the gates of the Lar, the well-painted clubhouse was shaded by tall palm and Sombreira or Sunshade trees and encircled by the flowers and shrubs which had been planted by Julia and the youngsters. Sloping, grassy grounds led to the basketball court, soccer field and barbecue, all of them protected by a thick umbrella of trees. Julia felt an immense and unexpected wave of satisfaction, realizing that this project was probably more important than her volunteer activities in L.A.

Sandra Cuza

Laura started the car and asked, "Any improvement in the *caseiros*?"

Julia ran one hand through her hair in a gesture of defeat. "Now you've ruined my day. Alda went to the hospital last week, sick again, and the doctor told her she's suffering from extreme stress and shouldn't work. So she mostly rests in her room and watches TV while Zé cleans and I cook."

Laura shot her friend a sharp look of disapproval. "So you're paying for a couple and only one half of it works? I think we've heard this one before."

"I know. I'm thinking of hiring a daily, since Zé is such a treasure."

Laura shrugged. "Do what you want, but there are other treasures that aren't stressed out and work as a pair."

As they turned out of the gate, Laura braked suddenly at the unexpected sight of a long line of cars. "What's happening here?"

"Probably an accident. I heard that São Paulo has something like two motor-bikers killed every day, and I forget how many car collisions."

Julia nodded. "My Portuguese teacher told me that there are more people murdered here with guns every year than died in something like thirty years in the Angola Civil war, and the fifty years of Israel's war with Palestine."

"That's cheery. I hope death isn't what's holding us up." Laura paused. "Or a police blitz. Remember, Mother's Day was just last Sunday."

Julia frowned, trying to make the connection, and then she chuckled wryly. "Oh, yes, I forgot that on holidays the criminals are let out of the prisons to be with their families and at least half never go back."

"Would you?"

"Of course not, but you'd think those idiot politicians would wake up to the fact that gangsters don't wish to get back in their cells after partying for a weekend."

"They know. Prisons are seriously overcrowded and I

94

think this helps to weed out some of the felons." Eyes narrowed, she tilted her head to one side. "Do you hear music?"

Julia rolled down the window and listened intently. "Definitely." Quickly she closed the window, guarding against the armed thieves that preyed on cars with open windows and unlocked doors throughout São Paulo.

Within a few minutes it became clear that they were hearing Samba music which, as they crept along the roadway, grew louder. At the intersection, traffic was snarled, voices could be heard raised in song and Julia saw dancing bodies at the far corner.

"Look at those telephone repairmen," she murmured gleefully, not quite trusting her eyes. Four men in uniforms and hard hats had abandoned the large, square metal box that contained the lines and connections for the neighborhood telephones and were dancing to music provided by their truck radio. Apparently, a beautiful woman returning from the market had wandered by, heard the music and, her potatoes and cabbage abandoned for the moment, was leading the dance. Several bystanders had joined them and now a few motorists parked their cars and ran eagerly toward the group. Forgotten, the door of the phone box stood open and cables spilled out onto the ground.

"So that's why the phones don't function," Julia said, as they drove slowly past. It looked like so much fun; how she wished she and Jack had taken those samba lessons. Sydney and Stephanie would love this. In fact, they'd be out there dancing, lessons or not.

"I'll bet they don't suffer stress over their work."

"That's a fact. Listen, before we go to the movies, can I stop at home to see if the plumber has finished?" Julia asked.

"What plumber?"

"This guy that was supposed to change the kitchen faucet and said it would only take ten minutes."

Laura grinned. "And you believed him?"

"Well, sort of. By the time you picked me up he'd been there for forty-five minutes, and then he'd gone out for some parts or tools. I was in such a rush to get my gardening things together and get out the door that I forgot all about him until five minutes ago."

"It's no problem to go see what's happening, but why didn't you ask Zé to change the faucet?"

Julia shrugged, feeling inadequate. "He's good at finding repair people, not doing the jobs himself." She turned toward Laura and blurted defensively, "I know, I know, I'm managing the servants all wrong, but this is not in my skill set." She folded her arms and stared out the window. Laura glanced at her, then reached across and patted her shoulder.

"You're doing fine." Traffic had thinned now that the dancers were left behind and Laura accelerated. "Did I tell you that the police solved the mystery of all those break-ins in my maid's home town?"

Laura's maid came from a small city in the interior where, for some months, homes had been plagued by strange break-ins. To the bafflement of the victims and police, only food was stolen but plates and glasses were always smashed. Until recently, there were no clues pointing to the culprit.

Intrigued, Julia looked quizzically at her friend. "No. Who was it?"

"It was a band of monkeys, would you believe. Somebody finally saw them at work and called the police, or what passes for the law in a village. It was amazing. First the gang cased the house for a couple of days and then, when they were sure all the household members had left the premises, a scout hunted for any unlocked or open window. When he found one he signaled the others. Three monkeys acted as lookouts while the others went inside and stole the food and broke the plates and glasses."

Julia chortled with delight. "Did they catch the

monkeys?"

"They did! And the thinking is to take them far into the jungle where they won't be tempted to use these skills again."

"Well, good luck. If they've figured out how to break and enter, then they'll certainly know how to swing through a few kilometers of trees to the nearest town."

They turned into Julia's driveway, a steep, winding strip of asphalt leading to the front door and carport just beyond. Almost immediately, Alda appeared in the doorway, an expression of distress creasing her pinched, mahogany face, her uniform apron twisted between her hands.

"I see trouble," said Julia, her spirits plummeting as she shut the car door and moved toward the house. "What's the problem, Alda?"

"José left and came back..."

"The plumber?"

"Yes, yes, he left and came back and left and..."

"Where is he now?" Julia had noticed his truck was not parked on the street and assumed he'd finished the job.

"He left again an hour ago."

"Do we have a new faucet?"

"We don't. And he took the old one with him. And the water's off."

Julia clenched and unclenched her fists and the muscles in her jaws moved spasmodically as she quietly ground her teeth. Stay calm, she told herself, staring at the maid with combined frustration and hostility.

"And where is Zé?"

"Out getting gardening supplies."

The maid's Portuguese was such a worried tumble of words that Julia asked her to repeat more slowly.

"That's great," she said in English, turning toward Laura. The two exchanged silent looks of understanding. "Let's take a look."

The kitchen sink was indeed without a faucet, although

97

the countertop was littered with washers and a number of other small, mysterious metal and rubber objects. Both women stared at the mess. Finally Julia spoke.

"I know I should be grateful that I have running water and a faucet—at least occasionally I have one—but sometimes I could just kick and scream and bang my head on the floor. After my cake last night, this is the last straw."

Laura was baffled. "Cake?"

"It was a great failure."

"Why? You're a very good cook."

"Yeah, well this was a chiffon cake that has to cool upside down, and when I took it out of the oven and turned it over the batter all ran out of the pan. The gas had run out halfway through the baking time, only I didn't know it. I can't get used to this bottled gas that goes empty with no warning and has to be changed."

"So, what does one cake mean in the bigger picture?"

Julia shrugged. "I guess it means just one more frustration."

"Do you have this plumber's cell phone number?"

"Of course, but my Portuguese is not advanced enough to do battle with a plumber or his wife or children, or whoever may answer the phone."

"Then call Jack's office and ask his secretary to phone. Let her deal with it while we go to the flicks."

Julia's stomach curdled. Ask the glamorous and much younger Eliana to deal with a problem that she herself couldn't manage? Admit failure to the chic secretary with the perfect figure, beautiful face and flawless English who seemed to accompany Jack to every meeting including luncheons?

"I can't do that. She's not *my* secretary."

Laura's face reflected disapproval. "For God's sake, everyone here uses their husbands' secretaries for messages and phone calls."

For a moment, Julia wondered if she could speak

commandingly in her pitiful Portuguese; maybe it was worth a try. Under no circumstances, would she ask Eliana for a favor. Then her eye fell upon Alda, thin and weak and leaning against the wall, and she discovered the solution. Moving to a pad of paper on the end of the kitchen counter, she held it up for the maid to see. "Here is José's phone number. The minute your husband returns, have him call and deal with the plumber. Forget the garden, forget the cleaning; tell him I want this fixed by the time I come back." Slapping it down on the counter, she stepped briskly toward the door, followed by Laura. "Come on, we don't want to be late."

Laura grinned as they rushed toward her car and then sped down the driveway. "Your Portuguese was pretty good back there."

"Thanks." Julia studied her friend's profile as they maneuvered through the São Paulo traffic. Over the past months, she had come to know Laura well and admired her active participation in Newcomers Club, the Catholic Church and an animal shelter. Her house seemed to be beautifully managed and her teenage children, Molly and Richard, were far better adjusted than her own daughters had ever been. Her biggest peculiarity, if it could be called that, was an obsession with dance movies, preferably oldies, and she saw every one that came to the city more than once, usually on her own. Laura once told her that she had trained to be a dancer but traded in the possibility of a career for marriage.

"Have you seen this film yet?" Julia asked. "And which one is it?"

"Years ago. It's Ginger Rogers and Fred Astair's *Flying Down to Rio* playing in the old Cinetex, which is probably as old as the movie itself and only shows vintage flicks. As a bonus they have a short documentary about seals, and you know how I love animals."

Julia thought it went beyond love into the realm of mania but she knew better than to voice that opinion.

Laura pulled into the parking lot and yanked on the handbrake.

"I saw *42nd Street* here just a couple of months ago. It was choreographed by Busby Berkeley and had the most spectacular dance scenes," she commented wistfully.

"Why don't you take some dance classes? I'm sure they have fabulous ones in São Paulo."

"I gave all that up," Laura replied shortly, "when I married Alan."

Reminded that she and Jack had also quit dancing when they moved to Brazil, Julia silently bought her ticket and followed her friend into the lobby. One end of the cramped lobby was devoted to the sale of popcorn, sodas and candy; a door just in front of them stood open and a man was fiddling with a projector.

"Look, Laura, this is so old-fashioned," Julia cried in delight.

"That's what I told you. The flicks are old, the equipment is ancient, and the building is prehistoric. Let's find our seats."

Once inside, Julia's enchantment evaporated. It was exactly the kind of theater that she, not a major movie fan, distinctly disliked. Shabby, it had worn plush seats that offered virtually no leg room, dim lighting and walls that were in need of a paint job. Worst of all, the smell of rancid fat filled the air.

"Phew," she breathed. "They should outlaw popcorn, especially if it has fake butter poured over it." She paused. "I hope they don't have fleas here."

Laura shot her a look of fond tolerance as the lights were suddenly extinguished and the screen illuminated. After a series of advertisements that convinced Julia she never wanted to buy any product displayed, a deafening blast of trumpets announced the beginning of *O Futuro da Foca*, the documentary about seals. The title gave way to credits that rolled heavenward against a background of seal hunters chasing baby seals and clubbing them to a bloody death or, more frequently, conscious immobility. Julia heard Laura gasp and felt her friend's arm stiffen on the armrest; a moment later she was on her feet shouting, "Pare! Stop this film. Take it off right now."

Through the theater Julia could hear hisses and boos as Laura swiveled to face the beam of light from the projection room.

"Do you hear me? Stop this film."

Stunned by her friend's ferocious reaction to the images, and aware of the hostile reaction of the increasingly noisy audience, Julia jumped to her feet and murmured, "Let's go."

But Laura was already gone, pushing her way over the knees and feet of those in her row and darting up the aisle to the curtained doorway, the shouts and catcalls growing louder. Julia followed more slowly, wishing they were invisible or, better yet, back at the Lar weeding the garden. Before she reached the exit, images on the screen underwent a violent series of spins and jerks and finally vanished altogether; simultaneously, the angry bellow of a male voice was heard from the projection room. Breaking into a sprint, Julia burst into the lobby and ran to the projection room where she saw Laura tearing film from the reel that she held in one hand. The projectionist attempted to grab her but Laura hit him with the reel and he tumbled to the floor just as a milling crowd spilled from the exit of the theater and the manager flung open the door of his office. Cries of "Polícia! Polícia!" were heard.

Julia ran to the projection booth, wrestled the reel from Laura's hands and tossed it to the ground. Grimly, she grasped her friend by the forearm and yanked her from the booth, dragging her back into the theater against the exiting crowd. Inside, red emergency lights flashed, and Julia paused for a moment to assess the situation. Intent on fleeing the theater, no one in the crowd identified Laura as the guilty party.

"Thank you God, for this crappy lighting," Julia

thought, pulling Laura toward one of the side exits.

"What are we doing?"

Police sirens could be heard and the muffled sound of feet running in the lobby.

"Trying to get out before we land in the pokey."

"But did you *see* that?"

"Do not say a word. Not one word until we get in the car." Julia felt her heart beating in her throat and perspiration running down her back as they exited into the parking lot. Laura was tall, certainly much taller than most Brazilians, but the theater had been dark and Laura's demented departure had been a solo one; with luck, her height might not have been noticed.

Glancing around as Laura handed the attendant her parking ticket, Julia noticed a couple whispering and staring at them. She felt sick, her head ached and she was sure she had a fever. Putting on her dark glasses, she stared at the ground, her body now covered with perspiration as they waited for Laura's car to arrive. Just as the couple spoke to a security guard, gesturing first to the theater and then toward Laura, the car drew up and the manobrista emerged, holding the door open for Laura. Hesitantly, the guard approached the car as Laura accelerated and slipped out through the open gate.

"What in the hell did you think you were doing?" Julia's voice was tight with rage as she twisted to look through the rear window.

"Protesting. There has to be some action taken or seal hunts will just go on and on with nobody caring."

"Laura, we could have been tossed in jail and deported. Ever think of that while you were protesting? That would have been a lovely reception for my family."

"There's always that possibility when you take action." Her voice was calm and serene, further infuriating Julia.

"Well, I don't want to see my children through bars for something I didn't do, so next time please give me the chance to count myself out."

They drove to Julia's house in silence. Inwardly seething, Julia realized that, although Laura was her best friend in São Paulo, she actually didn't know the woman at all. Going berserk in a one-person spontaneous protest movement was not a normal adult reaction to anything and, unbidden, Marilyn's voice echoed in her mind. "In your home territory you have jobs, friends, family, you know the language and the culture and the area and then you come here and have none of that. Women react in different ways."

Taking a deep breath, Julia looked out the window at the streets clogged with cars and suddenly felt acutely homesick for her job, her daughters, Mary Beth, and her old way of life in Venice, including the old Jack. She had lived in São Paulo for just about a year; twelve months ago she would have rushed home and stammered out her fear, anger and edginess to Jack and they would have discussed it, dissected the incident and reached some kind of a conclusion. Now she didn't intend to say a word.

ELEVEN—SÃO PAULO, BRAZIL

*S*tanding squarely in front of the double glass doors, Julia watched as passengers filed out of airport Customs, most of them alone, some in pairs. Sporadically, arrivals were assaulted by shrieking groups of friends and relatives who rushed forward the minute their loved ones appeared, tearfully grappling with the travelers in joyful embraces that effectively blocked the Customs exit. Luggage spilled onto the floor, children scampered excitedly around and between the feet of the adults while human traffic stopped. Eventually, luggage was retrieved, children were collected and the groups moved on, unaware of their disregard for others which was viewed indulgently by Brazilians but indignantly by almost everyone else.

Where were the girls and Gail, Julia wondered? She glanced at her watch—almost eight-thirty. United Flight 909 from Chicago to São Paulo, landing at seven in the morning, was the information she'd received from Gail but, arriving at 6:30, Julia found no such flight listed on the monitor. Plenty of other planes had landed more or less at that hour, and three of them were United but not from Chicago. After checking with Airport Information, Julia discovered that the flight number Gail had given her did not exist.

How perfectly predictable, Julia thought as she dialed Gail's house. Why did I expect my sister to behave any differently than she has for her entire life? After four rings she heard Gail's cheery voice on the answering machine, indicating that her sister and the girls might be either in the air or in Brazil. Julia had then spent nearly an hour running between the two International Terminals located at opposite ends of the airport while reflecting on the fact that confusion had always followed Gail like a little cloud. Standing vigilantly in front of first one and then the other Customs doors, she was acutely aware that her sister and daughters might, at that moment, be arriving at the other terminal. How Brazilian, she thought, to complicate the situation by building two International terminals instead of one.

She pulled out her cell phone and called home.

"Jack, has Gail or one of the girls called?"

"No, why?"

"There's no United flight of that number, or any United plane at this time from Chicago."

"How did she get from L.A. to Chicago?"

"Another United flight, I suppose, but that's just a guess."

"That doesn't give us much to go on."

"What do you think I should *do*?"

Jack's voice was rich, deep and self-assured. "I think you know that I'm preparing for a Board meeting this afternoon that is crucial to my job. You're dealing with adults who are either there or they aren't, and I can't help you out."

Julia knotted one fist in frustration. "These *adults* are your daughters and sister-in-law and all you're worried about is impressing board members who don't like you

105

anyway."

"I am not going to let you upset me before this important meeting. I'm just as concerned as you are about the girls and Gail but there is nothing I can do about it now." His voice was now smooth and calm, serving to irritate her even more. "They can't have been kidnapped, so at some point they'll turn up."

Kidnapped? She hadn't considered that. There were lots of kidnappings in Brazil, although she hadn't heard of any at airports. Looking vigilantly around the waiting room, she was struck by a sharp feeling of deja-vú. This was exactly where she and Jack had watched the one-woman samba demonstration. Although only a year had gone by, it seemed like decades.

Another fifteen minutes passed and Julia decided it was far too late for the group to emerge from Customs. Or maybe not, depending on where they were. One United flight was listed as eleven hours late; maybe her daughters were on that one. Moving slowly, searching the crowd, she took the escalator to the first floor. The space above the arrival exits was open to the ceiling and encircled by a deep balcony with bookshops, restaurants and bars. It was Julia's plan to sit at a table next to the gallery's brass railing, have a coffee and phone Mary Beth who might know what was going on.

Moving to the railing, she took out her phone, punched in Mary Beth's number and heard an invitation to leave a message. Of course, she thought grimly. With the time difference, Mary Beth would be sleeping, and she always turned the phone off at night in spite of Julia's lectures about emergency calls.

Turning toward a café that was just opening, her eye was caught by a swirl of unnaturally bright, platinum hair in the throng below. Hope caught in her throat as she bent over the rail for a clearer look at the woman who seemed to be pressing close to one knot of travelers after another as though eavesdropping. She couldn't be sure from this angle but it did look like Gail, and the clothes, jeans and a brief black top that might be some form of underwear, were certainly her sister's non-business style. But if that was Gail, where were Sydney and Stephanie? Julia turned and raced to the escalator, forcing her way past stationary bodies in order to jump down the steps two at a time. At the bottom, she ran toward the area where the blond woman had bobbled in a sea of humanity, squeezing between couples and darting around the edges of groups. She pushed past a loaded baggage cart propelled by a uniformed porter and found herself facing Gail.

"Julia, where have you been?"

"Where have *I* been? Looking for you!"

Julia stared at her sister and then the women rushed toward one another and met in a hug that was followed by several kisses on both cheeks. Relief flooded Julia's body.

"Where are the girls?"

Gail waved vaguely toward a coffee shop, ringed with tables and chairs, in the center of the floor. "I told them to change some money and have a coffee. I've been creeping around here trying to find someone who might speak English, but nobody does."

"That's because the language in this country is Portuguese. Look, I've been here since 6:30 to meet your United flight 909, but there is no such thing. What happened?"

Gail covered her coral mouth with one perfectly manicured hand and her brown eyes opened wide in shock. Of the two, Gail had always been the prettiest, possibly because, since childhood, she had been very concerned with beauty and had concentrated on appearing glamorous, or close to it, at all times. She spent a lot of time working out, having massages, facials and manicures, sessions with the hairdresser and now, Julia thought with a tiny tinge of jealousy, it had paid off. Four years her junior, Gail could easily pass for a woman in her early thirties.

"I can't believe no one told you that flight was

cancelled. When we got to Chicago we were switched to American and they said they'd phone you and give you the information."

"Well, they didn't," Julia commented tartly.

"I would have called when we landed but my cell phone won't work here and the pay phones take some kind of weird coin and nobody could speak English and help me." Gail's mouth drooped and she looked as though she might burst into tears. Julia put an arm around her sister and steered her toward the coffee shop.

"Well, you're here now. Your hair looks a little lighter. And longer..."

Gail fluffed the casually spiraled tresses that spilled over her shoulders and smiled, good humor restored. "I changed hairdressers. Alain is very French and has wonderful taste. His wardrobe is unbelievable."

"Is that underwear you've got on, or some sort of beach top?"

"It's the latest fashion in L.A. Do you think it's too low?"

"Yes."

"Mom! Mom, over here!"

Julia whirled and was almost immediately enveloped by her daughters in a massive hug. Intertwined, the three rocked back and forth, and Julia felt her eyes prickle with tears. More than ever, as she felt their bodies and smelled traces of their coconut shampoo, she realized how much she had missed them both, how her life had been impoverished by their absence.

"Uh, Mom, you're standing on my foot."

Reluctantly, Julia released the girls and moved back a few steps. "I'm sorry; it's just so exciting to see..." Her voice faded for a moment and then climbed. "Good grief, Sydney, what's that in your nose?"

"A nose ring. And I have a pierced belly button too." She smiled, and Julia's heart twisted. "Lawrence thinks it's sexy."

Julia's euphoria at having her family with her was considerably dampened. "Ah yes, the married sculptor with several teenage children."

"Only three..."

"What a relief. Where's your luggage?"

"Right here." Stephanie linked one arm with her mother and pointed to the luggage cart. "You push, Syd."

"I'm not your servant," Sydney snapped, fishing a packet of cigarettes from one coat pocket and lighting up. Julia decided not to discuss this new habit or her daughter's very short hair which was magenta with a sort of florescent green streak, nor even notice that, although she still dressed in a sort of faux Annie Hall style, she was wearing a jacket and short shorts of the same length along with cowboy boots. With a flounce, Sydney stuck the cigarette between her lips and shoved the baggage cart ahead of the trio.

"What's wrong with your leg?" Julia stared at Sydney's right leg that seemed to have a snake wrapped around the calf. Sydney stopped, tipped her head back and peered at it, brushing her coat collar with her lit cigarette.

"That's a tattoo, Mom. And I have a tarantula on my left bicep and a butterfly on my butt."

For a moment, Julia's mouth hung open as she stared at the tattoo and then she found her voice. "Are they permanent?"

"Of course."

"I told you we were having a few difficulties," murmured Gail.

"That looks hideous," Julia said, upset. "You have eternally marred your beautiful skin.

"You are so old-fashioned." Sydney began pushing the cart again.

"When you're my age that ink's going to be a big shapeless blot and everyone will think you were in the Navy."

"Now that's a thought. Maybe I'll join up."

"Do *women* in the Service go in for tattoos?" asked Gail as they exited the building and started toward the parking lot.

"Anyway, I may never *be* as old as you," Sydney announced.

Julia felt a sudden chill. "Don't say that," she admonished. "And I certainly hope you aren't thinking of getting more tattoos."

"Maybe... Maybe not. Anyway, you and Dad abandoned me, so what do you care?"

"Sydney, you know perfectly well that your father was offered a job that he basically had to take for a couple of years. You could have come but you wanted to stay with Gail."

"And Angelique and Oso," Sydney corrected. The cat and dog seemed to be preferable to life with her parents in a new country, despite the fact that the animals hadn't moved to Gail's, Julia reflected as they turned into the parking lot. "So, how was your flight?" she asked Gail.

"Not bad, but the plane was full of Mormons about sixteen years old arriving for missionary duty in the wilds of São Paulo. I felt very jaded," her sister responded, looking the antithesis of jaded.

"How do you know they were Mormons?" asked Sydney.

Her younger daughter might be tattooed and pierced and have a married boyfriend but she was amazingly naive at times, Julia thought.

"Because they were in a large, totally male group, all blond and pale, wearing white shirts and ties, and they folded their jackets carefully before putting them in the overhead compartment," Gail explained.

"Oh."

"That blue car is mine," Julia announced.

Sneaking a look at the snake on her youngest child's leg, Julia remembered Sydney as a laughing, loveable toddler and suddenly felt as though her family, for whom she would give her life, were strangers. Silently, she unlocked the trunk of the car and stowed one suitcase inside. Before she could hoist another, her sister pointed to a non-descript black bag on the cart.

"That's not my suitcase."

Dramatically, fingers glittering with diamonds that would have to be immediately removed before they were appropriated by a thief, Gail fanned the air in front of her face. "This is a disaster. That's supposed to be the one that has your Wedgwood replacements and Mother's sterling and one of her Belgian lace tablecloths and I've forgotten what else."

Julia's world settled into an old, familiar pattern. In a dispassionate tone that she maintained with difficulty, she asked, "How do you know this isn't yours?"

"Mine doesn't have yellow and green braided ribbons. This one does."

For a moment they all stared at the colorful plait.

"Didn't you check the luggage tag?" Julia asked, knowing the answer to her silly question.

"I never do."

Suddenly, Gail sprang forward, lifted the wheeled suitcase off the cart and raised its handle. She turned and, dragging the bag behind her, dashed back toward the Arrivals Terminal.

"Don't move," Julia cautioned her daughters with a hand upraised in warning before pursuing her sister. "Wait up, Gail," she called.

Her sister took no notice. Passengers emerging from the terminal stared curiously at the racing women and one young man began jogging beside Julia.

"Do you need help?" he asked. "Has she stolen something?"

"No, it's all right. She's my sister."

Julia dodged oncoming human traffic, finally catching up with Gail at the barrier in front of Customs.

"I have to go in there," Gail told the guard, pointing to

the closed doors. Gasping for breath after her unusual long-distance run, Julia repeated the statement in Portuguese, explaining that her sister had the wrong suitcase. After a brief, blank look, the guard murmured, "*Um momentinho*" and slipped into the inner sanctum.

A few minutes later, the double doors opened again and a women and child walked out; Gail darted inside and disappeared.

Oh my God, they're going to deport my flakey sister, thought Julia, dashing after Gail before the doors slid shut. As she ran down the corridor leading to the Customs lounge, she saw Gail come to an abrupt stop in front of a cluster of pale blond young men wearing white shirts and ties who seemed to be confronting a Customs official. When Julia reached them, she saw that the officer barred the way to a large room containing tier after tier of suitcases, knapsacks, bedrolls, carryalls, cosmetic cases— every conceivable kind of luggage—and beside the man was a suitcase identical to the one in Gail's possession.

"There it is!" exclaimed one of the youths, pointing to the bag. "That's our suitcase." He waved to a large group of matching young men gathered at the far side of the room and shouted, "We've got it. Look, here it is."

Joyfully, the men surged across the room, smiling at Gail and Julia and casting thankful upward glances. One of the men held out his hand to Gail and, releasing her hold on the suitcase, she shook his hand. Deftly, another young man took control of the bag.

"Thank you so much for bringing it back. It has all our Books of Mormon in there so this would have been a calamity. We're missionaries bringing the word of God."

Julia and Gail exchanged glances.

"You almost traded my Wedgwood, Mother's sterling and the antique tablecloth for dozens of Books of Mormon?" Julia asked tonelessly.

Gail lifted her shoulders in helpless affirmation. "You have to admit it looks like my suitcase."

"And now we'll probably have to pay the earth in duty," Julia murmured as she and the missionaries looked enquiringly at the Customs officer. Clearly sick of the entire scene, the latter made shooing motions with his hands.

"*Va embora. Va. Va.*"

"What did he say?" asked Gail.

"Flee. Run. Get out of here; so let's do that before he changes his mind and sends us through Customs."

Grabbing the handle of her sister's suitcase, Julia began retreating quickly down the corridor toward the Arrival lounge and freedom, followed closely by Gail. As they stepped into the terminal, Julia experienced her second wave of relief in less than an hour. Muscles sagging as the tension evaporated, she wondered what further surprises this family visit might bring.

TWELVE—SÃO PAULO, BRAZIL

"*A*re you about ready, Gail?" Julia called.

"Not really."

A moment later, Julia's sister appeared in the doorway of the living room wrapped in a towel; Sydney and Stephanie glanced up and then returned to their magazines. Obviously, not much about their Aunt came as a surprise to either one. Julia eyed her sister's platinum tresses that were now flying about like Medusa's famous locks and asked, "What happened to your hair?"

"This just isn't my day. I accidentally confused my hair lacquer and deodorant sprays so now I have to wash my hair all over again. And I can't plug my hair dryer into any of the outlets."

"That's because you need to file off the grounding," advised Julie. "It's that little hump in the side of one of the flat prongs."

"I know what the grounding is but I'm certainly not going to electrocute myself and set the house on fire just to dry my hair."

"Everybody does it here if they use American appliances.

"Unbelievable," her sister responded.

"Use Mom's dryer, Auntie Gail. It's on the dresser in my room."

"Please hurry," Julia urged. "Laura said lunch at one o'clock, and it's already one-fifteen."

Forgetting electricity, Gail stared at her watch. "Golly, that's impossible. My watch says eleven-fifteen." Lifting her wrist to one ear, she listened intently. "It's running. Yesterday I set it to Brazil time but maybe I was a little off."

"So it would seem."

"Fifteen minutes is all I need."

Normally, Julia wouldn't have minded arriving moderately late since Brazilians were never on time, but Laura was giving this luncheon to introduce Gail, Sydney and Stephanie to the ex-pat community. It was, Julia assumed, Laura's way of apologizing for the cinema incident and Julia didn't want to appear discourteous. It was, she knew well, a very small community.

Gail called from the bedroom, "I forgot to bring my umbrella."

"It's not raining and we have plenty of umbrellas," Julia replied, adding under her breath a disgruntled, "God!"

She had forgotten how idiosyncratic and eccentric her sister could be, but this visit was a forceful reminder that a highly successful businesswoman was not necessarily efficient and organized in her personal life. The first two days after her arrival had been spent replacing the contents of Gail's cosmetic bag which, somehow, had been left behind. Finding facsimiles of her toothbrush and paste, skin soap, hairbrush, night crème and a dozen other items had taken some time but the insurmountable problem was medication. Despite Julia's assurance that prescribed medication couldn't be obtained on demand either in the U.S. or in Brazil, Gail insisted on visiting several

115

pharmacies where she described, in English, what she wanted. The pharmacists were puzzled and polite and told her no.

"But this is Brazil. It's a Third World country full of corruption and people who bend the rules," Gail complained, finally giving up.

"Pharmacists are not known for their law-breaking tendencies," Julia said. She paused thoughtfully. "At least I've never heard of it here."

"It's really only aspirin, anyway."

"I have aspirin at home."

"Aspirin and a little extra something in case I get too stressed out from my work."

"You're not at work."

Now, Julia tried to quell her anxiety. She loved having the girls and her sister here so that her life felt once again complete, but she had also grown accustomed to regulating her days in accordance with her own time frame and wishes. Her family was beautiful and very precious to her but this was real life and they could also be difficult and trying.

"Is this lunch a big deal?" asked Sydney. "I mean, I don't see why your friend's asking us since we're perfect strangers."

"That's the reason. In the ex-pat community, when relatives visit, it's the custom for friends to meet them and introduce them to others. And I hope you'll be a little more charming when we get there."

Sydney shrugged and crossed her legs, which were completely covered by tuxedo pants over which a short, green skirt had been layered. An interesting and profuse collection of bead necklaces, medals on ribbons, and rosaries covered her white blouse which was topped by the tuxedo jacket. A lavender sailor cap and a pair of riding boots completed the outfit. Diane Keaton had retreated into the distance.

"*I* think it's a very sweet gesture," said Stephanie.

"Well, I hope they don't serve meat."

"Why?" Impatiently bouncing her car keys in one hand, Julia stood up and moved to the hallway. The door to her sister's room was firmly closed.

"Because I'm a vegetarian now," Sydney responded. "I don't eat anything with eyes."

Julia turned and looked at her younger daughter in astonishment. "Vegetarian?" she asked, turning toward Stephanie. "You too?"

Hazel eyes sparkling, Stephanie laughed and a deep dimple appeared in her right cheek. Her skin had lost its tan and was now very fair, her mop of expertly permed curls was a dark brown that matched her thick eyelashes and finely plucked brows.

"Not a chance. Any vegetarian at college would starve to death."

"Is that your natural color?" Julia peered at Stephanie's hair, which was a different shade and shape every time she saw her parents.

Stephanie shrugged. "Pretty close."

With a clatter of very high heels, Gail burst into the room. "Ready," she announced. In her wide-striped white and green linen trouser suit and designer scarf, her recently rewashed blond hair cascading over her shoulders and her wrinkle-free face perfectly made-up, she looked like a film star. Julia felt a twinge of jealousy.

"Let's go," she urged Sydney. "Where did you get that tuxedo?"

"Cool, huh? At the *Second Is Best* used clothing store."

"You know," Gail announced, as her stiletto heels carved tiny holes in the mahogany floorboards, "I might get a face lift while I'm down here."

As they stepped outside, Julia looked heavenward and pled, "Strength!"

Laura's house was perfect for entertaining, which was one of the main reasons she and Alan had chosen it.

Unlike most São Paulo homes, it was one story, octagonal and mostly glass with deep, shaded verandas. The main building curved around a large, slightly hilly lawn slashed by a lap pool painted black. Beyond the pool, a flagstone path led to a guest house; on all sides, there was a forest of trees and shrubs. Despite the armed guard at the gate and high, electrified fence, it was a friendly and welcoming house, one with casually scattered rugs, comfortable sofas and chairs and an eclectic array of bowls, sculptures, beaded objects and Brazilian paintings, all obviously selected by the owners rather than by a decorator.

"Although you can't see it, there's a little lake beyond the guest house," said Julia.

"Wow," said Stephanie. "What a layout. These people must be millionaires."

"You both know very well that it's vulgar and boorish to speculate about the amount of money other people have, but most ex-pats down here live in a style they've previously only seen in movies. Before we came, we very carefully explained that one of the attractions of your father's job was not just the higher salary and his title as President but the fact that Claymore Cable pays almost all the expenses. Rent, condo fees, electricity, telephone, car, an annual airfare home.....since you're both in school, they paid for your trip here." She looked meaningfully at Sydney. "If you had joined us, they would have paid your school fees here, which are horrendous." Sydney shrugged and Julia glanced at her older daughter. "Jack keeps most of what he earns, so we're extremely lucky. And we're typical of the community, as you'll see when you visit some other homes."

"But this is huge."

"That's right. A great big house is supposed to be a perk. Some companies designate São Paulo a 'hardship post' and even pay for maids and guards and buy furniture and appliances for the employee."

"Wow!"

"Claymore, of course, doesn't go that far."

Walking over the concrete path to the house, they could see that waiters and waitresses were serving drinks and hor d'houvres to a crowd on the terrace. Sydney, silent until now, exclaimed, "Oh, how fancy." Her resentful, belligerent shell dissolved, revealing an awed and insecure adolescent.

Two toddlers, watched closely by a hovering, uniformed nursemaid, waddled from the house and rolled on the grass. On the veranda, an elegant, very dignified, white-haired woman was seated on a wicker chair, one hand resting on a silver-topped cane as she spoke to an attentive young man. The pair was joined by Marilyn's gray-haired husband, Dr. Mauricio Coelho. Spiffy in a white shirt, dark suit, bright flowered tie and monocle, he bent to kiss the woman's hand.

"There's your plastic surgeon, Gail," Julia said.

Her sister squinted critically. "Is he any good? I actually had Dr. P. in mind. He was written up in Newsweek not too long ago and sounded fabulous. *And* he's an author."

"Although he's the most famous, he's not the only one around."

"Well, this guy's way too old for a pony tail," commented Stephanie.

Sydney's smooth forehead creased in a frown. "But if this lunch is to introduce us to people our age, what's the story with all these babies and old folks?"

"In Brazil, parties are family affairs; if you have a birthday celebration for a three-year-old, the invitation includes entire families, not just little children," her mother explained patiently. "Everybody gets along and besides, a party's a great opportunity to talk, which is the Brazilian leisure activity of choice."

As they stepped onto the veranda, Laura emerged from the airy entry hall, her arms linked with her teenage children. Although severely strained for some time following the movie theater incident, the relationship between the two women was now at least cordial.

"What happened?" asked Laura. "I know it's Brazilian to be late or not show up at all, but you're always on time." Before Julia could answer, the hostess turned to Gail and the girls. "Welcome to São Paulo. These are my children, Molly and Richard. And I know who you are from photographs."

"Cool tuxedo," said Molly.

"Thanks."

I must be aging fast, thought Julia. Although she knew Molly was sixteen, in her tight jeans, tank top and doubly-pierced eyebrow, Laura's daughter looked older than Sydney. The three girls eyed one another briefly and then Molly smiled and beckoned them toward the house. "Let's go find some food." Trailed by fourteen-year-old Richard, they vanished into the house.

"Excuse their manners," said Laura. "They've been taught to kiss cheeks and say something appropriate like 'hello'".

Julia shrugged. "It's the age. Don't worry about it."

Laura beckoned to a maid and whispered a few directions then turned to Julia. "Before I forget, Jack phoned his apologies a couple of hours ago. Apparently, he has a conference or something?"

It was a question that left Julia floundering helplessly. Her husband was supposed to join them for lunch at about one-thirty and, if there was a radical change of plan, why hadn't he phoned *her*? The fact that he had contacted Laura and ignored Julia left her feeling embarrassed and humiliated.

"I don't know," she answered truthfully, aware that distress must be reflected on her face. "The girls will be disappointed."

Laura reached out and gave her hand a sympathetic squeeze. "Men are sometimes so thoughtless," she said softly, adding in a louder tone, "Look who's here."

Marilyn, Diva and Jesse MacEntire strolled out of the

house. Jesse clutched a nearly empty drink and had highly flushed cheeks; Julia prayed that she wouldn't jump in the pool today. After Gail was introduced, Diva asked Julia, "How's the new caseiro working out?"

"He's very cute," commented Gail.

Julia grimaced. "Ze's fine, Alda's a dud, and I don't want to ruin this glorious day by discussing her."

"Okay with me," Jessie said, waving her glass at a nearby waiter. "Did you hear what happened to Mauro's partner's wife?" She enunciated her words carefully.

"No," Julia answered, casting an apologetic look toward her sister.

"Kidnapped over in Itaím when she was waiting for their daughter to finish her ballet class."

Shocked, Gail asked, "Kidnapped? Is she all right?"

Jesse took a big gulp of her fresh drink and nodded hazily. "You bet. Right as rain, however right that's supposed to be, but those guys drove her to three bank branches and had her take out thousands of reais, then dumped her in Morumbí and took off in her car. With the money, of course."

"Oh please, she drives a new Mercades, which marks her as a rich target. And sitting in any car on a São Paulo street is just asking to be robbed."

"My cars are all armored," Diva volunteered.

"Is it really that dangerous here?" asked Gail anxiously.

"Of course not," her sister replied. "But you do have to be careful and vigilant. And not drive a big imported car."

"I do," said Diva.

Marilyn turned to Gail. "Julia says you've got a wedding business called *A Ring and Roses*, which is a fabulous name. What exactly do you do?"

"Put weddings together, basically. It started as one shop where I rented out bridal clothing but I kind of grew into a consultant and now I'm in two locations. I practiced on my own weddings, of which there have been many, so I think I'm probably an expert."

Startled, Laura's eyebrows shot up while Jesse, sensing gossip and scandal, leaned forward.

"Really? How many would that be?" she asked.

Gail gave her a radiant smile and waved her perfectly manicured hands which, Julia noticed in dismay, once more were studded with diamond rings. "I've lost count." It was actually three, Julia reflected in amusement.

Jesse tottered back toward the house, gulping the last of her drink along the way. Accompanied by her hulking, fifteen-year-old son Denver, Pearl edged through the growing group, unhappy that others had been able to greet the guest of honor first.

"What have you lost count of?" she demanded, pulling Gail forward and kissing her on both cheeks. "I'm Pearl DeMott, the one that's giving the dinner party for you next Thursday, and this is my darling Denver who longs to meet your girls." Pearl looked around the crowd, her sharp eyes missing nothing. "Where are they?"

"Inside, I....."

"Here's where you're hiding." A bulky figure shouldered into the group and, for just a moment, Julia saw the cluster of women through Gail's eyes. What a disastrous collection of misfits, she thought. Wishing this lunch were over, Julia said, "Celeste, this is my sister Gail."

"I know, I *know*. The guest of honor," she boomed.

Gail smiled graciously."I'm happy to meet you," she said politely, whisking her tumbling curls away from her face and stretching out her right hand which Celeste clasped firmly. Leaning forward, she planted two wet kisses on Gail's cheeks.

"Celeste, what is on your head?" asked Fay Macedo, standing on tip-toe to see over the wall of female shoulders.

"A mantilla, of course." In addition to the bit of lace draped over her hair, Celeste wore a long black skirt and black blouse topped by a black leather coat.

"Celeste is either an art history professor or a nun,"

Julia explained to her sister.

A burst of laughter erupted from Celeste, causing even the tumbling toddlers to sit up and look in her direction. "I'm still jousting with the Sisters, making sure I'll have health insurance, although I'm wondering if the Antiochian Orthodox Church wouldn't be more...*me*. Antoun refers to a town in Egypt where there was a vision of Mary back in the sixties, you know, and is much revered by the eastern Orthodox members." She patted her mantilla. "I'm in mourning for the painter Portinari."

"I thought it was Princess Di."

"I switched."

"Portinari died quite a while ago."

"Nineteen sixty-two... I'm also deeply prayerful for my family, which is just falling apart. My parents have separated, and since my father's retired, he's either at Mom's house drinking beer and watching T.V. or at his mistress's house. She's married too, or living with a man, so it's tricky."

"Certainly sounds like it," commented Laura, beckoning urgently to one of the waiters. Pearl and Denver detached themselves from the group and moved toward the house.

"And Mom's having lawyer trouble. The first one was fresh out of school so she got another one who had a nervous breakdown and disappeared, or at least is incommunicado, and now Mom needs several thousand dollars to get a third one. And my brother Bunky's in the pokey again. At least Mom has the company of a guinea pig."

"Have drinks," Laura urged, her brown hair flying with either electricity or desperation as the waiter arrived with a tray of caipirinhas. "Our local rot gut okay?" she asked Gail.

Celeste watched as the others helped themselves to squat glasses filled with sugar-cane *cachaça*, limes, sugar and crushed ice.

"You know I never drink alcohol. Only caffeine-free sodas or fresh juice," she announced.

Laura gestured to a nearby maid who nodded almost imperceptibly. "Let's sit down so lunch can be served," the hostess said in a strained voice, motioning to the round tables that had been set up inside the dining room, family room and second entry hall. Embroidered, white linen table cloths had been set with crystal and silver, and bowls of flowers graced the center of each table.

"How beautiful!" exclaimed Gail. Leaning toward Laura, she whispered, "I'll just go wash my hands."

"Inside the *sala*, first door to the right".

As her sister vanished into the house, Julia sensed the expansion of their group then felt the light pressure of Laura's fingers on her forearm.

"Julia, I don't think you've met the Calhouns," she said. "Shirley's a therapist and school counselor, so she almost never comes to Newcomers or the Bridge Club or any of our other time-consuming activities."

"I'd love to but I'm too busy," said Shirley, kissing Julia lightly on one cheek. "Laura forgot to tell you we also have three children at home."

A small woman in her mid-thirties, Shirley had dark brown hair flecked prematurely with gray, a nose that was slightly too long for her narrow face and a friendly smile revealing teeth that were somewhat out of alignment. She wore no make-up and her clothes—Birkenstocks, a short Levi jacket and long, muslin Indian-type dress—pre-dated *Annie Hall* by several years, but she nonetheless exuded a warmth that mesmerized everyone.

"How nice to finally meet you," exclaimed Julia who had heard enthusiastic stories about Shirley, her perfect children, her work with troubled families in the city's international schools and her success with private patients.

"And this is Max, her husband, who's the Congregational Church pastor and was able to sneak away from his flock today."

As they shook hands, Julia felt her heart give an unexpected little leap that both annoyed and surprised her. His hair line was so recessive that he first appeared to be completely bald or shaved; when he turned his head slightly, Julia saw a long but sparse ponytail of red-blond hair that matched his well-trimmed beard and mustache. Deep brown eyes were magnified by rimless glasses, and in one ear he wore a small gold earring. In jeans, a dark blue, long sleeved shirt under a black velvet vest, he certainly didn't strike Julia as one of God's messengers.

"A pleasure," Julia said. "I would never peg you as a minister."

"I can spread The Word anywhere, anytime, wearing anything." He grinned and tilted his head to one side. "I'm pleased to meet you, Julia. Why haven't we seen you at Troubadours South?"

"Because I don't sing, act or dance," she replied. Laura had repeatedly asked her to join the only English-speaking amateur drama group in São Paulo, assuring her that there were plenty of backstage jobs available.

"We desperately need a props person," he encouraged.

"What would I do?"

"See that everything that goes on the stage gets there at the right time and place. It's not hard, and the whole thing's fun."

"I'll think about it. What production are you working on?"

A rumble of laughter rose from all those within earshot.

"*Introduction* by Brayton Harris, but I think we're going to have to forget it."

"Why?"

"None of the schools will lend us their auditorium because the play takes place in a brothel *and* I play the part of one of the customers," Max explained.

"It's a pity school authorities are so narrow-minded, because it's a fantastic piece and quite short," said Diva from the edge of the group.

"Diva plays the Madam," Shirley explained.

Marilyn adjusted a silver bracelet and surreptitiously looked at her watch just as a maid, obviously flustered, beckoned frantically to Laura. Detaching herself from her guests, the hostess listened with growing concern as the servant spoke in a low voice. After replying tersely, she returned to the group and said, "I'm sorry, there'll be a slight delay. Gail seems to have somehow imprisoned herself in the bathroom and we have to send for a locksmith."

Julia felt her face flame as the others flicked quizzical glances in her direction. After a moment, she broke the uncomfortable silence. "But how is that possible? The powder room has a latch." Even Gail should be able to operate that, she thought.

"Apparently, she somehow passed the powder room and went down the corridor to Richard's bathroom where the lock has always tended to jam. For that reason, we never lock it and just haven't had it fixed. Fortunately, Richard needed to use the restroom, or we'd never have guessed where Gail was."

"How long until the locksmith arrives?"

Laura shrugged, her exasperation apparent.

"Who knows? Fifteen minutes, two hours..."

Julia felt perspiration gather along her temples. "Why don't we eat without her? There's no point in ruining your lunch; she can join us when she gets out of the bathroom."

Laura, and most of the guests, looked relieved.

"Sounds good; we can do our welcome toast later."

"The way most locksmiths here work, that'll be at cocktail hour," said Max, looking directly at Julia. Whether it was a spontaneous twitch, very subtle wink or her imagination she later couldn't say, but his left eyelid fluttered briefly before they all turned toward the dining tables. Once again, she felt a faint, unfamiliar palpitation and wondered if she might be coming down with something. The nagging feeling that Jack had deserted them in favor of a more interesting lunch had vanished; in fact, all thoughts of her husband had evaporated.

THIRTEEN—SÃO PAULO, BRAZIL

$\mathcal{A}$s Christina Ortiz's fingers flew over the keyboard in an impossible sequence of chords that surged toward the finale of Rachmaninoff's Concerto Number 4, Julia's eyes strayed to the ceiling of the Sala São Paulo. There, over four stories high, acoustic blocks to fine-tune the sound quality of performances had been installed, and now a few of the carefully selected squares were fractionally lower than the others for this performance. Scanning the heights of the concert hall she wondered, not for the first time, how anyone learned to adjust those blocks to enhance the musical instruments.

There was a brief moment of total silence following the final note and then, nearly in unison, the audience at the Sala São Paulo leapt to its feet, clapping, cheering and shouting, "Bravo!" Julia snuck a glance at her youngest daughter. While the pianist took bow after bow and then played an encore that elicited the same enthusiastic audience response, Sydney remained firmly in her seat. At last the applause died and, as the packed theater began to empty, Sydney rose to her feet.

"I wanted to see Grace Jones sing in her fishnet stockings and silver gloves and that dress that looks like red balloons," she sulked. No one bothered to comment but Julia felt a stab of exasperation. She wanted her visitors to see the best of São Paulo and, hopefully, be impressed by the things she had discovered, but Sydney seemed determined only to tolerate each event or activity. What had happened to the perfect little girl of just two years past?

"That was fantastic, Mom and Dad," Stephanie said with a wide grin. "Thanks."

"You two are so lucky," Gail said, adjusting the straps of her green-lace over orange-silk dress. "You can come here all the time, and this theatre is absolutely amazing."

"That's a fact," commented Stephanie.

Julia slipped her arm around her oldest daughter's waist and gave her a hug. "It used to be a train station. Usually when they modify buildings for another purpose they just wreck the original charm. But here," she half-turned, her arm arcing in a swooping gesture that encompassed the massive, three-story high pillars, their pristine whiteness emphasizing the sophisticated elegance of the blond wood and chestnut upholstery décor, "they've managed to convert it from a train station to a state-of-the-art concert hall without losing anything."

"Except the trains," mumbled Sydney.

"Not even the trains were sacrificed," countered Jack. Guiding his daughters into the lobby, he pointed to a glass wall that separated the Sala São Paulo from a railway platform at which a train idled. As they watched, another slowly glided toward them, stopped by the platform, and was immediately boarded by waiting passengers.

"And look over there," Jack said, as they pushed close to the wall. A train rushed past on tracks beside the concert hall. A moment later it was followed by another.

"Can you get to the platform from here?" asked

Sydney, staring in fascination at the trains. Grace Jones seemed to be forgotten.

"Nope," her father answered, tugging affectionately at a tuft of her short hair. "The station and concert hall are both totally separate."

"Nobody at school's going to believe that I sat at a concert in an old railroad station while trains went by on two sides and you couldn't hear them or feel them."

"Nobody'll believe you went to a concert," Stephanie said archly. Sydney glared at her sister.

"Ha-ha, very funny."

"One reason we came to a matinee was so you could see the trains," Julia said. "We weren't sure that they run late at night."

Looking up at her father, Sydney said, "I'm starving."

He grinned and kissed her on one temple. "Well, let's go. Most restaurants here don't open until eight, but I know a couple of really good ones that have earlier hours."

Gail looked at her watch which was, to Julia's dismay, the one encrusted with diamonds. "Seven-fifteen. It *is* a little early."

"That dress is too fancy," Sydney told her aunt critically.

"It's cool," commented Stephanie. "And you certainly have no room to talk about anyone's clothes." Raising her finely plucked eyebrows, her glance roved meaningfully over Sydney's white satin shorts and wide gold lamé belt over a flowered, sequined bathing suit. Wedge cork sandals with plastic flowers, an armful of pink plastic bracelets and a wide red hair bow completed her outfit.

"It's casual," said Sydney stiffly.

"That's not what I'd call it," commented Stephanie with a sniff.

Ending the squabble before it escalated, Julie herded them toward the stairs, confident that her own black trousers suit with the faint silver stripe was the most appropriate of all for a late afternoon matinee and dinner.

She studied Gail's dress; a little too much but it *was* stunning and the hem, mid-calf in front and dipping to the floor in back, was an eye-catcher.

Joining the mob at the top of the stairs, they slowly eased down the steps and then out into the covered parking lot. On their left, trains clattered past, their noise level almost matched by hundreds of parked cars roaring to life. Sydney plugged both ears with her index fingers; Jack and Julia exchanged amused glances. As they moved toward the far end of the area where their car was parked, Julia felt buoyed by an inner sense of peace and serenity, as though she were floating over the pavement. In spite of Sydney's current negative behavior and defiant attitude, they had somehow recaptured their family unity, the easy camaraderie, affection and understanding that had been blotted from their lives since the move to Brazil. Edging close to Jack, she threaded her fingers into his and gave him a squeeze of happiness.

Twenty minutes later they drew up in front of La Casserole, an old restaurant that specialized in French food and was located at the center of town. Directly across the street was a plaza with towering trees, shrubs, paths and benches and, facing the restaurant in the square, a row of flower stalls, open at night and brightly lit. Muted lighting inside the Casserole illuminated the long bar to the left and, directly in front of the windows, tables set with white linen, crystal and silver.

"Boy, this is really elegant," exclaimed Sydney.

"First class!"

With a pang, Julia remembered how captivating Jack could be and, since their arrival in São Paulo, how little he had used that charm at home. Catching her husband's eye, Julia fleetingly wondered if the management would admit Sydney despite her outrageous attire.

Stephanie frowned in consternation. "Is this place open? It doesn't look it."

"Barely," said Julia.

They were the first customers of the evening and were shown to a table by the window where Sydney spent a lot of time studying the flower stalls across the street while the others scrutinized the menu.

"Those shops don't seem to do much business," she commented, her chin resting on one fist.

"Enough to keep them going for the past decades," her father answered. "Aren't you interested in food? I thought you were starving."

"I think we should all have drinks," announced Gail. "It helps me to think."

"It has the opposite effect on most people," commented Jack. Gail curved her lips in a pained smile.

Caipirinhas arrived, they ordered dinner and the restaurant began to fill up. Stephanie leaned toward her father.

"You know, I wish you could have come with us to Florianopolis," she said.

His white teeth flashed in a smile. "And so do I, but I had to work and earn money so you could spend it."

"I work and I also take time to enjoy myself," commented Gail, smiling seductively at the waiter.

Jack's easy, relaxed attitude vanished. Julia saw his facial muscles tighten, his eyes narrow almost imperceptibly and his shoulder muscles flex. Her stomach soured with tension. She glanced quickly around the table, hoping she was the only person aware of her husband's shift in mood.

"I think that's great," Jack said coldly, "and if I only had to support *myself* I might be able to flit around the world too."

Silence hung over the table and then Sydney spoke: "Hey Dad, what's wrong with you? Loosen up. Get a life."

Stephanie just stared at her father; Gail lit a cigarette and blew two smoke rings at the maitre'd. Suddenly aware that she had been holding her breath, Julia exhaled as Jack's infectious smile returned.

"Sorry, everyone, I just have a lot of pressures at the

office right now." He stroked Sydney's hand, his eyes moving from one daughter to the other. "So tell me what was so wonderful about Florianopolis."

"The beach," enthused Sydney. "It was long and curved and had these fields of tiny clams that were uncovered when waves washed the sand off and then they quickly burrowed down completely out of sight. And there were almost no people around."

"A little different from Venice Beach," he commented with a chuckle.

Still staring at her father, Stephanie said, "It was all perfect. The sun, the hotel on the beach with our balcony in front, the water..." She shrugged. "Pity we only had three days."

"They had this weird fruit at breakfast, all rumpled up and wizened and absolutely ugly," Sydney told her father. "Guess what it's called?"

Jack grinned. "That's got to be a *maracujá*, which is wildly popular in Brazil as a natural tranquilizer. They call it passion fruit in the States."

Sydney made a face. "Passion? I tried one and it was *so sour.*"

"That's because you wouldn't add any sugar, which I told you to do," said her mother.

Sydney shrugged. "And one morning we followed this bizarre black and green iguana with huge scales and nasty toe-nails up the path from the beach. He was at least this long." Her stretched arms indicated two feet.

But Jack was no longer listening. A noisy group of perhaps a dozen people had tumbled into the restaurant and had managed, in the space of a few seconds, to capture the attention of everyone on the premises. Gesturing dramatically to the others and ignoring the Head Waiter, a middle-aged man threaded around the tables and led the way into a private dining room. Conversing in self-consciously loud tones, his beautifully dressed and perfectly coiffed entourage drifted through the dining room and disappeared into the inner sanctum which began to reverberate with raised voices and bursts of laughter. As the last guest vanished inside, a burly guard in a dark suit, white shirt and dark glasses stationed himself beside the open door to the private chamber.

"Do you know who that is?" asked Jack, clearly dumbfounded.

Involuntarily, the others turned to look at the guard.

"Who is he?" asked Sydney excitedly.

"I'm not talking about that guy at the door. I mean the leader of the pack, the one that strutted in first."

"Is he married?" asked Gail.

As though unveiling a secret, Jack leaned forward and looked intently at the others. "That's Jovair Salgado."

Julia's lips curved into a broad smile. "Are you sure?"

"Absolutely. That crook, that filthy scum-bag." Jack was visibly disgusted.

Baffled, Stephanie asked, "But who *is* he?"

"He's now the President of the Senate, and he was our mayor a few years ago. Before we arrived here, actually. He's stolen so much public money and invested it in other countries for safe-keeping that he's now wanted in those countries for fraud, extortion, money laundering, theft and God knows what else."

"So why isn't he in jail?"

Both Jack and Julia laughed at Sydney's naiveté. "Because in Brazil, elected public servants never go to jail," Julia explained, shaking out her napkin and spreading it on her lap. "They either bribe the investigators and judges or have done so many 'favors' for them in the past that no one dares to convict anyone else."

"After this guy was arrested in France and interrogated by the police for a full day about accounts he had there, he came back, ran for Senate again and was elected with the highest number of votes any candidate has ever received."

Laughter spilled from the smaller dining room.

"And he's at it again," continued Jack angrily. "He owns

a lot of phantom companies that are paid with public funds; his relatives are all on the payroll and make exorbitant salaries and when anyone disagrees with what he's doing or questions the ethics and legality, he buys them a house. With public money!"

"Is this true?" breathed Sydney, her eyes wide. "How do you know all this?"

"The media," her father answered. "It's the only reason we know anything."

"When we came here and heard about this fraud or that bribe I thought they were just little glitches in the system, but now I think that corruption is so endemic that the system's broken," said Julia. "That's one of the major headaches your father has to deal with."

Gail laced her fingers primly together and shook her head as though to rid her blond tresses of nasty particles. "Even if Mr. Salgado were in the market for a wedding, I wouldn't dirty my fingers and my reputation."

"He's definitely not a potential client," chuckled Jack, exasperation gone as he opened the wine list. "Salgado's been married for years and has a mistress that's been headlined for her own misdeeds lately."

"And everybody knows about it?" asked Stephanie, aghast.

"We're not talking about quality," Julia said.

The Head Waiter moved toward the private room, briefly conversed with the guard and shut the door, muffling the noise. Once again, the restaurant was calm, elegant and tranquil. Julia looked contentedly at her family and then gazed through the window at the illuminated banks of flowers on the other side of the street. Of course Jack was stressed; he was working incredibly long days, often weekends as well, and his workplace was steeped in the dishonesty he had been sent to eliminate. It was possible that she had magnified her husband's mood shifts all out of proportion, perceiving them as threatening the stability of their marriage when it was clear, both that their family unity was still intact, and that Jack's job was ruining his normally easy-going disposition. As the others discussed wine preferences, Julia studied her husband, her eyes pooled with love. He was a good man, she thought, and they had gone through too many wonderful years to let a temporary position in a foreign country damage any part of their relationship. She would have to be more understanding and less affected by his frequent absences.

Jack's cell phone rang. Annoyed, he extracted it, glanced down at the number, and his expression changed very subtly, becoming both softer and more wary. It might have been the way he rounded protectively over the phone or maybe it was the shifting of his expression once again, but suddenly Julia was certain that this wasn't a business call. Her mouth felt dry. Was she the only one that had noticed the abrupt shift?

Jack shot a swift glance around the table and met Sydney's glare. "I don't believe this," she complained. "Can't you even eat dinner without talking on the phone?"

His smile was strained as he simultaneously clicked on the cell with one hand and reached out with the other to smooth Sydney's hair. "I'll get rid of him," Jack reassured his youngest daughter. Julia latched onto the masculine pronoun with fierce hope, as she pointedly studied the flower stalls through the window.

"Jack here." Julia noted that his voice was gruff and almost stern; her spirits rose and she snuck a glance across the table. "I'm sorry, I'm dining with my family and it will have to wait. We can talk tomorrow."

As he disconnected, both girls sighed noisily, signifying their disapproval. "Maybe you forgot but tomorrow is Sunday, Dad," Stephanie said. "Even God rests on the seventh day."

"He doesn't have my office problems. Anyway, I've rested today instead of tomorrow and I don't plan to ruin my dinner arguing about it." Arching her back and tilting her head to one side, Gail bestowed a brilliant smile on a hovering waiter and said, "*Mais uma caipirinha, por favor.*"

Good humor restored, Jack grinned. "I see you've learned a little Portuguese."

"Just the bare necessities," she responded modestly, adjusting a small diamond earring. Absently, Julia noticed that the nail polish on her sister's perfectly manicured hands exactly matched the orange of her dress and lipstick. With a touch of incredulity, she heard her husband's jolly tone as he attempted to rise above the unwelcome phone call.

"Does everyone want another caipirinha, or should we concentrate on the wine list?"

Aware that Stephanie was surreptitiously studying both her parents, Julia pushed any troubling thoughts into the background and smiled. "Let's skip the caipirinhas and think food."

Arriving home later that night they were met at the front door by Zé, who claimed an urgent need to speak to his employer.

"Can't it wait until morning, Zé? I'm tired and want to go to bed," Jack protested irritably in Portuguese. Sydney, Stephanie and Gail drifted into the house while Julia hovered beside her husband on the front steps, wondering why Brazilian domestic help always picked the least opportune time to bring up problems or important issues. If she were late for an appointment, on the way to the airport, or frantically preparing for ten guests who would arrive in five minutes, she could count on being waylaid for a discussion about salary, vacation, or which trees should be pruned next.

"Yes, that's a good idea, Senhor," agreed Zé pleasantly, "but I have a problem. I agreed to pay Djalma one thousand reais to recommend me for this job and I've already paid him half that amount but need to borrow the rest. From you, please. Djalma said he'll pick up the cash tomorrow."

Julia and Jack tried to digest this amazing news. Smoothing the skin under his eyes with both index fingers, Jack gazed at Zé and finally spoke.

"You paid him for the recommendation," he stated.

"Yes, Senhor," Zé beamed cheerfully.

"And if you hadn't paid him, he wouldn't have suggested you as his replacement."

"No, Senhor."

"I see." There was a long pause during which Julia struggled to maintain a serious demeanor and suppress the laughter that rose in her throat. No one in Venice Beach, including Mary Beth would believe this. Actually, Gail and the girls would find it hard to swallow. "All right, have Djalma come and see me and I'll negotiate with him."

The gardener's smile vanished. "Djalma doesn't want to talk to you, Senhor."

"I don't imagine that he does, but you can tell him that I will pay him directly or not at all." He turned to Julia. "I'm beat. Let's go to bed."

Arms around one another, they strolled into the house and down the corridor to their bedroom where, quivering with laughter, Julia sank onto the chaise-lounge. Stripping off his tie and unfastening his cuff-links, Jack grinned and shook his head. "Is that a shake-down or what?" he asked.

Wiping tears from her cheeks, Julia reflected that right now, this minute, they felt very close.

FOURTEEN—BERTIOGA

"*M*om, this is fabulous," Stephanie exclaimed as Julia drove down the dirt road and turned into a large vacant area that was serving as an impromptu week-end parking lot for countless cars. "That has got to be the biggest circus tent ever."

"Those banners look a little tacky," Sydney commented.

"No," advised Cristaldo Macedo from the back seat, "those are the names of the stores sponsoring the Festival. Advertising, you know?" Cristaldo, Mauro and Fay Macedo's eighteen-year-old son had attached himself to Sydney at Laura's lunch party and had been her adoring acolyte ever since. Julia's hopes that the Notre Dame sophomore might depose Sydney's married sculptor were shattered when her daughter announced, "Cris is just a summer replacement."

"There are hundreds of people here," Gail breathed eagerly, pulling out a compact and scrutinizing her face in the mirror. Unlike her sister, but in common with most

Brazilians, she had always loved crowds, adored talking to strangers and had been happiest sharing too little space with too many people. Julia turned off the engine and set the emergency brake.

"Sure looks like it."

"Thanks for driving, Mom," said Stephanie. "I don't know how you find the courage to get on the road with these people. Once they get behind the wheel they are completely insane." She looked at Cris. "Excuse me, but it's true."

"Don't pay any attention to her," Sydney stage-whispered in Cris' ear.

"Not only courageous but you can find your way around São Paulo, which is impossible with all those winding streets that change their names every block," added Gail.

Julia's self-esteem floated upward. She had tackled and conquered yet another obstacle, the traffic, without resorting to a driver.

"Thank you, fans," she said, opening the door and getting out.

After hearing that the Twenty-seventh Annual Tainha Festival would be held over the weekend in Bertioga, a small seaside village two hours from São Paulo, Julia had decided that this would be a perfect day trip. Enthusiastically, she urged the others to seize this wonderful opportunity and, along the way, see the 'mata atlantica'. The latter, she explained, was the tangled forest that had once covered the Brazilian seaboard but was rapidly disappearing to make way for ever-expanding cities. Her exuberance had not been shared by her houseguests.

"A *fish* festival? Get away," commented Sydney lounging on the sofa with one foot hanging over the arm. "I just want to relax with Cris and hang out at the beach."

"He can come along, and this is *on* the beach."

"Why can't we just go to a fish restaurant?" asked Gail as she plucked her eyebrows.

"Because it's not the same thing," Julia replied, her temper rising. "I think you're very lucky that a typical Brazilian event is so close to São Paulo while you're visiting."

"Does that mean we're going?" asked Stephanie, studying the pages of *Vogue*.

"That's just what it means."

Her younger daughter's short-lived sulks and pouts had only stiffened Julia's resolve, and during the drive to the coast the silence was thick, prompting her to pray briefly but intensely for a happy and successful day. Apparently, the Almighty had granted her request; all four passengers tumbled willingly from the car, enthralled by the sight of an enormous tent under which dozens upon dozens of plastic tables and chairs had been arranged. Most of the seats were filled with people hunched over foot-long, curved ceramic containers heaped with food. On a makeshift platform at the far end of the tent a trio played and sang Brazilian country music into a microphone that was over-amplifying the hillbilly tunes. Several of the diners had risen and were dancing a polka around the tables while others sang along with the performers.

"What's with the weird music?" Gail asked. "I thought it was all Bosa nova and samba and that kind of stuff."

Cristaldo smiled indulgently. "Usually, but this is June and we hear a lot of this music from northern Brazil during the month."

"Why?" asked Gail.

"I guess it's because we have these carnival type events called Festa Junina all during the month and everybody dresses up like hillbillies and dances the polka and has games and food. You can tell this fish fry's not a Festa Junina because it's got only the music and food."

"Thank God," commented Julia, wondering what ensemble Sydney would have concocted for a country bumpkin theme. She watched her youngest daughter lurching ahead on high heeled chartreuse polka dot wedgies, the fingers of one hand intertwined with those of Cristaldo. Wearing a tiny mini skirt and gauzy, off-the-shoulder print midriff, ruffled at the top, Sydney had accessorized by adding at least a dozen huge bead necklaces and matching bracelets. A paisley silk scarf had been wrapped around her head and tied at the top in a bow and large hoop earrings swung from her lobes.

"It looks like she's moved on to Carmen Miranda," commented Gail in a low voice.

"I can't wait for the Grace Kelly mode," responded Julia.

"Don't hold your breath."

A long, open-air shed with a counter in front and a thatched roof supported by poles was situated on the far side of the tent. A trench filled with smoldering charcoal over which dozens of fish were being barbequed ran the length of the shelter and was shaded by the palm frond roof. Cooks in white aprons waved tongs and enthusiastically danced the polka in independent solos, ignoring both the fish and the very long line of customers that waited in front of the counter and extended a good distance beyond. No one seemed to mind the delay and nearly all were chatting amicably with their neighbors.

"They all seem very friendly," commented Gail, delicately brushing invisible flecks of dirt from her stunning, white sun dress, bought two days ago at Daslu. Shocked at the outrageous price her sister had willingly paid for the garment, Julia explained that a skillful Brazilian dressmaker could duplicate any creation at very little cost.

"But it won't have the label," Gail protested. "Daslu is famous."

"I assume you know that the owner and her brother have been accused of fraud and tax evasion," Julia informed her with some heat.

"I did hear that. Poor things," Gail said.

"That's *theft*."

"You yourself told me everyone steals down here.

Remember that Salgado guy the other night? Anyway, in spite of the fraud and tax evasion, you could use a new wardrobe with *zing*."

Her sister was right but Julia was exasperated by Gail's blunt statement.

"*I* shop at used clothing stores and the Salvation Army," said Sydney.

"We know."

Remembering Gail's comment about friendly Brazilians, Julia glanced at the queue of convivial would-be customers.

"Brazilians adore talking to anyone, any time, any place."

"I love it! It's so me," said Gail enthusiastically. If I could only speak the language..."

Thank you God for that merciful blessing, Julia thought.

Cristaldo and Sydney, followed by Stephanie, were already threading their way between tables. Julia had been surprised and pleased when her older daughter had caught on right away that ironed jeans and tee shirts were the São Paulo city uniform; now she was correctly dressed for the beach in a halter top and bikini bottom, the latter covered by a large gauzy shawl called a kanga tied around her waist. With her coloring and frizzy hair, she could, and did, pass for a Brazilian.

Julia waved the girls and Cristaldo toward the food line which now moved along nicely since the musicians were on a break and the cooks had temporarily given up dancing. She and Gail joined the crowd in front of a makeshift ticket booth.

"I called Mauricio Coelho, Marilyn's husband, about my face lift," said Gail.

Face lift?

"I was going to make an appointment for the surgery but he said I have to be here much longer and I certainly can't get on a plane right afterward."

For a moment Julia held her breath, waiting for the announcement that her sister would stay in Brazil for several more weeks.

"So I asked about an eye lift and a neck job, because I *am* getting a chicken neck, and it was the same thing. I think maybe a little liposuction is the answer."

Julia was torn between amusement and disbelief.

"Liposuction? *Where*, may I ask?"

"I guess either at his office or in the hospital. It just popped into my mind a few minutes ago so I haven't really gone into it with Dr. Coelho."

"I meant what part of your body? You don't need that, you know."

Tickets in hand, the women slowly moved toward the food line.

"Maybe not now," she retorted, "but I will in a few years, so I may as well get a jump start on it. And this *is* the only country for plastic surgery." She paused thoughtfully. "Maybe I'll just spend the money on gemstones and a few more clothes instead. Those are very Brazilian."

Julia felt slightly out of focus and wondered if it was the pitiless, mid-day sun or her sister's idea of a major dilemma. In addition to being a very successful, hardheaded business woman, Gail also served as the Director of Volunteers for the Venice Public Library, facts that had baffled Julia for years. Maybe, she thought, this was a classic example of a split personality.

"Mom, Mom, give us the tickets."

Jolted, Julia looked up and saw the three adolescents approaching the food counter. With apologies to those behind them in line, Gail and Julia stepped behind the trio just as Sydney was handed a whole fish, about a foot and a half long, on an inverted roof tile approximately the same size. The teenager looked at her mother in confusion.

"What's with this creepy plate?"

"It's not a plate, it's a roof tile. Like the ones on our house in São Paulo."

"Is it a used one?" She bent over the roofing material and carefully examined it for signs of dirt or damage.

"I shouldn't imagine so. Move on down the line, please."

Mechanically, Sydney accepted a plate loaded with rice, 'farofa', bread, and some sauce along with a bottle of red wine, plastic eating utensils and a tiny paper napkin.

"Do we share this?"

The group started toward the tent, searching for an empty table. "You can see we all have the same thing, including a bottle of wine each."

"But it's way too much. I can hardly carry it. Was this very expensive?"

"Very cheap. Quick, there's a table."

As they unloaded their lunch, a teen-aged girl appeared with a wine opener and five mugs. *XXIII Festa da Tainha* along with a large Lions Club logo appeared on both her apron and the drinking cups.

"Guess who's the main sponsor?" said Cristaldo.

"*Brinde*", the girl announced with a smile, putting the mugs down and deftly opening one of the bottles of wine.

"What did she say?" asked Gail

"The mugs are presents," responded Cristaldo, as Julia signaled the girl to open only two of the bottles.

"Let's dig in," prompted Stephanie, following her own advice and starting on the fish. "This is delicious, but it's got mammoth bones."

"And a lot of them," added Julia, pouring the wine.

"You were right, this is great fun. Too bad Dad had to work," said Stephanie, taking a bite of bread.

"Yeah," agreed Sydney.

"*I* work on weekends, too," stated Gail defensively.

"Because that's when your customers get married."

Silently, Julia cut into her fish. The work problem again... Because of the tangled ownership, Jack had made little headway in curbing company corruption, which put him and his ethics in a very uncomfortable position. Like many other ex-pat executives, Jack left early and came home late but, unlike the others, he also worked nearly every weekend. More and more frequently, Julia found herself pleading—perhaps nagging—that constant work meant less, not more, productivity while he claimed that a huge backlog of work could only be handled in the peace and calm of a weekend. Julia often wondered if she needed an attitude adjustment with the help of one of the several psychotherapists in São Paulo that dealt with culture shock and ex-pat marital difficulties. Jack didn't seem to understand that she felt alone and isolated, but then again, maybe the fault was hers; she could no longer tell.

Stephanie's voice broke into her thoughts. "Dad does have a beautiful office, though."

"And a beautiful secretary," added Sydney.

"Oh, please."

"Well, she is."

Julia didn't miss the exchange of glances, or the silence that followed, and her face reddened, as though secrets were being whispered behind her back.

"What's this grainy stuff, Mom?"

"Farofa. Coarsely ground and toasted mandioca. I think it is called manioc in English, but I'm not sure since we never had it in California. Brazilians eat it with everything." Julia heaped farofa onto her fish and rice. "*Saúde!*" She lifted her mug, followed by the others, and took a sip.

"Oh, my God," gasped Gail, swallowing with an effort and gazing at the mug with startled eyes. "I've been poisoned."

The other four appeared to be strangling.

"This is breathtakingly bad shit," proclaimed Stephanie.

When she could speak, Julia looked at the wine label and said, "It's made locally, like bathtub gin, and maybe also used for insect control. We should have gotten beer."

Cristaldo quickly rose and collected the three unopened bottles.

"I'll go exchange these for beer."

"And while you're gone I'll eat some of your food," said Sydney. "And Auntie Gail's and Mom's as well. We have way too much and I'm saving my lunch to give to the poor."

Gail looked over the throng. "I don't see any poor here."

"That's not amusing," Sydney said crossly. "I'm thinking of those horrible favelas."

"You mean you want to ride back to town carrying that fish in the roofing tile and spilling rice all over my car just to give it to someone in a favela?"

"Yes, I do. What's wrong with that?"

Suddenly, Julia remembered handing out pineapple to favela dwellers not so long ago. "Not a thing."

Cristaldo appeared with the beer, and a few seconds later the musical trio returned from their break and thundered out an ersatz Patsy Cline tune making conversation impossible. Idly, Julia wondered how anyone could dance to country western.

Later, they made their way slowly out of the tent and across the sandy ground toward the car. Sydney carried her tile with the fish and a bag of bread that she had obtained from a mysterious source while Cristaldo balanced two tiles of rice.

"If she wants to be Lady Bountiful, you should make her carry it herself," Stephanie said to Cristaldo in a firm voice.

"He's being a gentleman," Sydney snapped.

"Do you think they have any really good shops around here?" asked Gail.

"No."

"What kind of store?" asked Cristaldo.

"Any kind. My sister likes to buy things." Julia thought of the purchases, ranging from geodes to paper mâché lamps to lace tablecloths and designer clothes that Gail had already accrued on this trip.

"I have a list of gifts to buy and I haven't even started."

"Mom, look at that," exclaimed Stephanie.

They stopped and stared at the nearby highway which had been completely blocked by an enormous crowd led by a band and a coffin. On the front of the coffin was a huge photograph of a playful goat, and as the throng drew nearer they saw many people in tears.

"What is going on?" asked Sydney.

"It must be Frederico`s funeral, although I didn't know it was today," said Cristaldo.

"Frederico?"

"The goat. It was in all of the São Paulo papers. The town got so sick of politicians and their corruption and lies that a group of citizens put Frederico up as a candidate for mayor. The polls showed him winning almost unanimously in the election, which is next week, so two days ago someone poisoned him."

"Oh, that is *sad*," said Sydney. "I'm so glad I'm a vegetarian."

"I believe I need a drink," Gail commented. "If we can't find any shops, would a little *barzinho* do?"

FIFTEEN—SÃO PAULO, BRAZIL

"I wish you could stay longer and go back with the girls," Julia said, wondering just how sad she really was to be driving her sister to the airport. She loved Gail, no doubt about that, but her sibling was unpredictable and exhaustingly energetic. Since the arrival of her family, there had been non-stop lunches, dinners, trips to the theater and museums; she was drained by this frenetic compression of fun-filled activity into a two week time frame although she knew that she would be despondent the minute they were gone, their absence leaving an empty hole in her orderly life.

"Believe me, so do I," answered Gail. "I'm missing out on my Brazilian liposuction just because that overly-indulged Adriana Talbot is having pre-wedding hysterics. Of course, she's egged on by her nouveau-riche mother."

She stared glumly through the car window at a favela on the margin of the highway where children of all ages flew kites scant feet from speeding cars. "Is that a prison?" asked Stephanie from the back seat.

Julia's eyes darted briefly toward a gray concrete building just behind the favela. "It is. There are several around here."

"In a crowded urban area? That must make the residents feel secure and comfortable," commented Sydney.

"I doubt it," said Julia, "since they constantly have prison rebellions and break-outs. Prisons here are so overcrowded that they pack the criminals into outdoor patios where they sleep and wander around, doing nothing except receive visitors en masse. And some of them that have committed really monstrous crimes like kidnapping and murder can opt for an open prison where you leave in the day and go back to sleep at night."

"You're joking."

"I'm not. The idea is for them to go to work, but a lot of them use the daytime to assault and kill people or deal drugs."

"Look at those empty watch-towers," murmured Stephanie as they passed another prison. "Not a guard in sight."

"Prisons run on the honor system," offered Sydney. Her sister pursed her lips in disgust and rolled her eyes. They swung around a curve and the offending gray building dropped from view.

"Occasionally one thinks so," said Julie absently, glancing at her youngest daughter in the rear view mirror. Her present concerns were of an entirely different nature. "Are you sure you want to go to college at Santa Cruz instead of Northwestern with your sister? It's not too late to change your mind."

"Please, Mom, it's freezing in Chicago, and besides, Santa Cruz is me, all cool and laid back."

"Hah!" sputtered Stephanie. "You know you'd have to work your butt off at Northwestern and that's not about to happen at U.C. Santa Cruz."

Julia pondered, not for the first time, the fact that in

less than a year her daughters had switched roles. Who would have dreamed that studious, conservative, beautifully mannered Sydney would be transformed into a rebellious, unorthodox hippy while Stephanie metamorphosed into a serious, mature creature? Except for her hair which, for the last two days, had become a metallic auburn that didn't suit her skin at all.

"You just want me to go there because Northwestern is close to Notre Dame where Cris goes and you hope I'll give Lawrence the heave-ho and take up with Cris. Which is not going to happen..."

"Cristaldo is a very nice boy," commented Julia.

"Yes, he's a *boy*. Lawrence is a *man*."

Julia and Gail exchanged sidelong glances. Stephanie said, "That stud carries a lot of baggage."

"You're just jealous." Sydney noisily lit a cigarette.

Stephanie laughed.

"Please, do not smoke in this car," Julia ordered. Sydney rolled down the window, flung the cigarette out and then slumped back in the seat, arms folded tightly across her chest.

"Cristaldo is polite, seems intelligent and is one of the best looking males around," said Gail, critically studying her long, coral-tipped nails. "You couldn't want much more."

"Why not?" The tone was belligerent.

"It is amazing that he's so handsome when his parents are really pretty homely," observed Stephanie.

Julia turned down an embankment, crossed the intersection and pulled up at the entrance of the airport parking lot. "And the family goes to daily Mass."

"Daily Mass?" mused Sydney. "I hope Cris isn't religious."

Julia knew better than to ask if this meant Cristaldo was again in the picture but her spirits did a cautiously joyous leap. Goodbye, Lawrence, she thought hopefully.

Sliding into a parking space, Julia pulled the handbrake.

Rather than jumping out, Gail rummaged in her enormous handbag and fished out a foot-long, dark brown, dried seed pod she had collected at Bertioga. She waved it slowly through the air.

"This comes from such a beautiful tree that I just must plant it in my garden, but U.S. Customs is so weird that I know they'll never let it through."

"That's probably right," Julia agreed as her daughters got out and moved to the trunk of the car where they began unloading suitcases and bags.

"Well, what I want are the seeds," Gail explained, getting out of the car and placing the pod on the ground, "so that's what I'll take."

Heavy silver earrings swinging wildly, she jumped on the pod several times, failing to demolish the tough casing, while passersby stared curiously.

"You're going to ruin that dress," cautioned Stephanie, glancing at the sleeveless, flowered silk gown with a plunging neckline, dropped waist and long, pleated skirt. Gail claimed it had cost the earth; it was clearly not a garment designed for exercise.

"Why didn't you think of this at home where we have a hammer?" asked Julia, joining her sister. Futilely, they bounced up and down, Gail's high heels and Julia's sandals proving equally ineffectual. Lips pursed, Sydney took a tire iron from the trunk of the car.

"I can't believe you two," she said. "Stand back".

"Don't crush the seeds," admonished Gail.

Two whacks, witnessed by several passing travelers, sufficed to open the pod. Gail quickly picked out the seeds and dropped them in her bag.

"Thank you, Sydney. That was quick thinking."

"What if Customs asks what they are?"

"I'll say I'm making a bracelet for my dissertation."

Stephanie tried to stifle a grin. "A doctorate in seed jewelry?"

"Why not? Oh, my God, I can't manage all this." Gail

was trying to carry three paper bags from as many museums as well as her cosmetic case in one hand and two plastic sacks in the other. Her right shoulder, weighted with a monstrous shoulder bag, was several inches lower than the left.

"Put the stuff on the cart for now, Auntie Gail."

"What have you got in there?"

"I have a paper lamp in the shape of a bird and a geode and some cards from the MAM gallery. I can't remember it all. Lots..."

"I told you to bring a carry-on or to buy one here. You always do this," Julia said crossly as her sister deposited the assortment on top of her suitcases in the wire cart. Dropping behind the other three, Julia wondered whether these months of separation had enabled her to see her family more realistically or whether they had changed in her absence. Gail had always been a little hair-brained but not quite this loopy. Or maybe she herself was a different person; certainly that calm, well-ordered, secure life she had led in Venice seemed out of a different world.

Gail checked in, they drank caipirinhas, said tearful goodbyes and, loaded with bags and sacks, Gail struggled through the doorway into Immigration Inspection. The line was long, threading back and forth across the room between wooden rails, and it was nearly twenty minutes before Gail reached the head of the line. Suddenly, as Julia and her daughters watched from the outside area, a handle on one of the paper museum bags tore and the bag ripped; as Gail bent to catch an assortment of objects, a second bag began to tear. Clutching the geode and paper lamp to her chest, Gail deposited the other sacks and bags on the floor and moved them along with her feet until she disappeared from sight. Stephanie, Sydney and Julia stared at one another.

"Can't we help her?"

"No, of course not. You're only allowed in with a valid ticket."

"But what will she do?" Sydney sounded like a small, worried child.

"I'm not sure, but I know what she *can* do. There's a Duty Free Shop just beyond Immigration designed to catch any shoppers with spare time and money. She can shuffle her bags in there and buy a carry-on. After all, shopping is one of her favorite pastimes."

"Let's make a bet," said Stephanie with a wicked smile that showed the deep dimple in one cheek. "I think she's going to toss her blond curls, make sure her legs are on display, look really, really helpless and get some guy to carry the stuff for her."

"Forget the legs in that long dress," said Julia, "unless she wants to go in for some gymnastics. Anyway, there's nothing we can do about it, so let's head for home."

A subdued trio, each one worrying silently about Gail's predicament, had reached the parking lot when Julia's cell phone rang.

"Guess what?" It was Gail's voice. "I'm so sorry but I forgot to give Jack's phone back. You know, the one I borrowed in case of emergency."

Julia momentarily closed her eyes. Fortunately, her sister had Jack's back-up. "Did you get through Immigration okay?"

"Barely. I had to stuff all the things from the broken bags into those thin plastic sacks and my shoulder bag and guess what?"

"What?"

"I just now peeked into the bag and the creams and oils I put inside have spilled all over everything including the cards from the museum. And the paper lamp has a few holes poked in it."

Julia closed her eyes. "Why didn't you buy a carry-on at Duty Free?"

"It's just one more thing to lug around. I have to go through the x-ray machine now. I'll send the phone back somehow, and I love you."

Julia clicked off and unlocked the car. "She says she's going through the ex-ray machine. Do you think she really means that literally?"

"She might try. Can we stop by Dad's office? We've hardly seen him since we've been here."

"Good idea." As she started the car, Julia reflected that she hadn't seen much of him either, not for quite some time.

SIXTEEN—SÃO PAULO, BRAZIL

Several months later, a uniformed, armed guard opened a pair of massive bronze and iron gates and Laura swung her car up an incline to the parking area on one side of the house. Beside her in the passenger seat, Julia observed the circular driveway fronting the massive stone dwelling.

"You mean to tell me Fay and Mauro live *here* but they can't pay their help?" she asked.

Laura switched off the engine and fished on the back floor for her handbag. "Of course they can pay, they just don't want to. They have plenty of money, but they're dead cheap."

"Which makes it even worse..."

"Eventually they pay the salaries so that the servants won't quit and take them to court, but the amounts are always very, very low and always in arrears."

"I thought you said they lived beyond their means." Julia spoke carefully. Although their friendship had survived the cinema episode, gradually assuming a superficial closeness, Julia was reluctant to return to the

156

unquestioning intimacy that they had once shared. There was, she realized, too much about Laura that she didn't know or understand; in Venice, with work, family and other close friends, the relationship would have died long ago.

Laura shrugged. "They might. Since they take from everybody and give nothing, it really doesn't matter."

"But Cristaldo is such a nice young man."

"And so is his older sister, Maria Luiza. It's one of those miracles that can't be explained in scientific terms, and also a big reason why the ex-pat community puts up with the parents."

Both women got out of the car and walked down a stone path toward the wrought iron and stained glass doors that now stood open, each flanked by a uniformed maid. As they started up the half dozen polished granite steps that swept in a half moon before the doors, Laura spoke.

"Are your daughters coming to visit again soon?"

"Not until another school holiday."

After a pause, Laura said, "Did you know that Fernanda Pimentel was robbed last Saturday?"

Julia stopped and stared at her friend. "But they live here in the Chacara, where it's supposed to be totally safe."

Laura smiled wryly and nodded toward the guard, now stationed with his back against the gate. "Nothing in São Paulo is totally safe. Remember, you were robbed before you even moved in."

"Is Fernanda all right?"

"Fine, fortunately. She and Ricardo had taken their four-year-old to one of those massive Brazilian birthday parties, and when they came back a few hours later they found the house a shambles. The thieves took a ton of stuff, including the computers."

Julia paused, trying to digest this bit of news that was an unpleasant reminder of their robbery. "And the maid didn't hear anything?"

"She doesn't work on weekends, but the police think it's an inside job. Otherwise, how would they know the house would be empty for four hours on a Saturday afternoon?"

"Did they catch whoever did it?"

Laura shrugged. "Of course not; they never do. Fernanda fired the maid and guard and said she and her family were lucky to be out of the house at the time."

Julia shivered involuntarily, unwilling to even imagine a confrontation with thieves. Changing the subject, she asked, "Why do you think Fay's giving this afternoon bash?"

"She does it every year. It's her one attempt at entertaining, presumably to pay back all the people she's been poaching on for the last twelve months."

Julia hadn't previously been invited.

Nodding to the maids, they stepped into the foyer which was large, round and crowded with antique stands and tables that were covered with collections of small objects. Silver pill boxes, Fabergé eggs, miniature porcelain tea sets and dinner services, tiny blown glass wine goblets and decanters, baskets that would hold two marbles at most and books the size of pendants were squeezed together on polished wood or marble surfaces. Oriental rugs obscured the floor, a crystal chandelier hung from the high, domed ceiling and dark, gloomy paintings featuring Madonnas, angels and monsters fought with round ceramic frescos for wall space.

Julia's steps slowed and, with an effort, she stifled a smile.

"I wish my mother could see this," she whispered.

"Your mother has passed away, right?"

"Yes, a few years ago." Her smile faded. Her mother had died of a burst appendix while on a cruise in Greece with her new husband, himself recently divorced from one of her Junior League chums. The marriage had taken place almost immediately following the death of Julia's father, causing both Gail and Julia to wonder whether their mother hadn't been having affairs as well. It had been a murky scandal on top of the ongoing ones generated by their father's extra-marital dallying and a lesson to both daughters; nothing good came of infidelity.

Moving forward, they stepped into an enormous round room. Directly in front of them a profusion of plants, flowers and moss were entwined on a central rock garden, partially obscuring a stream that trickled over the stones. Large marble columns rose two stories from the inlaid wood floor to support a vaulted roof with a circular opening at the top. Shaking off the film of gloom induced by past memories, Julia stared upward for a moment, and then turned to her companion.

"That round bit of the roof is open."

"They were inspired by the Pantheon, I understand."

"What happens when it rains?"

"They press a switch and a piece of bullet-proof glass slides over it."

"I see."

A shriek of welcome rose from one end of the room and Fay tottered toward them on high, strappy sandals. Her arms were spread wide, echoing those of Christ in the life-size marble crucifix just to the right of Julia, allowing the sleeves of her tiger-printed silk dress to flutter in the breeze. Around the room women, seated in conversational groupings of sofas and overstuffed chairs, chattered in high decibel tones that seemed trapped, rather than dispersed, in the vast living room. Fay's driver, now doubling as a barman/valet and serving drinks, picked his way around the clutter of tables and magazine racks while two maids offered trays of savory snacks.

"How wonderful that you could come, Julia," Fay gushed enthusiastically, kissing her noisily on both cheeks.

"Thank you for inviting me," responded Julia. She glanced quickly at her surroundings, taking in the religious paintings depicting gruesome atrocities and the sculptures of every size and material that had been deposited on the floor and tables. "You have a very unusual home."

"We like to pick up things around the world."

"Yes, I can see that."

"Gossip says you just got back from a quick trip to California."

"Very quick," replied Julia. "I visited *Angel and Friends* and my old television station and checked up on the house, but I went basically to settle the girls into college, especially Sydney who's just entering her freshman year."

"At some state school, I understand." Her tone held the slightest trace of contempt, and Julia bristled.

"Actually, no. It's the University of California at Santa Cruz."

"Ah, I remember now. That hippy place." She linked her arms with theirs and steered them toward one end of the room. "I hear they have lots of drugs and orgies."

Withdrawing her arm, Julia silently fumed. "It has an excellent reputation or we wouldn't have sent her there." Actually, Julia was worried enough without hearing Fay's nasty comment. Gail had caught Sydney smoking marijuana one Saturday afternoon, so who knew what might go on at a university with no supervision?

"Did you girls bring your White Elephants?"

I've got one next to me, Julia was tempted to say, saved only by the memory of her mother's disapproving face. As a child many years ago, Julia had attended a friend's birthday party and, for reasons long forgotten, had called the hostess an old fool. Julia was pulled from the celebration, Mother's grip on her arm like steel with a voice to match. "Young lady, do not ever, *ever* again insult, embarrass or humiliate your hostess, no matter how obtuse she might seem."

"Yes, we brought the elephants," Laura said. "They're small, so I've put them in my handbag."

"Why don't you sit down and have something to drink and I'll try to round up the others for our game." Releasing their arms, she half-turned and, in Portuguese, bellowed at the driver, "Fraga, bring these ladies some Prosecco. Quickly!"

As Fay clattered away, the women looked at one another.

"What game?" asked Julia.

"She always has one. That's why she asked everyone to bring a white elephant."

"I thought she was collecting them for her church rummage sale."

Laura laughed. "Of course not. She only does things for herself."

Julia raised one eyebrow and glanced critically at her surroundings. "Well, I can see why she doesn't have any spare cash for the servants."

Plucking two glasses of wine from the tray offered by Fraga, they moved toward the nearest cluster of sofas and chairs in response to a wave from Marilyn. The psychotherapist was sitting beside a woman who looked quite familiar even though her head was bowed, her hands clasped lightly in her lap.

"How was the trip, Julia?" Marilyn asked. Without waiting for an answer, she glanced at her companion and said, "You remember Kathleen Lamb, don't you?"

Laura and Julia stared as the woman raised her head and smiled weakly. The Kathleen Lamb that had disappeared in Seattle with her Internet lover many months ago had been a lively, beautiful, energetic and witty creature, a unique combination of delicate fragility and determination. Now all the sparkle was gone along with her physical charm; Kathleen looked tired and beaten. Julia was the first to recover.

"How great to have you back..." She paused, wondering what other tactful, bland comments she might make. "Are you here to stay?"

There was a sudden silence that grew as tears gathered in Kathleen's eyes and rolled down her cheeks. Deeply embarrassed over her inadvertent faux-pas, Julia felt a flush creep from her neck to her face. Marilyn slid one of her hands over Kathleen's. With her other hand, she rummaged in her handbag for a tissue, then handed it to Kathleen.

"I'm so sorry if I said something wrong," Julia murmured.

Kathleen shook her head, wiping her face.

"It's not your fault; and yes, I'm going to stay in Brazil, although Randolf won't have me back and he won't let me see Heather. He says I'm contaminated, and I am..."

"That's absolutely untrue," exclaimed Marilyn as Laura and Julia eased into two nearby overstuffed chairs.

"You just don't know the whole story."

Fraga served more Prosecco and then withdrew.

"Maybe we should join the others," suggested Julia. "Cheer you up a bit."

"Nothing's ever going to cheer me up," claimed Kathleen. "I was such a fool to give up everything thinking Willard and I would marry and blend our families and our lives." Willard, thought Julia? That name alone should have been her first clue. "Even though we'd only dated on the Internet, I fell in love with him the minute I saw him." She stopped to blow her nose and then continued, "I did have serious misgivings about his sexual practices and fidelity since I knew he'd been unfaithful to his wife, and he was disloyal to me as well. And he insisted on having unprotected sex!"

"What do you mean, *disloyal?*" asked Laura.

"He had a...relationship with another woman. Maybe more than one..."

"While he was having one with you?"

"Yes."

"You caught him *en flagrant*, so to speak?" Laura's voice was tinged with anticipation.

"Not exactly... They were getting dressed when I came home early one day. They said they'd been playing tennis and just came back to shower, but I didn't see any tennis clothes or racquets. And he'd never mentioned tennis before."

In the strained silence, Julia searched surreptitiously for an escape, deciding there was none

Laura spoke: "Was this after he was divorced?"

"He's still married, because it's almost impossible to get a divorce in Washington State."

"That is not true," stated Marilyn calmly. "My sister lives in Edmonds and she's been divorced twice."

Julia stared at Kathleen who was slumped to one side of the sofa. "You don't have to go into all this," murmured Julia.

"No, I want to. You have to understand that I'm not the same person I was a year ago. Anyway, to make a long story short, I asked him to marry me, and he not only refused, but that's when he left me."

Julia studied the pattern of the Oriental rug at her feet, at a loss for words. In the uncomfortable hush, they could clearly hear Fay's voice urging the other guests to unite in one area.

Finally, Julia spoke: "I don't understand his motive in all this."

Marilyn answered briskly, "Obviously, Willard's a very weak man. He needs the security of marriage, must have the approval and support of his children and has to have continuous new conquests to boost his ego. It's always a pattern."

"I feel so used and betrayed," Kathleen mumbled.

"I think you need to get into therapy right away," said Marilyn.

"I know. I'll make an appointment with you tomorrow."

"Not me. I don't take on friends as clients, but I can refer you to someone else."

"No, I don't want to see a stranger, Marilyn." Panicked, she clutched possessively at the psychotherapist's hands.

Before Marilyn could respond, the brisk click of heels announced the arrival of their hostess, who chirped cheerfully, "Sorry girls, but the others refuse to move, so you'll have to join them over by the library."

Abruptly, Kathleen jumped to her feet and rushed out of the room.

Fay seemed shocked. *I can just imagine this story circulating with a whole lot of embellishments*, Julia thought, standing up and brushing vaguely at her silk dress.

"Whatever's the matter with Kathy?" enquired the hostess in a low, conspiratorial tone. She looks exactly like a reptile licking her chops with forked tongue, Julia thought.

"Nothing really," answered Marilyn, standing and striding toward the library. "She has a touch of grippe, which I sincerely hope she hasn't passed on to us."

Good for you, Julia mentally applauded.

Disappointed, Fay caught up with the psychiatrist.

"Are you sure?"

"I'm sure I don't want the grippe, if that's what you mean." She turned and beckoned to Julia and Laura. "Here are some spare chairs, ladies. Let's sit."

"What a witch," whispered Laura. "I don't know why I come here."

"Yes, you do," answered Julia. "As you told me, the community is small and we can't afford to offend anyone. And also it helps beat back feelings of loneliness, isolation and boredom."

The other two stared at her, and then Marilyn nodded.

"That's true. The old 'fish out of water' syndrome," she said.

Laura spoke slowly and thoughtfully. "A lot of my ex-pat friends have been here for twenty or twenty-five years and none of them feel like natives, no matter how fluently they speak Portuguese or how many Brazilian functions they attend. We're outsiders, at least to a certain extent, and always will be. Even those that are naturalized

Brazilians."

Standing in the center of the large circle of women, Fay clapped her hands for attention.

"First, I want all of you to put your white elephants over on that wall table, and then take a number from the bowl Valerie is holding." Laura rose and deposited two small gift-wrapped items on the designated table, then returned to sit down beside Julia.

Valerie, one of Fay's faithful acolytes with no discernable personality of her own other than perpetual grumpiness, passed a glass fishbowl with bits of folded paper. As their hostess' tubby disciple gave the bowl an impatient shake, Julia began to hum "Let A Smile Be Your Umbrella".

"Now, girls, let me explain the game," Fay barked, clapping her hands for attention.

"Oh, God," whispered Laura. "What did I do to deserve this? I could be at home practicing self-flagellation."

"The person who draws number one will choose a gift and unwrap it for all to see. Number two can either choose a wrapped gift or, if she covets the one that her predecessor has picked, she can take that one. Number three can select a wrapped gift or instead take the ones that either number one or two have chosen. And so on. At the end, if number one has no elephant, she can pick one from all those acquired by the others, and that's the end of the game. I think you'll find this is very exciting and a lot of fun. Are there any questions?"

"I wish I were fertilizing the tomatoes at Lar Christina Angelica," Julia whispered.

"Yes, Julia?" asked Fay brightly. "You had a question?"

"Not really."

"Good. Then let's get started. Who has number one?"

Wordlessly, Valerie stood up, shambled to the table and made a great show of poking and shaking each package while Fay giggled and snorted.

"No fair, Valerie," she admonished as her guests began to chatter in low tones.

Valerie dramatically picked a beautifully wrapped, oblong package, tore off the wrapping and triumphantly held up a box on which was printed, *Electric Oyster Shell Opener*. Fay screamed with laughter and appreciative chortles ran through the room while Laura, Marilyn and Julia exchanged resigned glances.

"I'm sure everyone will try to get that from you, Val," Fay tittered, "since every home needs one. Who's number two?"

Julia was number five and found herself with a bottle of sweet, white vermouth, which she disliked, and Laura, number ten, drew a pair of beautifully hand embroidered guest towels.

"I see they're not all white elephants, thank God," she said, just as number eleven whipped them from her hands. Minutes later, Julia felt her muscles freeze and her breath stop as Jessie Macintire unwrapped an inlaid picture frame, its intricate design achieved through the use of many woods of varying colors and patterns. Swaying, Jessie clutched her wine glass with one hand and held the frame aloft with the other. Before the wave of admiring comments had faded, Marilyn claimed the picture frame and, moments later, it was swept away by Diva.

"What on earth is the matter?" Laura asked in concern. "Don't you feel well?"

Inhaling deeply, Julia blinked and then turned toward her friend with what she hoped was an easy smile. "I'm fine. It's just that picture frame..." Her voice faded.

"Oh, right. Maricarmen brought that. I was over at her house when she was wrapping it and I told her then that I thought it was absolutely gorgeous and obviously very expensive. I still have no idea why she thinks it ranks as a white elephant."

That is a good question, Julia thought, her body numb. Not only was it expensive, but she had bought it as a birthday gift for Jack and given it to him with a photo of herself and the girls, a photograph that had now been replaced with a magazine portrait of a model or movie actress. The last time Julia glimpsed the frame it was on her husband's desk in his office, but clearly it had somehow, sometime found another home. Unless, she thought with a leap of hope, the artist had created two or more identical pieces, a not improbable assumption. When the game ended, Pearl was the owner of the prized picture frame. Fay noisily began to herd the crowd toward the dining room for a buffet lunch.

"I'll just be a minute," Julia whispered to Laura and Marilyn before standing and edging her way toward Diva.

"Excuse me," she ventured, interrupting a conversation between Pearl and Diva, "but I wonder if I could take a closer look at your picture frame."

"Just a quick peek. I was lucky to come away with one of the two outstanding pieces amidst all this crap." Handing Julia the picture frame, Pearl sniffed, tossing her head in dismissal of the other elephants.

"We *were* told to bring rubbish," protested Diva.

"No, we were not. White elephants are often quite nice items that just aren't needed in one's home," countered Pearl as Julia examined the frame, then slipped the model's picture out and stared at the backing. "I myself brought that lovely crystal bowl that Jessie's taking home, which is the other treasure of the day. Of course," she whispered, "Jess hasn't the cultural background to appreciate it."

Julia heard the harsh voice through a fog as she hastily slid the commercial photo back in place, covering the hand marbleized paper backing she'd asked the artist to use. At the time, Jack had admired her originality, or at least that was the impression he gave, and now that paper served as absolute identification of a rejected present. Clutching the frame, Julia turned to Pearl.

"I wonder if I can buy this from you."

"What?" Pearl was genuinely taken aback. "You want to

buy this?"

"Unless you'd like to give it to me," Julia said in what she hoped was a jocular tone. "Or you can trade me for my bottle of vermouth."

A mask seemed to slip over Pearl's face.

"Darling, I couldn't possibly give you the frame," Pearl protested. "Maricarmen would be crushed to think I just tossed her gift away. And I'm allergic to vermouth." Pearl held out her hand for the frame. "Why do you want it?"

Because it belongs to my husband, ran through Julia's mind as her mouth opened and another story sprang out. "Stephanie's been longing for a momento of Brazil, something unusual that can't be found in the States, and this inlaid piece would be perfect. I'd love to send it to her with a photo of Jack and myself at the beach in Guarujá." Such lies, such a brilliant smile frozen on her face while her body was on fire, her stomach boiling with anger, pain and humiliation. With this talent she should have been in front of the cameras rather than the TV station's Public Relations Director.

"You could ask Maricarmen where she got it," suggested Diva helpfully as the last of the ladies straggled past and crowded into the dining room.

Julia shook her head. "This looks like a one-off piece to me. I'd really love to have this frame if you could bring yourself to part with it." This was followed by her most persuasive smile, her head tilted to one side. "Whatever price you'd like. Within reason, of course."

Diva and Pearl stared pensively at one another while Fay's shrill voice again summoned them to lunch from the dining room. With a sad and sorrowful face, Pearl turned to Julia.

"All right, for Stephanie I'll do it. One hundred fifty *reais*, and at that I'm giving it away."

Pain vanished and Julia's anger doubled. The frame cost eighty-five *reais*, and as a champion consumer Pearl probably had a pretty good idea of the actual price. Julia's facial muscles were paralyzed in a grin while her body was wet with sweat.

"I'll write you a check after lunch," she promised. "And thanks."

Hugging the frame to her chest she hurried to the dining room where the other game players were helping themselves to an enormous, if somewhat odd, buffet. Without interest she glanced at the squash risotto, tomato and mozzarella tart, fish stew, sun-dried beef, mashed potatoes, white rice, black beans, fried yucca and Provençal shrimp and edged her way toward Maricarmen.

"Excuse me," she said, nudging into the line beside her quarry, aware of the grumbles of those who thought she was jumping the food line. Maricarmen turned with a smile of recognition, and then glanced at the frame.

"Hello, Julia. I thought you might join the Bridge Club."

"Bridge is just not for me, Maricarmen." Julia extended the frame and both women examined it. "I fell in love with this as a perfect gift for Stephanie and persuaded Pearl to part with it. Where on earth did you get it?"

Maricarmen moved down the table, helping herself to rice and fish stew, then stepped out of line. "It was really quite lucky. I was at our country home one weekend and asked everyone what I should take to a strange American daytime party 'for women only' that featured unwelcome or bizarre gifts and my niece, Eliana, came up with this."

For a moment, Julia's mind refused to function.

"Eliana?" she echoed.

"Your husband's secretary. She said it was a present that she found unattractive." Maricarmen drew back, her face flushing pink with embarrassment. One dance Brazilians know as well or better than the samba is the avoidance of a confrontation, and Maricarmen quickly took the first graceful step to repair her faux pas. "That's because it really doesn't fit into Eliana's sophisticated, modern apartment. You know, all glass and steel. Of course, I myself think it's a lovely frame. Very unusual. "

"And a perfect present," responded Julia, immediately remembering that the frame had been Eliana's unwanted gift and the comment was therefore tactless. "Although not for everyone," she amended, dancing rapidly with a spate of words. "Stephanie loves handmade Brazilian pieces of art and has just the place for this." Although well aware that Brazilians were generally disdainful of their country's hand-made products no matter how beautiful, she also knew that they loved hearing that these items are internationally much admired and coveted. Both women relaxed.

"I'm sure she will enjoy it," said Maricarmen. "But aren't you going to eat?"

Nauseous, the frame cold in her clenched fingers, food was about the last thing Julia wanted. Smiling easily, she dipped her head in assent.

"I'll just get in line," she said.

The front door closed softly. Standing in the center of her living room, Julia held the frame, facing out, against her chest. The model's photo had been removed and the marbleized lining shimmered in the early evening dusk. Jack's footsteps moved down the entry hall then rounded the corner where he stopped abruptly in front of his wife. There was no sound at all as he stared at the frame, expressions of shock and guilt sweeping over the rugged, handsome features that she had known intimately for so many years but now blurred into those of a stranger. For a fraction of a second, Julia was triumphant, knowing that her suspicions were correct, but almost immediately she was engulfed by a wave of misery, regret and finally deep loneliness. She wanted her old life back, wanted her family close and together again, with laughter and arguments, anger and happiness, but for reasons she didn't begin to understand, that was all gone. Tears clogged her throat; the man she had trusted and loved had lied to her repeatedly, deceived her in the most basic way and turned their marriage into a sham.

Recovering, Jack smiled, the deep dimples not quite concealed by his beard, the perfectly even teeth.

"Where did you find that?" he asked, stepping forward. "We turned the office inside out looking for it and finally decided the night cleaner must have helped herself to it. I'm so glad that..."

Without a word, Julia hurled the frame at her husband and then turned and fled from the room.

SEVENTEEN—SÃO PAULO, BRAZIL

*T*he telephone rang, startling Julia who was having difficulty deciding on a suitable outfit to wear to a lunch meeting of the Troubadours South which, this time, was meeting at Laura's house. Finally succumbing to her friends' entreaties to join the drama group, she was about to put in her first appearance and didn't want to look too conventional, but what did actors and stage hands actually wear? With one hand hovering over the telephone, she leaned toward the mirror, staring critically at her reflection. The well-pressed jeans and gaucho shirt were probably okay, also the tennis shoes, but the face. Where had those crow's feet come from? Her thick hair was still brownish auburn with only a few sprinkles of silver, her tanned and freckled cheeks and forehead smooth, all ruined by those tiny lines around the eyes. No wonder Jack had lost interest.

Hit by a sudden wave of sadness, she clamped one fist around the receiver as though throttling her husband. They had battled savagely over the picture frame, with Jack shouting his innocence and accusing Julia of paranoia and insanity, while she sobbed in misery and beat her fists on the furniture, aware that the only evidence of infidelity other than her own suspicion was the appearance of the frame. Since then they had abided by a wary truce, each covertly observing the other while maintaining a polite and cool distance, each waiting for the other to apologize. Julia wanted to go home.

Lifting the receiver from the cradle, she frowned at her image.

"Hello." She hoped Mary Beth was at the other end of the line.

Jack's smooth baritone, now oddly overlaid with a touch of excitement, came over the line. "Julia, I thought I should tell you the news before you hear it over the local grapevine."

"News?" Now what, she wondered warily.

"About our posting here..."

Julia's heart gave a little leap of joy followed by a stab of caution. They had five months left in Brazil but maybe Jack was being sent elsewhere immediately. Like London... Or home... "What is it?"

"Believe it or not, Home Office thinks I'm doing a terrific job and they want me—us—to stay for a two-year extension."

Julia's mind was blank, her breathing shallow while she stared sightlessly at her reflection in the mirror. Her mouth was dry and when she tried to swallow, her tongue clung to the roof of her mouth.

"Are you there, Julia?"

Jack's voice cut through her numbness and she became aware of a crushing melancholy that seemed to envelope her mind and body.

"Yes, of course." Her tone was even and noncommittal. "But it's such a stressful job and you always say you aren't really getting anywhere. Couldn't you tell them that it's affecting your health?"

"Julia, companies don't want to know that their president is a delicate flower." His voice held a hint of truculence. "Anyway, I'm beginning to make headway and this will give me a chance to really do the job right."

Julia took a deep breath, puffed out her cheeks and then slowly let the air escape from pursed lips.

"I have a lunch appointment in ten minutes," he continued. "I just wanted to let you know."

"Thanks. And congratulations."

As she slowly replaced the receiver, Julia wondered why she was so disappointed. After all, aside from the language, she really did like Brazil enormously, had carved out a life here that would never again be duplicated, and enjoyed the company of some good, if not close, friends. And she knew that Jack had to accept any promotion or posting or even demotion that Claymore thought was fitting if he wanted to continue his employment with the company. So was she just being selfish and self-centered? Perhaps because he wasn't as affectionate and attentive as he was in the past? In the back of her mind, she knew that going somewhere else wasn't going to fix *that* problem.

The phone rang again. Julia jumped and then stared at the instrument as it rang four more times. More good news? Reluctantly, she lifted the receiver.

"Hello."

"Julia? What's wrong? You sound terrible."

Hearing Gail's voice, she made a conscious effort to modify her tone which she knew was tense and nervous. "I'm sorry. I was just on my way out."

"The papers up here are full of that creepy Fernando guy in Belem and I was worried about you."

Sadness vanished and Julia smiled into the phone. "It's the media gone mad again. Belem's about three thousand kilometers away, and Fernando's dead."

"But we're hearing stories about the police. How they shoot innocent people in those shanty towns, and now it seems they're involved with this."

Five months earlier, a criminal, Fernando, and his gang kidnapped the twenty-year-old daughter of a television personality and collected a huge ransom before releasing the young woman. A short time later, three police officers located Fernando in an upper middle class apartment in a district far from their own territory. During the ensuing confrontation, Fernando shot two of the lawmen and wounded a third, then ran back to the house where he had kidnapped the woman, and this time took her father hostage. The state governor negotiated surrender with guaranteed safety for Fernando and his cohorts; instead, they were all sent to prison in Belem where, last weekend, Fernando was poisoned and had died.

"There's always been a question about how and why the three police officers confronted Fernando since it wasn't their area and they didn't phone for backup."

"The papers said they were trying to extort money from Fernando".

"Probably, but no one will ever really know for sure. Don't worry about it. This is Brazil."

"Don't you have internal police investigations down there?" Gail asked.

Julia chuckled. "I sincerely doubt it. The justice system's so slow that everything drags on and on, and there are about a thousand appeals that take years, by which time everything's forgotten. Meanwhile, the guys involved usually move or die or some judge decides they're not guilty because there isn't enough proof. It's a rotten, corrupt system."

"When I was there, you told me the prisons are stuffed."

"They are, but only with the poor and Black. A couple of years ago a girl of nineteen or twenty, along with her boyfriend and his brother, killed her super-rich parents for their money. After two years the three were out free because the courts hadn't gotten around to having a trial."

"How can you live there?"

Julia's smile faded. "You get used to it."

The minute the words left her lips she realized what she had said. Had she really become so calloused, so inured to violence and injustice that she no longer noticed? What happened to the indignation she felt a year ago when Jack told her that one of his colleagues had finally had a court case settled after eighteen years, and added that this was not unusual? Critically, she scanned the mirror searching for clues that might indicate a loss of compassion, a hardening of her soul, while thinking about two more years.

"What's up with your caseiro?"

"Don't ask. Alda's still too sick to work and we still can't fire them because of the penalties, and we keep avoiding the subject." And most others, she added mentally.

"Your life is better than any soap opera," Gail said. "So prepare yourself for some hot news. Sydney's given the sculptor the old heave-ho."

Julia was engulfed by a rush of joy. "I'm so relieved," Julia cried. "This really makes my day."

"Wait, I haven't told you the rest of it."

Wariness replaced elation. "What?"

"The sculptor's replacement is a welder that rides a motorcycle, dresses only in tee shirts and jeans that aren't very clean and wears a hard hat the way some people wear hair. He also has a lot of tattoos. Sydney says he wants to marry her."

"Marry?" Julia echoed. Couldn't anything in her life go right?

"On the positive side, he's single, no children that he's yet revealed, and is only twenty-seven."

"Twenty-seven?" Julia repeated hollowly. "That's eight years older than Sydney."

"I wouldn't worry one bit," Gail advised. "I'm sure this is just a phase. Remember, I'm in the wedding business, and I can tell instantly who's about to take the plunge and who's playing a game."

"How do you know all this? Sydney's hundreds of miles away at college."

"She came home for the holiday and brought him with her. I think there was a little bit of marijuana going on after hours, but not much more."

"She's not living with him, is she?" Julia clutched the phone with one hand and massaged her forehead with the other. She should go back to California, restore some kind of order to the family, but now both girls were in college and independent and, if she left, who knew what Jack would do?

"She lives in the dorm, you know that."

"But what happened to Cristaldo, so patiently waiting? I thought Sydney was in the Carmen Miranda stage and we all know Carmen would never have a welder for a boyfriend."

"I can tell you're upset. For upset try this. Marcia Sidebottom—she pronounces it Siddybowtem, accent on the tem—can't understand why her wedding next May can't be in the Sistine Chapel, never mind the fact that neither she nor her groom is Catholic and that she's been divorced twice already. I told her it wouldn't work, but she said 'Money talks'. Well, it didn't speak very loudly to the Vatican. When they turned down her proposition, she had a temper tantrum, actually stamped her foot, threw a few things, yelled and screamed. Not at the priest but at me. Talk about shooting the messenger. What a bitch! As a consolation prize she's trying for the Getty, but she's not happy. I'm not happy..."

"...And I'm not happy," Julia interrupted.

"This welder business will all blow over, but to make us both feel better, I'm coming to visit you. It'll just be a short trip, maybe only a weekend, so we can go hiking. Get some exercise and fresh air."

Julia felt that she might be strangling. "I see. Hiking... I'll have to do some research on places to climb. Places that have fresh air..." Although Gail was very athletic, spending at least an hour and a half each day working out in the gym, playing tennis or jogging, Julia's only forms of exercise were swimming and walking. And she really didn't want to expand her repertoire.

"I've got to get back to Marcia," Gail said. "She's quite a large girl but wants a strapless velvet gown that's a mini skirt, a feather boa to toss over one shoulder and a sequin crown. All in blinding white, after two divorces. I ask you..."

"When are you coming down?"

"Soon. Bye."

Where have I gone wrong, Julia wondered, replacing the receiver and glancing in the mirror with disinterest. Gail's going to pop in here any minute and want me to exercise all weekend, I'll probably live here for the rest of my life and never learn to speak Portuguese, Sydney plans to marry a welder and have fourteen children before she's thirty, and who knows what's up with Stephanie? Snatching up her handbag, she left the house, slamming the door behind her and running to the garage. As she backed hurriedly out, her eyes focused on a motorcycle parked in the far corner and she abruptly stopped the car.

A strange motorcycle on the property? Had the welder and Sydney driven down for a visit? Opening the door, she stepped out and bellowed for Zé who was pruning the dwarf Ipé. As he approached, she pointed to the motorcycle and called, "What is that doing in the garage, and who does it belong to?"

"It's mine. I bought it a few months ago," he responded with a broad grin. "It's usually covered up, but I'm going to wash it today."

At least her daughter and the boyfriend wouldn't pop out of the bushes.

"Does Senhor Jack know you have it?"

Still smiling, he shrugged.

That meant no. "Do you ride it?"

"I don't have enough money for a registration, but I will soon. Anyway, I don't know how to ride a bike."

"You can't ride it and can't afford to register it," she repeated slowly, glaring at her grinning caseiro and aware that an essential piece of this equation was missing. Glancing at her watch and jumping back into the car, she decided it didn't matter if she understood or not, just as long as the motorcycle remained stationary in the garage.

"Sorry I'm late, Laura, but Gail called just as I was about to leave." Julia noticed that Laura, like probably nine-tenths of the city, was wearing jeans and a tee shirt and she immediately felt more comfortable.

"This is supposed to be a planning session, although all we've done so far is talk about everything but the play."

"Should I have brought something?" Julia asked in consternation. She'd been so nervous over her first appearance at the drama group that she'd forgotten to ask.

"Like what?"

"Well, I don't know," she mumbled lamely. "Maybe a shitake tart or my roast pepper and goat cheese timbales?" She felt like a fool.

"It doesn't matter," Laura answered, holding the gate open for Julia then leading the way across the lawn. "We've got way too much food, although yours is always a gourmet treat."

Hearing shouts of laughter and splashes of water, Julia glanced at the pool and stopped, suddenly self-conscious and reluctant to continue. "I thought you said this was a small group."

"I guess you misunderstood," Laura countered, beckoning Julia forward without turning. "It's a big *amateur* organization where everybody has a great time."

Watching Laura's receding back, Julia felt trapped. Her heart fluttered and her hands were slick with perspiration as she slowly followed Laura to the veranda where the latter was clapping her hands for silence. In the sudden hush, Laura stepped to Julia's side, encircled her friend's waist with one arm and raised her voice.

"This is Julia Elliott, one of my close friends, whom a lot of you already know. Her past life included work as a television executive, she's a semi-professional chef and she's going to join us, even though she claims to know nothing about the theater. Julia is very nervous, also very hopeful that you won't perceive her as an imbecile with no talent or ability."

A rumble of laughter and a wave of applause and cheers followed Laura's announcement. Julia struggled vainly to think of a clever protest or greeting.

Before anything was forthcoming, Laura shouted over the din, "Those of you in the pool will kindly get out, so we can eat and get down to business."

At the magic mention of food, the pool was instantly abandoned by the few bathers that had been bobbing and splashing about in the water. Female swimmers hastily wrapped themselves in kangas and the men donned polo shirts, both genders kicking into Havianas while shuffling forward toward a buffet set up on the veranda. In the modified scramble, Julia was pushed toward a long, curved table that held several kinds of salads, risotto, spaghetti marinara, palmito torte, barbequed chicken, rice, beans, and farofa. Picking up a plate, Julia stared at the food. "Good grief," she commented to no one in particular, "I was expecting a sandwich."

"Laura always does this. Or rather, her maid does it and Laura takes the credit, probably because she pays the grocery bill."

The voice was familiar. Reaching for the salad tongs, Julia half-turned toward the speaker and was startled to find herself looking into the deep brown eyes of Max Calhoun, the Congregational minister. Again, she experienced a tiny flutter of excitement as they stared at one another through his thick spectacles and she inhaled his lemon-scented after-shave. As her arm brushed against his bare forearm she felt her flesh tingle, and the hairs rise but at that moment there was an impatient surge in the line; Max stumbled and stepped on her toe.

"Oh, I'm so sorry. Could I kiss your foot and make it well?"

Blushing furiously, Julia turned her attention to the salad. "Thanks, that won't be necessary. You just keep on saving souls and I'll tend to my toes." She took a spoonful of rice. "Do you give a sermon or read a psalm at rehearsals?"

"I don't even say Grace."

"Then shame on you. This food is amazing. No wonder the Troubadours is a popular group."

"Word has it that your culinary creations are much more spectacular."

"Yoo-hoo, Julia."

Julia and Max exchanged wry glances at the familiar voice. Julia swiveled to look over one shoulder, her lips curved in a wan smile.

"Hi, Celeste."

"Guess what my brother Bucky did last week."

Turning back to the food, Julia moved along the table, selecting a piece of chicken and sprinkling it with farofa. Behind her, Celeste's voice blared out the news.

"Bucky and his wife Elva got into a huge argument because he took her car and wouldn't tell her where he'd gone so she trashed their lovely apartment in Cicero. She slashed the sofa, cut the legs off all Bucky's pants and the sleeves from his shirts and then ripped the phone off the hook and broke all the dishes and began hitting and tearing at Bucky. My brother called 911 and then escaped to Weezie's Pizza Parlor so the cops wouldn't find him."

"Pretty classy," observed Marilyn who had suddenly elbowed her way into the line.

"I'd think he'd welcome the police," commented Max mildly, taking a slice of palmito pie.

"No way," brayed Celeste. "He was stoned *and* drunk

and on parole so that wouldn't do. My Mom had to get him from Weezie's, and then he found out that Elva had filed grand theft auto."

Her plate full, Julia stepped away from the buffet table.

"That's not even the worst of it," Celeste continued without pause. "Elva went to Bucky's boss, who fired him, and it's hard for an ex-con to find work." The woman's round face, unadorned by make-up, reflected worry. Julia was struck by a wave of pity for this hefty woman who wanted so badly to be liked, to be a part of any group, and yet seemed destined to forever shoot herself in the foot.

Turning to face Celeste, Julia spoke softly, her freckled face sympathetic. "Well, I'm sure he'll find something to do."

Celeste laughed a series of hollow barks. "You can bet on that," she said. "And it won't be legal, either. Bucky's headed back to the pokey for sure. Poor Mom, but then it's really her fault for being soft on him."

Max, his plate heaped, rejoined them. "Aren't you eating, Celeste?" he asked.

"Just a few grains of rice. There is absolutely nothing else I can bear. I'm only here to see if there might be a religious part in the play that I can audition for."

"I don't think there is," Max said regretfully, "but you might want to participate in some other way. Wardrobe, or makeup, or prompter?"

"We'll see. It would have to be very interesting."

"If you'll excuse us, we'd better eat so we can get on with the meeting. Marilyn and Pearl are right over there," Julia said helpfully. "Kathleen too, I think."

"Thanks," Celeste said gratefully. "I'll join them."

As Julia herself turned toward Marilyn's group, Max lightly grasped her forearm and steered her to a small table with two chairs. "Oh, boy," Max breathed, "No wonder her university doesn't object to a nice, long sabbatical."

"It's very sad," said Julia, spearing a quail egg and keenly aware of Max's leg just inches from her own, "but she is so damned *annoying*."

"Enough of her," the minister said dismissively. "In what way would you like to help with this production?"

Startled, Julia lifted her head, noticing for the first time the touch of sunburn on his face and arms and seeing the slight smile that crinkled the skin around his eyes.

"I'm just here to listen in and see what I might be able to do. Like I told you, this is a whole new area for me." His foot shifted under the table and touched hers, which she quickly tucked under her chair. "Is your wife here?"

"Shirley has no time, between the kids and counseling her patients, and besides, she doesn't go in for theatrics."

Julia felt a simultaneous leap of joy and stab of wariness. "Have you decided on a play? One that the schools will approve?"

"We've done that much. It's going to be Albee's *American Dream*, and I play the part of Daddy and Laura is Mrs. Barker. That's about as far as we've come. Do you know the play?"

"I've read it, but I'd better bone up on it."

"Well, we decided Diva would be perfect as Grandma, but she totally refused because it might make the community think she actually is a grandmother."

Julia laughed and shook her head.

"Don't look at me. I'm not an actress." Tipping his head to one side, Max stared quizzically at her. "And I'm not anxious to be a Grandma right now, either." Realizing that her comment could be taken any number of ways, including a hint for compliments, Julia suddenly became very involved in winding spaghetti onto her fork. Max began to chuckle and then reached over and squeezed her knee. For a moment, she felt dizzy; how long had it been since Jack had touched her knee—or any other part of her body, for that matter? Moving her leg to one side, just a beat too slowly, she looked up, aware that the reddish hair on his bare forearms was glinting in the sunlight. As his laughter gradually subsided, Julia asked in a level tone, "Do you always take acting parts, or do you work backstage sometimes?"

"Usually I'm in front of the lights. I guess extroverted ministers that like to preach tend to be hams at heart. If I hadn't answered the call of God, I probably would have gone into the theater as a profession."

Abandoning her pasta, Julia studied Max, searching for signs of irony, but her luncheon companion was now intently demolishing the food on his plate.

"And what do you do for God in the way of tending to his flock?"

Ignoring the hint of sarcasm in her voice, he grinned and stretched, the muscles in his arms flexed, his legs, partly bare in Bermuda shorts, extended.

"Among other things, I visit the sick, counsel the deranged, try to keep the church finances afloat and direct a teenage group from our congregation that works in the favela over in Morumbi."

Forgetting emotional and physical attraction for the man, Julia leaned forward, her eyes bright with curiosity. "What do they do?"

"Right now we have the girls helping with kindergarten one afternoon a week, and the boys laying sewer pipe. When they finish, which won't be for a while, the boys are going to paint what passes for a community center."

"I think that's wonderful."

"Well, it teaches them a little bit about the less privileged."

"I think everyone has an obligation to help others in some way," she declared firmly. "At home I worked with undocumented families at *Angel and Friends*, and here I teach gardening to the boys at Lar Christina Angelica a couple of times a week. I'd have been much better as a cooking instructor, but that didn't work out for a number of reasons."

He sprawled on an overstuffed chair, fingers interlaced behind his head. "Laura told me about your gardening work."

Instantly wary, she wondered what Laura and the minister had been saying about her. Glancing toward the far end of the veranda, she watched their hostess pour coffee for Diva and Pearl, then move to the next table. Max straightened and leaned forward, elbows on his knees, chin on both fists.

"If you're interested, you could come see what the kids do in the favela. We go out from church every Wednesday at 3:00 o'clock, and you're welcome to join us."

Why not, she thought, feeling vaguely that this was not a good idea.

"Thanks, I just might do that." Her forehead creased with a frown. "But not right away. I think my sister's coming to visit again."

"Bring her along."

"Oh, no. You've met Gail."

"Only briefly, before she locked herself into Laura's john."

They both began to laugh.

Half turning in her chair, Julia watched Laura stride toward them, her face set and unsmiling.

"You too are very unsociable. The rest of us," she flung an arm backward to indicate the crowded veranda, "have been discussing the play and trying to assign tasks while you've been over here having a private conversation."

Max stood up and thrust both hands into his Bermuda pockets. "We've decided that Julia should be prompter," he said, smoothing his pony tail.

Startled, Julia opened her mouth but before she could speak, Laura's voice bit into the still, hot air. "That is a *group* decision, and while you've been having your tête-à-tête, the *group* gave that job to Celeste."

Julia stood, her friend's abrupt outburst serving as an uncomfortable reminder of their ruptured friendship. Allowing Max to move ahead, Laura grasped Julia's arm and hissed, "Don't be led astray by that Man of the Cloth crap. You are headed for big trouble. Think 'wolf in sheep's clothing', and remember this is a very small community that sees everything, imagines a lot more and loves to gossip."

EIGHTEEN—BOTUCATÚ and POÇOS DE CALDAS

Standing in front of the double doors at the Guarulhos Airport customs exit, Julia felt a strong sense of dejá vu. The surge of passengers from Gail's flight had rapidly dwindled to a few stragglers and then to the occasional lone traveler, but her sister the wedding consultant had still not emerged. Half an hour more then I'm going home, Julia thought, feeling a mixture of helplessness and irritation.

Twenty minutes later, the doors opened and Gail stepped into the waiting room dragging two enormous black garbage bags. Staring at the sacks with a hollow feeling in the pit of her stomach, Julia rushed around the steel railing to greet her sister in a welcoming embrace. She'd told Gail to bring at least one extra suitcase to hold all the things she was certain to buy, but an international voyage with garbage bags?

Releasing her hold on the sacks, Gail gripped her sister in a hug, kissed her cheeks and said, "You won't believe what happened."

"Probably not," said Julia.

"I did just as you said and packed two suitcases."

"I said to bring an *empty* one."

"Really? I don't remember that part of it," said Gail. Julia signaled for a skycap, immaculate in his white jacket, and pointed to the bags, which he reluctantly lifted onto his handcart. Obviously, he wasn't accustomed to hauling garbage and was overly sensitive to the curious stares of the few remaining people in the lounge.

"Anyway, I forgot one. Except for the fact that half my clothes got left behind in L.A., there was no problem until I got off the plane here and they unloaded the baggage. Mine was the last suitcase onto that trailer thing and while the guy was driving over the tarmac it fell off and a plane ran over it."

Julia eyed her sister skeptically. "Are you making this up?"

"I have a little style, you know, and this is not it." She waved one hand toward the sacks. Julia remembered very clearly her glimpse of Gail going through São Paulo Immigration, shoulders hunched as she clutched ripped paper and plastic bags, her purse and cosmetic case, but she decided to let it pass.

"Was your medication in the suitcase?" Julia asked anxiously.

"Of course not," Gail answered airily, patting a huge designer handbag. "I'm not a nitwit." Julia took a deep, calming breath.

"So," continued Gail as they exited the airport and started toward the parking lot, "does the airline run out to Duty Free and get me a new suitcase? Of course not! Those uniformed robots stuffed all my things into these bags and made me fill out a form, first telling me that they aren't responsible for either the driver of the baggage trailer or the plane."

"Here we are," Julia said to the skycap in Portuguese, unlocking the trunk of her car. Gingerly, the man deposited the two bags inside.

"Well, I just lost it," said Gail. "I shouted a little and told them they were totally unable to take responsibility for anything, a character failing that they must have learned from their crooked politicians. No wonder this country's in a huge mess."

Julia paid the skycap and opened the passenger door for her sister.

"They must have loved that."

"They can't speak English, remember?"

"Some of them can."

"Anyway, guess what happened when I was going through security at LAX?"

"I can't imagine," Julia responded truthfully.

"You remember this slip?" Gail lifted her mid-calf linen skirt, revealing a satin undergarment with a wide lace hem.

"Not really."

Gail dropped the skirt and both women got into the car. "I thought you had one of these too. It's got this zipped pocket in the lace so that you can carry money and jewelry, which is what I did, and then going through security the guy with the wand stopped at my knee and said, 'You've had a knee replacement?' I told him no, not yet, but he kept it up and kept it up and the wand kept blipping at my knee. It was the jewelry, of course, but that was none of his business. Finally, he called two of those women security people over who escorted me into a little cubicle and patted my leg and then grappled with my knee."

Choking on an escaping bubble of laughter, Julia started the car and drove out of the parking lot.

"It's not funny, Julia. They were really weird. One said, 'What's this?' like she'd found the Holy Grail. When I told them it was money and jewelry they didn't believe it until they saw it. *Then* they searched my purse and found two dozen Heath bars, which I said I was bringing as a present for my sister, and they wanted to know why you didn't buy them here. I told them I could hardly find them in L.A., let alone here." She looked at Julia, her expression one of pained disbelief. "Have those people ever been out of L.A.?

"Probably not," said Julia.

"They finally let me go, and the last thing one of them said was, 'Love your hair'. I thought that was just so sweet, especially since hers looked like a rat's nest. I gave her my card and told her I'd give her a discount for any wedding she might have. And then I got here and the plane ran over my suitcase."

"Okay, calm down. We're going home, and I'll make you a large caipirinha."

"...and I'll peek at the clothes in those sacks which will all be rags now. We'll have to go shopping immediately since I need an entire wardrobe."

Why was it, Julia wondered, that she did so much praying when her sister was around?

"I thought Brazil was the land of sunshine," commented Gail as Jack steered the car through the narrow, badly paved streets of Botucatú. Although it was only one hundred fifty kilometers from São Paulo, he had been driving for nearly four hours, most of it in inclement weather. Torrents of rain cascaded over the windshield, distorting the driver's vision as he swore inventively and tried to identify deep potholes that had filled with water and were now invisible and extremely hazardous. They were called *quebra rodas*, or axel breakers.

Clouds hung heavy and low, slate-gray streaked with silver and shaded with lead, bringing a gloom to the late afternoon that would soon shift abruptly into a dark, wet night. During their drive from São Paulo, the wind had picked up and now blew in occasional gale-force gusts that tore at the branches of the tall, overhanging sibipiruna trees, ripping off the delicate yellow flowers and long green pods and tossing them against walls and buildings. Looking out the passenger window, and trying to ignore her husband's scowling face and the unpleasant atmosphere in the car, Julia wondered what lesson she should learn from this circumstance. Not to cave in to Gail's pleas to go hiking, especially when it involved the purchase of an entire new sports wardrobe? Not to persuade her reluctant husband to accompany them for a fun weekend? She sighed as they climbed another hill then swung around the corner.

"There", she cried in relief, spying a *Hotel Jacarandá* sign on the top of a building. "That's the hotel."

Jack turned the car into a driveway that they all assumed led to the parking area of the *Jacarandá* and stopped. Parking spaces beside the hotel currently sheltered stacks of lumber, a huge pile of sand and sawhorses with planks of wood upon them, upon which two men with chain saws were busily working. A cement mixer and tall, mysterious mounds covered with plastic sheeting took up a great deal of the open area.

"Oh, my God," breathed Gail, peering over her shoulder. "What a dump!"

Julia glared at her husband as he parked next to the cement mixer. "I thought you said Eliana researched this completely."

Jack shrugged. "There aren't a lot of choices in Botucatú."

I wouldn't bet on that, Julia reflected sourly, convinced that her husband's secretary had probably picked the very worst accommodation available to spite them all and teach Jack that it wasn't wise for him to devote a weekend to his family. Of course, she still had only her unconfirmed belief that her husband had strayed, but nothing in their slowly disintegrating relationship indicated otherwise.

"Let's go," Jack ordered, opening the driver's door and trotting through the rain to the sheltered area where he paused to speak to the chain saw duo.

"Did he do this on purpose?" asked Gail. "He seems changed, somehow."

"I know he didn't arrange for this weather, and his secretary is responsible for the hotel," Julia replied evasively, distressed that her husband's coolness was obvious to Gail. He used to be charming, and still was around others, but his charisma was short-lived when extended to his wife and sister-in-law.

Jack disappeared behind the sawhorses; Julia and Gail dashed after him through the downpour and stepped into a short hallway that opened onto a deep veranda facing a garden. Large pots filled with trailing vines and flowers lined the edge of the terrace while thick wooden posts supported the red tile roof. Intertwined trunks and branches of bougainvillea grew in a profusion of vibrant magenta, orange and rose hues that swept across the roof and cascaded toward the tile floor. Although the view was partially obscured by driving rain, the women could see garden paths that cut through an expanse of lawn and wound around a free-form swimming pool and rock garden before disappearing into dense shrubbery overhung by tall trees.

"How beautiful," Gail screeched over the din of the rain, the chain saw and the heavy pounding that had begun somewhere in the upper reaches of the building. "And look, those are actual hammocks. You never see that at home."

Julia followed her sister's gaze and saw a brick barbeque, sheltered by a deep, red tile roof, just to the left of the swimming pool. Two sodden hammocks sagged between the support posts, the waterlogged fabric now only inches from the tile floor. There was no hint of sarcasm in Gail's voice, and when Julia glanced at her sibling, she saw only an expression of delight in a hotel garden that would be exquisite in better weather. Julia was swept by a tide of affection for her sister, the good sport with the happy attitude in spite of Julia's increasing dismay over the entire venture. Gail's objective was to hike strenuously and burn off non-existent fat, while Julia wanted to extract more information about her daughters; neither had succeeded in reaching their goals.

"Ladies, this is Sr. Herminio, the hotel owner." It was Jack's public voice, the animated one he used at the office and at parties, the tone guaranteed to win friends.

Both women turned toward a short, pudgy man in a polo shirt and Bermudas. With a double chin and thinning, gray hair, his broad smile crinkled the skin around his dark brown eyes and revealed an imperfect set of teeth. He immediately set about apologizing, in Portuguese, for the rain, which was unexpected, and for the construction that he was certain had been mentioned to Sra. Eliana when she phoned. It was, he assured them, by far the best of the four hotels in Botucatú, and he was expanding it to accommodate the demand.

Julia glanced into the long room opening onto the veranda and saw a steam table, buffet and a sea of wooden tables, only two of which had been set for dinner.

"Are there that many visitors to the town? We came because you're supposed to have some great hiking spots and rock formations, but it *is* a little remote," Julia shouted. The first hammer had been joined by several more.

For the first time the smile faltered and he bellowed, "This is a very rich town. We have two bus building factories, a plane manufacturing plant, the University and agriculture. And visitors come for the peace and quiet of the countryside."

The wind shifted and they were pelted with rain.

"Is there more to the hotel?" she asked hopefully. "A lounge? Or library?"

"At the moment, this is it. We'll have leisure rooms after construction." The wide smile was back.

"But where can we sit and read? Or talk?" she yelled with a tinge of desperation.

"Right here on the veranda." He beamed, his even teeth flashing. "Normally it's a perfect place to have a drink, talk, read. Play cards."

"What did he say?" shouted Gail.

"Aside from our bedrooms and the dining room, this is the operative part of the establishment."

"I'll have someone bring in your bags," said Sr. Herminio, motioning them forward. With definite misgivings, the trio followed the hotelier along the veranda into the building and up the carpeted stairway where all but the owner immediately fell to their knees. Herminio turned, his plump cheeks rounded beneficently.

"The steps are a bit tricky. Some are a little lower than the others."

"What did he say?" asked Gail.

"That he had cheap unskilled labor put in the stairs and then paid off the inspector to ignore the mistakes," responded her sister.

"A lot of Brazilians speak English," Jack whispered warningly.

"Truth often hurts," Julia said tartly.

Standing up and brushing off their knees, the group continued to the next floor. On the outside wall, rain had seeped through the paint and thin cracks were everywhere. Grouped around the first bedroom door, they were jarred by a sudden silence, broken almost immediately by a chorus of interior doors rattling in the wind and occasionally slamming shut. With another paternal smile, the owner announced, "Five o'clock and the workmen are gone. Now it'll be very tranquil."

Poised on the threshold, Julia asked, "Could you recommend a restaurant?"

"There's only the pizzeria. And our dining room."

"Nothing else?" asked Gail.

"Everyone eats at home."

"What did he say?" asked Gail.

"I promise, you don't want to know," said Julia.

Later, on the veranda, buffeted by the odd gust of wind and sprinkled with rain, the sisters sipped their second caipirinha. Jack had seated himself at a dining table inside and was tapping on his notebook.

"What's with Jack?" Gail asked.

"He has problems at work."

Gail tossed her blond hair over one shoulder. Carefully coiffed at the beginning of the day into clouds of long, white-blond ringlets, it was now transformed into damp, dripping strings.

"You think *I* don't have problems at work? He should have to deal with Lorraine van de Kamp who wants to wear her grandmother's wedding dress and shoes, both of which are about ten sizes too small. And don't even *mention* her mother!"

"This is trouble with his boss and the guys from the States, all of whom seem to be cheating the company."

Gail smiled, finished off her drink and waved to Herminio for another.

"Well, he'd better just relax and go with the flow on that one. As you keep telling me, this is Brazil." Handing her empty glass to the owner, she leaned forward and whispered to her sister, "I thought this guy was kind of cute in a fat way until I saw what a shitty hotel he runs."

"You haven't told me about the girls. You know, Sydney and Stephanie."

"Well, there's not a lot to tell. Sydney caught her welder in the act, so to speak, with one of her pals at the university, so he's out and it's propelled her into a sort of monastic Doris Day phase, complete with Peter Pan collars and twin sets."

"It pays to pray!" exclaimed Julia with happy satisfaction. After a few seconds her bliss vanished and a tiny frown creased her freckled forehead. "Why didn't you tell me this earlier?"

Gail shrugged. "We all know Sydney. By now she may have decided that work as a line captain in Vegas is her calling."

"We had a Consul General down here that started out as a line captain," Julia said.

"Male or female? Anyway, I don't see Sydney as a diplomat. For what it's worth, her grades are fine. I guess you know that Stephanie's thinking of grad school. And has no boyfriend at the moment."

"I don't understand that." Julia's forehead was knotted. "She's beautiful, fun, intelligent and should have packs of men after her."

"She probably does but nobody special. You worry if they have boyfriends and worry if they don't. Our parents never were upset, but then our parents didn't remember they had children," Gail said bitterly, "which is probably why they waited until Mother was forty-three to have me."

"They just thought other people were more interesting than their daughters."

"You're always defending them," Gail complained, reminding Julia of her sister's eager attempts to win their parents' approval. "If you ask me, they shouldn't have had us."

"You're right about that."

"I suppose it was a dysfunctional family," Gail concluded.

Julia chuckled. "Today *every* family in the States is considered dysfunctional, just like every child has dyslexia. And thousands upon thousands seem to be on Prozac and into therapy of some sort..."

"Let's eat."

Both women were startled by Jack's voice just inside the dining room doorway. Standing, Julia saw that he'd put away the notebook, a good sign, which meant he might not do any work for the rest of the evening. She stepped into the dining room, surprised when he gave her the old, warm smile she hadn't seen for weeks. And when he took her hand and laced his fingers within hers, her stomach did a small but hopeful flip. "Let's see if the food matches the rest of the establishment."

Gastronomically, the hotel was startlingly good. They each had another caipirinha, and when they stumbled and fell up the stairs to their respective bedrooms, all three were in mellow moods despite the rain that continued to pound the hotel and grounds. Closing and locking their door, Julia turned wordlessly into the bathroom, shucked off her clothes and stepped into the shower, a nightly routine that no longer included Jack. Months ago she had stopped trying to interest him in sexual activity, or even after-dinner conversation, since he was preoccupied, short and tense, claiming stress at work and worries about his position. For many months they had slept in the same bed but touched only accidentally, a situation Julia didn't initially understand but one that had caused her deep unhappiness. Gradually, she had risen to a level of lonely solitude in which she constantly planned to ask him about Eliana but never could quite find the right moment.

Rinsing shampoo from her hair, she gasped in fright, her muscles froze, as a pair of muscular arms snaked across her stomach, pulling her backward into a nude male body. Too terrified to speak, she felt a beard brush her neck and twisted her head slightly.

"Jack? What are you doing?" Sudden relief transformed her paralyzed muscles into trembling rubber blocks. Lifting her wet hair with one hand, he soaped her body with the other.

It rained all night. Neighborhood dogs barked constantly and hotel doors rattled and banged, but Julia was oblivious as she and her husband embarked on inventive, athletic sex for the first time in many months. Dozing happily, she wondered if she'd leapt to the wrong conclusion; maybe it really *was* only stress and worry that was devouring their marriage, not an extra marital affair. Too happy to sleep, she drifted contentedly, feeling Jack's body curled around hers. She would have liked to talk with him about his obvious transformation, as they would have done in the old days, but was afraid to break the happy spell.

Next morning the downpour seemed to intensify. The trio, apparently the only guests in the hotel, met in the early morning gloom of the dining room.

"Nobody's around," muttered Jack. "And no coffee..."

"We can't waste two more days here," said Julia, turning to her sister. "I just had an idea. I know you wanted to hike, but that's impossible with this rain, and you leave next week, so why don't we get in the car and drive to Poços de Caldas. Diva and Marilyn say it's absolutely charming and has a few easy trails and a lot of other things to do."

Silently, the other two digested the suggestion. Impatiently, she frowned at them both.

"This is not a revolutionary suggestion, folks," she lobbied.

Gail came to life. "That's a fabulous idea! Luckily, some of my garbage bag clothes were fine, and those that I bought are sophisticated." She patted her very tight, very fashionable leather trousers and jacket with pleated, puffed sleeves. "I'll just run up and get my suitcase."

"We can wake somebody to bring down the baggage," Jack said.

Fluffing her newly curled platinum hair, Gail smiled.

"That's a bad idea. I left my window open, and when I woke up at about three this morning, the bedding and mattress were all soaked. We should just go."

Any question of coffee was forgotten as both Jack and Julia jumped to their feet and followed Gail, who had once again fallen on the uneven stairway.

"What about the bill?" asked Julia.

"We'll load up the car and then wake Sr. Herminio," Jack announced impersonally, and Julia wondered if last night had been only a wishful dream.

The weather in Poços de Caldas, a charming Colonial town known for its curative mineral spas, was glorious. Jack had booked them into the Palacio Hotel, an old, grand establishment built in 1815 and patronized by kings and heads of State until gambling was outlawed in Brazil and the elegant casino next door closed. Only three stories high, it faced a wide expanse of tree-shaded, well-trimmed lawn in front and a park with rivers, footbridges, flowers, pergolas, fountains, tall trees and densely massed shrubbery in the back. A deep, covered veranda ran the width of the hotel façade and, although this was now divided into small shops, one could easily imagine beautifully gowned women seated in wicker chairs having tea with friends. The reception and entry hallway were enormous, as was a room that had previously served as a ballroom and others that still were used as a games room, library and writing room. An enclosed bar faced the tiled, indoor thermal pool and individual spas beyond; domed ceilings rose loftily throughout the ground floor.

"I could only get us suites," Jack announced as they followed the bell hop down a wide, carpeted hallway and up a staircase built by skilled labor. "Bedrooms were completely booked and the hotel is totally sold out all of next month."

"This is more like it," exclaimed Gail as she was ushered into her suite. The ceiling of the huge room soared above a thickly carpeted floor and four poster mahogany bed. Striped satin draperies were tied back over lace curtains that fluttered at French doors opening onto a balcony. The floor and walls of the bathroom, which was the same size as the large sitting room, were completely covered with antique Portuguese tiles.

"It's wonderful."

"It's also late, so let's just drop our suitcases and go for a walk in the park before dinner," suggested Julia.

Gail raised her finely sculpted eyebrows in

astonishment. "We've been riding all day in the car and you think we should have cocktails and dine in our travel clothes?"

Julia glanced down at her khaki skirt and white linen blouse; they *did* look a little casual. The dining room, which they had glimpsed, was enormous with windows overlooking the park and round tables draped with white linen. Bedraggled clientele probably would be seated in the pantry.

"Well, maybe you're right. Let's meet in the library in fifteen minutes."

Half an hour later, while Jack studied financial reports and Julia pretended deep interest in the latest issue of the magazine, "Isto È", Gail stepped lightly into the room. She was wearing a long sleeved, gray silk blouse with a plunging neckline and satin cuffs, a crème skirt with horizontal pleats, and very high heeled gray pumps with enormous silk bows over the Achilles tendon. Countless bead necklaces were draped around her neck, her hair had been swept back into an elaborate pony tail and she would have been a smash hit at any gala evening. Julia felt instantly dowdy in her blue print silk dress that was comfortable and best described as a classic.

Jack stood, gawking at Gail. "You're going to walk in the park like that?"

Gail pivoted lightly toward him.

"Actually, no, I'm not walking in the park right now, I'm going to the crystal shops."

In 1954, Mario Seguso of the old and venerated glass-blowing family in Murano, Italy, immigrated to Poças de Caldas and there, in 1965, founded his workshop. Seguso men had been glassmakers since the fourteenth century; their pieces famed for delicacy and color and, for a number of years, Mario's signed objects had been sold at Tiffany's. Brazilian apprentices were trained in the art, and the industry expanded both in size and reputation; by the end of the twentieth century, other glass-blowing firms had appeared, but none quite so distinguished as Mario's. Now he had an elegant shop only a block from the Palacio as well as a more casual one in his `factory` with a tempered glass wall where visitors watched craftsmen create glass animals, vases and paper weights from molten glass.

Julia tossed the magazine onto a table and stood. "We can do that tomorrow, Gail," she said.

"Tomorrow I want to go to the Japanese park, up to the Cristo on the ski lift, to the aquarium, to the cultural center and to the glass blowing factory. May as well see the whole town..."

"No hiking?" asked Jack.

"Only if I can squeeze it in," she said.

"How did you get all that information?" Julia stared at her sister.

"I asked at the desk, of course. Are we going or not?"

"I'll wait for you here," announced Jack, sinking back into the leather chair.

Thank God, Julia thought, knowing how much her husband hated to shop for anything. "We'll walk in the park when we get back," she called to Jack.

Feeling like a page, Julia trailed after her sister, witnessing the purchase of signed vases, etched liquor glasses, decanters, candlesticks and serving plates, all of which were packed in boxes and delivered to the hotel. Remembering Gail's disastrous exit from Passport Control, Julia tried not to wonder how hand-blown, signed crystal would make the journey.

Later, the three walked in the park, had cocktails in the bar and a gourmet meal in the restaurant; Gail was the center of attention everywhere. Leaving the restaurant, they stepped into a throng of beautifully dressed men and women in the hallway. When Julia asked a waiter what was going on, she discovered there was a wedding in the adjacent room, which clearly was not large enough to hold all the guests.

"A wedding," breathed Gail, turning her eyes up to the

crystal candelabra. "Thank you dear God!" Beaming at her sister, she said, "Marvelous! This is my chance to find out how the Brazilians do it. See you at breakfast." And she edged through the overflow crowd into the packed room where the nuptials were to be said.

Jack gave his wife a crooked smile. "Crashing a wedding?"

Julia shrugged. "Let's have a drink and go to bed."

At eleven-thirty, just after Julia had drifted into a deep sleep, she was jolted upright by a blast of music from the floor below.

Beside her, Jack squinted at his watch, then got up, shuffled to the French doors and batted the lace curtains aside. Laughter was heard, cheers, and then an old-fashioned waltz shook the walls. Jack stepped outside, leaned as far as possible over the balcony and remained motionless for a few minutes before turning back into the room.

"It's the happy couple and their two thousand guests dancing up a storm down there, to a three hundred piece orchestra."

"It's so loud," Julia complained, turning on the light.

"That's because we're right over the ballroom. Lucky us."

The waltz ended and a samba took over amidst cheers and shouts.

"How long do you think this goes on?" Julia asked, reaching for her book.

"No idea. I'm glad I brought my notebook."

At four o'clock the party, and orchestra, disbanded and Julia fell at once into an exhausted sleep, only to be jerked into full consciousness at seven by a high decibel jumble of cowboy music, car horns, announcements and motorcycle engines. Next to her, Jack struggled to a sitting position, his face gray with fatigue.

"What the hell is going on now?" he asked, punching at the sheet to disentangle his legs. Lurching toward the

French doors and then out onto the veranda, wearing only the under shorts in which he slept, Jack stood immobile and silent for several minutes, his back muscles rigid. *Well, this weekend has turned out to be just perfect*, Julia thought, pulling her dressing gown closed and joining her husband on the balcony.

"I don't believe it," she breathed. Below them, the street and park teemed with men and women wearing cowboy outfits and drinking beer while hillbilly music in Portuguese blared from three flatbed trucks. A pickup truck bearing the banner, *Annual Jeep Fest*, and holding a group of cheering, drinking enthusiasts, led a crush of multi-colored, honking jeeps up and down the street and around the park while a vast number of motorcycles revved their engines and wove through the crowd. The din was appalling.

Julia suddenly grasped her husband's elbow with one hand and pointed with the other. "Jack, isn't that Gail?"

Squinting, he leaned forward and watched a chartreuse motorcycle drive slowly between a mass of parked jeeps and stop beside other bikers. The driver dismounted and removed his helmet as did his passenger, a striking blond with long, shining curls loosely held in a ponytail. With a smile, she handed her helmet to the driver, accepted a beer from a bystander and clapped a ten gallon hat onto her head.

"I'll be damned, it *is* Gail," exclaimed Jack in wonder. "I thought this was going to be her hiking weekend and she's brought a wedding outfit, some cowboy clothes and travel outfits and seems to have snagged a boyfriend in six short hours." He leaned over the railing and bellowed, "Gail! Up here!"

The crowd looked up. A few revelers snickered at the middle-aged man in his underpants while Gail waved cheerfully and then returned her attention to her companion. In spite of her exhaustion, Julia began to laugh. Mary Beth would be so envious of this weekend.

"You think it's funny, but I need my sleep," Jack said, shuffling across the room and flopping face down on the bed.

Her laughter faded and Julia stared at him for a moment, trying to remember the night before last in Botucatú when he had been so loving, so like the man she had known in Venice Beach. It was impossible to connect that amorous, tender man with this humorless stranger. Instead, she thought of Max leaning close to her, his knee brushing hers, his kind, humorous eyes magnified by the round spectacles, his voice low and intimate. It was a dangerous image, one that she should banish from her mind, but Max was fun, caring and made her feel special, as Jack had once done. Suddenly, she couldn't wait to get back to São Paulo.

NINETEEN—SÃO PAULO, BRAZIL

*D*espite her immersion in Newcomers Club, her gardening classes at Lar Christina Angelica, participation in the Troubadour South production of *The American Dream*, and a flurry of therapeutic bread-baking, Julia felt lost after Gail returned to California. Her sister was undeniably irritating, often the typical blond bubblehead, but she was a link to Julia's old familiar world peopled by family and friends, where there were few surprises and she herself fit in. When Gail left, Julia was very aware of the six thousand miles that separated her from Venice Beach and her family.

Although she expected her sister's departure to be dramatic, Julia hadn't envisioned the reality. A procession of sky-caps pushed carts bearing a variety of suitcases and an array of Poços de Caldas boxes across the Guarulhos Airport terminal. The parade was led by Gail, wearing a silk georgette print dress that fluttered as she walked, and wood and satin platform shoes. Julia, more modestly attired, accompanied her sister as they swept up to the United Business Class check-in, and that's where the difficulty began.

Initially, there was a verbal tussle in which Gail refused to believe that her luggage exceeded the permissible quantity and she fought these pesky regulations with tosses of her blond curls, seductive smiles and gestures of feminine helplessness. Julia watched the scene with a certain amount of cynicism, thinking that perhaps her sister would like to stay and play the lead in *The American Dream*. Gail and her adversary were haggling over the price of overweight luggage when the wedding consultant made a mistake.

"But you shouldn't charge that much. These are national treasures."

In the sudden silence, three ticket clerks on the other side of the counter exchanged glances and then one turned and spoke into what seemed to be his cupped hand. Almost immediately the group was joined by two men in dark suits.

"I understand you're taking national treasures in these boxes."

"Yes."

"That's illegal."

"How can that be?" Her eyes conveyed innocent astonishment and she pressed one hand to her throat. Julia felt a severe headache approaching. "I told them to wrap for shipping and they did."

One of the men whipped out a notebook and pen. "Who was doing this?"

"The factory at Poços da Calcas."

It was time, Julia thought, to end this before the check-in queue behind them grew violent. "She means modern treasures, not old ones. These are glass vases."

"Crystal," Gail corrected huffily. "Crystal."

"...wine glasses, bowls..."

"I'm a wedding consultant, you know, and I can use all these beautiful things in my business. Look!" Gail pulled a small photo album from her handbag and opened it for the inspector to see. "Won't it be glorious to have crystal urns from Brazil holding the flowers by the altar instead of these nasty ceramic ones?" A small crowd of ticket clerks and baggage handlers gathered on the other side of the counter, studying the picture. Gail flipped the page. "And I bought the perfect etched punch bowl and glasses, signed by Mr. Seguso himself, that will be fabulous on a table like this." She lifted her chin, tilted her head to one side and looked steadily at the inspector. "Are you married?"

"I am."

"Oh, too bad. I could have done a beautiful wedding for you in Santa Barbara, or maybe La Jolla." She paused thoughtfully. "Would you like to renew your vows?"

Puzzled, he frowned. "I don't understand."

"You know, get married again. To your wife, of course..."

For a moment the employees and officials looked at one another in confusion and then muffled chuckles spread through the group. With a broad grin, the inspector shook his head and said, "You Americans, always repeating your mistakes." Bowing slightly, he handed Gail her passport and ticket, then gallantly waved her through. "*Boa viagem.*"

Since her sister's departure, Julia had taken charge of props for the Troubadour South production as well as occasionally serving as stagehand and make-up girl. One Saturday afternoon, not long before the play was scheduled to open in the American School auditorium, the tense, highly strung cast was rehearsing. Laura, a co-director, dashed past Julia.

"Having fun?"

"Definitely." But Laura was gone, shouting to Marilyn that she was on the wrong side of the stage and anyway it was time to quit so that those with children could pick them up. Julia stuffed the script into her leather book bag, straightened and found herself facing Max. Startled, she jumped and her heart began to race.

"Don't creep up like that. You scared me."

He smiled, a broad, easy grin.

"Sorry, I didn't mean to frighten you. I have a proposition to make."

Clutching her book bag to her chest, she studied his face carefully. "What?"

"I'll walk you to your car," he offered, "and we can talk about it."

Julia shook her head. "We can talk now."

"Okay. I thought you might like to come with me on Monday to see what my youth group does in the favela."

This was about the last thing Julia had expected to hear. She smiled in relief.

"Oh. Yes. I've never been into a favela." Nor had she previously been tempted, but now Max was casually suggesting a foray into alien territory.

"They're not major tourist attractions, certainly not for this collection of thespians." As they watched the theatrical group silently collecting their belongings from the auditorium, Julia was intensely aware of Max's single gold cross earring that swung rhythmically back and forth."Is agriculture somehow involved?"

Lifting his head, he laughed, a merry sound that sent a warm blush of mortified discomfort through Julia's body. What had she said? What unknown gaffe had she made? A few members of the cast and crew glanced briefly in their direction before smiling and hurrying toward the exit.

"I'm sorry," he apologized. "It's just that the idea of horticulture in *this* favela is...well, wait till you see it."

Looking into those soft, brown eyes, Julia felt her instant of embarrassment blur into a twinge of desire. *Stop it*, she thought. *This is a married clergyman who has thinning hair in a ponytail, which I cannot bear, and clothes that I am sure came from his church rummage sale. And a lovely wife who is considered a near-saint by the entire community."*

"All right," she heard herself say. "I'll go. Shall I meet

you there?"

Max shook his head, the earring swinging, his thick glasses flashing. "Definitely not. You'll never find us. Why don't you come to the church tomorrow around one o'clock and we'll ride in the van with the kids?"

Laura skidded to a stop beside them, looked from one to the other, and said, "Let's *go*, Julia. The children are waiting for me even as we twaddle and dawdle."

Max drew his slim figure into a straight line, saluted with one finger, and tipped his head cockily to one side. "Yes, Ma'am." Grinning, he turned to Julia. "See you tomorrow afternoon."

As they hurried out of the auditorium and across the school grounds toward the parking lot, Laura scowled at Julia. "I told you to keep away from Max if you want to stay out of trouble."

Irritated, Julia hoisted her book bag onto one shoulder. "Exactly what is his crime of choice? Serial killing with dismemberment? Cannibalism? Rape and robbery? I don't know what I'm being warned against."

They reached the parking lot, now nearly deserted, and crossed to Laura's car. Waving to the guard, Laura opened the trunk and they both stowed their bags inside. Before unlocking the driver's door, Laura paused, crossed her arms on the roof of the vehicle and stared across at Julia.

When she spoke, both her expression and voice were stern.

"I don't know anything specific, just rumors here and there in spite of the fact that he's apparently devoted to Shirley and to his children. But then, nobody likes to come out and say bad things about ministers, even if they're true. Look at the scandals about priests and altar boys."

"You think Max is a pedophile?"

Laura smiled uncertainly and then burst out laughing. As she shook her head, her sculpted cap of shining, chestnut hair swung from side to side. "You are totally impossible. Of course I don't think he is, at least I hope not. But I know you pretty well, and I know you're not completely together lately. All I'm saying is *be careful*."

"He only asked me to go into the favela with his youth group," she countered defensively, realizing once again how the gap between the two had widened.

Laura unlocked the car. "Favelas can be dangerous."

The next afternoon, Julia sat sedately in the passenger seat of Max's car. The church van, he explained, had gone ahead, driven by Lou Griffiths, a volunteer who supervised the older boys. During the twenty-minute journey, Max chatted, telling her about the students, most of whom were high school seniors, while she remained silent and apprehensive.

Her anxiety didn't diminish when they turned into the rutted, semi-paved favela road lined with crooked brick, plywood and cardboard dwellings. Turning again, Max carefully crept down a wide muddy road pitted with craters and sprinkled with boulders, and then stopped in front of a small, run-down building.

Julia got out and stood looking uncertainly at the desolate street; its unpainted, ramshackle buildings were squeezed together while a few trees served only to emphasize the misery of the surroundings. Several people emerged from the hovels and stopped to stare.

"Let's go." Max grasped her elbow.

"Is it safe? I mean, those people don't look very friendly."

"It's okay, they're used to us."

Just outside the building, a few boys squatted on the cracked concrete, diligently painting old playground equipment.

"Hi, guys," said Max. "This is Mrs. Elliott who's here to see what we're up to."

Smiling, mumbling greetings, the boys returned to their tasks. Max and Julia stepped inside the diminutive, windowless room, its walls smeared with the grime of years. Neatly dressed small children sat at desks arranged in tidy rows; bent over workbooks, they were helped by several girls.

"The object here is to teach the children the basics of reading and writing so they'll be able to enter school. The local mayor decided to guarantee school placement to every child participating in the program, which is great."

"What do you mean, guarantee placement?"

"There aren't enough spaces available in public schools. Here they learn how to hold a pencil, to go over lines, match pictures with objects—all that."

Julia was confused. "If they don't do this, then they can't get into *public* school?"

Max grinned. "It's a pisser, isn't it?" They walked between the rows of children who were currently tracing numbers. "The children learn to play team games, too, like 'Simon Says', and bean bag games. They love it."

"Did you think this program up?" she asked.

"Not all by myself. My congregation is very privileged and the kids all go to private schools where they become totally self-absorbed. Frankly, they're often spoiled, selfish and just vaguely aware of real life. These projects are good antidotes."

An older woman, whom Max introduced as the teaching supervisor, approached and, after exchanging the mandatory greetings, cheek kisses and health inquiries, she handed the minister a list of needed supplies. He glanced at it and nodded.

"We'll see what we can do, Fernanda."

"Thank you, Reverend."

Reverend? Julia was sharply reminded of the contradiction between Max's profession and his personality. He just didn't seem like a man of God to her, but then she had to admit that she had a fairly stereotypical idea of God's representatives here on earth. Quietly, the three adults moved to the door and out onto the dirt road. Max turned to Fernanda.

"Mrs. Elliott works with some boys in Embú Guaçu so I thought she should see what we're doing here. We're going to check up on the older boys now."

"Vai com Deus," advised Fernanda in parting. "Go with God."

"I always try to."

As they passed Max's car, Julia looked at him quizzically.

"It's easier to walk than to drive and it's not far," he said.

Julia glanced at the watchful, unmoving figures across the street and said doubtfully, "I guess you know what's best."

Five minutes later Max announced, "Here we are. Now be careful you don't slip in the mud." He waved at a steep, narrow downward path that had been churned into slime by rain and countless feet. As she hesitated, the minister laughed and said, "I'll go first and catch you if you slide. We're parked on the only real favela road. The rest are just dirt trails and, believe it or not, this one is a major thoroughfare. The older boys are putting in a sewer line at the bottom."

Carefully, Julia started down the hill, lost her balance and skidded to a halt beside a meandering stream lined on both sides with shanties built on stilts. The stench was appalling and, with a jolt, she realized that the creek was actually a sewer. She and Max were joined by four very dirty, gloved and rubber-booted teenage boys who had been leveraging a huge length of concrete pipe into place not far away. A small collection of favela children suddenly appeared, jostling one another for space near the group.

Julia smiled at the adolescents. "I'm Mrs. Elliott. Max told me about your projects and I wanted to see them for myself. This is quite a job."

All four chuckled.

"The hardest was the beginning", volunteered the smallest boy. "We thought we were just going to dig a small gutter for rainwater. What a shocker to find out the residents didn't have this already."

"We didn't know where to start," added another. "Then Reverend Calhoun pointed out that the sewage stream had to be diverted before we could even begin on the ditch."

"We spent a whole school term digging the trench and somebody asked `Okay, where's the machinery to lift the pipes?'"

They all laughed and nudged one another.

"We figured it out, though."

"Yeah, right, after Mr. McNair pointed to our hands."

"And Mr. McNair is...?" Julia asked.

"Our school principal."

"Well, I'm very impressed and filled with admiration," said Julia truthfully. Since her slide down the hill, she had been aware of numerous residents skidding down to the sewage stream, jumping to the other side and slogging up into the favela, often greeting the boys and glancing at her curiously. "How do you get on with the locals?" she asked.

The burliest boy shrugged. "Great. At first they just ignored us but when they figured we really were going to stay and do some work, they got friendly. Sometimes they help out, especially the unemployed men, which is about half of the favela."

As if to prove the truth of the boy's statement, a small crowd had gathered by the cement pipe. One of the men waved his arm.

"We'd better get going," said one of the boys.

"You guys are doing a great job," Max said earnestly. After the boys moved away, he glanced up at the heavy gray clouds shaded with black. "Let's get back to the church before it rains again," he said.

As they struggled up the muddy pathway, Julia was consumed with enthusiasm for the work Max had fostered in the favela and felt a profound admiration for the minister. How, she wondered, could Laura have gotten him so wrong? On the way back to the church, where Julia had parked her car, she chatted companionably about her previous work at *Angel and Friends* and now at the Lar while Max regaled her with lively and amusing tales of the adolescents and their companions.

"And your own children," she asked, realizing that she knew almost nothing about Max's private life. "How old are they?"

For a moment, he didn't answer and Julia had the feeling that she had blundered into private territory.

He responded curtly, "Sarah's seventeen, Alex is fifteen and Martin twelve."

"So you're well-grounded in adolescent behavior."

"Yes." They turned into the church driveway, passed Julia's car and swung around the back where Max stopped and turned off the engine. Piqued by his brusque reaction to a question she considered very neutral, Julia picked up her handbag and opened the car door without a word. Instantly, Max's hand was on her forearm.

"I'm sorry if I was a little short. It's just that I have a lot on my mind at the moment." Later, Julia was to wonder about the nature of these weighty matters but, at the moment, she was silent. "Come into my office for a coffee, why don't you?" he offered. "I'd like you to see photos of the school and the sewage stream before the kids started there." His tone was once more beguiling, his expression one of warm enticement.

She hesitated. "I don't know," she answered. "I should get back."

Max got out of the car, slammed his door and helped Julia out, his hand under her elbow. "It's a little messy inside," he said, taking out keys and guiding her toward a door in the back of the church. While he shut off the security system and opened the door, Julia still vacillated, a feeling of vague unease urging her to step firmly away and go home, yet tempted by the hope of a return to their previous easy, intimate conversation. Jack left home early and often didn't return until she was asleep and, when they were together, the focus was on his business problems, Julia rationalized.

Max stepped inside and held the door open. "Come in," he invited.

Hesitantly, she moved into a room that was smaller, darker and more airless than she had expected. Much later, she was to think of it as walking into a spider's web but, at the moment, she was oddly unable to leave, mesmerized by the sight of the minister moving about the office, turning on a fan, opening the windows, shifting piles of paper from a sofa to small tables and, finally, stooping to open the door of a small refrigerator that was tucked into one corner. After rooting around for a few moments, he stood up, brandishing a bottle of Proseco in one hand and two wine glasses in the other. The spell was broken and Julia found she could move and speak once again.

"I thought we were going to look at photos."

"We certainly are, but we may as well drink champagne while we're doing it."

Julia smiled. "That's decadent."

"Not at all. It's only decadent when we take the Proseco to the favela and drink it while watching the kids stumble around in the mud and slime."

Carefully, expertly, he coaxed the cork from the bottle, easing it silently into the palm of one hand. He poured two glasses and handed her one. "Sit," he commanded, gesturing with his free hand toward the sofa, its ancient leather clearly bald in spots. Julia sank down on a well-worn cushion and tilted to one side. Self-consciously, Max grimaced. "This couch is pretty beat up. You have to sit right in the center of the pillows."

Her heart twisting at his discomfiture, Julia carefully eased into the middle and turned toward her host.

"Cheers! And good luck with your project. It's quite amazing," she said.

After Max had seated himself beside her, they clinked glasses and drank. Diffused light slanted through the partially closed blinds and glinted on the reddish-blond hair covering Max's forearms; Julia felt again that disturbing leap in her stomach. Rapidly draining her flute of champagne, she carefully placed the glass on a side table and turned toward Max.

"I must go."

Intending to thank him for the excursion and his hospitality, she looked directly into his dark mahogany eyes and her breath caught in her throat. For a moment—or perhaps many minutes—they studied one another, connected by invisible magnets locking them together. Vaguely aware that she should break free, stand up and march toward the door, Julia saw Max's face draw closer, felt his arm around her and then his lips on hers. Without any hesitation, she pulled him close, his beard brushing her chin, his ponytail now loose and sweeping over them both. Despite her usual caution, she did not think about the open windows, or the closed but unlocked door, nor was she conscious of their tumble from the sofa onto the floor where they frantically shed most of their clothes.

Unlike Jack's infrequent hurried and impersonal attempts at coupling, apparently a duty he must discharge occasionally, Max's lovemaking was gentle, erotic and slow. Like Jack in the past.

Later, Julia rolled away from the minister, her eyes focusing on the dust-bunnies under the old leather couch and then scanning the gritty floor and bunched, dirty Peruvian carpet on which they lay. Obviously, the church cleaner didn't include the office in her routine but it was a long time before Julia questioned the reason. She turned toward Max, who lay on his side, tanned face propped on one palm as he gazed at her.

"This can't become a habit, you know," she murmured. Why, she wondered, did she feel no guilt at all? In fact, her only sensation was one of peace and contentment.

"I don't see the harm, as long as it doesn't bother anyone else."

She'd heard that old line before when she'd refused propositions and advances, and always felt nothing but contempt for the speaker. This time, her reaction was one of disappointment. Surely Max could think of something more original.

Sitting up, she pulled on her clothes, and then stood up, horrified.

"Oh my God, you can see right through the windows. What if someone came by here?"

Max stood up and dressed. "No one did."

It was not the right response.

"How do you know? I can see the gardener over there in the corner and here come a couple of very old ladies with church vessels." She was torn between irritation and panic.

"Trust me. That's Vera Summers and Blanche Diaz and they're turning into the church, not coming here." He moved close for a kiss but Julia backed out of range.

"This is really very dangerous behavior, and anyway, I have to go."

He shrugged. "Okay. I'll walk you to your car."

Julia was worried, not about her infidelity but about the possibility that someone—a faithful member of the congregation, Max's wife, children from the youth group—might have observed them through the window. Only gradually did she become aware of the fact that, by not leaving Max's office after her glass of champagne, she had altered the rules and direction of her life.

TWENTY—SÃO PAULO, BRAZIL

*P*erplexed, Julia studied the ground under and around her tall, previously very leafy fichus tree, and then knelt for a better look. Black pellets the size of allspice peppercorns were sprinkled liberally on the parquet floor and piled in the dirt of the planter as though they were ripe fruit shed by the shrub.

"Mara," she called, standing up. "Mara, *vem cá, por favor.*"

A moment later, the new maid appeared in the doorway. "*Sim, senhora?*"

Julia gestured toward the floor. "Look, they're here again," she said in halting Portuguese.

Lifting her shoulders in defeat, the maid crossed the room and joined her employer to stare at the pellets. "I sweep them up every morning."

"But they're getting bigger. Soon they'll be the size of coconuts."

"*Não entendo,*" Mara responded with a puzzled grimace. I don't understand.

"Neither do I, but there has to be some explanation.

Can they be some kind of tropical seeds only found here?" Followed by the maid, she began to search through the branches, turning over the leaves to examine their undersides and running her hand over the rough trunk of the tree. "Or is it some weird disease? There's less foliage, you know."

Silently, diligently the women searched for some clue to the mysterious daily harvest in the drawing room. Half turning toward Mara, Julia asked, "Have you asked Zé about this? He *is* a gardener."

"He doesn't like me."

Julia looked sharply at the maid who had turned her full attention to the tree.

"That's nonsense. What gives you that idea?"

Silently, Mara shrugged. Just then, Zé crossed the lawn, rake and clippers in one hand, his walk jaunty, and his bronze body trim and muscular. Zé couldn't afford to dislike Mara, Julia thought irritably. Although Jack was still paying the wages of a couple, sickly Alda had taken a job in a factory and they had hired Mara as her replacement. Julia's annoyance, she realized as she scowled at the tree, was directed at herself; she and Jack needed a crash course in servant management. Absently scanning the tree, she knew she would have to enlist Zé's help herself or, better yet, hire someone from a local nursery.

The phone rang; Julia answered and Mara vanished in the direction of the garden.

"Julia," Gail began, "this should make your day."

"What?" Julia glanced anxiously at her watch, hoping this wouldn't be one of her sister's marathon talk-fests; today she really didn't have the time. Moving to the large Peruvian mirror, Julia hoped that her silk trousers, crocheted blouse and paisley jacket were what a fashion show commentator should wear. Probably not, but she couldn't remember ever actually noticing the announcers, who generate enthusiasm not through their own attire, but through garrulous running monologues during the events.

"I'm sorry, Gail, but could I call you back later? I'm supposed to be the commentator at a fashion show and lunch over in the International School auditorium and I'm running really late."

The event, a benefit for Lar Christina Angelica and Gotas de Esperança, had been organized by Diva and Marilyn on São Paulo's Birthday, a city-wide holiday, and she had been persuaded to participate despite the fact that she had absolutely no experience in the field.

"Fashion commentator? That sounds so un-you, and like so much fun," her sister enthused. "But listen! I called to tell you that Stephanie has a boyfriend. He's a doctor doing his internship at Cook County."

"That's just great." At least one of the girls is on the right track, she thought in relief.

"And Sydney has decided that maybe art school would be more interesting than college and maybe she made the wrong choice."

Nor was this disclosure a bombshell. She now only expected surprises from her younger daughter.

"Does that mean she's planning on dropping out of Santa Cruz?"

"I doubt it. You know Sydney. Want to know what she's currently wearing?"

"No."

"Okay. And I'm thinking of getting married again."

This was a genuine shocker. "You're *what?* To whom?"

"Oh, I haven't got anyone specific in mind. It just seemed like it might be fun to share expenses with someone else."

"You've tried that before and it was a jolly laugh for about two days."

Gail sighed. "Well, I'll let you go now. You're so lucky—you never have to work."

Julia's face tightened with anger and perhaps just a touch of guilt.

"I know you think I have this fabulous, pampered life

in an exotic country but let me remind you that, when I did work, I loved my job. It was a real sacrifice for me to give up my career, friends, volunteering—everything—and come down here. Besides, money from this event goes to the Lar."

"Oh, I know. It's just that after my restorative nap I have to deal with Mona Winters who has added Von in front of the Winters because she heard it denotes nobility and now wants me to research royal wedding gowns. Where do these people come from?"

"Got to go."

"Bye. Love you."

Julia shouted to Mara that she was leaving, snatched her handbag from the wingback chair and ran to the garage. Only when she was halfway to the International School did she realize that she had forgotten her notes. Now she really would have to wing it.

"Fantastic, Julia, just a stupendous job. I can't believe this is the first time you've been a commentator."

Emily Feingold, an American married to a Londoner, had lived in São Paulo for nearly a decade and, during that time, had designed clothes that were then made by her seamstress. Her customers were other ex-pats over the age of thirty, primarily American and British, who didn't want to squeeze into the tight, skimpy Brazilian garments favored by the local population. Emily had sold her popular soft print cotton skirts, gossamer dresses of silk and voile, linen blouses, dressing gowns and batiste nightgowns—never trousers—in a local boutique and the clothes appeared bi-annually in a charity fashion show. Now her husband, Larry Bloom, had been transferred to Poland and this was Emily's professional swan song.

"It was a lot of fun," Julia said truthfully, forgetting her previous tension and anxiety. Now that the show was over, she felt limp with relief. A makeshift boutique consisting of racks of Emily's clothes and a table with two cashiers had been set up at the back of the auditorium and was now engulfed by women in search of garments they had just seen on the runway and were determined to buy.

"I have a tradition," continued Emily, pushing back her dark gray hair, cut in a severe flapper style. "Since I don't pay my commentators, they can pick any item of clothing they want." She smiled. "Go ahead and join the fray before everything's gone."

"Well, thank you. I may do that," she said doubtfully. It was a very generous offer but Julia just couldn't see wading into the tangle of women and joining their genteel battle over the clothes. "I'll probably see you at the dinner later on."

It was the 451st anniversary of the founding of the city of São Paulo, an annual holiday that was celebrated through a frenzy of public and private events. As soon as they could leave, Julia planned to drive to Ibirapuera Park with Marilyn and Laura who were meeting their husbands, Mauricio and Alan, for a few hours of musical and acrobatic performances, flower exhibits, dancing and singing. Unfortunately, Jack had seized on this holiday as a golden opportunity to spend time working in his office, so she would be more or less on her own. Later, there was a Newcomers Club black-tie dinner at Mo's house with food produced by five of the members and their maids. Her husband had promised—*promised*—he would attend this function. For just a moment, jostled by the throng of women clawing at the racks of clothes, the floor seemed to tip beneath her feet and she fought a sudden sick realization; she was no longer important to Jack in any way.

"We're ready when you are."

Laura's voice yanked Julia back to the present. Her eyes lingered on the mass of women grabbing garments and shoving others out of the way, clutching hard-won prizes to their chests, and her mind veered to the favela. There, sewer pipes were magical gifts and anyone with the knowledge and time to teach gardening or first grade reading was a treasure. She was ashamed of her brief wallow in self-pity.

"Then let's go," she said.

"Aren't you going to pick one of Emily's creations?" asked Marilyn.

Julia nodded toward the mob, her hair swinging against one cheek. "Would you be tempted?"

In response, Laura laughed, her straight teeth very white against the weekend tan she'd acquired at the beach near Paraty.

"Not a chance. All else aside, Emily's clothes are great but they're for Henry James women. Not me and you."

Julia scanned her companion's face for any hidden meaning, maybe an allusion to her affair with Max. Not that she had confided in Laura or anyone else; in fact, she had been very discreet, or at least she thought so, meeting her lover at his office behind the church or occasionally in the guest room of her home, but only after Mara had gone for the day. Far from Puritanical in their sexual attitudes and habits, Brazilians nonetheless did not use their homes for adulterous or illicit affairs. Instead, they patronized motels. Charging by the hour, varying in quality from rudimentary to luxurious, the sole purpose of Brazilian motels was to provide a safe place for sexual liaisons. For this very reason, Julia had not suggested that their rendezvous' take place in one of the many hundreds of motels in São Paulo; trysts in those locales would force her to face the reality of their situation. As it was, their assignations were hasty and tense, with ears listening for footsteps or a hand on the doorknob, and eyes on the lookout for a human shadow on the window shade. To her, sex with another woman's husband in these dangerous and forbidden places meant it was clearly and totally wrong, whereas relaxed coupling in a chic motel would indicate that there was a possible future for them. Which certainly was not the case.

Pushing through the crowd of women, Julia followed Laura, wondering why she had never felt guilt. Her mind flashed suddenly to her conversation with Marilyn many months ago. Without naming or describing the woman, Marilyn spoke of a client who was having a torrid affair with a prominent member of the ex-pat community and experienced no guilt or regrets, nothing but pure pleasure and happiness.

"I ruined it all, I'm afraid," Marilyn said, "when I gradually led her to understand that she was happy because she was punishing her husband, getting even with him for neglecting her, even though he knew nothing about the affair."

Had this conversation not taken place long before Max entered the picture, Julia would have suspected Marilyn was analyzing her relationship with the minister.

"This is fantastic," Julia exclaimed as she threaded her way toward a stage that had been set up in Ibiripuera Park. The park was centrally located and home to four museums, one of which was used to house the International Biennal in the years that São Paulo hosted the event. The park was a woodland in a city of twenty-two million people, with huge trees, some of them hundreds of years old, grass, shrubs, and a lake that meandered into a serpentine replete with fish. Ibirapuera also boasted soccer fields, children's playgrounds, wide, paved avenues for bicycling or skating and an outdoor stage where hundreds of thousands heard live music or saw dance performances on Sunday mornings.

Now, it seemed to Julia that the entire city had converged on the park, their attention currently focused on a group of Brazilian musicians. Performing on a stage high above the crowd, their music amplified by a state of the art sound system, the band played Brazilian oldies while hundreds, maybe thousands, sang along. A good many of them, men and women alike, enthusiastically danced a samba alone.

"They all know the words," shouted Julia, the skin around her eyes crinkling as she smiled.

"Yes, they do. In case you haven't noticed, Brazilians love to party," answered Laura.

"Is that an accordion?" Julia asked, staring at a man who was bouncing up and down beside the drummer.

"Isn't it strange? They love that instrument. I don't know how it got to Brazil but I assume it came with the German immigrants, of whom there are many, especially in the Southern part of the country," called Marilyn, her voice barely rising above the song fest.

A moment later, when the sound level of the music lowered, Laura asked, "How's the caseiro situation?"

The women exchanged glances and then began to laugh. Julia shook her head.

"Mara has decided that Zé doesn't like her."

"I've told you before, he's a power-nut, like most men from the *Nordeste*, and I'll bet he's tried to boss her around," said Marilyn, raising both arms in a Charles Atlas stance and glowering into space. "*Muito macho.*"

"We should go over to the Bandeirantes and see if the men are there," shouted Laura.

As they turned away from the stage, there was a sudden commotion nearby and the crowd began moving backward, pushed by uniformed police officers who had formed a flying wedge through the mob. Laura, Julia and Marilyn stood on tiptoe, straining to identify the somberly-suited men who stepped briskly along this cleared pathway.

"It's our favorite senator and his henchmen," announced Laura.

"Which one's the senator?" asked Julia, thinking that they all looked pretty similar.

"The one in the middle doing the gracious wave to the crowd. Always politicking."

"That crook," exclaimed Marilyn in disgust. "He's squirreled away millions in public money in European bank accounts and still he gets the votes."

"He got more votes than any of the other candidates, and most of them came from the favelas."

"I think it's just disgusting."

The tiny procession disappeared from view and the three women again threaded their way through the crowd. The music grew fainter, the throng thinned and Marilyn waved vaguely toward the right.

"The annual Japanese flower sale is set up over by MAM Museum. I'm going there later to buy some orchids for the garden, if I can coax Mauricio to come with me."

"How long does this go on?" asked Julia.

"Until everybody gets tired and goes home, I guess. They have a lot of different bands that are scheduled to play and acrobats and God knows what else. Food, of course, and those carts with the booze. There's some big name singer performing downtown in the Sé—maybe Maria Monte or Daniela Mercury, I don't remember who, but it's way too far to go."

Skirting the lake, they reached the edge of a road which was now closed to traffic and scanned the concrete monument just opposite. Dedicated to the *bandeirantes*, those latter-day adventurers who explored the interior of Brazil and paved the way for settlers, Brecheret's enormous memorial depicted larger-than-life size men on horseback galloping into the future. It was occasionally decoratively embellished for use in campaigns, most notably the one against AIDS, and was frequently climbed by children.

"I don't see Mauricio," said Marilyn.

"He's right across the street with Alan," said Laura. "And Max."

Julia felt her heart jump and then begin to thump as she focused on her lover. Wearing sandals, a tee-shirt and cargo pants, his unrestrained hair falling to his shoulders, Max was speaking animatedly to his companions as they crossed the road. Alan waved and Mauricio glanced at his watch.

"Did you know Max was coming?" Laura asked Julia in an odd tone.

"Of course not," she answered truthfully, "but since everyone else in town is here I don't see why he should stay home."

Marilyn waved to the men as they crossed the street.

"Hello all," said Laura, turning immediately to Max. "Where are Shirley and the kids?"

"They were here a while ago and then my children went off with yours and Shirley had an emergency call from one of the families she counsels and rushed away. So I'm by myself." He lifted his shoulders in a helpless shrug and smiled, his brown eyes hidden behind aviator glasses. He turned to Julia. "Where's Jack?" he asked.

"At his office, of course; I'm just tagging along."

"Okay, I'll join you."

"Mauricio, could we go see the flower exhibit?"

The plastic surgeon, spiffy as ever in a dark designer suit, white shirt and monocle tucked into the breast pocket, frowned severely.

"As I recall, the last time we went to one of those I ended up staggering around for hours with a huge box of plants."

"I'll control myself; just two little orchids."

"I have to get something to eat first. I'm starving," said Max. "How about the rest of you?"

"I was too nervous for food today, so yes, I could go for something," confessed Julia, looking enquiringly at the others. They all shook their heads negatively.

"We'll have a quick bite and then meet you at the exhibit," said Max.

After the other four had disappeared into the crush of people, the minister took Julia's arm and guided her back toward the Bandeirantes Monument. After a few steps, she stopped and pulled free.

"Hey, we're going the wrong way. The food cart is back

there."

"We're going to get in my car and drive to your house. Servants have the holiday off, remember?"

"But Marilyn and Laura expect us to turn up at the flower exhibit," she protested, aware of the flutter of excitement and foreboding in her stomach. Emotionally and intellectually she knew this affair was insane, she was flirting with disaster and there would be no happy ending to their story, but Max was exciting and a wonderful lover. For a moment she stared at him, acutely aware of the muscular body that was enhanced rather than hidden by the snug tee-shirt.

"Where is the car parked?"

After making love, Julia drowsed, her mind dipping in and out of a dream in which Sydney, wearing a bikini with a bridal veil and followed by dozens of masked former boyfriends, discovers her mother in bed with Max, Alan, Mauricio and Jack. Disturbed, Julia jerked herself into full consciousness and looked at her watch, then rolled out of bed.

"Oh, my God, it's nearly six o'clock. Get up, get up, Jack will be here any minute." Worried, she shook her head. "Besides that, we have to get back and find the others."

Sitting up, Max shook his head. "This is Brazil. Nobody will miss us."

Max slid out of bed and snatched clothing from the floor while Julia hastily smoothed the sheets on the guest bed. Silently, she tossed the cotton blanket over the top and then the bedspread, jumping in fright when the phone rang. As Max slipped into his tee-shirt and underpants, she picked up the receiver.

Listening for a few minutes, dazed relief altered the pinched features of her face and Max, observing, automatically slowed the pace of his movements. After hanging up, Julia turned to him, weak with the unexpected reprieve, yet affected by a vague sense of fright. Her life was definitely out of control.

"That was Jack," she said slowly, running the fingers of one hand through her hair. "He says he's at the church with you and won't be home for another half hour."

TWENTY-ONE—SÃO PAULO, BRAZIL

As parties went it was a good one, this Newcomers Club event at Mo's house, and it should have been a wonderful evening for Julia. Jack kept his word and attended with her, replacing the discontented, bored expression that he now wore constantly in her presence with an affable grin the moment they stepped over their hostess' threshold.

"Adilson," he cried, spying a business friend. Stepping aside, the two exchanged manly hugs.

Julia sighed glumly, remembering the disagreeable scene in their bedroom less than an hour ago. How, she wondered, could he undergo such an instantaneous and magical transformation?

"I see you made it, although we missed you at the Flower Show." Julia flushed, hoping Jack wasn't listening, as Marilyn kissed her on both cheeks. With annoyance she recalled Max's glib assurance that their absence would not be noticed.

"I decided to go home and wait for Jack."

"Isn't it amazing how everyone at a party looks like

they're in mourning?" Marilyn continued breezily. "A colorful outfit would be scandalous. And then you go to a Brazilian funeral and they're all wearing jeans or sleeveless yellow dresses or strapless outfits."

Julia was relieved at the change of subject. "I hadn't thought about it but you're right. Women here never wear anything but black to evening events, and yet you see halters and shorts in church."

Cocking her head, Marilyn peered curiously at her friend. "I didn't know you went in for religion."

"Not very often," she amended. "My current favorite religious celebration is one I read about in the college Network News that I got yesterday. It said that, on December 6, they held the annual Festival of Light and Dark on campus to celebrate Solstice, Christmas, Hanukah, Advent, Ramadan, Santa Lucia, the Buddhist Celebration of Life..." she paused, aware that she was babbling but unable and unwilling to stop, "...three more, I think. Oh, now I remember. The Virgin of Guadalupe, Kwanzaa and the end of the semester."

A quick glance in the immediate vicinity apprised her of the fact that Jack had disappeared. Resolutely, she pasted a smile on her face.

Marilyn laughed. "How politically correct!"

"*And* the celebration involved candles, music and the community."

"No chicken blood?"

Julia chuckled and shook her head. "Let's eat." They walked toward the dining area, open to the living room but elevated and separated by three steps.

"I haven't had a chance to ask how the new maid is working out."

Julia clapped her palm to her throat and thrust out her tongue in mock strangulation. Jack vanished from her thoughts.

"You know, I am so sick of this whole domestic servant business. I used to be busy working, playing, running my house and now I mediate between the maid and the caseiro. And his wife who occasionally pops up. When people say 'get a life', I know what they mean."

"I guess things aren't going well."

"You guessed right. I hired Mara because she's a nursing student, even though she takes a lot of time off work for studies and class. I think she's darling and so nice, but as far as Zé is concerned she does not do one thing right. He wants me to fire her and hire Evangelista, the maid next door, and I know that's because he's having an affair with her. And Mara hates Zé because he tried unsuccessfully to seduce her and now just bosses her around."

"And where is Zé's stressed-out wife in all this?" asked Laura who had joined the two.

"She's still working in the less traumatic factory job but living with us."

Laura gazed at her sternly. "Fire everybody and start again.

Julia nodded her head. "You may be right."

They again moved toward the dining area. "This is the first time I've been in Mo's house," Julia said.

"She almost never entertains, but when she does I hear the food is divine." Laura added quickly, "Of course, yours is better."

As they mounted the steps, Julia was surprised to feel her husband slip an arm around her waist and she was stung with melancholy. The special closeness they had shared in Venice had vanished; now they arrived at events together, left together and spoke to almost everyone at a party but one another. Their confrontation earlier in the bedroom, when she demanded the truth about her husband's alleged visit to Max, had somehow become the norm in their relationship rather than an anomaly. Acidly dismissing Jack's flimsy alibi, she said Max had been part of their group at Ibirapuera, and even a man of God couldn't be in two places at once. Jack confessed; it was a lie, he wasn't with the minister at all. Bracing herself to hear the admission that she dreaded, Julia momentarily forgot her own adulterous behavior.

"So where were you?" she insisted waspishly.

"You won't like this," he murmured.

"Go ahead."

"Zé took his motorcycle out and had a minor accident."

She was stunned. "But he doesn't know how to ride."

"Which is why he had the accident. He hadn't registered the motorcycle so he was arrested and I had to get him out of jail. That meant a few bribes here and there plus the registration fee." He smiled boyishly, appealingly. "I should have told you the truth but I really wasn't up to a scene about our caseiro and his irresponsibility, so I said the first thing that popped into my head."

Flooded with relief, Julia had commented, "I'm sorry."

A moment later she was crushed by shame and guilt. What right did she have to question her husband when she was in bed with another man while Jack was dealing with both Zé and the police? Silently, she vowed to break off her relationship with Max, regretting that first trip to the favela. And the worst of it was that she could never apologize for her infidelity because Jack must never know.

Steered by one of Jack's fingers on her spine, Julia ascended the steps into the dining area which was packed with guests, many of them squeezed around the large, oblong table, others waiting in what appeared to be a queue. Standing on tiptoe, Julia surveyed the buffet; she was suddenly very hungry.

Large silver bowls contained chicken xim-xim, shrimp moqueca, shrimp with polenta, bacalhãu, and numerous salads while platters held carne seca in a pumpkin, salmon with fresh palmito, fried squid rings, cold roast pork wrapped in bacon, fresh tuna in a soy sauce and cold sliced roast beef and turkey. A large Murano chandelier hung over the damask-covered table; it, together with a multitude of candles and candelabra arranged throughout the room, provided the room with far too much light.

"She has really gone overboard," breathed Laura at her shoulder.

"Is this the end of the line?" Julia asked a woman to her right. The woman shrugged. "Who knows? I think so."

"We'll say it is," Laura announced, planting herself on Julia's left.

"Hello there," shrilled Celeste in a high soprano. Both Julia and Laura briefly closed their eyes; Jack's arm around Julia tensed. "I just love this commemoration of the founding of São Paulo. It's the most fabulous holiday," she bellowed. "That's why I'm wearing the national colors, in case you haven't noticed."

The three turned toward Celeste, taking in the yellow, light wool suit, blue and green silk print blouse and green felt beret. Julia felt a twinge of combined envy and irritation. Why was it, she wondered, that noisy boring Celeste, who was overweight and not at all attractive, had a wonderful clothes sense? Even when she was in mourning for someone, which was most of the time, she managed to look chic and fashionable.

Julia smiled at her. "Very pretty ensemble you've got on, and a nice change from black," she said.

"Do you think it's too gaudy for church?" she asked. "Because I've just been in São Bento saying a novena for Mauro and Fay Macedo. He's one of the two thousand people being investigated by the government for possible tax evasion."

All three stared at her uncomprehendingly. Heads turned and a few other party-goers drifted toward the group as Celeste continued.

"Mauro?" asked Jack in disbelief.

"He hasn't paid taxes for years. I thought everybody knew that." She was clearly elated to find that apparently no one else was privy to this exciting information. "I told him a long time ago it was very risky to declare no income and have no bank account, but did he listen? No, he just kept right on using only cash from off-shore and now, what a mess. It's like my brother Bucky. I worry about him whenever I find time to think about him. When, *se Deus quiser*, he finally gets off the coke and booze and crack and manages to stay out of the clink, if that ever happens, he'll have lost years' worth of Social Security."

Julia blinked at the change of subject and then turned to Jack. "Did you hear any of that about the Macedos?"

Jack shook his head. "Absolutely not, but even if it's true, I doubt that he'll do any jail time."

"Of course not," interjected Celeste. "Guys who steal millions in this country can pay for innocent verdicts and never go to jail. It's the Brazilian way."

Nearby, a woman nodded in agreement. "That's a fact. Remember that senator from Acre who was the Chief of the Polícia Militar and was also the head of the local assassination squad that killed a couple of hundred people by chain-sawing off their arms and legs before shooting them?"

"His name's Hildegard or Hildebrand or something," commented Celeste, "and he was, or is, the main drug dealer in the state as well. He's never done any jail time."

Where did Celeste get this information, Julia wondered, and when did she have time for her own professional art naïf research? This dirt took a lot of digging.

"A little cash here, a little there," tittered a voice on one side.

"I know a lawyer who hires a *despachante* to go into court records and wipe out any trace of his clients," added Jack.

"You *do*?" said Julia. 'Does he work for your company?' she wanted to ask, but refrained. She suddenly felt very naïve.

Inching forward, they reached a tea cart loaded with porcelain plates. Julia handed one to her husband, then to Laura and Celeste.

"I can't eat any of it," said Celeste. "I prefer clear soups and white meat or poultry."

Julia replaced Celeste's plate on the tea cart and stepped up to the table. Ravenous, Julia scooped rice, chicken xim-xim, fried bananas and salad onto her plate and, followed by Jack and Laura, stepped out onto the terrace. A balmy breeze replaced the stuffy heat of the house; Julia took a deep breath. Edges of the patio, paved with granite tiles that extended from the house to the swimming pool, were outlined with tall, bamboo stakes topped by glowing, conical candle-sticks. Across the expanse of lawn, a thicket of trees had been outlined by candles in brown paper bags and were backed by a tall, brick fence that marked the property boundary. Lawn chairs and tables, all occupied, had been scattered across the grass and terrace and, from a well-lit pool house at the end of the garden, the strains of last year's Carnival music blared forth in competition with a number of strident voices.

Julia looked around quizzically and then shrugged her shoulders.

"I don't see any place to sit."

"Inside, I guess," said Laura.

"No thanks. I'll stand out here."

Marilyn, balancing a glass of wine in one hand and her plate in another, approached, accompanied by a stunning Brazilian woman somewhere in her thirties who wore a very tight, beautifully cut, ebony designer dress. Black again, Julia thought.

"Julia and Jack, I don't think you know Mafra Bernini. She owns the elegant bird and animal hotel, *Rei Rainha e Filhotes* and the pet shop next door on Alameda Cidade Jardim. Between Faria Lima and the bridge."

While kissing Mafra's smooth cheeks and smelling her Bulgari perfume, Julia tried, and failed, to recall seeing anything resembling an animal shop in that neighborhood. It was not an area she knew well, and now that she was pet-free, the care and feeding of domestic livestock was not in her range of interests. All she could think of to say was, "Oh, really?"

Marilyn continued, "Mafra has the most gorgeous cockatoo for sale now and I would love to buy it but Mauricio says no."

Laura leaned forward animatedly.

"I adore cockatoos. I had one when we lived in Australia and it was like a guard dog. They're very loyal, one-person birds that don't need a cage. Ours sat on a chair in the house or on the fence just outside where he observed visitors and expressed either approval or disapproval. And they can carry on conversations."

"I didn't know you lived in Australia," exclaimed Julia, acutely aware that she really didn't know all that much about her friend, even after three years in São Paulo.

"I'm sure I told you. Right after we were married we lived in Brisbane. It was fabulous and we loved it but the company sent Alan for only four years."

"Cockatoos are native to Australia," offered Mafra in slightly accented English. "In my shop, at night the birds all sleep and the dogs bark, but one night I was there for inventory and, after I thought I'd taken out all the dogs, I still heard barking. When I went inside to find the stray that had been left behind, I found that it was the cockatoo, not a dog, making all the noise."

Amused smiles appeared on all the faces.

"How much is the asking price for the bird?" asked Laura.

"Four thousand, eight hundred reais."

"Ouch", grunted Jack.

"That's why Mauricio said no."

"They live to be about eighty," mused Laura. "Tell you what, Marilyn. You and I can buy it jointly and I'll keep it for the first forty years and you can have it for the last."

The others laughed and Marilyn commented, "Oh, great idea." Sobering, she gazed toward the pool house where a small group had gathered around her husband

Mauricio. The plastic surgeon seemed to be examining the skin behind the ears of another man and inviting the others to follow suit.

Baffled, Julia asked, "What're they doing?"

With a resigned sigh, Marilyn explained. "My life-long partner is advertising."

"He's doing what?" Jack asked.

"Moacyr had a face lift and Mauricio is pointing out to the entire world that the scars are almost invisible."

"*Moacyr* had a face lift?" asked Jack, incredulous.

"Amazing, isn't it? He looks just the same to me. Maybe my precious husband should have the prescription of his monocle checked."

Julia was riveted to the group. "But doesn't he mind a mob peering at the back of his head?"

Laura gave a short grunt of mirthless laughter. "Moacyr is so busy talking about himself I'm sure he doesn't notice and, if he does, he just thinks they're adoring acolytes."

Clearly stunned, Jack murmured, "Moacyr is the president of the Banco Marques do Sul, and he has a face lift?"

"This is Brazil, my dear, cosmetic surgery capital of the world, and not only for women."

They were joined by a sudden surge of fellow guests unable to find empty chairs; Celeste's voice boomed from the nearby crowd.

"Guess who just arrived at *this* hour? Max and Shirley, and she's wearing that gold Indian sari outfit with a red dot on her forehead." Julia felt her breath quicken and her muscles tense. Max had told her he wouldn't be at the party because they couldn't get anyone to stay with Stephen, their twelve-year-old. Resolutely, she kept her eyes on her plate, sliding a slice of banana onto her fork. "I think it's just disgraceful for her to dress like a Hindu when her husband's a man of God," Celeste continued.

"You know," Marilyn interrupted quickly in a clear tone, "the media must be desperate for news items other than corrupt politicians. It's not even approaching summer and today I read this article about how, on New Year's Eve, you have to wear the color underpants that match your wishes for the coming year and, if you do, the wishes will come true."

"I read that too," said Mafra with a chortle. "They said the colors are green for hope, blue for health and black for a radical change, so I'm going to wear black all year." A few snickers ran through the crowd.

"Excuse me," said Laura. "I'm going to get some of that divine polenta."

"There's more," said Marilyn. "Orange is energy, rose is love and I think yellow is for money."

"That's for me," called a voice nearby, eliciting more chuckles.

"White is peace," added a woman. "Naturally."

"And red is passion," said Jack softly.

Involuntarily, Julia's head jerked up and she found herself staring into her husband's clear, azure eyes. What was he telling her, she wondered in confusion? Was this a silent confession, an accusation, or a plea to try and recapture the ease, love and camaraderie of their former relationship? Heavy with guilt and feeling suddenly breathless, she moved closer to Jack, her hand reaching for his just as his eyes flicked away from her and focused on the far edge of the lawn. Julia followed his gaze and she was instantly suffused with hot anger. Wearing dark glasses and a short, elegant taffeta ivory dress topped by an unlined black lace coat, Jack's secretary, Eliana, stood on the lawn chatting with Jessie, Mo and Maricarmen. Julia stared venomously at her, hating the woman's perfect figure, her long, carelessly curled brown hair, and the white teeth that managed to flash even at this distance.

And then her eye was drawn to a movement in the shadows of a gigantic tree that sheltered the pool house. For an instant, she couldn't breathe or swallow, her eyes riveted on Laura and Max. The pair might have been engaged in a pleasant social chat, but something in Max's boneless slouch, a stance she knew all too well as one of his forms of flirtation, and Laura's nervous shift from one foot to the other, hands clasped behind her back, suggested otherwise. And then she saw, or thought she saw, Max's hand stray to Laura's hip bone and drop over her buttocks before being thrust into his trouser pocket. Was it a trick of the light, or lack of it, or was she hallucinating, her over-worked guilty conscience attributing her sins to everyone else in a kind of alternative reality? A moment later, the two separated and walked in opposite directions, both melting into the moving mass of guests.

Julia's forehead beaded with perspiration, her knees trembled and her hands felt too weak to support the plate of food that she could no longer eat. Nauseous with undirected anger, she took a deep breath and looked toward Jack, only to see that he too had vanished. She was aware of conversations that rose then fell, laughter that swirled around her and the shifting of bodies as guests moved from one group to another, but she felt as frozen as a block of dry ice. For the first time she looked clearly at her own situation and understood that sneaking around to see Max was not exciting or fun, just cheap and tawdry. Her life had become a mountain of lies, one tumbled onto the other and, unless she extricated herself quickly, there would be no happy end to this story, just an eventual scandal to titillate the bored ex-pat community.

She turned slowly and walked toward the house. It was time to resolve this, but not tonight. Maybe tomorrow...

TWENTY-TWO—SÃO PAULO, BRAZIL

Nervously, Julia studied her image in the hallway mirror, wondering if the long cotton-jersey dress with the slits up the side, the one her friends called an overgrown tee-shirt, was an appropriate garment to wear when ending an affair. Twisting to look at the back of the dress and then staring at her silver and citrine necklace with the matching earrings, she decided that she looked a bit like a schoolteacher. Shaking out a blue paisley silk shawl, she tossed it over one shoulder, slipped on her dark glasses and decided that was better. Although she didn't plan to see Max romantically ever again, she certainly didn't want to leave him thinking that he was lucky to be free of a dowdy frump.

"Senhora! Senhora!" called Mara just as Julia opened the front door.

Always perfect timing, Julia thought sourly. All I have to do is jangle my car keys and the maid appears, urgently needing to discuss her salary, vacation, sick mother, daughter's lack of school books and supplies or a friend/sister/cousin/aunt who is a treasure but out of work and needs employment.

"Yes, what is it?" she asked impatiently as Mara appeared in the hallway. "I'm really in a hurry."

"Dona Julia, I found out what those black balls are under the fichus tree."

"You did?" This was worth a little delay. "What are they?"

"Cocô." Turds.

"Excuse me?" Maybe the word had another, more genteel, meaning in Portuguese.

"Follow me and I'll show you," Mara beckoned, scurrying into the living room.

Julia strode behind her, the shawl billowing like Superman's cape. The two women stopped inches from the tree, now seriously denuded, and the maid pointed to a nearly bare branch a foot or so overhead.

"See?" she crowed triumphantly as the pair stared, mesmerized, at the limb.

Not quite believing her eyes, Julia dragged up a chair and climbed onto the seat. She leaned forward until she was a few inches from the bough in question, staring at a caterpillar at least six inches long, and of a green hue that matched the few surviving leaves. As she watched, the enormous creature inched forward and began to chew on the foliage, excreting a few round balls that plopped onto the polished wooden floor.

How nasty," whispered Julia, horrified by the larva that had been sharing her home and plundering her plant. Shuddering as though chilled, she stared for another moment and then jumped down. Turning to Mara, she saw that the maid was clearly amused. "Get that thing out of the house, *please*," she ordered tersely in Portuguese. "When I come back I want it gone."

Mara's smile faded.

"But how?" Obviously she didn't consider herself hatchet-girl for a worm.

"I don't know," responded Julia in annoyance. "Call Zé, cut off the branch and throw it into the compost pile, flush it down the toilet...you figure it out, but I don't want to see it again. And then spray the tree and give it some bone meal and water."

Disgusted by the discovery of an organism that seemed to belong to the prehistoric era living in the bosom of her family, Julia stepped out of the house wondering if the caterpillar might not hatch into some form of flying dinosaur. It simply was not possible that, even in the tropics, an ordinary butterfly or moth could emerge from that grotesque worm.

Distracted, worrying about the possibility of other giant caterpillars populating her home, she got into her car and drove out of the garage. As she turned the corner, her aversion to the creature faded into general weariness. Her life with Jack was a tangled mess and their domestic help complicated an already poor situation. Not only did she and her husband have to deal with their own problems, they had to solve those of their employees, like the continual Zé-Mara battle of wills and the household items that occasionally vanished. Vera had helped herself generously to some kitchen equipment when she left, but there was nothing Julia could do about that because she didn't even know where the maid had gone. Breakage was another matter. Julia was legally entitled to ask an employee to pay for a broken item but she knew it wasn't possible, on a domestic's salary, to reimburse even the cheapest article. Life had been so much easier in Venice Beach when she did her own housework.

Not until she reached the church and parked the car in the shade of a leafy tree did her mind shift onto the reason for this visit. All thoughts of the caterpillar, and of Zé and Mara, vanished as Julia turned off the engine and sat for a moment staring at the church and gearing up for a confrontation with Max. This affair had initially been exciting, she reflected, sharply reminding herself that a good part of the thrill had been the danger of deceiving Jack without getting caught, as well as the satisfaction of payback for his neglect and possible unfaithfulness. And, when she thought about it honestly, it wasn't entertaining or even steamy, because she knew it was wrong and it made her feel shabby and wicked. This was not the way to deal with her marriage problems, and she was going to end the affair now.

She left the car and began walking down the gravel driveway, her feet crunching noisily upon the stones. There were no vehicles in front of the church, which appeared to be locked. However, as she moved around the side of the building, she saw Max's car parked at the bottom of the incline beside his office. At least he was in, she thought, anxious to put this behind her, yet dreading the approaching scene.

The windows of his office were open, the shades half open and, as she moved toward the door, she imagined that she saw movement inside the room. I hope he's not practicing a sermon or, worse yet, counseling a student, she thought, her resolve beginning to dissipate at the idea of interrupting the minister at work. Nor did she want a church visitor to think she had any connection with Max outside the theater group.

Usually, she simply opened the door, but Max and she had always arranged assignations in advance. Now she hesitated, her hand on the knob, listening intently and hearing nothing from within. Uncertainly, she tapped lightly on the wood and then, in the silence, knocked more insistently. Still there was no response. Her spirits lifted with the knowledge that, although he was obviously somewhere on the premises, she wasn't going to interfere with his job.

With edgy courage, Julia twisted the handle, pushed the door open and walked into the office. After just two steps her mind, muscles and heart froze. She couldn't breathe or believe what she was seeing. The room was not empty, as she had expected, but filled with the presence of Max and Laura, both of them crouched between the desk and the sofa where they couldn't be seen through the window. Both were nude.

For an eternity, no one moved. Julia stared at the pair, her eyes flicking from one figure to the other, as her mind at last began to register what she was witnessing.

"My God," she whispered, as shame rose in her throat. Or maybe it actually was nausea, physical revulsion at the memory of her own disgraceful behavior in this same study now displayed so graphically in the scene before her. The moment of sickness passed and she felt an almost hysterical urge to laugh, followed immediately by anger so enormous that her entire body was suffused with heat. Her front teeth clamped against one another as her jaws ground back and forth and her hands wadded into fists as she once again began to breathe.

"Get up," she commanded, her voice hoarse with rage. Neither of them moved. Julia stepped to the desk and, with a slashing motion, sent Max's papers and books flying across the room. "Did you hear me?" she shouted. "I said get up." The pair remained immobile. Julia picked up the desk lamp and hurled it through the open window where it crashed onto the gravel, shattering the glass. Without pause, she yanked several books from the shelves and threw them after the lamp. Max jumped to his feet which, Julia could now see, were still encased in black socks.

"Stop that," he ordered. "Are you crazy? Those things cost money."

"Am I crazy?" Julia echoed. "I don't think so. And why don't you cover up, Reverend Calhoun?"

Silently, Max picked up his jockey shorts and stepped into them, then pulled on his chinos. Still squatting by the desk, Laura had wiggled into an orange tee-shirt and was attempting, unsuccessfully, to maneuver into her underpants.

"Oh, grow up," Julia said, staring disdainfully at her

friend. "Stand up and put on your clothes."

Max glanced fearfully at the window as Laura rose, her shoulders hunched and her back half turned to Julia as she stepped into her bikini pants and then a short white cotton skirt. Bending down, she peered beneath the desk, then under the sofa and finally retrieved a pair of orange Havianas.

"Have you humped every ex-pat in São Paulo, *Reverend,* telling them all that this is the *only* affair you've ever had? Fed them your favorite heart-warming tale about how you've never before strayed from Shirley's bed?" Julia continued in a loud, angry voice. "Is your work for the Lord that very special attraction that pulls in the ladies, making them feel blessed?"

His face skewed in dismay, Max took a step toward her. "Do not touch me," she warned, picking up a floor lamp. Max moved backward.

"I'm expecting three women from the Education Committee shortly," he whispered.

"Well, congratulations, Reverend Max. You've moved on to a threesome." She glanced around the small office. "Although there's scarcely room in here... Planning to use the church? Perform on the pews, perhaps?" Her voice was scathing.

"Please," he begged softly, with another quick peek at the open window.

Julia turned toward Laura. "My friend," she said sarcastically, her tone a notch higher. "My *good* friend, always warning me away from the man of God, trying to save me, and hinting that you'd heard tales about his womanizing. You were too gutless to just come right out and say he was, for the time being, your property. As I'm sure he has been for every other ex-pat female under the age of seventy."

Laura's face flushed and her eyes flashed in anger. "Hey, wait just a damned minute before you get too self-righteous. You have no room to talk or make any accusations *at all* considering what you've been up to." Glaring at Julia, Laura bent stiffly and snatched her handbag from the sofa.

Julia's face burned. Was Laura just guessing? Or had she, Julia, been the subject of discussion between the two? "Leaving so soon? Please don't do that. I'm on my way out in a few minutes and then you can screw each other into infinity, maybe even entertain the education committee." She turned toward Max. "Your little hobby must be an open community secret. What should have tipped me off were those open windows, the unlocked door, the meetings in public...you *want* everybody to know that you may talk about the Bible and the Lord but you're also a stud!"

Laura's face suddenly paled while Max almost preened. Julia paused, panting in anger, her hands rhythmically clenching and unclenching. She stared at her former lover, taking in the hunched shoulders, the hippy pony tail that was supposed to disguise the sparse hair growing ever thinner, the brown eyes, magnified by rimless glasses, that even now looked at her flirtatiously, the carefully casual chinos and short sleeved check shirt that aimed to belie his profession, and she wondered how she could have ever been attracted to this man. She felt physically dirty.

Abruptly, Laura's face twisted into a rye, mirthless smile of triumph as she tipped her head to one side. "I wouldn't worry about Max and me, if I were you, since the whole town's talking about Jack's affair with what's her name—his secretary, Eliana. I hear they even had a nice little weekend in Bonito, or maybe it was Florianopolis— someplace they thought they wouldn't be seen, but of course they were."

Julia's heart seemed to stop. For a moment she couldn't see or think, couldn't hear for the deafening silence in her ears. Then her mind began to function again and she knew it might be—had to be—Laura's shot in the dark, her attempt to strike and destroy. Well, that wasn't going to happen. Automatically, Julia straightened her spine just a bit more, narrowed her eyes and stared straight at Laura who returned her gaze, hostility crackling between them. Swiveling to include the minister, she snapped, "You make me sick, both of you."

Body stiffly erect, Julia turned and stepped across the threshold, then moved around the corner of the office. Gravel crunched noisily under her feet as she marched up the driveway toward the parking area, her muscles tense and rigid. She felt sharp pains in her chest, her throat was thick and clogged and her brain seemed to ache as she moved woodenly toward her car.

As she moved up the incline, she realized she was furious, not with her former friend and lover, but at herself for being such a fool. How could she have gotten involved with a con-man who had clearly only wanted one more notch on his belt, one more name in his black book?

Three middle-age women wearing jeans, tee-shirts and tennis shoes got out of an SUV, assisted by a driver dressed in a white shirt and dark tie. Chatting companionably, the trio paused to study a nearby bougainvillea in profuse, full bloom, its magenta flowers a splash of vivid, almost obscene, color against the tropical green of the trees and shrubs. One of the women bent to pick up a fallen blossom and then the three again strolled toward Max's office. As they neared Julia, all three fell silent, their faces tightening with concern, and only then did Julia realize that tears were running down her cheeks and marking the front of her carefully chosen dress.

TWENTY-THREE—SÃO PAULO, BRAZIL

*J*ulia floated on her back in the swimming pool and stared at a gossamer cloud that was threading its way across the silver-blue sky. Private pools in Brazil were almost never heated and this one was no exception, but in spite of the chilly water, Julia didn't feel cold. In fact, she felt nothing at all, not the goose-bumps that involuntarily rose on her arms and legs or the sting of the cool breeze as it brushed her wet skin.

"I was such a fool," she confided to the cloud. "And I've made it even worse by holing up like a hermit so that everyone in town wants to know, what's the matter with me? Everyone but Jack, who either doesn't notice or doesn't care."

In response the cloud shredded into lacy particles that were immediately swallowed by a larger, fatter cousin. Julia frowned and closed her eyes, wishing she could give her brain a wash and erase the times she had spent with Max. Not just the memory—the whole experience.

"Senhora, you will get grippe and die in that water," warned Evangelista from one side of the pool. Startled, Julia splashed to an upright position wondering, not for the first time, how her new maid managed to creep silently around the house and garden.

"You don't catch flu from cold water," she responded. "Russians and Eskimos swim in the ocean." She added in a whisper, "At least I think they do." After a prolonged pause, Julia asked impatiently, "Well, what is it?"

"Senhora Coelho is here to see you."

"Dona Marilyn?" No one had come to see her during her two weeks of self-imposed hibernation, although countless messages had been sent from her friends and co-workers at the Lar. Now Julia suffered a moment of panic, wondering if Marilyn knew why she was hiding away and, most of all, what she, Julia, would say to her friend.

"Tell her to come out. And bring us some of that Bolo do São João cake, please." Julia began sloshing through the water toward the pool steps.

"I can't."

"Why not?"

"I didn't make it."

Puzzled, Julia climbed out of the pool and lifted her towel from a chaise lounge. "I thought you did that yesterday."

Evangelista had promised to treat her employers to this special Brazilian cake consisting of fine corn meal and guava paste.

The maid's cheeks turned pink and her shoulders rounded with embarrassment. She glanced furtively at Zé who was pruning a manacá tree some distance away, then moved to Julia's side and whispered something unintelligible. Her forehead gathered in perplexed furrows, Julia looked at the maid and shook her head.

"*Repita, mas mais devagar.*" Tell me again but slower.

Evangelista repeated her message, not once but three times before Julia finally understood. "What?" she barked sharply in English, staring incredulously at the maid who twisted her hands together and gazed steadily at the wall. She couldn't have understood correctly. Unaware that the gardener had become far more interested in this exchange than in his work, Julia switched to Portuguese. "You can't beat eggs or make a cake during your period?"

Still avoiding her employer's eyes, Evangelista nodded and mumbled, "Women can't eat pineapple then, either."

Julia closed her eyes and covered her face with both hands, squeezing down a belly laugh. For a moment it was a frozen tableau; Zé straining to hear the conversation, Evangelista examining the wall with great interest and the lady of the house seemingly in the throes of a deep emotional crisis. Mutely, Julia dropped her hands and, without looking at the maid, picked up a tee shirt she had left on the chaise lounge. Slipping it over her head, she slid her feet into a pair of havianas.

"Tell Sehora Coelho to join me, and bring us a bottle of white wine from the fridge, if you're allowed to do that during your period."

"*Sim, Senhora*", Evangelista whispered, scuttling quickly toward the house.

"I let myself in," Marilyn announced cheerfully, walking across the lawn. "Who is that?" she asked, nodding toward the retreating maid.

The two friends exchanged obligatory kisses on both cheeks and Julia gestured toward chairs shaded by a beach umbrella.

"I'm so glad to see you," Julia said, realizing that it was true and in that moment understanding just how much she had missed her friends. She was definitely not cut out for the life of a recluse. "Let's sit."

Settling onto one of the chairs, Julia reached for her towel and vigorously dried her hair, then smoothed the damp, shoulder-length strands away from her face.

"That's my new maid, Mara's replacement."

"New maid? What happened to the old one?"

"She and Zé had one fight too many and she quit. On the spot, but I think she'd been planning it for a while because she walked into another job the next day."

"Ah..."

"Although they both deny it, I know that Zé and this new one are having an affair, even though Alda still lives here." Seeing Marilyn's blank face, Julia prompted, "Remember Zé's wife Alda?"

Pursing her lips, Marilyn slowly shook her head. "Vaguely, although I'd rather not."

Julia smiled then laughed aloud. "You won't believe what Evangelista just told me." Leaning forward, her forearms pressed against the metal patio table, she repeated the maid's statements in a tone of incredulity. "And she actually believes it!"

Taking a deep breath, Julia slumped against the back of the chair, her lips now curved in an easy smile. It had been, she suddenly realized, a very long time since she had found anything amusing.

Marilyn chuckled. "Of course she believes it, and probably a lot more incredibly absurd nonsense. But you have to remember how poor public education is in this country. Can she read and write?"

"She thinks she can write, but I can't understand the messages she leaves."

"Well, there you go. She's functionally illiterate and her information comes from old wives tales learned at Granny's knee and from the television, which is not much more enlightening. Maids don't usually watch Discovery Channel."

Evangelista emerged from the house carrying a tray with two glasses, a bottle of wine and the opener. No one spoke while the maid carefully placed the tray in front of Julia.

"*Obrigada*," Julia said in her normal tone of voice. Silently, the maid retreated to the house while Julia reached for the bottle and opener.

"Now, why haven't we seen either you or Laura? We've missed you both at Newcomers Club. The Lar is not happy that you've vanished and the theater group doesn't know what to think. Have you and Laura had some kind of falling out again? Or is there a problem with Jack?"

For a moment Julia was tempted to tell Marilyn everything; after all, her friend was a therapist. Therapists were like doctors or priests when it came to keeping secrets, and besides that she would certainly have some kind of objective advice to offer. Almost immediately, the desire to spill every bean was smothered when she realized that she and Marilyn were just friends, not client and therapist. She could feel her muscles tense as she mentally sifted through the lies and half-truths she could tell.

Her face hidden as she pulled the cork, Julia responded, "I've had to sort out the maid problem. And you're right; Jack and I haven't been getting along too well." She lifted her shoulders in a quick shrug. "I just felt like holing up for a while." It was all completely true.

Marilyn frowned in concern. "Are your daughters okay?"

Mercifully, both seemed to be doing a lot better than she. Concentrating on the wine, Julia carefully poured the chilled liquid into the two glasses and offered one to her guest. "They're fine."

"Is your sister coming to visit? I know that always makes you nervous," Marilyn prodded.

Thankfully, Julia grasped the life jacket her friend was offering. "Yes, she is. I think we'll go to the beach for a few days."

What was one more lie when her whole life was composed of them? But the minute Marilyn had left, she'd get on the phone to Gail and invite her for a visit. Even though her sister was flakey, she was also bright, even occasionally experiencing sparks of insight, and Julia could confide in her without worrying about shocked, judgmental proclamations or a rush to break the news to the world.

The women lifted their glasses in a silent toast, and Marilyn took a sip before speaking. "You shouldn't agonize over Gail's visit. I know she's a little...unpredictable, which probably brings on anxiety attacks, but I can tell you that we all think she's fun and amusing and a whole lot different than most ex-pats." Placing her glass on the table, she studied Julia carefully. "Sometimes this group gets a little ingrown. I know that it can be overwhelming at times."

Julia smiled, wondering if her friend was making a veiled observation or simple chit-chat and decided she couldn't worry about everything, certainly not about Marilyn's possible hidden meanings.

"When is she coming?"

"I'm not sure. I have to call her."

"Well, let me know. I'd love to have a dinner party for her."

Julia began to chuckle. "You'd better child-proof the bathroom first."

Both women laughed, leaned toward one another over the table and clinked glasses. Julia felt better than she had in weeks, possibly since she began her affair with the minister.

"I just love coming to visit. All these parties," Gail enthused as she unpacked an enormous suitcase, tossing underwear, tee-shirts and socks casually into an open drawer while hanging other garments haphazardly on padded hangers.

Determined not to interfere by folding and arranging her sister's clothes more carefully, Julia slouched on a wingback chair and watched. How, she wondered as she had for the past forty years, did Gail manage to always look perfectly groomed, pressed and elegant when she showed no respect for her clothes at all, chucking them indifferently into and onto any available space, including the occasional table? As children, their father had inspected their bedrooms armed with a basket, picking up stray garments from the floor and depositing them in the basket, promising to return the confiscated items when the girls showed signs of neatness. Julia had been a quick learner but Gail didn't seem to care. For years, Julia had thought her sister was rebelling but lately she had changed her mind. Gail simply operated with a different set of values and often the things that were important to others—like tidiness or the eternity of marital vows—simply didn't have a place in her life.

"There are a lot of parties, which gets tiresome pretty fast, but this may be different," Julia said, as Gail rooted about in her cosmetic kit with increasing frenzy. "Kathleen and Randolph Lamb are sort of back together and at a raffle for charity at the Anglican Church they won a weekend in the Presidential Suite of the Meliá Hotel. They decided to invite everybody they knew, along with some perfect strangers, for a black tie cocktail event in the salon of the suite."

Gail looked up with sudden interest. "Isn't she the one who ran off with the boyfriend she met on the Internet? I seem to recall that she planned to marry the guy, and then he dumped her and she came back here.

"That's her."

"I thought her husband wouldn't have her back."

"He changed his mind, but rumor has it that he now has a girlfriend on the side."

"Maybe I can help him with his wedding plans." Gail once again scrabbled about in her cosmetic case, her forehead creased in a frown of worry.

"I wouldn't bet on it. He *is* living with Kathleen." Julia thought briefly of her own botched marriage and decided that she wouldn't bet on any relationship.

Gail straightened and dramatically passed one palm across her forehead.

"I forgot my hair dye."

"Why do you need hair dye?" Casually appraising her sister's silver-blond coiffure, Julia couldn't see the reason for Gail's concern.

"My roots. My *roots*!"

"I don't see any roots."

"Of course not. You're clear across the room. Come here and *look*," Gail cried.

Catching sight of her first gray strand somewhere around thirty years of age, Gail had spent a short time bewailing her advancing age and then had begun to dye her hair. Since she was naturally a dirty blond with increasing gray, her roots, when they showed at all, seemed to blend into the bottled platinum. At least, that's the way it looked to Julia.

With a resigned sigh, she crossed the room and the two women studied Gail's scalp, Julia sifting through the hair with her fingers while Gail followed her progress in a hand-held magnifying mirror. "It hardly shows, Gail."

"But it does show." Straightening, Gail threw the mirror on the bed and faced her sister. "I have to find some hair dye or I can't go anywhere."

Julia felt the irritation that her sister always managed to generate. "That's not very considerate. I promised Kathleen we'd be there tonight, and tomorrow we're going to Ilha Bela, to a luxury hotel just like you asked."

"Not with this hair."

"Oh, for God's sake, then I'll call Daniel and get you an appointment this afternoon."

"I don't know Daniel and he's not familiar with my hair.

"He's a *hairdresser*. It's his business to be familiar with all kinds of hair." Julia wanted to reach out and sharply yank the carefully coiled, platinum locks that were causing so much trouble.

"Don't they sell dye here?"

For a moment Julia wondered if her happiness in having her sister as a houseguest wasn't perhaps because

Gail really did push any other problems into the background. Sometimes they even disappeared, although that hadn't yet happened on this visit. Julia stood up, knowing she should have been prepared to chase after items that her sister had forgotten.

"Let's go right now and pick some up. While we're out, is there anything else essential that's been left behind?"

Julia leafed through an issue of *Veja*, the weekly São Paulo magazine read by every literate person in the city, trying to concentrate on the listings of current museum exhibitions. There was a sudden crash in the guest bathroom followed by a wail. Tossing the magazine onto a table, she walked quickly into the hall, stopping in front of the bathroom door.

"Gail, what's going on in there?"

The door flew open and Julia confronted her tearful sister whose face was smeared with touches of the same thick, purple dye that plastered most of her hair to the top of her head in a moist, glistening pile. Gail's hands were black and the yellow bath towel in which she had wrapped her body was streaked with ebony.

"Just look," Gail said in a tone that bordered on hysteria as she gestured to the room.

Speechless, Julia stared at the olive-green marble tiles that covered the floor and walls, the ivory ceiling, the circular crocheted rug, one of the two hand-painted basins, and the primly folded lemon-hued bath set alongside the embroidered hand towels. All were spattered with the same deep violet-black color that shone on Gail's head. Lodged behind the toilet, the plastic dye bottle dripped the remains of its contents onto the floor.

"My God, what happened?" Julia breathed.

"I don't know," she moaned. "I have so *much* hair that I decided to use that second bottle, and then I remembered I hadn't put cream on my face and the dye was dribbling down onto my skin. So I was trying to unscrew the face cream jar with one hand and shake the dye with the other and I noticed my fingers were black and I got so nervous that the bottle just flew out of my hands."

Julia shook her head. "Why weren't you wearing the rubber gloves that came in the package?" The question, she knew the moment she spoke, was quite beside the point in view of the chaos in the bathroom.

"I forgot."

My problems don't vanish when Gail is around, Julia realized—they're just diminished by new, overwhelming emergencies that appear.

"Get into the shower and wash that stuff out, then we'll rub cream into your skin. I'll have Evangelista come clean up."

"Who?"

"The maid," she snapped.

"Another one? You must have hired half the domestics in São Paulo. You don't have to use that tone with me and anyway, the half hour isn't up yet."

"What half hour?"

"I have to leave this on my hair for half an hour."

Trying to tamp down her anger, Julia stepped gingerly across the floor and opened the jar of skin cream. "While you're waiting, rub this on your skin. You won't mind if Evangelista comes in to clean, will you?"

"I'm really so sorry. The bottle just seemed to fly away."

"You have a serious problem with bathrooms."

Forty minutes later, Gail appeared in the service area where Julia was trying to convince the maid that, although Brazilians never washed garments in anything other than cold water, it might be a good idea to try hot on the dye-streaked towels.

"Look!" Gail cried. "Just look at this!" She pointed to her light brown hair with a hand that now looked slightly dirty. "Now it's your color, and I still have roots."

Julia had had enough. "You've got two choices," she

replied tartly. "Leave it as it is, or we go to Daniel."

As the sisters entered the elegant *Daniel & Marcelo* salon, the hairdresser rose from a leather sofa to greet them. Wearing Dolce & Gabbana signature loafers, snug leather trousers and a leather jacket partially unzipped from both top and bottom over his black tee-shirt, Daniel was the portrait of chic. His eyes hidden behind tinted glasses, his hair short and his goatee perfectly trimmed, he raised both hands in horror at the sight of his client's sister.

"*Aieee, que cabelo feio,*" he cried, patting his chest rapidly with one hand. "*Meu Deus! Meu coração.*"

"What's the matter with him?" asked Gail.

Julia thought it better not to tell her sister that Daniel had cried 'what ugly hair' followed by a dramatic appeal to God to help his failing heart. Since she had explained the problem when she made the appointment, the sight of Gail's tresses should not have been a total surprise to the hairdresser, and anyway Gail didn't look all that bad. Granted, the hair color wasn't nearly as glamorous as usual. And the roots were still showing.

"Nothing really, he's just being dramatic. Ignore him and he'll calm down."

Which he did, striking a matador pose as he snapped his fingers for Marialisa, his drudge for all work, to attend to Gail's hair.

"I *love* thespians," Gail burbled as she and Marialisa headed toward the washbasins. Julia's face crinkled in pained amusement.

Slipping onto the chair next to Daniel's station, Julia again flipped through *Veja* while Daniel preened in the mirror, observing himself from all angles and adjusting the zipper of his jacket a fraction of a centimeter. Julia lifted her eyes to the mirror.

"Can you see through those glasses?" she asked in Portuguese.

The salon owner lifted both hands and allowed them to

float outward from the wrists. "Of course," he responded. "They're Prada. To go with my bag." Picking up a large handbag emblazoned with the designer's name, he tossed it over one shoulder and strutted the length of the salon and back, to muted applause from clients and operators. Julia sighed and turned a page of her magazine, relieved when Gail returned and settled onto the adjacent chair. Her sister's spirits had been magically transformed.

"I have total confidence in this salon," she declared cheerfully. "It's so chic and elegant and everyone speaks a foreign language. Very refined..."

"They're all speaking Portuguese, Gail, and it's not foreign to them."

"It's very romantic."

Daniel bent to his work, delicately separating and raising strands of Gail's hair, leaning first to one side and then the other, studying the offending tresses from every angle. With one finger he gently tipped his client's chin back and stared at the loathsome roots while Gail rolled her eyes toward her sister.

"Could I ask you something?" asked Gail.

"I imagine you're going to do that no matter what."

"You seem sort of depressed." Gail's smooth forehead was creased with concern. "If it's because of the bathroom, I'm really, really sorry about that and you know I'll replace or repair anything I wrecked, like the tiles or the towels or anything."

When she thought about it later, Julia could not fathom why she blurted out in *Daniel & Marcelo*'s domain the secret she had planned to share in the strictest privacy. Maybe she was caught off balance by her sister's kind offer and her obvious anxiety over the ruined bathroom, or swayed by Gail's eternal optimism in the face of any and all disasters, or perhaps the busy clients and operators who spoke no English made the airy salon seem particularly safe—whatever the reason, she answered without hesitation.

"It's not the bathroom. I've been having an affair...with a married minister who has several children and a faithful wife."

Gail's hair slipped from Daniel's fingers as he, Marialisa and Gail stared at Julia. After a brief, heavy silence, Gail smiled contentedly.

"How wonderful! At last you've joined the rest of us who make mistakes and have to clean up the mess."

"Mess?" questioned Daniel indignantly in English. "I would like an affair with a minister."

"Me too," said Marialisa.

Julia was horrified as she watched Marialisa scurry away to share the glad tiding with the others in the salon.

"I thought you didn't speak English," she said accusingly.

The hairdresser adjusted his dark glasses, inspected the zipper of his jacket and lifted a wad of Gail's hair. "Marialisa and I are learning."

Have learned, Julia corrected mentally.

TWENTY-FOUR—ILHA BELA

Heading toward Ilha Bela, an island where she and Gail planned to spend three or four days, Julia drove at a leisurely pace along the southern coastline of Brazil, the two lane road occasionally winding and hilly, the frequent view of beaches and ocean spectacular. Hills on the left were covered with *mata atlantica*, thick jungle vegetation that was disappearing at an alarming rate to make way for condominiums and pousadas. Dozens of islands showing no sign of human habitation were visible just offshore, their lush green hues shading into deep blue. Julia swung around a curve and immediately pressed the brake pedal.

"What's going on?" asked Gail, sitting forward.

"It's a blitz, I guess, where the state cops check the papers and driver's license of everyone who comes through."

Off the highway, partially hidden in the shrubbery, they could see a police car and two officers, one leaning against the door. A third, standing on the edge of the road, flagged them down. Julia pulled onto the dirt shoulder and stopped. One of the policemen wearing jack boots to the knee, a belted khaki uniform and a captain's hat, stepped around the front of her car. His gun was clearly in evidence.

"They look like storm troopers," whispered Gail.

"They probably were, not so long ago." Julia rolled down her window and looked at the officer.

"Papers, please," he demanded.

In silence, she handed him her driver's license, followed by a sheaf of papers related to the car, all of which he studied meticulously. After a moment, he looked at Julia and then back at her driver's license and the papers. Finally, reluctantly, he handed the papers to Julia and waved her on.

As she drove slowly and carefully away, Gail turned toward her sister: "He wasn't very happy."

"He was hoping to find a missing paper so that we would have to pay a bribe or have the car impounded."

"That would never happen in the States," Gail stated firmly.

"That's right."

Lights flashed behind them and, when she lifted her eyes to the rear view mirror, Julia saw a car closely tailgating. A few minutes later, the vehicle hurtled around them on a curve then swung back into the right hand lane just as an oncoming truck lumbered around the bend. Gail flopped back against the seat, one arm dramatically covering her eyes.

"God, this country!" she exclaimed

"I just love our hotel. Remember the one with the homemade stairs and leaky windows?" queried Gail.

Julia smiled. She recalled every one of her sister's visits with vivid clarity.

Eyes closed in contentment, Gail flopped onto the hammock that hung at one end of the balcony and immediately rolled onto the floor. Julia stopped unpacking and glanced briefly at her sister, now crawling on all fours under the hammock.

"It's not a mattress, Gail. Sit down carefully, with your feet on the floor, then pull the sides out with your hands and lie down."

"There's always some trick to everything in Brazil," Gail grumbled shortly, standing up and brushing off her yellow linen shorts and adjusting her halter top. Tentatively, she stretched out on the hammock, then dangled one foot over the side and kicked it against the floor. The hammock began to swing gently from side to side. Relaxed, she pulled up the sides of the canvas, concealing all but her calf and a few strands of blond hair from sight.

"I just can't get over that cop." Gail's voice was muffled.

Julia closed the empty suitcase and stored it against the wall, then stepped out onto the veranda where Gail was now batting at the folds of the hammock, struggling to sit up without falling out, and moved to the railing. The view gave no hint that the hillside pousada, with only six rooms and a magnificent restaurant, was located within the island's only town. A lush growth of magenta bougainvillea wound around the balconies and pillars of the building, framing the sight of the beach umbrellas, tables and chaise-lounges grouped around a blue, rectangular pool just below. Beyond the wooden deck, trees, tangled shrubs and undergrowth, accentuated by occasional coconut palms, spread over the hillside, an emerald carpet ending in the azure sea and the darker blue of the mainland not far away. Although she could see no other signs of civilization, sounds of traffic from the island's sole paved road, competing strains of samba music and sporadic shouts rose clearly up the hillside. She was joined by Gail who looked at her intently.

"Should I start smoking?" she asked.

Julia's face mirrored the bewilderment she felt. "Why?

Everybody else is quitting, or at least trying to."

"That's just the point. I'd be the only one in my crowd with one of those long, thin cigars." She paused thoughtfully. "I've been looking at old movies recently and the stars all smoked and looked so glamorous and sophisticated." She plucked a twig from the nearby window box, held it between her fingers and, with head back and one hand on her hip, pantomimed a theatrical inhale and exhale.

"They're all dead too, most of them of lung cancer," said Julia.

Gail tossed the stem away, fluffed her platinum hair and stretched, standing on tip-toes in her chartreuse polka-dot cork wedgies. "You may be right," she declared absently, transfixed by the view.

"I thought you were going to ask Mary Beth to come down too."

"I did, but she can't get away."

Slowly, Gail extended both hands and gestured sweepingly toward the sea. "This is so perfect for a wedding. I'm going to persuade that snotty bitch Marion Campbell to have her daughter's wedding here. She and that old husband she drags around have nagged mercilessly for nuptials on a grand scale equal to their nouveau-riche position in Beverly Hills. This could be it. I'm sure they would love to marry off their mousey Judy-Ann here, since the island was a clandestine landing place for slaves and the headquarters of that sly old pirate, Thomas Cavendish."

She looked at her sister in amazement. "How do you know about the slaves and Cavendish?" Julia asked.

"While having my refreshing swing in the hammock, I read the brochure I picked up at the desk. I am not just a blond fluff, you know." She paused, gazing into the distance. "Daniel *did* do the most fantastic trim and coloring job. Maybe I'll have him do my hair regularly." Julia's expression altered to one of acute alarm at the thought of monthly visits from Gail, who now picked up the brochure and waved it vaguely toward the water. "In this English language publication, I also discovered that the canal we crossed in that rickety ferry is one of the deepest in the world," she announced. Closing her eyes, she placed a sheltering hand lightly over the lids while tilting her face to the sun. "I think Judy-Ann and that nitwit Marvin Keane she's engaged to should be married in one of the pirate caves."

Clasping her hands together under her chin, Gail's eyelids flipped open and she smiled angelically, her white-gold hair floating around her head like a moveable halo. "Bertie Campbell may live in Beverly Hills now but he's a recent arrival from Cerritos where he was a semi-legal bandit operating a poker parlor and had illegal immigrants working for him for slave wages. This would be so suitable."

Julia shook her head. "It won't work."

"Why not?" Gail asked.

"The caves are all on the other side of the island and there's just one very bad access road. You have to have a jeep and a guide, so they're virtually inaccessible."

"Then we'll go by boat. It's much more romantic."

"That's open sea. You'd lose them overboard before they ever landed."

Gail smiled broadly, "Not a bad idea if I can get payment in advance."

Julia looked at her watch. "We're going to lose our guide if we don't step on it."

Gail darted into the apartment. "And miss our hike to the waterfalls? After all, hiking is why we're here."

The afternoon was a huge success, at least as far as Gail was concerned. Eighty-five percent of Ilha Bela was a State Park, covered with thick forest and undergrowth and boasting nearly three hundred waterfalls. Their guide, Geraldo, was a tanned, stunningly handsome surfer type, much too young for the sisters, and quite shameless in his blatant flirtation with them both. He arrived in a green jeep decorated with bird decals and swept them, at high speed, along the island's only paved road and then onto a dirt trail where he parked.

"Now we walk," he announced in Portuguese, immediately striding ahead and disappearing into the forest.

"Isn't this fun!" cried Gail, slipping nimbly down a narrow path made muddy by the rain forest and scooting quickly out of sight behind Geraldo.

Trudging along behind, stumbling over concealed roots and grasping slender branches for support, Julia learned the meaning of martyr. Never an athlete, she found this 'walk' grueling and reminded herself repeatedly that this was a sacrifice for her sister who, along with the guide, seemed to have forgotten about her. The path was indistinct, sometimes obscured by rocks, undergrowth and mud, and her sense of righteous suffering dissolved into apprehension. Frequently the trail seemed to diverge; what if she had taken the wrong turn and was lost forever in the outback of Ilha Bela? Her mind focused on Stephanie and Sydney, concentrating on their college achievements, winning personalities, good looks—anything to avoid panic at her plight.

Sweat sheeted down her face and body, gumming her hair to her scalp and plastering her tee-shirt and shorts to her body. Clearly immune to the thick coating of insect repellent covering her skin, mosquitoes clung to her exposed flesh, only soaring lazily away when bloated with blood.

For some time she had been subconsciously aware of a noise that now became louder, and as she lurched around a thicket of trees with wicked thorns and vines hanging almost to the ground, she realized it was the sound of running water. Seconds later, she saw a waterfall tumbling over vertical layers of rocks, a froth of spume rising from the transparent pool below as the water struck. Her somber mood lightened as she realized she was no longer lost but could follow the stream to the ocean and, hopefully, civilization. Swiping at a cobweb adhering to her throat, she stepped out of the tangled vegetation and saw Gail and Geraldo swimming in the pool. How fortunate, she thought, that she'd insisted they wear swim suits under their shorts and tee-shirts; otherwise, her sister would most probably be splashing about in her underwear...or her birthday suit. Gail waved happily.

"Come on in, slowpoke," she called. "The water's great."

Slowpoke? Julia wondered. *I'm lucky I got here at all.*

Peeling off her outer garments, she jumped into the pool. For a moment her heart stopped and her breath caught in her throat as the icy water closed around her overheated body. Is my sister, who abandons me for an athletic adventure, worth this torture, she wondered, swimming wildly to warm her chilled skin? After a few minutes she stopped, panting and out of breath, and watched Geraldo emerge from the pool and adjust his testicles.

"Ugh", said Gail, averting her eyes. "It's bad enough that he wears Speedos, but that's nasty. And embarrassing!"

Her body temperature now almost normal in the frigid water, Julia's humor had been restored. "They all do that. It's a Brazilian thing and so are the Speedos, which are called sungas here, by the way."

"Zunga? As in Zunga Din?"

"Funny."

"*Vamos la,*" called Geraldo, pulling an orange tee shirt over his head and flexing his biceps.

"What's he want?" asked Gail, her silvery hair now pulled into a sodden ponytail.

"He says it's time to go."

They followed a difficult hiking trail and, four hours after leaving the jeep, they arrived at Praia do Bonete, their goal. Covered with sweat and mosquito bites, their attention was divided among the nearby fishing village, the spectacular beach and their own red welts.

"This is gorgeous, and the little village is so quaint, just like in a tour book," said Gail. "And look, Julia, there's a tiny river."

"Probably a lot of them since there are something like three hundred waterfalls on the island," her sister replied, examining her exposed skin.

Geraldo lowered one long-lashed eyelid in a sly and sexy wink that only slipped into comedy because he was trying to include both women.

"He thinks he'll get a big tip," said Gail, dousing herself with more repellent.

"He's just being Brazilian, like adjusting his balls and wearing a sunga."

Gail gazed surreptitiously at Geraldo, who smiled and flexed his abdominal muscles again. Enough, Julia thought, and hired a boat for the return trip.

"What a fantastic afternoon," crowed Gail happily, stripping off her clothes in their room and flinging them to the floor. Yes, it was an extraordinary day, Julia agreed, as she slouched on the hammock and wondered if she would ever walk again.

Gail stepped into the bathroom. "Julia," she called a moment later. "What's a garden hose doing in the john?"

Now what, Julia thought, creeping stiffly to the bathroom door. Her sister was examining the douchette, a thin articulated metal hose next to the toilet that had replaced the old-fashioned bidet in most hotels and many homes.

"You use it to clean your bottom instead of using a bidet. I don't like them very much, but what can you do?" She shrugged indifferently and turned back into the room as Gail closed the bathroom door. Several minutes later there was a sharp shriek.

"Oh no, it's the bathroom syndrome again," groaned

Julia, limping across the room and throwing open the closed door. Her naked sister was hopping around the white marble floor, the douchette coiled near the toilet that seemed to be making weak, coughing sounds.

"Just look." Gail pointed toward the douchette.

Relieved that her sister was unhurt and dramatizing again, Julia was nevertheless baffled. "What's the problem?"

"I thought it would be fun to test the garden hose," she said, plucking a towel from the rack and wrapping it around her body. "So I sprayed it into the john and the water was boiling hot. What if that had been my butt?"

"Gail, this is only hooked up to cold water. Look, I'll show you."

Grasping the hose, she aimed the nozzle at the toilet, an appliance that was having its own difficulties as little waves of heaving, gurgling water jounced about in the bowl. Julia pressed the release button and a jet of scalding water hit the toilet, raising a cloud of steam and creating a small tsunami in the bowl. Alarmed, Julia released the hose as Gail added, "And the toilet doesn't work either."

As they dined that night in the expensive, elegant hotel restaurant, maintenance workers toiled in their bathroom, managing to repair the toilet and douchette. The water in the latter apparatus was blessedly cold but so was all the bathroom water. In addition, whenever they turned on the tap in the basin or the shower or flushed the toilet, the douchette was activated and sprayed the room. By the time they had showered and were ready for breakfast, water was an inch deep in the bathroom and both women had decided to dress in bathing suits—now wet—and shower caps, whenever they had to use the bathroom.

"What's *wrong* with these people?" complained Gail. "Can't they even manage simple plumbing?"

"Not really. Tradesmen don't have any formal training or certification—they learn by trial and error."

"On other people's property..."

"Exactly!"

Julia remembered having the same indignant reaction nearly four years ago when she arrived in Brazil. And then, at some point she'd begun to accept hit or miss workmanship as normal. "Our guide is probably waiting," she said.

Wearing a sport shirt with an American flag printed on the front and "I love Newark" on the back, Geraldo greeted them with effusive kisses on both cheeks.

"I love America," he announced in English, grinning and gunning the jeep's engine.

"He speaks English?" asked an astounded Gail.

"I don't think so. Probably he figured out our nationality and has that big tip you mentioned in mind."

Peeling rubber, the vehicle sped wildly down the paved street, dodging pedestrians and honking at dogs.

"He'd better remember that dead clients can't pay," cautioned Gail, clinging to the side of the jeep.

"He's just showing off. Brazilian men think they're undiscovered race drivers and the public streets are their practice areas."

"I've noticed that."

On two wheels, Geraldo turned onto the only road that connected the two sides of the island and they bounced eleven kilometers to the gatekeeper of the Ilhabela State Park. There they left the jeep and hiked to Agua Branca waterfall, stopping at five crystalline pools for a swim. Along the way, Geraldo surprised them both by pointing out a variety of birds, identifying them all and giving information about the species.

"So he's not just a pretty face," commented Julia as she translated for her sister.

"Maybe he figured his muscles and a teeny weeny gunga din weren't enough for a tip."

"Sunga," Julia corrected. Her sister could be right.

Sitting on large boulders beside one of the pools, shaded by the surrounding thick mata, they ate a lunch of cold artichokes stuffed with crab salad, eggs in aspic, marinated mushrooms in white wine, palmito wrapped in prosciutto, slices of fresh mangas and French apple tarts that had been prepared by the hotel and packed in a specially constructed thermal backpack. Geraldo, muscles rippling, had toted their feast without effort.

"I wish the hotel was as good at plumbing as they are in the kitchen," commented Gail. "How much is this lunch costing us?"

"A bomb," Julia answered, determined to finish every bit of the astronomically expensive fare. Delicately, she speared a mushroom with a colored toothpick. Unbidden, the image of Max invaded her mind, his chair tilted slightly against the wall, eyes soft and appealing behind the rimless glasses, beard and ponytail glinting red in a shaft of sunlight. Ruthlessly she banished her former lover from her thoughts.

Gail looked at their guide, who was sitting on a rock some distance away and eating his own lunch from what appeared to be a tin bowl. "What's he eating?" she asked, straining for a better view. "And why the funny pot?"

Popping the mushroom into her mouth, Julia slipped two palmitos onto the porcelain plate and then glanced at Geraldo.

"I can't really tell, but I'd bet it's rice, beans and either chicken or beef. And that pot is the bottom half of a workman's lunch pail—he had it clamped onto our backpack." Her gaze shifted to her sister. "You'd better focus on our lunch, not his. We're paying through the nose for this and we're going to clean our plates."

Later that afternoon, Geraldo whisked them at high speed to the hotel where, bestowing a lingering, meaningful gaze first on one and then the other, he gallantly helped them from the Jeep. With a bow, he warned the sisters that he would arrive at nine o'clock the next morning, their last day on Ilha Bela, for a boat trip along the beaches on the mainland side of the island.

Amused, they watched him lay a strip of rubber as he peeled away from the hotel and disappeared down the hill.

"He can't decide who's going to cough up the tip."

"Let's see what's new in the bathroom."

They climbed up the stone steps to the hotel and into the hotel lobby, cool and elegant with bamboo furniture, plants and a fabulous view of the channel and mainland beyond. As they approached the desk, the male clerk drew their key and a slip of paper from a compartment.

"This telephone message arrived about an hour ago," he stated in a neutral voice. "She said it was urgent."

Julia's stomach knotted in a cramp of premonition. Her fingers felt thick and unwieldy as she unfolded the pristine paper and stared at the name and number. Frowning, she looked at Gail.

"It's Marilyn. What do you think she wants?"

Gail lifted her eyes, their size and color enhanced by skillful eye shadow and a few false lashes, to the ceiling and splayed her hands in a dramatic gesture. "How should I know? Why don't you call and find out?"

Hurrying to their room, Julia dialed Marilyn's number on the hotel telephone. Her breath was rapid as she clutched the phone and listened to the rings, her thoughts skittering fearfully from one possibility to another. The children? Not likely. Jack? Possibly. A car accident? Everyone in Brazil was insane behind the wheel.

"Hello." Marilyn's voice was tired and hollow. Julia's stomach sank.

"Marilyn, it's me. You called and told the desk clerk it was urgent. What's wrong?"

The pause was long and eerie. Julia sat on a rattan chair with plump, white cushions. On the other end of the line, her friend sniffed and cleared her throat.

"There was an assault on Laura's car and Alan and Richard were shot."

Julia's mind was blank.

"Shot? Are they all right?" Of course they were. They

had to be.

"Her son Richard will be okay. He was shot in the arm. But her husband is gone."

"Gone"? she echoed.

"Alan's dead," Marilyn explained gently.

It wasn't possible. This happened to strangers in the newspaper, not to her friends, not to Laura and Alan, or to their children. Julia's mind was crowded with tumbling thoughts that made no sense along with pictures of the Paterson family in a jumbled kaleidoscope of scenes from her memory.

"Julia, I have to go. I know you and Laura had some kind of a row in the recent past but that doesn't matter now. You must come back at once. She needs her friends. All of them."

"I'll be there as soon as I can." Woodenly she stood up and turned toward Gail who raised questioning, plucked brows. "We have to pack and leave. Alan Patterson was shot and killed, and their son wounded."

Gail's gasp was nearly obliterated by the ring of the phone.

"Yes?" Julia said.

"Julia, you've been out all day," Jack said, his voice sharp.

Not an argument at this point, she thought. "I've been hiking and swimming with Gail."

"You have to come back immediately. There's an emergency situation here."

Jack's interest in her friends was unexpected and very kind. In the center of her inner turmoil she felt that soft spot of love for her husband that she thought had nearly disappeared.

"Yes, I know."

"You do?" His voice cracked with something like dismay. In her despair, Julia barely noticed. "How did you find out?"

"Marilyn called and told me. We're leaving right away."

TWENTY-FIVE—SÃO PAULO, BRAZIL

"Where are you going?" Gail asked in surprise as Julia drove slowly past cars lining both sides of the road. Laura's street in Chacara Flora was normally quiet and tranquil with few cars in sight. Now parked vehicles, some with uniformed drivers either standing on the cobblestone pavement chatting with other chauffeurs or polishing chrome on the cars, stretched almost to the condominium gate. "Aren't we going home to change?"

Edging into an empty space, Julia shook her head. "No time for that."

"But we're wearing beach clothes. What kind of respect for the dead does this show? You wear black when someone passes on."

"Not here," Julia said as they left the car and walked rapidly toward Laura's house. "By law the dead have to be buried within twenty-four hours, and people often show up at funeral services wearing jeans. And beach clothes. The difficulty is getting the word out fast enough."

"I didn't know that Brazilians pay attention to *any* law.

And this one is just barbaric...it's like trying to have a fancy wedding with only one day's notice."

Julia let that pass.

"Shouldn't we take a casserole or something?"

"I really don't know the protocol here," Julia confessed, "but I don't think so."

A uniformed guard just inside the open gate of Laura's house nodded permission for them to enter. The trip from Ilha Bela had taken four hours and it was now dusk. Although Julia had been in Laura's house countless times, she was gripped by a sudden sense of unreality, as though she were visiting it for the first time. The silence, unbroken by music or voices, was eerie and threatening.

Shivering in the heat, Julia hurriedly stepped onto the veranda. Silently, almost furtively, she wove her way past empty tables and chairs. Followed closely by Gail, she crept toward the dimly-lit entry hall and moved inside. Julia's skin prickled and a spasm ran through her body; gooseflesh rose on her arms. Gail caught her hand and held it tightly, whispering, "Boy, am I glad I'm into weddings instead of funerals."

The air was compressed, close and suffocating and she became aware of an unpleasant, cloying odor that reminded her of decayed flowers. A hushed murmur, pierced by occasional sobs, was heard just beyond the partially closed door to the living room. Lifting her eyebrows, Julia stared at her sister who was very pale underneath her beach tan.

"Let's go."

Hands joined, they slowly pushed the door open and stepped into a room filled with women, most of them whispering in small groups. Laura sat on a white brocade sofa in front of a marble fireplace, her hands covering her face, her head shaking ever so slightly as though in denial. Kathleen Lamb squeezed next to her, an arm around the widow's shoulders, her head bent close to Laura as she spoke soft, inaudible words. On the other side, Pearl patted Laura's knee while gazing around the room, obviously more interested in the other guests than in giving comfort.

Julia felt a hand lightly grasp her forearm and turned as Marilyn wedged between her and Gail. The psychotherapist's face, usually animated, was haunted and raw, showing signs of recent tears. "I'm glad you came," she whispered, attempting to smile at Gail, "both of you."

"Of course we came. But what *happened?*" Julia's voice was very low, forcing the others to bend close.

"You hear about this all the time—read it in the papers, but never think...not to someone you know..." Marilyn's voice quavered into silence and her nose and the rims of her eyelids reddened. She ran the fingers of one hand across her forehead and closed her eyes briefly. To Julia, who had only seen her friend as a decisive, firm professional who stepped easily into leadership roles, this side of Marilyn was unknown and definitely unsettling.

Marilyn opened her eyes and began again in a husky voice: "They'd been out to dinner and parked in the usual space in front of the house. Alan opened the car door and got out and two men with guns appeared from nowhere. Laura didn't hear what they said because she was on the other side of the car, but Alan yelled, "What do you want?" Marilyn dropped her head into the palms of her hands and sniffled. Julia could feel her eyes begin to sting.

"And then they shot him?" prompted Gail, clearly appalled.

Marilyn lifted her head and swiped at the tears on her cheeks. Clearing her throat, she continued: "The guard came running out and one of the men shot Alan and Richard, then shot at the guard but he missed. Then the pair just vanished."

Gail pressed both hands to her throat. "Who is Richard?" she whispered, swallowing twice. Her face was a light shade of citrine.

"Laura's sixteen-year-old son. Fortunately, the bullet

went cleanly through his forearm."

"Where is he now?"

"São Luiz Hospital."

Julia's mind felt mushy and slow as though the facts were too difficult to comprehend. "But I thought the Chacara was safe. That's why people live here." She paused. "It's why *we* live here."

"In theory it's safe," answered Marilyn slowly. "I do think this is the first murder, but there are robberies that you never hear about."

Julia's mind jumped to the terror she had felt when discovering their break-in four years ago.

"Why wasn't the guard outside?"

"He was unlocking the gate when it happened, and I guess it was all very fast."

"Did they catch the two men?"

"No, of course not; and they won't either. As you well know, the Chacara has trees and lakes and vacant lots...plenty of places to hide before they jump over the wall to the street."

The small group was silent for several minutes and then Gail sat down on a nearby straight-back chair. Obviously uncomfortable in this situation, her hands twisted together in her lap.

"When is the *velorio*?" Julia finally asked, glancing at Laura who now had a new covey of attendants hovering around her.

Gail looked up, puzzled. "What's a *velorio*?"

"A wake," Marilyn answered. "It's at seven-thirty."

Julia glanced at her watch. "There's not much time," she remarked. "Where is it?"

"At São Luiz hospital, then he'll be cremated."

"A velorio at the hospital?" Perplexed, Julia frowned.

"That's where he died."

Somehow, knowing that Alan had lived for some time perhaps in great pain, maybe knowing he was dying, made it all much worse. Without a word, she turned and moved to the sofa. Kneeling in front of the widow, she looked around the circle of women. "May I have a minute with Laura, please?"

The others silently moved away and Julia slid onto a cushion next to Laura. "I know it's completely inadequate, but I'm so sorry—for everything."

Laura looked at Julia for a long moment, her face haggard and her skin blotchy. Wordlessly, she twisted to the side, slipped her arms around Julia and pulled her close. As Julia's arms enveloped her friend in a mute declaration of support, she felt Laura's body shudder with sobs and knew that her own tears were soaking Laura's shoulder. And yet, in spite of it all, the anger and awkwardness, the memory of lies and deception that had spoiled their friendship, remained.

"It's my fault," Laura declared thickly.

"What?"

"It's my fault that Alan is dead."

Julia felt her heart thumping irregularly. Whatever horror was in store, she didn't want to hear it. "Don't be absurd."

"But it's true." Laura's voice rose in a thin wail and, throughout the room, heads turned to stare accusingly at Julia.

"Hush," Julia commanded in a soft voice. "Don't say silly things".

"We had an argument, a really stupid one, about whether the food was worth the price at the restaurant," she blubbered thickly. "And I just lost it and told him he was the great complainer and a cheapskate." Her voice dwindled to a sob and she blew her nose noisily. Julia patted her friend's cheek, hoping the silence would continue. "And then when we got home," Laura resumed, "he jumped out of the car and yelled at those men the way he wanted to yell at me." She paused again, and Julia thought of all the times she had left her daughters or Jack or even Gail with a cross last word and how devastated she would feel if that had been their final parting.

Laura pulled away and sat up, facing Julia. Her face was puffy and mottled and her eyes nearly swollen shut with tears.

"Don't you see?" Laura continued weakly. "If I hadn't said all those horrid things to him, then he would have been cautious about getting out of the car, and certainly wouldn't have been belligerent toward two armed men. He was just too furious to control himself."

Scraping her mind for the most comforting, least trite words, Julia was saved when Marilyn knelt in front of them. Taking one of Laura's hands in both of hers, she said gently, "It's time to go."

Julia looked questioningly at Marilyn, who shook her head slightly.

"Mauricio and I will take Laura and her daughter to São Luiz. You and Gail can follow in your car."

Laura turned to Julia, their eyes interlocked, and both women remembered with pain and remorse the close friendship they had shared and lost through deception and lust. Laura collapsed against Julia's chest. "Thank you for coming," she whispered. "And I'm so sorry...about everything."

Julia felt her eyes again fill with tears. "We both are," she said as Mauricio and Marilyn helped the widow to her feet. At almost the same moment, her cell phone rang.

She stared blankly at the number before recognizing it as Jack's. Hesitating, she frowned at the instrument and then pressed it to one ear.

"Yes?"

"Where are you?"

"At Laura's, of course. Why aren't you here too? Laura needs all her friends right now."

"I just heard about Alan a little while ago."

Julia was completely confused. "What do you mean you just found out? You phoned me at Ilha Bela to tell me he'd been..." Her voice faded and then picked up in a hoarse whisper, "...attacked."

"I called you there because of *my* situation, the one you discussed with Marilyn."

"Marilyn told me about Alan. What's going on?"

"Not over the phone. Just come home."

"I don't understand this. Are you sick?" Her mind abruptly filled with stories of the many São Paulo kidnappings, assaults, robberies and, just a few hours ago, Alan's murder. "Is anyone there?" she asked carefully.

"No one is here except the caseiro and Evangelista," he said. "I'm fine, and the house is fine, but we need to talk at once."

Gail jiggled her arm. "What's wrong?"

Julia shook her head, signifying bewilderment. "I have to at least put in an appearance at the velorio. We'll leave right afterward."

Absently, she broke the connection and turned toward her sister, her face abnormally pale and her expression one of worry. "He scared the shit out of me for a minute. All I could think about was how Alan's last minutes on earth were spent fighting with Laura and how unpleasant Jack and I have been with each other lately."

"What's the problem?" Gail asked.

"I have no idea."

As they moved toward the front door with the other mourners, Gail murmured, "I should get back to California. Irma Blatchford's driving me nuts with her e-mails about bridesmaid dresses and whether pink or lavender would look best with red and white roses. Can you imagine? And you should see the so-called style of the dresses she's picked: fifties satin with scoop necks and large, sweeping collars that cover the shoulder and the boobs. And that's not all: dropped waists with big bows, if you can believe it." She sighed deeply. "I'm going to tell her that I just adore the Brazilian way where all the bridesmaids wear their own long dresses. She'll go for that as something exotic and sophisticated and at least the wedding won't look like a home video with period costumes." They stepped out onto the veranda. "Anyway, I feel like a fifth wheel here."

Dozens, perhaps hundreds, of Alan's friends and associates drifted quietly through the spacious room in São Luiz Hospital that was rimmed with eight-foot-high hoops of flowers, each bearing the name of the donor. A cluster of mourners huddled near the open doors of a smaller room that was also lined with floral tributes.

"Wow, those flower arrangements are enormous," breathed Gail.

"And they cost the earth."

"Tell me about it. I deal with flowers too, but at least my clients can enjoy them."

Julia shot her sister a warning look and Gail hastily apologized.

Slowly they moved toward the smaller room where they could see a casket surrounded by solemn men and women, some weeping and others seemingly in shock. As they approached the entrance to the room, Gail announced, "I didn't know him so I don't need to say a last goodbye. I'm going to admire the flowers and try to guess how much they cost."

Hesitantly, Julia stepped forward, inching her way toward the far end of the casket. Finally she stopped, wedged between two strangers, both sobbing loudly into handkerchiefs, just as her cell phone rang. Damn, she thought, realizing that she had completely forgotten to turn it off. Casting embarrassed, apologetic glances at the crowd, she shouldered her way toward the outer door, glancing at the caller's number. Jack again. How infuriatingly inappropriate! Stifling her anger, she pressed the phone to one ear and whispered hoarsely, "Jack, I told you I'd be there as soon as possible."

"I don't know what that means. Obviously I'm last on your list of priorities."

"Don't be petulant and childish," she snapped. "What's so overwhelmingly important that I can't come to the velorio of a friend's husband?"

"I don't know how important you'll find *this*, but I've lost my job."

It took a minute for her to grasp Jack's words. "You've what?" she breathed.

"I've been fired."

TWENTY-SIX—SÃO PAULO, BRAZIL

*J*ulia, followed by Gail, rushed up the front steps, jammed the key into the lock of the front door and then stopped. How, she wondered, staring at the elaborate ironwork directly in front of her, had she managed to trade a life that was nearly ideal for one that involved secret affairs, assassinations, and a husband that she no longer understood? What was she doing here? At that moment she envied Gail's freedom to come and go, do as she pleased and work at a job she enjoyed. Closing her eyes, Julia pressed her forehead against the cold, decorative iron and glass door, bracing herself for a scene that would be unpleasant at best.

"What's wrong?" asked Gail anxiously.

Julia straightened, twisted slightly and tilted her head toward her sister. "I was just thinking that maybe I'll come with you."

Gail sucked in her cheeks in an expression of sardonic humor. The siblings exchanged wry, mirthless smiles. Julia was aware that the guard, hovering near the gate and sensing something amiss, was watching them closely.

"Good idea," Gail said. "Why do you think I'm currently single?" Her smile disappeared and she added thoughtfully, "Although I am sometimes tempted by my own divinely creative weddings..."

After Julia opened the door, they stepped into the front hallway, taking care to close the door softly behind them. The house was quiet but, unlike the sense of peace and tranquility Julia usually felt when coming home, it now seemed weighted with an empty sadness. Or was it, she thought fleetingly, an extension of her own grim mood?

"Boy, this is spookier than the hospital," whispered Gail, answering Julia's unspoken question.

Julia frowned. The atmosphere was contaminated and the air poisonous but she didn't necessarily want Gail's confirmation of the fact. "You don't have to tip-toe," she said curtly. Almost immediately she regretted lashing out at the one person who, although notably flakey, was consistently her loyal supporter.

"Sorry." Gail's voice was slightly louder than normal and she didn't sound at all repentant as she moved toward the bedroom corridor. Her heels stamped forcefully on the hardwood floor and Julia thought, for a brief moment, that they had both regressed to childhood.

"I'm going to pack," Gail announced.

"I envy you."

They paused and Gail nodded slightly.

"I know."

That moment of discord was replaced by a familiar balance; once again Julia thought nostalgically of her scattered family and their former closeness. As she turned toward the living room she mused, Brazilians don't live like this, wandering all over the country and the world like nomads, abandoning each other and losing the threads of family life. They sometimes moved but seemed always to return for vacations and, if possible, weekends and holidays, in the family groups that include distant aunts and uncles and cousins, many of whom have lived in the same place for generations.

As she stepped into the living room, her mind was swept clean by the sight of Jack wearing an immaculate white shirt, Hermes tie and perfectly pressed suit, his work uniform. He sat in a wingback chair angled toward the fake fireplace that contained a permanent pyramid of kindling and logs on the grate. With a drink in one hand, the newspaper in his lap and the soothing sounds of Marisa Monte's most recent recording washing through the room, nothing indicated a crisis or even a ripple on the surface of their lives. Julia couldn't move.

Marisa concluded her performance and the room filled with an oppressive silence; Jack lifted his eyes and stared at her blankly. Irrelevantly, Julia noticed that the years had treated him well; his figure was still trim and the graying of his beard and hair as well as the few creases in his bronzed skin lent him an air of distinction rather than of age. He was a handsome man.

Crossing the room, Julia sat on the sofa, slumping spread-eagle against the soft cushions that had always felt like clouds to her. She closed her eyes, her head pillowed by down, and asked, "What happened?"

"I was fired."

With an effort, Julia sat up, crossing her legs primly at the ankles and clasping her hands over her knees. Her mind felt bruised by the series of shocks she had endured throughout the day and, for a moment, she could only stare at Jack.

"I know *that*, but I don't understand. You're the president."

"Not anymore." Although he still seemed to be relaxed, his tone was bitter. "The company is merging with McClellan Telecom and they're bringing down a new man to be in charge."

Julia blinked rapidly, studying her hands and trying to grapple with this new reality. "But are they sending you back home? I mean, what happens now?"

Jack snorted. "That's a really good question. If you mean will they ship all this stuff..." with one arm he gestured to the contents of the room "...back to the States, of course they will. It's in the contract. As to my professional status, they've generously offered me a position in Ohio as Director of Marketing, something that is completely out of my knowledge base."

Julia silently mouthed the word, *Ohio*. Finally finding her voice, she asked, "If they've offered you another job, you haven't really been fired."

"I'm toast. How many times have we watched other men get this kind of a shaft and shaken our arrogant, self-satisfied heads and smugly thought it would never happen to us. Remember Keith Devon?"

Everyone, Julia thought, remembered Keith Devon and his wife Beverly Jean as a sort of cautionary tale. When he was fifty-nine and one year short of mandatory retirement from a company to which he had devoted his entire working life, Keith was abruptly relieved of his job and sent back to his home base. Expecting a promotion, he discovered that there was no job waiting and, therefore, no retirement pay. After thirty-nine years with the company, he was unceremoniously screwed.

"Yes, I remember them very well."

"And you know he wasn't the only one. South America is the scrap heap for executives. No one has ever known exactly why they're side-lined, not even the ones who were dumped, and now I've joined the club."

They sat in tense silence as Julia tried to grasp this turbulent new twist in their lives. Her mind refused to function; she clung to the mental mantra, stay calm, stay calm, stay calm.

"What are we going to do?" she finally asked.

For the first time, Jack looked uncomfortable. He toyed with the edges of the newspaper. "For sure I'm not going back to a marketing job that's a predictable failure."

"All right... But what's your plan?"

Taking a healthy swallow of his drink, Jack took a long time before answering, carefully placing his glass on a wooden coaster. "I'm going to look for work down here. Thank God I have my permanent resident visa or I'd have a hard time even doing that."

"Jack, we've been here over four years, and they're just as age-prejudiced here as in the States. Perhaps more so. Here they legally ask your age, and then use it against you. You're fifty-one," she commented, and then added incredulously, "and I'm nearly forty-eight."

"I know how old I am, but I won't roll over and play dead in the hope that the head guys will admire my cooperation. I already have some interviews lined up, and one of them seems really positive."

"But where are we going to live? The rent here is paid by the company and they're not going to keep on supporting someone who's left the firm."

Although his face was free of expression, both hands began alternately twisting and smoothing the front page of the newspaper which seemed to be, Julia noticed absently, unopened.

"Of course we can't stay in this house. Actually, I think you should go back to California."

Unable to comprehend her husband's words, Julia's breathing was shallow.

"What do you mean?" To her own surprise, her voice was quite normal.

Jack's eyes no longer focused on her but had shifted to a small painting. His hands were still twisting and smoothing the newspaper, as though disconnected from his body.

"Just what I said: you should go back to Venice. Tell the boys they must move out of the house because you need it."

"What about you?"

"It shouldn't be too difficult for me to find a small

apartment here."

Julia's face flamed as she repeated carefully, "I go back to our house in Venice Beach and leave you here in a small apartment. Could you tell me why?"

"Life is very uncertain right now. I think I can find work but I'm not sure, and we can't afford a maid, nor can we keep two cars. Actually, I'm thinking of your comfort and welfare."

One hand pressing against her chest, Julia leaned forward. "Don't give me that bullshit. You're trying to weasel your way into a separation without actually saying so, and since you're so concerned with my comfort and welfare, I need to know the truth."

Jack abruptly stood, tossed the paper onto the coffee table and jammed both hands into his trouser pockets. Taking a long, slow breath, he turned to face his wife.

"The truth is that Eliana and I are planning to live together."

So, she thought numbly, the rumors were true and the nasty feeling she'd had whenever she saw them together was more than justified. Her vision was suddenly blurred, either by the tears that began to pour down her cheeks or the tight pressure that rose from her chest to encompass her head. Jumping to her feet she moved around the coffee table, her head thrust forward, fingers bent into rigid claws. Alarmed, Jack backed around the other side of the table, both arms extended as though to ward off an attack.

"So how long have the two of you been sneaking off to the motels?" She continued to edge around the coffee table toward her husband who silently continued to back away. Her voice rose. "I'm sure most of São Paulo knows about your sordid little affair—everyone but me, of course. I feel like a complete fool. People we don't even know pitying poor little Julia who does her good deeds out at the Lar and participates in the theater group and goes to lunches and laughs and giggles with her friends like some moron while her husband and his secretary are screwing like bunnies."

Julia stopped her advance and, as though moving in tandem, Jack halted.

"Well, don't you have anything to say?" she demanded.

Jack's outstretched hands now turned palms up in a silent entreaty. "I'm sorry, Julia. We just fell in love."

With that bald statement, Julia's world fell apart. Anger and humiliation were replaced by a vast sense of emptiness. Weakly, she stumbled to the sofa and fell against the cushions, one hand covering her closed eyes. With a shock, she realized that she was absolutely on her own, tossed away like a piece of old rubbish by a husband that clearly had no intention of helping her, while her daughters were far distant and unable to offer support or comfort. Nor would they, any better than she, comprehend what this was all about. Sometime later, she heard Jack's voice as though through a thick mist. Opening her eyes, she stared at her husband who still stood beside the coffee table.

"We should talk," he suggested.

Julia croaked a bitter chuckle. "We should have done that a long time ago."

"But we didn't," he said. "Of course I will give you the house in Venice Beach and your own bank account there. We can decide which pieces of furniture I'll need—it won't be much—and the company will ship the rest back to you in California."

He couldn't meet her eyes as he babbled on. Julia scarcely listened to her spouse slicing up more than two decades of marriage into neat little pieces. And then one statement jerked her from her state of paralysis.

"Don't worry, Julia, I'll be very fair."

Springing upright, she glared at him.

"Fair? My God, none of this is fair. Fair would be..." Abruptly, she stopped as Max's image flashed into her mind. She and Jack were guilty of the same sin, the only difference lying in the fact that her feeling for the minister had been lust and Jack's was love. And it didn't make much difference if she'd had the affair in vengeful retaliation for her suspicions about Eliana and her husband, it still had been wrong and damaging. Too late, she had realized that infidelity really did bring nothing but trouble, a truth that obviously still eluded her husband.

The flat tone of his last sentence echoed in her mind and she suddenly wondered if he knew about Max. Since she'd heard rumors about Eliana, it was entirely possible that Jack's ears had twitched at suggestive hints about his wife's infidelity. Not a trace of emotion flawed her husband's handsome face as she tried to discern any hidden meaning in his suggestion of fairness.

"We could see a marriage counselor," she suggested with sudden calm.

Jack paused, cleared his throat and loosened his tie. "I'm not one for shrinks, as you know, and I doubt that would help us now. We've been growing apart for a long time, Julia. Ever since we arrived in Brazil, come to think about it." He paused uncomfortably. "And I love Eliana."

"What do you want, then, a separation, or a divorce?" The words seemed to stick in her throat.

Jack removed his tie and rolled it from the slender end, then unrolled the silk and smoothed it.

"I don't see any point in dragging this out, especially the way Eliana and I feel about one another. I think we should get a divorce."

Julia felt the hollow emptiness spread until it encompassed her body, her mind, her world. How often she had seen this happen to other ex-pat women; she and her friends always felt a secret relief that they weren't the subjects of such humiliation and suffering. But now it was her turn, when she least expected it, when she was least prepared.

Julia felt an invisible band tighten around her forehead while bile thickened and rose slowly in her throat. Every muscle tense, she took one step toward her husband. When she spoke, her tone was biting but she chose her words carefully. "The reason Claymore fired you is because you're a failure, Jack. They sent you down here to bring in new values, mainly honesty, and you couldn't do it because you were so busy cheating and lying yourself. You thought you got away with it, but everybody knew about you and Eliana, even my friends to whom I didn't listen." Her voice lifted in a sardonic mimic. "Not Jack, he wouldn't do that. I trust him completely." Her tone dropped and flattened, her eyes narrowed against the haze of rage that clouded her vision. "What a fool I was! But you're the loser, my friend, because you've become just like those you were supposed to reform, and because of that you're a failure." She suddenly felt nothing but hatred for this stranger.

TWENTY-SEVEN—SÃO PAULO, BRAZIL

*J*ulia opened the old-fashioned mail-box at the bottom of the Chacara Flora driveway, swept the contents into one hand, and without looking at the envelopes, began to climb back to the house. Abandoning the asphalt, she squeezed through the tangle of hibiscus and jasmine lining one side of the driveway, and stepped onto the sloping lawn. The grass needs cutting again, she observed idly, moving up the hill and noticing that several of the plants seemed bedraggled and neglected.

A wry smile twisted the corners of her mouth. Her marriage had collapsed and now this Chacara Flora property was falling into ruin. Claymore, or whatever her husband's former company was now called, had awarded her a three month grace period in the house thanks to some clause in Jack's contract that her Brazilian lawyer had unearthed, but Zé, the gardener, now appeared only twice a month to take care of the most urgent horticultural emergencies. Loving plant maintenance was just a memory. And the swimming pool was a wreck. Previously Zé had been obsessively attuned to fluctuations in the water's chemistry, deeply concerned with floating leaves and horrified at the faintest discoloration of the tiles, but now he casually dumped a few liquids into the chartreuse water from time to time before speeding away on his motorbike. Obviously, he had learned to ride the vehicle but Julia doubted that it had ever been registered.

The house itself was never very clean, since Jack claimed an inability to pay for a full-time maid and the company certainly wasn't going to foot the bill. Evangelista had been replaced by Janaína, a cleaning woman who appeared on Tuesdays and Thursdays to deal with the build-up of surface dirt. *I used to clean my own house back in Venice Beach,* Julia chided herself, reaching the top of the hill and stepping onto the flagstone terrace, *but then we had a smaller, more manageable place. Keeping this one in order is a full-time job, and I have no intention of becoming my own domestic servant.*

House repairs in the way of blocked plumbing, chipped paint and roof leaks, normally problems quickly solved by Zé, demanded attention but this property owner, like most Brazilian landlords, would rather watch his real estate disintegrate than pay for regular upkeep. That was the responsibility of the tenant, even if the rental agreement said otherwise. Through the years, Julia had watched ex-pat friends undertake, at their own expense, repair of leaks under the house, faulty electrical wiring and the retiling of bathrooms; landlords ignored the problems, it would take years before a court case came before a judge and so, rather than live in what amounted to a crumbling home, renters did it themselves. Or actually, the work was done by their caseiros, and the renters footed the bill.

Well, thought Julia, I'll be gone soon enough. A little leakage here and there won't hurt at this point, and then someone else will have to deal with it.

She paused, swiveled and looked out at the garden that

she loved and in which she had spent so much time, her eyes flicking sadly over the tropical plants and trees, the neglected orchidário with its wilting collection of rare orchids and finally coming to rest on the wide, stone bird feeder. A broad smile crept across her face. An inordinately large, citron-yellow woodpecker was consuming the half papaya Julia put out daily, the long, golden feathers on his head whisking frantically to and fro like a winged rockstar as he demolished the fruit. Until settling into this house, she had never seen a yellow woodpecker nor, for that matter, had she seen or even imagined the flocks of green parakeets that regularly flew overhead and occasionally landed in her paineira trees, their bodies blending with the foliage, their presence revealed through their loud and unmelodic chattering.

Quietly, Julia settled onto a small upholstered sofa on the veranda, mesmerized by the ceaseless bobbing of the bird's head and the violent tossing of the bright, lemon-toned feathers. Why, she wondered, didn't she feel depressed? The three-month grace period was nearly up, and she had no idea what her next move would or should be. Since Jack's departure, she had written letters to her old boss at the business channel, her friends in Venice Beach and Santa Monica, Angel and Friends where she had volunteered every weekend, even museums and universities—anyone and everyone who might remotely be able to help—asking for a job. And the replies, when the recipients bothered to answer at all, were invariably no. The packet of mail felt very weighty in her hand and she considered throwing it into the waste basket without another glance.

Suddenly, the woodpecker was motionless, his head cocked attentively to one side, and then, abruptly, he soared upward and over the treetops, vanishing in an instant. The next moment, Marilyn's car came into view, struggling slowly up the steep driveway toward the level parking area by the front door, the psychotherapist's hand flapping a casual greeting as she drove past.

Tossing the letters onto a bamboo chair, Julia stood and stretched, hearing the vehicle's motor fade into silence, followed by the slamming of three car doors. A moment later, Marilyn, Laura and Kathleen appeared in the entry hall and she felt a surge of happiness at the sight of her friends, followed by a hollow sense of loss. She would miss them, even Laura. For the past four years these friends had been her family; now she would be going back to her sister and two grown daughters and a very uncertain future.

"Hello," called Marilyn, breezing into the entry hall. Laura and Kathleen appeared just behind her and then vanished in the direction of the kitchen.

"Yoo-hoo," called Julia waving both arms dramatically overhead. "I'm out on the veranda." She moved around the bamboo furniture and across the terrace. "Why didn't you tell me you were coming? I'd have gotten us some lunch."

"We brought lunch." Marilyn strode through the living room and onto the patio, lugging a large, covered basket which she plunked onto the mosaic table. "Surprise! We've come bearing food, drink and news."

"How terrific," she said. "Is there some sort of occasion? A happy event like a birthday I've forgotten, or a divorce?"

"Nope... We just thought we'd have a little get-together."

Marilyn dusted the cushions of an upholstered settee with one palm, and then sank down with a sigh, giving the swing a push with her foot. Laura, carrying plates and glasses on a tray emerged just behind Kathleen; after mandatory kisses and hugs, they began unloading the basket and setting up an array of food.

"I'm so glad to see you," Julia exclaimed, suddenly aware of her wrinkled chinos and the general air of dustiness in the house, "even though you look far too chic for a picnic on the veranda."

"Yes, well we wanted you to feel badly so we got all dressed up in these fabulous designer outfits," Kathleen said, gesturing toward her cargo pants and leather sandals. "A shame I couldn't find my tiara."

"Any news on the job front?" asked Laura, her hands momentarily suspended over the silverware as she gazed quizzically at Julia.

Julia shook her head, flapping the unopened letters. "Not a bite. I've written to just about the entire population of California and no one wants to hire me. Would you like to know why?"

"Sure," said Kathleen, arranging smoked salmon sandwiches on a large ceramic plate.

Julia dropped the mail on her lap and began ticking off the fingers of her left hand. "I've been away too long, I don't have any experience, they're laying off, not hiring, I need an extra doctorate or two, I haven't taken the correct civil service exams which are given irregularly and in a certain order..."

"So, what's your plan?" asked Marilyn.

"I don't have one." Smiling easily, she stood and selected a sandwich, some carrot sticks and grapes, then returned to her seat on the sofa.

"You don't seem too worried," commented Laura as she shook grapes from a plastic bag into a bowl.

"I was terrified for a while." She flicked one hand dismissively toward the heap of letters. "Every time the mail came my heart went into overdrive and every rejection brought another tear. Then I got to the point where I knew I'd get nothing at all from those thousands of begging letters and I decided I just didn't care." She grinned at Marilyn.

"You'd probably have a psychoanalyst's name for that."

Marilyn nodded. "I probably do."

"At least you don't have to deal with a caseiro and maid anymore," commented Laura.

Julia smiled. "I know, and I'd finally learned how to do

it."

Watching Laura, she wondered about the strength of their friendship. The relationship seemed to her like a cracked plate, holding together but so damaged and flawed that it could shatter with the least blow.

"Thank you for the lunch and your friendship. All of you."

"I hope you know that we've all more or less been in this boat," said Kathleen.

"I haven't". Marilyn again gave the swing a push with her foot. Kathleen shook her head.

"Your day might still come," she told Marilyn, settling onto a wicker chair, "and sooner than you think." She waved a celery stick at Julia.

"How're Sydney and Stephanie holding up?"

Julia gave a wry smile. "They both hate their father and have told him how they really feel. Sydney goes farther than simple loathing, though. She thinks he should be sent to jail."

"On what charge?"

"That was the problem. She didn't know."

They all smiled. At the foot of the driveway, a radio on full volume suddenly blared out a Carnival song from the previous year. The three visitors looked inquiringly at one another and then simultaneously turned to Julia who was demolishing a sandwich.

"*What* is happening down there?"

"That's Djalma getting even with me for some real or imagined past insult."

"Who?"

"My first caseiro. It only goes on for a few minutes. I've heard he has a job here in the Chacara so it gives him the chance to annoy me at noon or when he comes to work or goes home."

"Very Brazilian," commented Marilyn

As suddenly as it had begun, the music stopped. Gears ground and a car engine faded quickly into the distance.

"Guess it's time for him to go back to work."

For a few minutes the only sounds were birdsongs and the creak of metal as the settee gently swung back and forth. Kathleen broke the silence.

"You said you'd blanketed the world with resumes. What about your old TV station?"

"They were the first ones to whom I wrote, and they were just thrilled to tell me that the week after I left they replaced me with a *marvelous* person, implying that they were so lucky I'd flown the coop."

"Well, never mind. Let me tell you one of the reasons we dropped by."

"Okay..."

"Your former spouse has found a job."

Julia felt hollow and the food that she was industriously chewing suddenly had no flavor. "What?"

"He has a job, so he can't claim indigence as a reason not to support his wife".

"Soon-to-be-ex-wife," Julia corrected automatically, fighting the wave of acrimony that swept over her.

"We also wanted to give you the straight story before you started hearing rumors, which takes about three-quarters of a second in this town, and then the gossip is usually three quarters untrue."

"What kind of a job?" Julia asked warily, hoping it was as a doorman or clerk, maybe one of those city street cleaners—something Jack would consider demeaning and beneath his skill set and preferably something that would require a uniform.

"It's a good one. I don't know how he got it except that he must have done a really slick sales pitch. He's the new executive manager of an old Brazilian company called Pereira and Sons or Filhos or Sobrinhos or something. My own darling Mauricio found this out because one of the Pereiras is a patient of his. Apparently the firm has been torn apart by family squabbles so they've offered Jack a big salary, bonus, the whole bit to root out the dead wood and turn the company around."

For a moment Julia was speechless with rage and then she jumped to her feet. Forgotten on her lap, the earthenware plate tumbled to the ground and shattered into thick fragments.

"That is so unfair," she cried, stamping both feet violently on the flagstone terrace. "He does not deserve a good job. He and Eliana should starve, and now he's better off than he ever was, while I can't get any kind of work." She looked at them through furious tears that suddenly filled her eyes. "And we all know that it'll take me ten years in a Brazilian court to get a penny out of him. I hate this country, and I detest him, and I wish him the worst of everything in the world."

Suddenly, feeling totally empty, she sank onto the sofa, her chin resting on both fists. Marilyn moved swiftly, darting up from the swing and sliding next to Julia on the sofa. As she slipped an arm around her friend's shoulders, Laura unobtrusively shifted from her chair to Julia's other side.

"Well, let me remind you of my own glorious story," offered Kathleen. "I'm sure you remember what a sloth, what a whiney mouse, what a *weeny* I was when Willard dumped me. I was so humiliated and so guilty because I'd run away from my husband and daughter to be with Willard the Wonderful for the rest of my life and then he turned out to be an arrogant asshole who *used* me and chucked me out. I couldn't stand myself, and when I came crawling back, neither could anyone else. Do you remember?"

Reaching across the table, Kathleen uncovered a plate that held cold chicken; after a moment of deliberation she plucked a paper napkin from a pile and, with it covering her fingers as was mandated by Brazilian etiquette, selected a leg. The other three nodded.

"I remember," Julia murmured.

"So," Kathleen continued, "I hid away at Marilyn's until

one day I decided that I was wasting my time and I'd better snap out of it because this is the only life we've got and neither Willard nor Randolf were worth my spending it in misery."

Julia reached across the table, speared a chicken leg with a fork and placed it on a clean plate. She could see where this was going and it lifted her spirits.

"That's when I went out and got my job teaching business English to Brazilian executives. I told Randolf that if he didn't want me at home, he had to rent a place so I could move out of Marilyn's, and that's when he allowed me to come back." Methodically wiping her fingers on a napkin, she stared at Julia. "It's not working and I think he has a girlfriend, but so what? I'm living rent-free and building a bank account, and when I'm ready I'll make my move. Who needs Randolf?" She briefly studied her plate before turning her attention once again to Julia. "Think it over. You're the one being dumped, and you feel really shitty, but believe me, ten seconds from now it'll be ancient history. Which we can't rewrite but we can leave behind. I did, and so can you."

Julia felt her stomach jump. Was this a subtle way of telling her that the affair with Max was public knowledge? She gazed into Kathleen's pale aquamarine eyes and failed to detect any hidden message.

She nodded slowly. "You are absolutely right, Kathleen, and believe me, I'm trying but it's hard."

Laura patted her knee. "It might take more than ten seconds but you'll get over it."

"You'll be fine," Marilyn assured her impatiently, "but what actual decisions have you made? About staying here or going back, for starters. You're just about down to the wire in this house."

There it was, the request for a public statement about her future. For weeks she had agonized over every possibility, sorting out each in her mind, discarding those that were clearly impossible and vacillating over the ones that were simply unattractive.

"Well, I can't stay here. In Brazil, I mean." She looked at Kathleen. "I could probably teach English but I have no place to stay and I'm not at all sure that my visa wouldn't be rescinded once I'm divorced."

Sounding more confident than she felt, Julia carefully placed her plate on a footstool, edged broken crockery under the table with one foot and then picked up the pile of mail that had been abandoned on the sofa. The others watched as she slit the first envelope with a fingernail, scanned it and tossed it aside.

"So I've decided to move back into the Venice Beach house and have the company ship all this furniture to me. Jack wanted some of it but to hell with that. And when I get home I'll look for work. Don't ask me doing what, but I'm bound to find something." She picked up another envelope. "I'm not giving up, but I've realized that *this* is not the way to find a job."

The other three women returned to their food and the latest gossip while Julia continued opening the mail and tossing the pages aside. Well into the pile, she hastily scanned one of the letters, then hunched over the paper and re-read it carefully. Gradually, a smile grew, transforming her face.

"What?" asked Laura.

"I don't believe it. This is from Gary Marshall, the Executive Director at *Angel and Friends*. I worked for him as a volunteer—we were good friends and made a pretty slick team. He says he's trying to retire and has been looking for a replacement for months without any luck. Listen: 'Your letter asking about possible employment was a God-send. I presented it to the Board and we all agreed that you would be the perfect person to take over as Director. It has a nice salary and the usual benefits. If you agree, please confirm as soon as possible, and let us know when you can begin work.' Unless this is a mirage, I've been offered a fabulous job. I don't have to work as a waitress."

The four women stared at one another in silence before breaking into whoops of joy.

"I've been telling you not to worry," said Laura, as Julia read the letter again. Suddenly, she jumped up, clutching the page tightly as she edged around the patio furniture.

"Now what's wrong?" asked Kathleen.

"This letter was mailed nearly three weeks ago. They'll think I'm not interested and offer the job to someone else. I've got to phone right this minute."

Watching her disappear into the house, Marilyn said, "She worries over everything but maybe we'd better offer a short prayer that the job's still open."

TWENTY-EIGHT—VENICE BEACH, CALIFORNIA

"*L*et me help you with those bags," offered the taxi driver as he pocketed the fare plus Julia's generous tip.

"Thanks. It's the first house up the walkway."

Hearing the faint rhythm of the ocean a few blocks distant, Julia stopped and slowly scrutinized the Venice Beach neighborhood. Shaded by huge leafy trees, frame houses were surrounded by flowers and shrubbery, children skated on the pavement and shouted to friends across the road, a boy pedaled slowly past with a surfboard tucked firmly under one arm and old Mr. Parker sat on a glider on his front porch; nothing had changed. Her disappointment that Gail was working and couldn't meet her at the airport vanished and she felt buoyant with unadulterated bliss. Suddenly, Julia's vision blurred and her eyes stung as she turned to follow the driver down the pedestrian walkway, realizing only at that moment how much she had missed Venice and how completely happy she was to be back where she belonged.

She opened the gate and turned to the driver.

"Just drop the suitcases here. And thanks so much for your help."

Pulling one suitcase behind her, Julia slowly moved toward the front door, her eyes roving over the lap pool by the side of the house, flower beds, fruit trees and lawn and noticing how well the garden had been tended. At sight of the tire-and-rope swing that still hung from a branch of the enormous walnut tree and the basketball hoop attached to the wall of the garage she remembered how outraged the girls had been when she wanted to remove these remnants of childhood. Just before ascending the steps to the veranda, she stopped and stared at the outlines of the three stained glass geese, black in the sun's glare, which she knew were flying toward a brilliant sunset. That's right, birds, keep on going, she urged.

Julia pushed the heavy front door open, stepped inside the entry hall and was startled by tumultuous, excited shouts. "Surprise!" Dazed, Julia dropped the handle of her suitcase and stumbled into the living room where she was immediately surrounded by dozens of friends, cousins, nephews, neighbors. Unable to speak, she lifted one hand to her throat.

"Welcome back, Mom," said Stephanie, crushing her in a hug just as Gail swept through the crowd and planted two kisses on each of her sister's cheeks.

"We couldn't come to the airport because we had to get everything organized here, which was not easy," she explained breathlessly. "I don't know how you manage food. Even with three of us galloping around the kitchen it's still not quite ready." Gail's platinum tresses looked a little wilted and Julia detected definite traces of flour on her sister's maroon silk dress. And was that a little grease spot on the skirt? Julia found her voice.

"Thank you so much. What a fabulous surprise." It sounded pitifully inadequate.

Sydney slid an arm around her mother's waist and gave

her a juicy, noisy kiss on one cheek.

"Aren't you supposed to be at college?"

Sydney shrugged, giving her mother a squeeze. "I took five days off. You're more important than Santa Cruz. More fun, too."

Julia didn't know whether to be flattered or worried, and then forgot about it, engulfed by guests eager to welcome her back. She beamed at her daughters and then was caught in the tumult of the crowd, questions asked and answered, everyone talking at once, and the noise level rising as more guests squeezed into the living room.

It was the beginning of Julia's rush to see old friends, catch up on neighborhood news, unpack furniture as it arrived from Brazil and oversee a number of repairs to the house. Days sped by as visitors and family again filled the house with laughter and gossip while Julia, installed in her kitchen, churned out the cakes, pies, and hors d'houvres with which she welcomed her guests.

With a degree in Art History, Stephanie had returned to California to work in the Los Angeles County Museum of Art, renting a tiny apartment in nearby Marina del Rey which she shared with a female dentist, Marlene Roncatto. On weekends, and on some days after work, they could be found helping Julia with the garden and house and, whenever possible, they were joined by Gail. During this idyllic period, not a word of discord was heard among the women, and even Oso and Angelique deferred barking and hissing. The weather was sunny and mild, the ocean a distant thunder that lulled Julia to sleep, and the roads, unlike those of São Paulo, were swept clean of rubbish and well lit by street lamps. It was an enchanted time that surpassed even the most magical memories Julia could dredge up of her former life in the beach city; the past four years in Brazil faded quickly into a blurred memory.

After three weeks, life settled down and she reported for work at the not-for-profit *Angel and Friends*. She didn't know a single one of the volunteers, which wasn't entirely unexpected. One of the problems with NGOs was the unreliability of volunteers, many of whom tended to regard this unpaid activity as an optional choice rather than a firm commitment, only appearing when there was nothing more exciting or important to claim their time. So those new faces were not surprising to Julia, but she was not happy to find that none of the paid staff were familiar either.

As Gary Marshall, the previous Director, escorted her through the premises, introducing her to the staff and any volunteers who were present, Julia's expression gradually altered from one of easy affability to puzzled concern. After leaving the Social Worker's office, she turned to her friend and former supervisor.

"I don't understand this, Gary."

"Oh, it's a little daunting at first, but you'll get used to it."

A muscle in her cheek twitched. "That's not what I mean. I've only been away four years and yet I don't know one single person here. Why is that?"

Gary's eyes did not smile as he chuckled lightly and waved one hand dismissively in the air. "Not-for-profit jobs don't pay much, and when there's a better offer most folks snap it up. And you know the story with volunteers."

Although the two had always had an easy going relationship, Julia sensed a sudden tension in the atmosphere and a forced cheeriness in her friend's voice that she found disturbing. What was he not telling her? Taking a step forward, she stared into Gary's steel-gray eyes and said, "That doesn't make sense. Except for you, I see a complete employee turnover. Is there something you should be sharing with me?"

Involuntarily, the man glanced into the Social Worker's office to see if their conversation was being monitored and, for just a moment, hesitated. Then his lips again curved into a pleasant facsimile of a smile and he shook his head vigorously, gesturing for Julia to accompany him to her new office.

"Well, I imagine I should share the books with you along with the management system we use. That should help."

With a tightening of her muscles, Julia knew she had her answer. Something was definitely not right, and Gary wasn't about to enlighten her.

It didn't take Julia long to learn that she had eagerly jumped into a quagmire. Gary's elusiveness had not been a reluctance to divulge information; he didn't have much to reveal. During the first week she discovered that the organization had no annual financials, operating statistics, job descriptions, Five Year Plan, Plan of Action, Organizational Chart or training plans for staff and volunteers. She was shocked. At the Business Channel, they had bi-monthly staff meetings to review all these items and correct problems before they could blow up into disasters. So she was not surprised to find that the NGO was operating at a continual loss, partially covered by sporadic emergency donations by the founding angel, Angelo Corona, and a couple of his friends. The organization obviously leapt from crisis to crisis.

"Great," she thought to herself, reflecting on the fact that the view from the top was not the same one observed by a volunteer.

"The big mystery to me is how *Angel* has tottered along all these years," she grumbled to Gail. It was a Saturday afternoon and Julia held the telephone with one hand while whipping cream with the other.

"What's that racket? I can hardly hear you," said Gail.

"It's the beater. Marlene and Stephanie are coming over in a few minutes, and I want to give them something delicious." She turned off the electric beater. "Gingerbread and whipped cream and a choice of tea or gin. For me, it's a big gin and tonic to gear up for my first Advisory Board meeting on Monday night. The members seemed surprised that I wanted to attend, but I don't know how I can run the show if I don't know what's going on in the Board Room."

"Do you think Stephanie's gay?"

She could always count on Gail for an off the wall comment. "I don't know", Julia answered testily. "I don't really think about it, and anyway she seems very happy with her life."

"But where are the boyfriends and what happened to the doctor?"

"Why don't you ask her?" suggested Julia. "Right now, I've got bigger problems."

Monday evening, she was surprised to see Angelo Corona among those seated around a large table in *Angel and Friends'* work room. Julia had done her homework and knew that virtually all the Board and Advisory Board members were old friends of Angelo's, but she had been given to understand that the founder himself no longer participated in running the establishment. And yet, here he was. Sliding onto a nearby seat, she leaned toward him with a smile.

"I didn't know you were still involved here."

Angelo Corona had once owned and run two of the top restaurants in Los Angeles. A shrewd man, he had sold out while they were still fashionable, invested in Mount Washington property, sold that almost immediately for a vast profit, reputedly to an unpopular local cult, and had become a murky living legend. According to rumor and unfounded speculation, he was involved in drugs or prostitution or gambling or illegal wood from the Amazon or sweat shops in Mexico—it was all guesswork. No one had any idea what he did, if anything, or how much money he had or where it was located. The only certainty was the fact that he regularly bailed out *Angel and Friends* when they tottered on the brink of insolvency.

Julia and Angelo traded level gazes as she waited for a comment. A big man and trim, he was always beautifully dressed in perfectly tailored slacks and shirts, cashmere jackets and silk designer ascots. His mustache and hair, both far too black for his sixty-some years, were trimmed and his nails buffed. His eyes, brown and expressionless, had always made Julia feel uncomfortable although she wasn't quite sure why.

He shrugged. "I like to keep my hand in. See what's going on."

Julia nodded vaguely and sat back in her chair as the meeting was finally called to order by the president, Martha Morgan. A dumpy little woman nearly Angelo's age, Martha's professional experience had been as a first grade teacher at a Catholic school. There was no agenda and, after Julia was formally introduced to the group, they discussed whether or not to apply for more government cheese for the family food packages, if the refrigerator needed replacing, how single men should be treated if they arrived drunk for a sandwich lunch and if the social worker was doing her job adequately. It was chaotic, with on-going private conversations, several members speaking at once and no recommendations or decisions taken. Martha smiled through it all, suggesting that they have a party to celebrate Angelo's upcoming birthday while the former restaurateur remained totally mute.

Julia raised her hand. "Excuse me." No one noticed. She tried again, her voice elevated. "Excuse me."

Martha sent a warm smile in her direction. "Yes, dear?"

"I need some information. I can't seem to find it and thought maybe one of you could help."

Gradually, the group simmered down and took at least partial notice of her.

"What is it you need?"

After consulting her list for a moment, Julia began to read. "I've been searching for a Plan of Action, a Five Year Plan, Job Descriptions and operating statistics." Angelo stopped her.

"Why do you need those?" he asked. It was the first time he'd spoken during the meeting. Now she had the group's undivided attention.

Julia felt a twinge of annoyance. "Because they will help us figure out the problems here, of which there are many. And enable us to run more efficiently so that we don't have periodic financial crises."

"Who says we do?"

The atmosphere was suddenly distinctly hostile and, for the first time, there was complete silence in the room. Now Julia felt cornered as well as irritated; sweat ran down her back and her face flushed.

"I know it had financial problems when I was a volunteer, and Gary says it still does. I haven't been able to see current financials."

"Gary's not here anymore. Why do you need job descriptions?"

Julia spoke very slowly. "So I'll be clear as to what each employee should be doing. There seem to be duplications in tasks."

"Anything you need to know is in the files," said Martha.

Now anger flared throughout her body. "I'm sorry, but none of those are in the files. Or anywhere else. Any NGO should be run like a business but *Angel and Friends* is just wobbling along. To get it on its feet I need to look at everything on this list." She snapped the paper back and forth.

"It is on its feet". Angelo stood up. "I need to get home. What do you say, Martha?"

Martha studied her small, gold and diamond watch, and then looked up with a vague smile. "Oh, yes. Sorry. The meeting is adjourned."

Julia was suffused with rage over the rudeness and heard, or imagined that she heard, snickers from some of the Advisory Board members. Grinding her teeth, she stuffed papers and graphs into her briefcase and walked stiffly from the building, aware of the huddled, whispering groups just behind her. No one said good-night to her; in fact, no one said anything. As she drove away she saw the tall figure of Angelo, so anxious to go home, towering over diminutive Martha and surrounded by his hand-picked Advisory Board members. All right, she thought, her silk blouse glued to her torso with perspiration, I'll just figure out the answers for myself.

For the next few months she struggled unsuccessfully to unearth any information that would disclose plans for the future of the organization while trying to run *Angel and Friends* without any financial data. There seemed to be no provision for training of either staff or volunteers, not that many of the former stayed long enough to be trained. Hiring and firing appeared to be on an ad hoc basis, with decisions made in her absence and no concrete reasons or explanations given.

"But what was the matter with Alice?" Julia asked in an Advisory Board meeting. Martha had just announced the unexpected replacement of the Volunteer Coordinator, a woman Julia had considered very capable and efficient.

"She was much too familiar with the men," Martha replied after a quick glance at Angelo. "And she had no rapport with the women. Our volunteers are donating their time and must feel that their work is not just worthwhile but a vital contribution to the organization."

"I heard no complaints."

"We did."

"May I ask from whom?"

"I'm afraid that's confidential."

Julia felt the color flood her cheeks. "I was her supervisor and I think she was doing a fine job. We were lucky to have her here." She was uncomfortably aware that this was a pattern; since her arrival, the Public Relations Director had bitten the dust along with the part-time accountant. Now that she thought about it, there had been a noticeable turnover in staff even in her days as a volunteer.

"I need to see job descriptions for everyone, including

myself. Since I can't find any, I'll write them up for your approval." Martha looked puzzled.

"You've mentioned those before."

"But I haven't found any."

Angelo spoke: "Let's not waste time. What's next on the agenda?"

By now, she was used to the man's curt orders, but they never failed to generate a feeling of anger and disgust. Her initial enthusiasm for the job gradually diminished and was accompanied by a rise in anxiety about her own performance. She had been hired to run *Angel and Friends* and thought she was doing well but she had no way of knowing, especially without a job description. Jack and his problems at Claymore crept into her mind and she felt a reluctant rush of sympathy for her former spouse. Was her new career on the line, she wondered, and if so, why?

Not long after, she had her answer. She and Sheila, the recently hired Volunteer Coordinator, were in her office going over the schedule of male volunteers when Martha knocked timidly at the open door. Julia looked up, surprised. Board members didn't often pay a visit to the center.

"Come in, Martha. Is it important?"

"Actually, yes."

"Okay. Sheila, we'll get back to this later but you do understand why we assign only men to hand out lunch to the single men?"

Sheila nodded and stood up. A recent college graduate, she was well liked by both the volunteers and clients, just as Alice had been. Watch your back, Julia silently advised as the young woman moved out of the office. Martha, looking particularly dumpy in a powder blue polyester trouser suit, took the vacated seat.

For a few moments she sat, nervous and ill at ease, surveying the room and the bookshelves. Tapping one finger on the desk, Julia wondered idly if Martha had been a good schoolteacher and decided probably not. Finally the

Board President spoke.

"Didn't you get my e-mail?"

Baffled, Julia shook her head. "No. When did you send it?"

"Yesterday afternoon."

"To which e-mail address?"

"I thought you only had one."

"No, of course not. I have a business one for *Angel and Friends* and my personal address which I haven't checked for a couple of days."

"Oh." Martha looked like a startled rabbit. "That's too bad."

Martha gazed helplessly at Julia who looked pointedly at her watch and then began to search through the papers on her desk.

"I'm sorry, but I have a ton of things that must be done today. Could we make an appointment for another time?"

"But you shouldn't be here." The words tumbled out breathlessly.

"Why not?"

"As I told you in the e-mail, we no longer need your services."

Julia's first impulse was to laugh, and the second was to throttle the fat little messenger. In fact, she neither moved nor drew a breath for several minutes.

"Excuse me?" Her voice was light with disbelief.

Martha sat up primly and looked at her adversary with the disapproving expression of a stern and humorless teacher. "Your employment has been terminated."

"And this is how you do it, over the Internet?"

Martha stood, attempting to display authority and affronted dignity. "Please collect your belongings and leave at once."

Julia collapsed limply against the back of her chair, unable to move or think coherently. Fired. The word echoed through her mind, along with the awareness of a slender bank account dependent on the income from this job. Now what would she do?

TWENTY-NINE—VENICE BEACH, CALIFORNIA

*H*er chin propped on both palms, Julia stared glumly at the neat stacks of paper arranged on her oak dining room table. Directly across from her, Sydney filed her nails while Stephanie, seated next to her, jotted notes and figures in a spiral notebook. At the end of the long table, Gail studied bills, paid and unpaid, and sorted them into piles that she occasionally pushed down the table to Stephanie. There was complete silence until Julia spoke.

"I just don't see any way we can manage to keep the house."

"Mom", Sydney cried in exasperation, "I don't want to hear that. You're the one who always told me to keep going, don't give up, you can't be a quitter and many, many more tired old Elliott expressions. Those boring clichés pushed me through Santa Cruz and now listen to you." She flipped her emery board onto the table and glared at her mother.

Julia swiveled toward Sydney. With a sigh, she

straightened her spine in a stretch and then slouched back in her chair.

"Yes, I know, do as I say not as I do. But there just isn't enough money coming in. Those construction workers over on Millwood make more than I do as a teacher in a private school."

Stephanie looked up. "Boy, are you out of touch. Construction guys make a bomb."

"All of us are in crummy jobs that don't pay anything," grumbled Sydney.

"Speak for yourself," her sister countered snippily. "I have a great job and so would you if you'd had a serious major in college. Or gone to an important university."

"That's enough." Julia spoke sharply, sitting forward and crossing her forearms on the table. "I asked you all to this little family gathering because I want to hear realistic ideas that will get us out of this hole. And if there aren't any, I have no choice. I'll have to sell the house."

Stricken, Sydney stared at her mother. "For real?"

"Do you live in this world?" asked Stephanie. "We've been discussing this off and on for months now."

"But I didn't know you actually meant it." Her voice trailed away.

"I have an idea, although none of you may like this one," said Gail.

Warily, three pairs of eyes turned toward her end of the table.

"My assistant Grace is just not working out at all. She has no people skills and actually tries to convince the clients they can do my job. Tells them it's a snap, if you can believe it, and seems not to understand that her salary and my income depend on keeping that fact as our secret." She glanced at her hands, lightly folded on a sheaf of bills, then bent over one forefinger, examining it closely. With a grimace, she held it up for the others to inspect and announced, "Look at this. The polish is chipped and I only had the manicure yesterday. There's just no quality work anymore."

"So what's the idea?"

"Oh." She leaned toward Julia. "I thought that you might replace Grace. We could work together as partners and maybe the girls could join us on the weekends doing some decorating, scheduling, going over menus with the clients...all the things that I have to hire temporaries to do. That way the money could stay in the family and you could barely squeak by and not have to sell the house." Gail beamed at her sister and nieces, then caught sight of the offending fingernail and scowled severely at it. Raising her head, she looked at each of the three in turn. "Well?"

Off balance, Julia was torn between enormous relief and skepticism. It was so unexpected that it took her a moment to catch her breath, a tiny instant in which she heard Stephanie say, "Sure, that'd be fun and I know Marlene would love to help".

Julia had never been easily frightened but now she was cold with fear. What if she quit her secure teaching job with its regular and pitiful salary and made even less money intermittently? Or what if the pay was fine, better than fine, but working with her sister drove her crazy? There were no guarantees in life, as she'd clearly learned in Brazil, but this proposition had all kinds of pitfalls and they weren't even hidden.

"Sure," said Sydney. "I'll sacrifice weekends for the good of the cause. I'll even start to pay rent for my room here."

"You know, that's a thought," mused Stephanie. "I'll talk to Marlene and see if we can't move in too and pay you what we're laying out in Marina del Rey."

Unable to speak, Jullia gazed at her daughters and sister with love and gratitude. Turning away, she scanned the pass-through into the kitchen that was slightly too high, then the paneled walls and the indoor garden in the corner that had never worked because the room was too dark, an add-on, built when she and Jack had collected enough spare cash. But then the whole house had grown, bit by bit, from a three room beach cottage into a five bedroom residence with a second story, library, a very large living room and this dining room, all of it undertaken whenever there was money available. Julia and an architect friend had designed every extension and addition. It was flawed and spectacular and they all loved it, Julia most of all.

There was really no choice. If she stayed in her secure teaching job she would certainly lose the house and most probably have to move to one of the small, modern, faceless apartments in Mar Vista or Culver City or share her sister's ranch style home. And she might have to sell the property even if she went to work with Gail but this way there was a fighting chance that she, and her daughters, could keep it.

She gave them all a watery smile and cleared her throat. "Thank you. Thank you so much. Gail, this is so kind but I don't know a single thing about the wedding business. Maybe I don't have the skill sets."

Gail pressed one palm to her forehead and dramatically extended the other hand. "Of course you do. The work's exactly like your job in television—you meet the public and talk bullshit. You were very good at it."

Julia hesitated, not sure if this was an insult or a complement. "Are you sure?"

"Absolutely."

"I am really very humbled by your offers to pay rent and sacrifice your weekends," she said to her daughters in a low voice, "and I would give anything to be able to turn you down but I'm not in a position to do that. So I accept. I love you both a lot."

Sydney moved her chair close to her mother and put one arm around Julia's shoulders, then leaned over and kissed her cheek. Eyes down, Stephanie fiddled with a pencil.

"How about me?" said Gail asked. "Don't you love me a lot too?"

The atmosphere lifted and the other three smiled.

"Of course I do," Julia replied. Sydney removed her arm and moved her chair away.

"That's good because we have to do something about your clothes." She shook her head. "Before anything else, we'll go shopping." She tilted her head to one side. "Maybe you can borrow some things from me."

Gail was wearing a belted, black, cotton-knit dress that looked precisely like a thigh-length polo shirt over a long sleeved, turtle neck red and white stripe knit shirt and black cotton tights. On Gail, it was very chic. Julia knew she could never pull that one off.

"I'd look like a clown in your clothes. I'll have to do like the French and buy one outfit I can wear and wear and wear."

Gail pulled in her chin, wrinkled her nose and said, "Phew".

Sydney and Stephanie exchanged glances and then, in unison, emitted a prolonged moan. "Oh, poor Mommy. Only one dress." Sydney turned to Gail with a mock scowl and stamped her foot. "Bad Auntie. Bad, bad Auntie causing all these problems for Mommy."

With a grin, Gail stacked her papers and both girls stood up. Julia began to laugh. "Sorry. I guess it did sound pitiful."

"You *guess*?" asked Sydney.

"One more thing," said Gail. "Start using your maiden name like I did. From now on you are Julia Saunders. Again."

"When does this new regime start?" enquired Julia.

"Now, of course. What do you think?"

"But I'm in the middle of a semester."

Placing both palms flat on the table, Gail leaned forward, her eyebrows arched. She explained with elaborate patience, "Why do you have to be so responsible? I *know* it's the middle of a semester but if you wait until the summer break the house will be gone. You have to move now, faster than the speed of light, and this little scheme still may not work. Tell the principle anything but you're out of there this weekend."

Julia knew she was right; she also knew that, if this venture failed, she might not get another teaching job. Pressing her lips together, she looked at all three of them in turn. With no expression, they returned her stare.

Julia sighed. "Okay. You're right. I'll talk to him tomorrow."

Gail's business was located in a one-story frame house on Abbott Kinney in Venice. Thirty years ago the street had been West Washington Way, one of several Washington Streets/Ways/Boulevards in the beach city, and it was hopelessly deteriorated. A lumber yard, a bible center, three small used clothing stores, countless head shops, an organic vegetable co-op and a few junk shops masquerading as antique emporiums sprinkled on both sides of the street, all of them housed in one-story frame beach cottages urgently in need of extensive repair. On the corner of Washington and Palms Boulevard stood Brandelli's Brig, the neighborhood bar and a large one at that, with its adjoining parking lot. The entire side of the stucco building facing the parking lot had been painted with what was presumed to be the owner as a young, muscular biker accompanied by an extremely blond, curvaceous female. No one in Venice ever admitted to venturing into the bar but it was obviously a busy enterprise, as could be seen from the parking lot which was always filled with Harley-Davidsons and Hondas. Not infrequently, owners of the bikes tumbled out into the parking lot where they battled with the LAPD using fists, chains and other hardware, and the wise passerby didn't hang around to see which side was the winner.

In the late 1980's, the rest of Venice began the serious but sad process of gentrification as producers, directors and top film stars and singers began to buy up, tear down, and rebuild property near the beach. The artists, actors, writers, druggies and hippies who had lived for decades in the crumbling town could no longer afford life in Venice and began to move out while chic restaurants and expensive shops previously seen solely in Santa Monica sprang up.

For awhile, the only major street unaffected by this activity was West Washington Way where paint continued to peel on the clapboard houses and gardens were weed patches contained by picket fences. That was when Gail sold her shop in Pasadena, bought a ratty frame house on West Washington and moved the business to Venice. Julia thought she was insane and told her so.

"Washington is never going to change, Gail. You could have rented something really chic on Main Street or stayed where you were."

"Pasadena is not for me. Those people all want the same traditional thing which is dead boring. I might as well work in a bank."

"I still think this is a huge mistake."

Julia couldn't have been more wrong. Gail's off-beat style was perfectly suited to the beach community, and having Gail Saunders arrange your wedding became the stylish and fashionable thing to do. Her business thrived, her prices soared and she bought a small house on Shell, close to both her sister and her place of work.

She had definite ideas regarding the appearance of *Saunders Consultants* and, through the years, the exterior of the building would remain structurally unaltered although it was kept in perfect repair and painted regularly. A white picket fence enclosed the small garden with its sheltering trees and colorful, well tended flower beds.

The interior, however, had been completely revamped and the sophisticated informality of the large reception area was a pleasantly shocking contrast to the charming, old fashioned exterior. Floors were hardwood, paintings by local artists hung on muted green and gray walls, and comfortable, down-filled sofas and chairs had been arranged around a large coffee table in the reception area, with low book shelves and a smaller conversation group against the far wall. The actual office, never seen by clients, was in a converted bedroom and was crowded with metal files, a safe and two desks, both buried under computers, phones and stacks of paper.

When West Washington underwent an official name change and became Abbott Kinney Boulevard, in honor of the city's founder, it took everyone by surprise. It also signaled the beginning of a transformation in this tacky street, changes that were subtle at first and then more obvious. Head shops disappeared and were replaced by elegant restaurants, the lumber yard closed and junk shops either became genuine antique stores or sold designer clothing. The street had caught up with Gail's business. Only Brandelli's Brig remained outwardly the same; the mural with ageless Mr. Brandelli and his blond girl-friend now received fresh paint touch-ups every year but the motorcycles in the parking lot had been replaced by Mercedes and BMWs. And there were no fist-fights outside the front door. By the late 90's Abbott Kinney was a desirable and upscale business address and Brandelli's was affectionately regarded as a symbol of old-time Venice.

Myra Keller and her daughter Lily sat on the gray sofa facing Julia in the reception room of *Saunders Consultants*, the coffee table between them nearly covered with clippings, magazines and photographs. From time to time, Julia jotted notes on a clipboard balanced on her knees or leaned forward to flip through some of the papers on the table.

"I know you have your heart set on a wedding on the beach," she said to Lily, "but I'm afraid it can't be Malibu Colony. That's private property." Giving the pair no chance to protest, she rushed on, "besides, we have to think of parking and traffic. And the distance your guests will have to drive. You live in Los Feliz and that's an enormous distance from any beach."

"Mother had thought of two other places that might be nice," Lily said. She was a plain girl, nineteen years old although, in her pleated skirt, white blouse and loafers, she seemed much younger to Julia. "How about either the Hollywood Bowl or maybe the Rose Garden between the Science and History Museums?"

Where, wondered Julia hiding a smile, did they come up with these ideas? She had been partnering with her sister for eight months and found, to her astonishment, that she really enjoyed the work, liked meeting the clientele, no matter how off the wall they seemed to be, and found their stories and suggestions fascinating. Maybe when she had been in the business as long as Gail she would be less amused but right now it was a lot more fun than teaching and there was a surprise every day.

"How about a church?" Julia suggested. She knew the rules and foibles about churches, synagogues and home services and now felt confident enough to deal with any of them, but public places were an entire separate story. Both mother and daughter stared at her in consternation.

"A *church*?" intoned Mrs. Keller. "We aren't in the least religious. I thought I'd made that clear, Ms. Saunders." She looked piercingly at Julia, her yellow suit with black polka dots and yellow cartwheel hat seeming to set the area ablaze.

"Yes, I do recall, but weddings are much more difficult to arrange in public places."

"That's why we hired you."

Ulp, Julia thought. "I'll make enquiries about the Bowl and the Rose Garden but let's also think about a bigger beach with parking, like Venice or Santa Monica." She scribbled a note to herself and then looked at Lily. "Now we should discuss the gown. Do you have something in mind?"

The bride-to-be picked up a magazine and opened it to a marked page which she showed to Julia. "I like this one."

It was a perfectly plain ivory suit with a long skirt and small feathered hat that might be the choice for a second or third wedding although this was Lily's first foray into wedlock. Myra Keller held up another magazine for Julia's inspection. "And this is what I will wear as Mother of the Bride."

Now I get it, thought Julia as she studied the mid-calf, rose colored chiffon dress covered with beads and sequins and topped by a hat that was an elaborate swath of chiffon, silk and netting. This is Lily's big day but Mom's going to the center of attention.

"Very nice, both of them. We might see what else is available, just for comparison in the event that these can't be easily recreated." The front door opened and Gail stepped inside. "Here's my sister, Gail," she said in relief. "Let's see what she thinks."

THIRTY—VENICE BEACH, CALIFORNIA

*I*t should have been the world's easiest wedding to arrange. Julia had been working as a consultant for nearly a year, knew all the necessary suppliers and resources, was adept at handling emergencies and was skilled in solving problems in this new career to which she had adapted with surprising ease. And this, the marriage of Gwendolyn Hauser and Frederick Faux, had everything going for it; the ceremony and reception were to take place on the grounds of the bride's imposing home in San Marino, Gwendolyn's family was amenable to any suggestion, and all arrangements had been made with not a single snag. Then the day before the wedding it all began to unravel.

Flowers were the first crisis. Bushels of white roses, to be arranged with white and yellow orchids and clouds of baby's breath, had failed to materialize and the florist's suggested substitution brought a scandalized glower to Gail's face.

"Marigolds? *Marigolds?*" She held the cell phone away

and scowled at the offensive instrument before clamping it back to her ear. "I haven't time to listen to this rubbish. The orchids have made it all the way from Brazil and look wonderful and if your supplier in Oregon can't manage a few roses you'll just have to whip around town in your trucks and get all the white roses in L.A. Quickly. And I want you here by nine tomorrow morning."

"Can you believe marigolds?" The question was a general one but before Julia or her daughters could comment they heard a scream from the house. Exchanging horrified glances, the four women raced across the sloping lawn, pushing past a team of workmen setting up tents, tables and chairs on one side of the pool. As they ran across the veranda of the Georgian Revival house, Gail stripped off her gardening gloves, dropped them on the floor and, without knocking, dashed into the broad entry hall where they were stopped by a high pitched shout.

"It's ruined. Look at it."

It was the voice of the blushing bride followed by the equally strident and angry voice of her normally calm mother.

"I told you to keep the plastic over it."

Gail looked at the ceiling and crossed herself, and then stage hissed to the others, "They're in the library."

Stephanie stared at her aunt as she crossed herself. "Have you secretly converted?"

"No, but it's a precaution. He might be Catholic."

"And She might be a woman," Sydney reminded her snippily, but Gail was already sprinting across the entry and down the hallway, followed closely by Julia. Just inside the library they stopped. Julia covered her mouth with one hand; they all stared. Across the room the manicurist was placidly gathering her supplies and packing them up while Gwendolyn flapped her hands in dismay and Mrs. Hauser bent over the satin and lace wedding dress carefully arranged on a dressmaker's dummy. On the pristine bodice of the closely fitted dress was a very visible streak of crimson nail varnish.

"I thought my nails were dry," sobbed Gwendolyn, blowing on the offending fingers while, in the background, the manicurist stoically prepared to leave. Involuntarily, Gail glanced at her own, perfectly manicured nails.

Red faced, Mrs. Hauser straightened up and fixed her daughter with a stony stare. "If your gown had stayed covered it wouldn't have mattered but no, you had to have another look."

Quickly, Gail stepped forward. "Not to worry, we'll call the dressmaker and she can improvise a lovely lace rose..ah..flower..uh..or something and no one will be the wiser." Taking Gwendolyn by one elbow she steered her to the departing manicurist.

"I'll know," cried Gwen, "and besides that, I won't be able to pass a ruined dress on to my daughter."

"You don't have a daughter at the moment so don't worry about it," Gail said crisply, turning to face the manicurist. "Before you leave, redo the smudged nail, please." The cosmetologist was taken aback at the order; it had never occurred to her to repair the nail since her job was done. "Idiot," Gail intoned, not quite under her breath.

The sky clouded and a thin drizzle began, stirred by winds that threatened to increase; outside, everything was damp and slippery heralding more difficulties. The dressmaker was busy on an urgent job and only the promise of an outrageous sum of money persuaded her to turn her attention to the damaged dress, the Hauser family dog chewed up Gwendolyn's garter, steel supports for the largest tent failed to arrive, cases of glass tumblers were delivered instead of the crystal flutes that had been ordered, and then *Cuisine Internationale*, the caterers, cancelled.

Julia had answered the call from the manager of the latter and, for a moment her mind spun in giddy, senseless circles. It was far, far too late to try and engage another firm or even a restaurant or an independent chef, and no food at a wedding lunch would be truly the disaster of all time.

Julia found her voice. "What do you mean you have to break the contract? You can't do this. There's an enormous penalty, you know."

"I am aware of that," the voice continued calmly, "and we are prepared to pay. Chef Donatello broke his leg early this morning in a car accident and is in the hospital. He cannot possibly fulfill the contract."

"But what about his team?" Julia asked desperately. "Surely they can carry on without him."

"Certainly not. He is the director, the master chef, the one who holds the key to the production. The others are simply strands in the tapestry he weaves." The woman's voice was reverential; Julia' first thought was *such bullshit* and then she wondered if the caller was Donatello's devoted wife or adoring lover.

"I'll call you right back", Julia announced abruptly and hung up.

When she told Gail the latest bad news, her sister pursed her lips, shook her head and then her sour expression unexpectedly cleared. Gazing fondly at Julia, she announced, "Then I guess you'll have to take over."

Julia's eyes widened in shock and her eyebrows shot up. "What?" It came out as a whisper.

"You'll be the master chef and weave those little strands together. I've never understood why you like banging around in the kitchen but you are a gourmet cook and you can now lift those magical wooden spoons aloft and save the day."

"Gail, I wave those spoons for dinner parties of eight. I have never produced even sandwiches for two hundred people."

"It's a challenge," Gail admitted, beckoning to a gardener that was rolling a potted palm toward one of the tents.

"You don't understand. I've never even thought of doing something on this scale. It will be a monumental failure."

Forgetting the gardener, Gail stared crossly at her sister. "It certainly will be if that's your attitude. Don't be so damned selfish. Give it your best shot and if we go down in flames at least we—or rather you—tried."

She turned and stamped away. Her face burning, Julia glowered hatefully at her sister's back, wishing she had thought of some really nasty retort. Then her gaze shifted to the workmen in the garden struggling with the tents, Sydney, Stephanie and Marlene arranging chairs and counting out table settings, her sister directing the gardeners and checking up on missing plates, flutes, and the reluctant dressmaker and Julia realized that this was something that she had to try. She might land splat on her ass—and it wouldn't be the first time—but she couldn't refuse to do it.

She phoned the manageress. "I will replace the chef but I need to use his team. And I want to know the menu right now."

She heard something that sounded like a snicker over the line. "*You* will replace Chef Donatello?" Followed by a definite cackle.

"That's right."

"Well I'm afraid that won't be possible. You can't use Chef Donatello's team *or* his recipes."

The fury she had previously directed toward her sister was now revived and aimed at the supercilious voice on the telephone. "I don't want his recipes, I want the menu which I can certainly get from Mrs. Hauser who is very busy and will not be pleased when I tell her why I need to bother her at this moment." She took a ragged breath. "Our contract is with the catering company. I will not use the company's name out of courtesy to poor ailing Chef Donatello but I want the services of the team, who will be paid as we agreed. And if you refuse, I promise to dun you for the penalty and also to spread the word among our clients that you are not reliable and should not be used." She paused. "I will do my best to ruin your business."

The silence was so protracted that Julia thought the line was dead. As she was about to click off, she heard a subdued, cackle-free voice.

"Very well. Come by this afternoon and meet with Paul Murphy, Chef Donatello's assistant who will go over the menu and help with any readjustments. I will, of course, draw up an addendum to the original contract specifying that our name not be used."

"Perfect. I'll be there as soon as traffic allows."

Clicking the phone off, she was overwhelmed with an anxiety that bordered on panic. What was she doing? She'd never even taken a cooking class or watched a demonstration on TV, just pottered around her own kitchen trying out recipes and cooking for the fun of it. She had no idea of how a caterer worked, how many cooks were involved or what they did but she was certain that there was no way she could produce a wedding luncheon for two hundred on her own.

As she loped across the lawn to give her sister the latest news bulletin she was struck by their collective grubbiness. Only Marlene, recently arrived, was fresh and clean but Julia, her daughters and sister had been digging in the dirt, cleaning chairs and tables and uncrating dishes since early morning and they all looked absolutely bedraggled. As for Julia, her hair needed washing, her white tee-shirt was smudged with unidentifiable stains and her jeans could be termed filthy. She should make a great impression on Paul Murphy and his co-workers.

Consommé with Filled Pancakes
Salt Pastry
Salmon in Aspic
Filet of Beef Wellington
Duchess Potatoes

Ice Cream and Peaches
Wedding Cake

"Wow," Julia exclaimed as she scanned the menu. "Kind of elaborate isn't it?"

Paul Murphy chuckled. "You should see some of the requests we get."

Julia looked up quizzically. "And you do whatever the client wants?"

"Well, sort of. If they pay enough and we have some idea of how to do it." Julia nodded gravely.

Probably in his mid-thirties with reddish, close-cropped hair, light brown eyes, and freckled skin, Paul had been friendly and helpful from the moment they met. After escorting her around the premises, he took care to introduce her to the team of three with whom they would be working, explaining the background and expertise of each. She was expecting someone older, protective of his employer and his own culinary skills, and instead the assistant chef seemed genuinely interested in seeing that this potentially disastrous luncheon was a success.

They were sitting on stools in the kitchen of *Cuisine Internationale*, the menu propped on the butcher block between them. Julia's eyes strayed around the immaculate room with its industrial stove, freezers, refrigerators and dishwasher over which hung enormous copper and aluminum kettles and lids.

"I'm going to be perfectly honest with you," she said. "I know absolutely nothing about catering or providing any kind of food for huge groups. I've never taken a cooking class, so I guess I can say I'm a self-taught gourmet cook." She paused, debating the wisdom of confiding more to a total stranger who had the power and knowledge to make or break this wedding celebration, then decided there was no point in selective truth. "I'm not sure why you would want to help me make this a success, since *Cuisine Internationale* won't get the credit, but I'm hoping you will be my guide and guardian angel in this."

Paul smiled and nodded his head. "Of course I'll do my best. I'm an *assistant* chef, and it doesn't matter to me whether I'm assisting you or Donatelli. And I don't burn bridges or close doors, either. Who knows, maybe you'll be more gifted than the great master of *Internationale*."

"Thank you." Relief swept over her. Gesturing toward the menu, she said, "I have recipes for all these but since this lunch is being served, not set up as a buffet, I want to change the salmon in aspic to individual salmon mousse. And let's get rid of the salt pastry, whatever that might be."

"Done." He stood up and so did Julia. "This looks like an all-nighter so I hope you don't have a husband or boyfriend that expects you home tonight at seven o'clock."

For a moment, Julia stared blankly at Paul remembering when she did have someone waiting for her. It was another lifetime, she thought, one that she only remembered from time to time with a kind of wistful sadness.

Aware that Paul was watching her with an expression split between puzzlement and anxiety, Julia stood up, clutching the menu as though it were a life jacket.

"No one's waiting at home," she said crisply, "so we can work till we drop."

As bad as the previous day had been, the wedding was perfect. The sky cleared, winds died, roses appeared, a magnificent Belgian lace flower masked the stain on the wedding gown, threatened disasters failed to materialize and the guests, all two-hundred and twenty-one of them, had finished lunch and were lingering over coffee and champagne. Too tense and nervous to register the exhaustion that would soon overtake her or even to exult in the success of the lunch, Julia meticulously arranged small gift-wrapped parcels of wedding cake on a table in the garden. A uniformed maid stood at attention, waiting to hand a package to each departing guest.

"Well knock me down, if it isn't Julia Elliott."

The voice was vaguely familiar. Julia whirled around to face Frank Heller, program manager at the Business Channel with whom she had worked for many years. She was overjoyed to see her former colleague, a chubby, dimpled man with curly dark hair and pale blue eyes and, laughing, they folded into a hug. Pulling away, Julia said,

"I'm Julia Saunders now."

His face crinkling into a smile, Frank ducked his head and said, "I won't even ask."

"Don't. How's the Business Channel?" Her attention divided, she kept one critical eye on the table with it's trays of wrapped cakes interspersed with sprays of baby's breath.

"I've moved on to The Other One." This was the code name Business Channel employees used when referring to the national television network for which they would all kill to work.

"You didn't!"

"I have to admit, money and power were the bait and I've never regretted the move." He looked at her chef's jacket and white trousers. "You cooked that incredible lunch?"

Lifting her shoulders in a deprecatory gesture, she said, "Certainly not all by myself but yes, Paul Murphy and I did the food."

Behind them, guests had begun to rise from the tables, shake hands, wave enthusiastically to one another and embrace shallowly and impersonally. The maid moved closer to the table.

"You ever think of coming back?"

She shook her head. "I like what I'm doing."

"I didn't mean to your old job. It just occurred to me when I saw you that we've got a day spot, one hour once a week that I've been trying to fill with something interesting. Nothing's been right but you giving cooking demonstrations in that chef's outfit could be terrific."

Guests swirled around them, reaching behind Julia for the packets of cake, jostling her and then mumbling apologies. Staring at Frank, she moved abstractedly to one side, feeling a slow surge of excitement begin to build.

"I'll tell you right now I can't demonstrate cooking for two hundred."

"Of course not. We're talking about a dish or two for maybe four people."

"And also I'm in partnership with my sister."

He shrugged, impatiently jingling the coins in one pocket. "It's up to you. Just a few hours a week and you'd be great at it."

Pictures flew through her mind; the Business Channel, *Angel and Friends*, wedding dresses, pastry for two hundred, Jack, unpaid bills, her classroom and they all merged into one cohesive thought. It was a fantastic opportunity but would she be letting Gail and her daughters down after they had completely restructured their lives and professions to help her survive?

"It's a great offer and I'm truly very flattered," she said slowly, looking directly at Frank. "You know how I love to cook and I'm pretty good at teaching but I'm involved in this wedding business with my sister and daughters. But let's give it a try—say one month—and we'll see how it goes."

THIRTY-ONE—VENICE BEACH, CALIFORNIA

Gail and Julia huddled together at the kitchen table in Venice, their heads almost touching as they studied a folder full of charts, graphs, and designs. Angelique, the cat, strolled across the ceramic tile floor and leapt onto Gail's lap, purring contentedly. Automatically stroking the fluffy, gray fur, Gail swept an errant curl from her cheek with her free hand before picking up one of the papers.

Behind them at the steel counter, Stephanie frowned in concentration as she carefully scooped pulp from lemons and dropped the shells into a plastic bag. Her pink cotton sweater and embroidered trousers were protected by a spotless white chef's jacket and her dark brown, curly hair, just shampooed and towel-dried, was tucked snugly into a white cap.

"I think we could do this," Gail said, rattling a paper in front of her sister. "The projections look good and it ties right in with the catering. "How about it?"

Stephanie closed the bag, put it in the refrigerator and

began pressing lemon pulp through a sieve.

Julia's cheeks bunched in a grimace. "Don't you think opening an upscale kitchen shop would be kind of stretching the limits? Paul and I are busy enough running the catering company and the weekly TV cooking class, on which you all appear occasionally by the way, and you're in charge of the wedding consultancy which involves us all. Seems to me that's enough."

Elbows on the table, Gail propped her chin on both fists. "Look, be realistic. We don't all do everything all the time. You're least involved with the weddings because you and Paul run the Catering. And the girls and I just put in guest appearances on TV."

"Speak for yourself," said Stephanie, selecting green, black and white peppercorns from the spice rack. "I actually cook on screen."

"All right, what do *you* think of the idea?" Gail asked her niece.

"I think it's terrific. Marlene said she'd run the shop and she's a great administrator. That's her field."

Julia flung her hands upward in defeat. "Okay, we can discuss it when Sydney's here. And when we're not expecting a visitor..." she glanced at her watch, "...in just a few minutes."

"What on earth are you making?" Gail asked Stephanie.

"Olive tapenade in lemon shells to be served with thin Danish crackers, to be exact."

Gail shook her head. "All that work for someone you don't even remember."

"And for Mary Beth," Stephanie reminded her, "even though she'll be here later on."

"Anyway, Steph remembers Marilyn," countered Julia, looking again at her watch and shuffling the papers together.

"Barely, but this is a test run for the Richler wedding, not an elaborate welcome for Mom's friends," said Stephanie.

"You know," mused Julia, "it's been six years since I left Brazil and this is the first time anyone has come to visit. Amazing."

"It's not like Venice Beach is on the way to anywhere, Mom. You have to specifically come to L.A." Stephanie finished chopping black olives and tossed them in the food processor, adding crushed garlic, anchovies, tuna and capers before pausing to assess her unfinished creation.

Julia stood up and watched her daughter strip leaves from thyme stalks and drop them into the processor along with the peppercorns and lemon juice. "You're right and if Marilyn didn't have a conference in Century City we wouldn't see her now."

"That should tell you something," Stephanie commented, still focusing on the food processor.

Gail deposited Angelique on the floor and stood up, brushing gray fur from her tight black leather pants.

"Don't do that in the kitchen!" Stephanie snapped, glaring at her aunt.

"Ooops, my mistake," Gail said breezily, shooing Angelique out of the room and following closely behind just as the bell rang at the front gate. "Julia, do I have any more cat-fur on me?" she called to her sister.

Striding toward the front door, Julia stopped and glanced cursorily at her sister's pants, oversize black and white striped cotton knit turtle neck sweater and a half dozen black plastic chains looped around her neck. "You look fine," she said as Gail adjusted her black leather racing cap and donned a pair of enormous white-rimmed sun glasses. *But then she always looks good no matter what she puts on,* Julia thought without bitterness or envy as the two hurried across the deck and down the path to swing open the iron gate.

For a brief moment, Julia and her old friend stared at one another in silence, and then met in a fierce hug, with Brazilian kisses. Stepping back, Julia beamed joyously at her guest and exclaimed, "I'm so happy to see you after all this time."

"Almost six years". Their eyes locked, each recalling different scenes from their intermingled past.

Julia stepped aside and gestured toward Gail. "You remember my sister."

"Of course."

"And Mary Beth's coming around as well."

Julia surreptitiously studied the psychotherapist. She hadn't changed much; the long, curly hair, still without a trace of gray—probably thanks to the magic of chemicals—had now been shaped into a chic, short cap of ringlets and her wrinkle-free skin was certainly thanks to her husband's skill with the knife.

"You're looking very professional," Gail commented eying Marilyn's belted beige silk suit with short sleeves, short skirt, puffy patch pockets and epaulettes on the shoulders.

"Since I'm at a conference I have to look good or I'd never be taken seriously." Julia remembered the lace hipster trousers and halter top that had practically been Marilyn's Brazilian uniform.

Linking arms, the trio moved slowly toward the house.

"Why haven't you come back to visit?" Marilyn asked.

Julia turned toward her friend, feeling the first hint of estrangement. "At first I had no money and now I have no time. Since you've been in Miami nearly every year, I'd hoped you would come out here."

Marilyn lifted her hands expressively. "Oh those were just shopping trips. And then I had to see Mother in Detroit. You know how it goes." No, thought Julia, I don't.

They paused on the deck and Marilyn looked carefully around the garden, taking in the tall hedge that concealed the fence as well as the sheltering trees, flowers and lap pool. "This is wonderful," she exclaimed enthusiastically. "I had no idea your property was so spacious and charming, I suppose because you didn't really describe it in

São Paulo. You must be doing very well financially."

Julia's eyes met Gail's and held for a fleeting derisive moment. Marilyn had changed after all, Julia decided in disappointment. Or had her own memory built her São Paulo friends into larger-than-life heroines, or was she so insecure in Brazil that she was overly dependent on others? Maybe the years had tumbled them all in different directions; Julia didn't know.

They stepped into the entry hall and Marilyn again stopped, admiring the curved staircase directly in front and the library beyond. Turning slowly, she studied the four stained glass windows in the living room for a long time and then shifted her gaze to the paintings lining the staircase walls and then to her hostess.

"This place looks like you. Much more so than the house in São Paulo."

"That was.....just temporary." Gesturing toward the living room, she said, "Let's go sit down. Stephanie, who has turned into a fabulous chef, is concocting something in the kitchen for us to sample but she'll be out soon. I hope."

Marilyn lifted her enormous, designer handbag. "I took you seriously when you said we could walk on the beach and I brought clothes for it. Is there somewhere I can change before we settle down to talk?"

Ushering her guest through the living room and down three steps, Julia opened the door of her bedroom. "Make yourself at home. I've put clean towels in the bathroom."

Shutting the door, she hurried back through the living room, motioning to her sister. "C'mon, let's get the champagne."

"Absolutely. But first I'm going to make myself a martini."

In the library, they moved toward the built-in bar where Julia extracted a bottle of Dom Perignon from the small fridge. Gail poured gin, vermouth and a few ice cubes into the plastic juice jar that served as a cocktail shaker, clamped on the lid and shook it furiously. "What do you think?" she mouthed.

Julia hesitated, slowly arranging three champagne flutes on a tray. "Well, I don't know," she finally stage whispered. "She's...not the same. Maybe more materialistic than I remember?"

"Oh please. She's married to a plastic surgeon and comes to the US to shop a couple of times a year and as I recall she wasn't into charity work in Brazil. You're memory is faulty, dearest sister." Giving the container a final, vicious shake, she poured the concoction into a martini glass. "Anyway, people do change and it's been six years." Lifting the drink, she held it to the light and frowned. "It shouldn't have these bubbles."

Julia smiled, the skin at the corner of her eyes crinkling, and then she began to laugh. "That's because you didn't rinse it well, which I told you at the time. Those are soapsuds."

Abandoning the cocktail, Gail shrugged. "I don't do well in a kitchen."

Followed by Gail, Julia carried the tray back into the living room just as Marilyn appeared. Wearing a striped tank top, khaki Bermuda shorts and sandals, the therapist had been transformed, at least in appearance, into the old familiar friend that Julia knew so well. Gail sank onto the sofa and Marilyn smiled at her hostess who was wrestling with the wire top of the champagne bottle. Still standing, she looked thoughtfully around the room and then studied the four stained glass windows on the far wall. Against a cloudy sky, the three geese flew over a meadow filled with long-leaved grasses and white flowers, the lead bird on the far window heading toward a sunset. Lit by the afternoon sky, the colors, reflected on the hardwood floor, were brilliant. Carefully seating herself next to Gail, Marilyn asked, "Where did you get those fabulous windows?"

"I had them made by a friend in the business."

"I love them, love your house. The little veranda off

your bedroom, the high ceilings, polished wood floors.."

"Thank you. Later on, I'll show you around." Julia eased the cork from the bottle and bent to pour champagne. "This was a small shack when Jack and I bought it but we built on and renovated and added the upstairs." A sudden pain twisted her chest. "It was our dream house where we planned to grow old. Together." Handing drinks to her sister and guest, she settled into an oversize armchair. "Welcome to Venice."

They lifted their glasses and sipped. "So Stephanie's in the kitchen but where is your other daughter?" asked Marilyn.

"Sydney's at St. Paul's Church in Westwood setting up a wedding for tomorrow."

"And you've become a famous celebrity with your own show."

Julia's eyes flicked toward her sister as she took a sip of champagne. "Not at all. I just give some cooking classes."

"You're very modest. We see you on cable TV in São Paulo and everyone claims to have been your best friend, including Pearl, if you can believe that one. You should hear it at the parties. They will turn *green* when I tell them I've actually visited you."

Julia listened incredulously to Marilyn's rapturous praises and descriptions of her supposed international renown. Aware that her sister was watching her with a sardonic grin, Julia pointedly refused to look in her direction.

"Marilyn, it's just a *job*, part of our catering company which is part of the wedding consultancy. Not a big deal."

"But it's so glamorous."

Gail snickered and Julia chuckled.

"Mucking about in a kitchen all day? Chopping vegetables and measuring butter and flour? Dealing with temperamental directors who would much rather be working on a feature film? That's not my idea of glamour."

"But you're a famous TV personality. Even the name

of the show, *The Second Julia,* is wonderful. I'll bet you just have to beat the men off."

Unreal, she thought, feeling a wave of laughter building. So this is why I have a visit after all these years, and here I thought it was my sparkling personality.

"My only regular male companion is my catering partner, Paul, who is also about twenty years younger than I am."

Slipping on her sun glasses, Gail finished her champagne in one gulp.

"Well, that's what I mean. An affair with a much younger man," Marilyn commented. Gail covered her mouth with one hand, her shoulders shaking slightly as their guest continued. "Having a rich and famous ex-wife really serves Jack right, especially since he's in deep shit."

Gail sobered instantly, removed her dark glasses and peered at Marilyn with an expression that might be described as eager. "*Is* he now? Something *really terrible* has happened?" She winked slowly and dramatically at Julia who, hiding her face, leaned forward to refill the flutes.

Obviously delighted to be the bearer of news, especially since it was bad, Marilyn rushed on, "He thinks so. You know how he had the dream job of all time, with big bonus, big salary, masses of perks and all he had to do was root out the deadwood from this family-owned business."

The other two nodded.

"One of the owners of the company is a patient of Mauricio's and he told my husband that they hired Jack to improve the productivity, work habits and ethics of the various executives. Mauricio said this guy was furious with Jack because he was totally ineffective...said they had to cancel his bonus and perks. BUT when Mauricio went out to the São Paulo Golf Club, he ran into Jack and got the other side of the story."

For the past two or three years, Julia had basically forgotten about her former spouse. No longer bitter, hurt or angry, she didn't think about him at all unless his name came up and then her attention was remote, clinical and unemotional, as though he were a stranger. Now, she was amazed to find herself seething with fury and knew her face was taut with rage.

"The *Golf Club?* The initiation fee there is tens of thousands of dollars, as I recall, and the greens fees are several hundred. And he could never pay alimony or help the girls through college?"

"Membership was one of his perks before they were cancelled," Marilyn replied mildly. "So anyway, Jack said that his job was impossible because the owners wanted a big turn-around in the company but none of them had the slightest intention of changing. And because it's family-owned and run, he'd become the scapegoat."

"You never know what lies ahead," commented Gail, examining her nails.

"You haven't heard it all. Did you know that Eliana left him?"

Both women slowly shook their heads. To her surprise, Julia felt quite empty when she should have rejoiced, gloated over her ex-husband's complete downfall. Instead, she felt nothing at all. She turned to her sister. "I suppose it explains why he called and asked if we couldn't be friends." Gail nodded and Marilyn leaned forward, her expression alert.

"And what did you say?"

"I told him I didn't think it was possible. When did this happen?"

"The break-up? Maybe a year ago. I thought Laura or Kathleen might have e-mailed you. Jack and Eliana had been living together since you left and I heard they were planning to get married, but later I heard that Eliana wasn't happy with the relationship. And was cheating on him. Apparently, she was mainly attracted to him—at least according to gossip—because he had an important job and big salary and when it went sour, Eliana got out."

Gossip, thought Julia wryly. She had forgotten how São

Paulo floated along on a sea of gossip and rumor.

"So now that he's alone and his job is in danger, what's he plan to do?" asked Gail.

"I have no idea," responded Marilyn, finishing her champagne and placing the flute carefully on the coffee table. "Keep plugging away or maybe look for something else, although his Portuguese isn't really too wonderful. Or come back to the States."

"Not here I hope," Gail said firmly, studying her sister intently. "This has been a tough learning experience for us all."

A crooked grimace flashed across her face as Julia's gaze shifted to the lead duck straining to reach the promise just outside the stained glass window. *Learning experience?* she thought. She'd found out that nothing good came from extra-marital affairs but also that she could have a successful, happy life on her own terms as a single woman. Again, she realized that she really didn't care what Jack did or where he did it. She stood up.

"Gail, could you tell Stephanie that we're going to walk to the beach and we'll be back in half hour or so? It's always peaceful and beautiful at this time of day and Marilyn shouldn't go back to Brazil without seeing the Pacific Ocean close-up. Also, she can fill us in some more São Paulo gossip."

"I'm not dressed for the beach," her sister protested.

"You're fine," Julia answered, leading the way across the room. Suddenly, a blur of gray fur streaked across the room and plunged through the cat door, followed by Oso who squeezed through the opening. Just outside, Angelique soared gracefully onto a branch of the fig tree where he meticulously cleaned his paws and ignored the frantic dog below.

At the stained glass window, Julia paused and patted the lead duck encouragingly on one wing, then moved out onto the deck.